Voyage

to

Muscovy

MORE BY THIS AUTHOR

The Anniversary
The Travellers
A Running Tide
The Testament of Mariam
Flood
Betrayal
This Rough Ocean
The Secret World of Christoval Alvarez
The Enterprise of England
The Portuguese Affair
Bartholomew Fair
Suffer the Little Children

Praise for Ann Swinfen's Novels

'an absorbing and intricate tapestry of family history and private memories ...
warm, generous, healing and hopeful'
VICTORIA GLENDINNING

'I very much admired the pace of the story. The changes of place and time and
the echoes and repetitions – things lost and found, and meetings and partings'
PENELOPE FITZGERALD

'I enjoyed this serious, scrupulous novel ... a novel of character ... [and] a
suspense story in which present and past mysteries are gradually explained'
JESSICA MANN, *Sunday Telegraph*

'The author ... has written a powerful new tale of passion and heartbreak ...
What a marvellous storyteller Ann Swinfen is – she has a wonderful ear for
dialogue and she brings her characters vividly to life.'
Publishing News

'Her writing ...[paints] an amazingly detailed and vibrant picture of flesh and
blood human beings, not only the symbols many of them have become...but
real and believable and understandable.'
HELEN BROWN, *Courier and Advertiser*

'She writes with passion and the book, her fourth, is shot through with brilliant
description and scholarship...[it] is a timely reminder of the harsh realities, and
the daily humiliations, of the Roman occupation of First Century Israel. You
can almost smell the dust and blood.'
PETER RHODES, *Express and Star*

Voyage

to

Muscovy

Ann Swinfen

Shakenoak Press

Shakenoak Press
ISBN 978-0-9932372-3-2

Cover images
St Basil's Cathedral founded 1561
Contemporary drawing of Sami sleigh

Cover design by JD Smith www.jdsmith-design.co.uk

To the Memory of an Inspiring Teacher

Charles E Danner Jr

1921-1997

Chapter One

I had not been attending much to the conversation round the dinner table. To tell the truth, I had not wanted to come to the Lopez house that evening, despite knowing that I would be given an excellent meal. For two nights running I had hardly slept, for we had had three difficult births in the lying-in ward and the midwives had needed my assistance. In the dark watches of that morning we had nearly lost one mother and babe. Even now, I was uncertain whether they would survive, so I had left word that one of the errand boys at St Thomas's hospital must fetch me, should I be needed. He would have to take a wherry across the river from Southwark to the City, for the gates to the Bridge would be closed by now.

And besides, I did not much relish any company at the moment. It was barely two weeks since Sir Francis Walsingham's funeral, and the memory of that sad, miserly service by night in St Paul's still cast a pall over my spirits. The shock of discovering, next morning, that the offices in his house had been raided while we laid him to rest, had shaken me profoundly. All our precious and most secret files had been stolen, together with our code books, the locked cupboards ripped open, even Arthur Gregory's painstakingly wrought seals were gone. Fortunately, my own seal hung on a fine chain round my neck. Arthur had made it for me two years ago, when I was sent into the Low Countries. Everything else which had connected me to Walsingham's service was gone – my favourite ink pot, the pen knife I kept on my desk, my own collection of codes, many of which I had deciphered myself.

1

Since that terrible morning I had seen nothing of Thomas Phelippes or Arthur Gregory, who must now find themselves fresh employment. I had visited my horse Hector, given to me by Sir Francis before his death and kept at livery in the stables of his Seething Lane house. And I had spoken to Francis Mylles, his chief secretary, to confirm that Dame Ursula was content with the arrangement Sir Francis had made for Hector to remain there, because even though I now received the salary of a licensed physician, I could not afford the livery of a horse like Hector.

'All is in place, Kit,' Mylles had assured me. 'Dame Ursula will continue to live here in Seething Lane and she is happy with the arrangement for your horse.'

'Lady Sidney?' I said. 'Or rather, the Countess of Essex, as she is now – will she and her husband move to Essex House?'

Sir Francis's only child, his daughter Frances, had remained in the Seething Lane house even after her new marriage, for she and her father were very close and she had not wanted to lose any of his last hours.

Mylles shook his head, and I gathered from his expression that he did not approve. 'They remain here at present.' He pressed his lips together as though he would have liked to say more, but did not trust himself to speak.

'What will you do yourself?' I asked. 'Now that you have purchased a manor from Sir Francis, will you leave London for the country?'

'Not yet. Dame Ursula has need of my services. Creditors are gathering like vultures. She needs someone familiar with Sir Francis's business affairs to help her through the maze. Most of the claims are spurious, but some are genuine. When everything is in order, then I shall leave. There is a competent manager in charge at the manor. I can leave matters to him for the moment.'

He had paid me some monies owing to me, and that was the last I had seen of the inside of Walsingham's house, although I visited the stables every few days.

With all these affairs on my mind, and the demands of my work at St Thomas's, I was reluctant to accept Sara Lopez's invitation to dinner, but Sara was a close friend, the only person who knew my true identity, and I did not want to disappoint her. I was less fond of her husband, who was ambitious and (I suspected) sometimes unscrupulous in his attempts to achievement advancement. He was speaking now, and a name caught my wandering attention.

'That was why Sir Francis sent his man to Muscovy last year,' Ruy said. 'Because of the suspicions about what might be afoot there.'

I knew that Walsingham had been a shareholder in the Muscovy Company. So also were Ruy Lopez and my fellow dinner guest, Dr Nuñez. Although both had trained as physicians at Coimbra in Portugal, like my father, they had also become merchants after settling in London. Ruy Lopez merely bought and sold goods, though in some quantity, for he had a warehouse in the neighbourhood of St Katherine's Creechurch. Dr Nuñez, however, was an important member of the merchant community of London, as well as being a Fellow of the Royal College of Physicians like Ruy. He owned a number of ships. Indeed it was on one of his ships that I had escaped from Portugal eight years before. Like most of the important merchants in London, both of them held shares in the Muscovy Company, which sent a fleet north round the top of Norway every year to trade with that remote and barbarous country ruled by a Tsar, a country called sometimes Muscovy and sometimes Russe.

'Sir Francis sent an agent to Muscovy?' I said, shaking myself and trying to make an intelligent contribution to the discussion. 'I did not know that.'

'It would have been while you were away on the Portuguese expedition last spring,' Dr Nuñez said. 'It was done very quietly. The man was employed by the Company as a stipendiary, and was to look into certain matters that were causing concern.'

'Stipendiary?' I said. 'I'm not familiar with the term.'

'They are one rank below the agents. It is the agents who are in charge at each of the Company's households in that country. The stipendiaries act as clerks or secretaries or assistants. The most senior stipendiary in each household can take charge if the agent is ill or absent. Then there are apprentices, learning the business, together with various craftsmen and servants, both English and Russian.'

'I had not realised so many people were employed.'

'Oh, indeed. Some hundreds of Englishmen. And that is not to count the Russians. Then there are their dependent families. Even some Englishmen take their wives and children with them. However, as with all large enterprises, and certainly one extending over so vast an area, so far from home, the trade of the Muscovy Company is open to abuse.'

'Who was the man who was sent by Sir Francis?'

'One Gregory Rocksley. Do you know him?'

'Not well. I have met him once or twice, I suppose. But what is the problem now?'

He laughed. 'I suspected you were asleep, Kit. You have not been listening.'

I saw Ruy Lopez frown. He opened his mouth, no doubt to say something cutting, but Dr Nuñez forestalled him.

'I happen to know that Kit has worked through the last two nights without sleep. Don't be hard on him, Ruy.'

He nodded to the servant, who refilled his glass, but I placed my hand over mine and shook my head. My wits were dull enough already, without additional wine, particularly the strong (though excellent) red wine that Ruy Lopez imported from France.

'From the start of the Company, near forty years ago now, there has been the problem of employees engaging in private trade,' Dr Nuñez went on. 'They are forbidden to do so by Company regulations. All buying and selling of goods with the Muscovites must be done through the Company and entered in the ledgers. Employees are paid a salary. Shareholders bear the losses, as when a ship is sunk or captured by pirates, or goods are spoiled or sold at a loss. Over the years there have been many losses. When there is a profit, it is shared amongst those same shareholders.'

'I understand,' I said, 'although I can see that it may be very difficult to prevent men trading on their own, when they are so far from home.'

'Indeed it is, but we are happy to wink the eye over petty trading. Only if it reaches serious proportions do we take the offender to court.'

Ruy shifted irritably in his chair, as though he wanted to interrupt. Sara gave him a quelling look.

'And it was to investigate this illegal trading that Gregory was sent to Muscovy?' I said.

'Nay.' Dr Nuñez shook his head. 'That was used as the excuse, the pretended reason to the shareholders for Rocksley joining the Company as a senior stipendiary. He has some accounting experience, it seems, so the story was a convincing one.'

Ruy shifted again, causing the legs of his chair to scrape on the floor. Sara murmured something to the servant, who withdrew. Opposite me, Anne Lopez stifled a yawn. It seemed the affairs of the merchants in this distant country had little interest for her. Her elder brother Ambrose, however, leaned his chin on his hand and watched Dr Nuñez closely.

'You fear there is something more serious afoot,' he said. 'Or at least that was what I gathered before Kit woke up.'

I pulled a face at him and he grinned back. I struggled to sit up straighter and pay attention.

'I am not sure whether you know, for it was before you first came to England, Kit,' Dr Nuñez went on, 'but for some years the Tsar had seized possession of the port of Narva on the Baltic. He lost it again to Sweden in '81. So for a time, as well as the route round the North Cape to St Nicholas, we also had a much shorter route – and one free of all the ice-bound dangers of the northern passage. Narva is on the east shore of the Baltic. The only danger there was getting through the Straits without being either captured or fined by the King of Denmark.'

I could not quite see where this was leading, but I nodded.

'Narva was valuable because it also provided a much more direct route to Persia and the spice trade. Now everything has to go the long way round once again. When we pulled out of Narva, some of the Company's men left their employment with us and elected to stay, setting up as independent merchants. Narva is an important trading centre for many countries, not just those around the Baltic. Ships come in from the Low Countries, from France.' He paused. 'From Spain.'

'Ah,' I said.

'Aye.' He gave a grim smile. 'We suspect that vital information about England's navy, ports, state of readiness for war, is leaking out from some of the Company households in Muscovy to former agents or stipendiaries in Narva, and thence to Spain.'

'I see.' I was fully awake now. 'And Sir Francis would have been deeply concerned about that. Yet I do not remember him mentioning it. Or Thomas Phelippes either.'

'As I said, it would have been while you were away in Portugal. Our company governor, Rowland Heyward, consulted Sir Francis and they decided to send Rocksley with last year's fleet to Muscovy. Any communications with that country must perforce take months. Even so, Rocksley should have sent back coded despatches by now, by the land route through Poland, so that we could take any necessary action when this year's fleet leaves next month. Those were his instructions.'

'And you have received no despatches?'

He shook his head and I thought of the files missing from the office in Seething Lane. Had there been something there from Rocksley, overlooked in the last days of Walsingham's final illness?

'However,' Ruy said, unable to hold his tongue any longer, 'we have now received a despatch through Poland from our chief Muscovy agent, Austin Foulkes, who is based in Moscow. A despatch that is

5

causing us the gravest concern. Rocksley left Moscow in November last, and it was believed he was heading for Narva. In the meantime, war has broken out again between Sweden and Muscovy, so all that western part of Russe is in turmoil. The last news our people have is that Rocksley changed his plans and headed instead for Astrakhan and the Caspian Sea, that is, for the longer route that trade with Persia must now follow. He has not been seen since January.'

It sounded serious. For an Englishman, even one of Walsingham's experienced agents, to go missing in such a dangerous country did not bode well.

'He was alone, Rocksley?'

'There was a Russian interpreter with him,' Dr Nuñez said. 'Rocksley spoke a little of the language, having travelled there once before. That was why Sir Francis chose him for the mission. But he was not fluent. He would have needed an interpreter. The interpreter has also vanished.'

He looked grave. 'Anything might have happened. The true nature of his mission might have been discovered. He might have perished of disease or the fearful winter climate in those parts. And that route is notoriously dangerous. Company men on peaceful missions have been murdered there before.'

'So what do you propose doing?' Ambrose asked.

'There is to be a meeting of the Court of Assistants in a few days' time,' Ruy said. 'Dr Nuñez is currently one of the Assistants.'

'This year's fleet will leave some time in the middle of May,' Dr Nuñez said. 'A new chief agent will be travelling with it, Christopher Holme, to replace Austin Foulkes, who has served there for three years now. Long enough for any man, I should think, in such a barbarous land! The Company must decide before then what action should be taken. We might simply decide to wait and hope that Rocksley will reappear.'

I frowned. 'A weak course to follow, if a man you sent into that land is in trouble and in need of help.' I thought of the times I had found myself in danger abroad in foreign lands, and my sympathies were with Rocksley.

'On the other hand,' he said, 'we may send out another man to search for him.'

'You should go, Kit,' Ambrose said. I thought he was probably teasing. 'You have a talent for making your way in foreign lands. And I have heard that the Tsar is anxious for English physicians to come to his country. Is that not so, Father?'

Ruy nodded. 'Physicians, apothecaries, architects, skilled craftsmen. The Muscovites have been urging us to send such men ever since the time of the present Tsar's father.'

'Ivan the Terrible,' Ambrose said, with a certain grim relish.

I shivered. 'Few can have wanted to go,' I said. I certainly would not.

'The present Tsar is of a very different character to his father,' Dr Nuñez said. 'A weak, foolish creature. His brother-in-law is Tsar in all but name.'

'Aye,' said Ruy. 'Boris Godunov. An able administrator, we understand. Not so overtly cruel as the last Tsar, but not a man to be trifled with. He governs by stealth.'

After that the conversation wandered on to different things, in particular the struggle for power that was developing between the Earl of Essex and the Cecils, but I was growing very tired. There was still a long walk ahead of me, first from Wood Street to the river, then the crossing by wherry before I could walk to my lodgings in Southwark. I excused myself soon afterwards and Dr Nuñez rose too, saying he would accompany me.

At first we walked in silence. Of late Dr Nuñez had begun to move more slowly and I noticed that he was hunched forward slightly.

'Does your back trouble you?' I asked.

'Nothing serious. Nothing but old age. And sitting too long on those fancy chairs of Ruy's. Beautifully carved, of course, but scarcely comfortable.'

I laughed. 'They were very uncomfortable, weren't they? It had its advantages, though. It was the only thing that stopped me falling asleep altogether. They must be new, for I've never seen them before.'

'Despite his losses in the Portuguese affair, Ruy still seems to have money to spend.'

'He does. Take care, there's a patch of slippery mud here.' I took his arm and beckoned one of his servants nearer. Dr Nuñez had brought two lads carrying pitch torches with him, to light the way home.

'How is Dame Beatriz?' I asked. 'I was surprised not to see her tonight.'

Dr Nuñez's wife was an old friend of Sara's, but I suspected that, like me, she did not care over much for Ruy.

'She has a heavy head cold and decided to go early abed.'

'Nothing serious, I hope?'

'Nay, nothing a little care will not mend.'

7

We had reached the corner of Fish Street and Little Eastcheap where our ways parted, he to walk the short distance to Mark Lane, I to find a wherry at Old Swan Stairs to row me across the river. He laid his hand on my arm.

'Ambrose was right to say that you would be an excellent person for the Company to send, Kit, but it is likely to be dangerous. I should not like to see you coerced into such a venture.'

I looked at him in alarm.

'It surely was not meant seriously!'

He grunted. 'I would judge, by the look in Ruy's eye, that he was considering it very seriously. Take care, Kit.'

He gave a worried frown and seemed about to say something else, but then he shook his head and patted my arm.

'Off with you to your bed. You will do your patients no good if you get no rest. Ned will light your way to the stairs.'

'In any case,' I said, 'I could not go to Muscovy. I have my work in the hospital.'

At one time, Walsingham could have sent me where he pleased and managed all arrangements with the hospital, but Walsingham was gone and I was no longer employed on secret missions. Life had grown a little dull of late, but there was no denying that it was less dangerous. I had no wish to travel to Muscovy, even though Ivan the Terrible had gone. It was rumoured that he had perished in the throes of a murderous rage, like that in which he had killed his son and heir. The thought of such a country made me shudder.

'God go with you, Dr Nuñez.'

'And with you, Kit.'

I huddled in my cloak as the wherryman rowed me across the river. Although there were a few signs of spring by day, the nights were still cold and a cutting east wind was blowing upriver, funnelled between the arches of the Bridge. At St Olave's Stairs I paid the wherryman and scrambled ashore.

Light flowed from the windows of the whorehouse as I passed, and I could hear music and laughter from within, so I walked more quickly. The Winchester goose Bessie Travis was forever trying to invite me inside, from the kindest of motives, and I was forced to employ every strategy at my command to avoid her. There was a light, too, showing under Simon's door as I made my way up the stairs to my room in the lodging house, sheltering from the draughts the candle Goodwife Atkins had left for me.

8

I thumped on Simon's door and went in. He was crouched over his candle with some ragged sheets of paper in his hand, muttering to himself.

'Conning a new part?' I asked, placing my candle where it would benefit him and throwing myself down on his bed with my hands behind my head.

'Aye.' He rubbed his eyes. 'We have but two days to learn this new piece that Will has made for us out of an old story. I grant you this: the fellow writes quickly, but Master Burbage is in such a hurry to open the Theatre that we start to rehearse on Friday and perform the new play next week.'

'It's still mighty cold for playing in the open air,' I said. 'I thought you would stay on in the hall of the Cross Keys a few more weeks.'

'So did I, but Master Burbage thinks the new play will draw a larger audience than the inn will hold. Where have you been this evening?'

'Dining at the Lopez house. Shall I hear you?'

'Aye.' He passed me the handful of sheets and I heard his part until he reached the end. He was always quick to learn.

'And what entertainment did you have with the Queen's distinguished physician?' he asked, getting up to pour us each a mug of ale. It was a homely brew compared with Ruy's fine wine, but I liked it better. It would not fuddle me so.

'I was half asleep most of the time,' I admitted. 'And I must be off to my bed soon. 'They were talking about the Muscovy Company.'

'Were they, indeed!' Simon said, with more interest than I would have expected.

'Are you planning to invest?' I said.

I grinned. If Simon ever had more than the next month's rent put aside, I would wonder at it.

'Very witty,' he said. 'Nay. There is some talk of Master Burbage sending a group of us out with the Company fleet to perform abroad.'

'In *Muscovy*!' I gaped at him.

'Nay, not to those barbarians. We would go only part way, to the trading town of Wardhouse. We would mount a few plays there, then come back with the fleet when it returns to England a few weeks later.'

'Wardhouse?' I said. 'That is somewhere off the north coast of Norway. And its true name is Vardøhus.'

'Well, Master Burbage calls it Wardhouse. He says they are starved of entertainment and will pay us well. Cuthbert Burbage will be in charge. I have put myself forward to be one of those chosen. I enjoyed our time in the Low Countries last year. It will mean I have the chance to play better parts than here in London, for I doubt Christopher Haigh or Dick Burbage will want to go, they are too busy making a name for themselves here.'

He sounded somewhat bitter. Usually Simon was resigned to the fact that a player must accept the parts allotted him, though he grumbled when he was obliged to play a comic. He had not long moved on from taking women's roles, which he had done since he left St Paul's as a boy and joined Burbage's men, but now he was eager for the better parts mostly allotted to Christopher and Dick.

'Well, I shall miss you if you go,' I said, keeping my voice casual, 'but I can understand that it would be a great opportunity. However, I have heard that the journey is bleak and miserable to those northern parts. The North Cape is said to be the furthest north any man has ever ventured. I should not care for it myself.'

He shrugged.

'You have far more experience of the world than I have, Kit. That trip to the Low Countries was the only time I have ventured outside England. After listening to Raleigh and Harriot speaking of the New World, I am restless here on our little island.'

'Be grateful for a peaceful homeland,' I said, somewhat sharply, aware that Simon knew nothing of those aspects of the wider world with which I was all too familiar.

'It is a strange coincidence that you should speak of travelling on the Muscovy fleet,' I said, in a friendlier voice. 'This very evening Ambrose Lopez was trying to persuade me to go to Muscovy on Company business.'

'Indeed?' Simon raised his eyebrows. 'Why should that be?'

'Oh, they need someone to hunt for a missing man sent out there last year by Walsingham. Ambrose spoke in jest.'

I remembered, however, that Dr Nuñez had warned me that the suggestion might be considered seriously.

'Would you go? If you were asked?'

'I no longer work for Walsingham,' I said.

As I spoke the words, I felt a sharp pang. Over the years I had learned to admire the man known as the Queen's Spymaster. Even, a little, to love him, for since my father's death he and Dr Nuñez had come close to taking his place.

10

'No one works for Walsingham now,' he said, 'and no one knows who will replace him. But I suppose someone will need to search for this fellow. Who is it? Someone you know?'

'Gregory Rocksley,' I said. 'I barely know him. I think I would recognise him if I met him, though I am not sure. But that is all.'

'And how many could say the same? Did you not tell me that most of Walsingham's agents have drifted away to other employment? It began even before his death.'

What he said was true.

'That does not mean I am the *only* person who would recognise him,' I protested, aware that Simon's argument might be used by Ruy and other Company shareholders.

I swung my legs off the bed and sat up.

'I must away to my bed, or I shall have a third night without sleep. Besides, poor Rikki will have given me up in despair.'

'I took him for a walk earlier this evening,' he said, 'and invited him to stay with me until you came home, but he whined and scratched at your door until I let him into your room. I expect he feels the need to guard your belongings.'

I laughed as I picked up my candle.

'My only possession of value is that porcelain bowl of Drake's, which I came by somewhat illegally. And the medallion Leicester gave me.'

'Both valuable,' he said. 'And so is your horse.'

'Fortunately, Hector is not required to live in my room. I bid you good night, Simon.'

'God be with you,' he said, as I closed the door softly, so as not to disturb the other lodgers.

Rikki had no such inhibitions, leaping at me like a furry whirlwind and nearly knocking me over. I was accustomed to this when I had been obliged to leave him for a few hours and braced my shoulders against the wall in order to withstand the onslaught of his welcome.

'Easy, lad,' I said, trying unsuccessfully to dodge an enthusiastic licking. 'I am home now. Did Simon feed you?'

There was water in one bowl, and another was licked spotless, where I suspected Simon had fed him, although Rikki's eager glances toward my hanging food cupboard implied that he thought it was high time for another meal. I had a cup of broth left over from the previous day, so I poured it over some stale bread and gave that to him, while I locked my door and drew the curtains before I changed into my night

11

shift. That porcelain bowl which had once been Drake's stood on the windowsill, next to the medal Leicester had given me. Not a personal medal, of course. One of many, lamenting his departure from the Low Countries. Beside them lay another object, of no value to anyone except to me. I picked it up and ran my thumb over the silky surface of the glossy wood. A simple figure of a seal, carved by a surly Spanish fisherman.

Although my time with Simon had woken me up briefly, I was suddenly so tired that I could barely take the trouble to fold my clothes neatly for the morning. By the time I had crawled into bed, Rikki had finished his meal and leapt up beside me, even before I had blown out my candle. There had been no fire in my room all day and it felt damp and cold after the warmth in Simon's room. I pulled my feather bed about my ears and fell asleep almost at once, glad of Rikki's warmth against my back.

But my sleep was troubled with dreams of snow and bitter cold, and a strange dark land full of cruel-faced savages.

The following morning held more promise of spring than we had yet experienced. Although my sleep had been haunted by those strange dreams, I seemed to have recovered from the mind-numbing fatigue that had nearly sent me to sleep over the dinner table at the Lopez house. I walked briskly east along the river bank toward the hospital, with Rikki frisking about me, discovering new and intriguing smells to investigate every few yards. At the gatehouse to St Thomas's, I found Tom Read, the gatekeeper, perched on a stool and enjoying the thin sunshine. His elderly wolfhound, Swifty, was stretched out on the cobbles at his feet. There was not much sign of swiftness about the old dog to be seen now, but Tom assured me that in his youth he had been remarkable.

'Fine morning, Dr Alvarez,' Tom said, grinning up at me. He had the end of a pie in his hand and broke off a piece for Rikki, who took it delicately between his lips, then lay down beside Swifty. He was trained now to know that he would spend the day with Tom and Swifty while I was at work in the hospital.

'Aye,' I said, 'though perhaps a little chilly for sitting outside.'

'It won't be for long. There's a load of firewood to be delivered from Kent, coming in this morning. And three crates of hens from Bermondsey, that'll need moving into the chicken yard.'

'A busy morning you'll have then.'

I gave him a grin, and made my way into the hospital. St Thomas's was more like a village than a single institution for the treatment of the sick and the housing of the elderly and infirm. There were important workshops on the premises, left over from the days when this had been an abbey with a reputation for fine craftsmanship. They still supplied skilled work in wood and stone carving, in the printing and binding of books, and perhaps most notably in the making of exquisite stained glass, famed even beyond England. Adam Batecorte, a soldier I had first known on the Portuguese expedition, had been taken on as a labourer in the glass works, but had recently begun to learn how to work the glass himself.

The hospital had its own orchards and vegetable gardens, a fish-pond, poultry yard, beehives, piggery and small dairy herd. We could not feed ourselves entirely, but our own produce helped to keep our costs down, something which was a constant worry to Roger Ailmer, Deputy Superintendent of the hospital, who ran its day-to-day affairs.

When I reached the lying-in ward endowed by Richard Whittington, I was relieved to find that the woman who had seemed on the threshold of death the previous day was much recovered. She had lost that gaunt, grey look and her eyes no longer seemed to be staring at something she could see beyond this earthly world.

'She has eaten a little porridge with cream this morning,' Goodwife Appledean murmured, after I had finished my examination. She was the senior midwife, competent and trustworthy. 'And she slept well.'

'The babe?'

I turned to the wicker cradle beside the bed. The baby was very large, while the mother was slender-hipped, the source of our trouble in the delivery.

'He is beginning to be restless. He has not wanted to feed yet, the poor mite was as exhausted as his mother, but I think we might try now.'

I left them to it, while I visited my child patients in the adjacent ward. With the passing of winter there were fewer cases now of chest and throat complaints, but April is a hungry time of year, when winter supplies are exhausted and the new season's food not yet available. Spring may seem full of promise, but for the poor it can be a wretched time. There were many pauper families in Southwark, and amongst them the man of the family must always have the best of the food. If his strength fails, he cannot support his family and all will perish. That is the principle by which they live, though I knew many families in the

13

neighbourhood where the woman earned more, and more reliably, than the man. Aye, and kept house, cooked, cleaned, cared for the children, too. There were some families where the woman was the only earner, while the man spent her wages in the tavern and their children ran half naked and hungry in the streets.

At least the children admitted to St Thomas's were fed well and given clothes from our store of charitable gifts. None of these garments were new, but they were whole and clean. Some of the waifs were in a pathetic state, flaccid skin holding together fragile bones and very little flesh. I would keep such cases in the hospital longer than Ailmer altogether approved, refusing to turn them away until they showed some signs of recovered health.

Today all my young charges were in good spirits, none giving me concern, so I spent much of the day assisting on the other wards, especially the men's. There were always many – too many – cases of injury amongst the Southwark labourers, for they worked at some of the harshest and most dangerous trades. I was surprised to see a familiar face amongst the patients.

'Adam!' I said, 'what are you doing here? I hope you are not seriously injured.'

Adam Bellacorte gave me a sheepish grin, holding out a badly blistered palm.

'My own fool fault, doctor,' he said. 'I am learning to carry the blowpipes with the molten gather from the furnace to the blow-man, then act as his assistant while he spins the glass into a sheet. Idiot that I am, I went to pick up a blowpipe without putting on the thick glove we use. I was thinking about how soon we should have our midday break, for it was very hot in the glass works, and I let my attention slip.'

I examined his hand. It was a nasty burn and must be very painful, but was not at bad as it might have been.

'Aye,' he said, seeing my expression. 'When I dropped the blowpipe – and ruined the glass – one of the journeymen grabbed my arm and thrust my hand into a bucket of water. It must have slowed the burning.'

I salved his hand and bandaged it.

'Keep it clean and come back tomorrow,' I said. 'In a day or two it will be best left open to the air. I'm afraid you will have a scar.'

Instinctively, my fingers closed over my own scarred left palm.

'I hope I suffer no worse than that,' he said grimly. 'I must see the master when I go back. Say a prayer for me, that I may not be dismissed for my stupidity.'

'He's a fair man,' I said, 'and everyone makes mistakes when they are learning. Apologise and do what work you can with your left hand to show that you are anxious not to lose your place.'

'Aye, that's best.'

He went off, trying to look cheerful, but I knew he must be in considerable pain, though he refused anything to ease it.

That evening I had yet another supper engagement, though it was one I had accepted much more readily. These days I did not often see my former mathematics tutor, Thomas Harriot, but I was always glad of his company. Moreover, he did not mind Rikki coming with me to the suite of rooms he currently occupied in a wing of Durham House, Raleigh's fine mansion on the Strand, overlooking the Thames.

I was the only guest, so we dined informally at a small table beside the fire in a room crowded with tottering piles of books and strewn with papers covered with diagrams and calculations. We shared a love of puzzles and ciphers, which had led (inadvertently) to Harriot recommending me for Walsingham's service when I was but sixteen. He had also introduced me to optics and tutored me in both optics and the theory of harmony as well as mathematics. To some, such subjects may seem dull or baffling or a kind of magic, but they are not. Those early explorers of the Muscovy Company would have lost themselves forever amongst the fogs and ice flows of the uncharted north, had they not understood celestial navigation, which is based on mathematics. Even after nearly forty years of those perilous voyages, such knowledge was a matter of life and death.

That evening we talked a little of Harriot's latest attempts to map the face of the moon, but after we had eaten and played some music together, Harriot poured us each a glass of wine and our conversation turned to the topic which was now often on men's lips.

More and more, as Lord Burghley had became enfeebled with age, his younger son, Sir Robert Cecil, was undertaking the burden of his father's work as the Queen's most valued counsellor. The old order was passing. Leicester dead soon after the victory over the Armada, my father the following year, Walsingham only weeks ago, Burghley worn out with age, and – although his mind was as sharp as ever – Hector Nuñez, growing visibly weaker ever since our ordeal on the Portuguese expedition.

'Essex continues to parade about the City and the Court,' I said grimly, staring into my wine as I swirled it about in the glass. 'Attended by his band of undisciplined followers. It's clear, even to the common citizen like me, that the struggle for power will now be between Essex and Robert Cecil.'

'You are hardly a common citizen,' Harriot said, 'after your years of working for Walsingham. But matters are indeed in a state of flux. For decades, Burghley and Walsingham managed England's affairs between them. In matters of defence, though, Burghley has been ever cautious, Walsingham was more warlike in his approach to our perpetual enemy, Philip of Spain.'

'And despite his reputed poor health,' I said, 'the Spanish king seems likely to outlast them all, all our great leaders. Burghley and Walsingham may have differed in their approach to the problem of Spain, but they respected each other's views.'

'Aye, and worked, for the most part, in harmony.'

'With Essex and Cecil, it will be a different matter,' I said.

'They loathe each other,' Harriot said. 'Big, handsome, blustering, arrogant Essex, with money and charm, who can sway the Queen his way.' He gave a wry smile. 'That is, when he remembers to conduct himself towards her with respect and propriety.'

I nodded. 'Aye. And little hunchbacked Cecil, stunted and ill since birth, with his long face, pale with suffering, and his fragile hands – he'll never gallop about in a mock tournament defeating all comers.'

'But a man who has a mind as sharp as a razor and as subtle as a master thief,' Harriot said. 'They will never work together for the common good. Theirs will be an unending struggle until one of them achieves supremacy. Any man caught in the pincers of that struggle risks destruction and death.'

'You are right,' I said. 'Best for the rest of us to keep out of the way until the battle is settled, one way or the other.'

I sipped my wine thoughtfully, glad I was safe away from them and remembering the subtle mind of Walsingham. 'In the end,' I said, 'I would put my money on Cecil, but Essex will probably do a great deal of harm first.'

'I fear he will.' He shook himself, then poured us more wine, though I stopped him when my glass was half full.'

'I am falling asleep by your fire,' I said, suppressing a yawn. 'I must go soon.'

'Will you come to Raleigh's *conversazione* next week?'

Harriot grinned. I could not remember who had first employed the pompous Italian term, probably Marlowe, but we both thought it absurd.

'I shall try.'

'Make sure you do. I have something remarkable to reveal. It will delight you.'

'Indeed? And what is that?'

He tapped his nose. 'Wait and see!'

Chapter Two

*A*s my services to Walsingham had declined during the last months of his illness, I had been able to visit the gatherings at Durham House more frequently. The meetings of the group of scholars and scientists who congregated around Raleigh and the Earl of Northumberland were always exciting and reminded me of the evenings at our home in Coimbra, when my father's colleagues from the university would explore new ideas, while I sat in a corner with my arms about my knees, listening avidly.

Harriot was always to be found at the Durham House meetings, always glad to see me, even though my increased duties at St Thomas's no longer allowed me time to study with him. Dr John Dee was often of the party too, the Queen's astrologer and alchemist, who was said to possess a remarkable library. He shared many interests with Harriot, but he veered more towards magic than my former tutor. He spent less time than Harriot developing celestial navigation charts for seamen and instead more time conjuring angels. Or so he said. I never saw him do it, though he swore he had pages of manuscript, direct transcriptions of angelic messages which passed to him through his medium and assistant, Edward Kelley.

Sometimes I went to Durham House with Simon, but, if Marlowe was in his company, I would make some excuse and either stay in my room or make my way to Durham House on my own.

On one occasion about the middle of March I had found Marlowe at Durham House without Simon and regretted at once that I had come, for he sauntered over to me, swaggering in a new velvet doublet with satin slashings. How could he afford such attire? Surely a maker of plays, even one as popular as Marlowe, would not earn enough to dress in clothes to rival those of Raleigh and

Northumberland? Even if you added whatever he earned as an occasional spy for Walsingham.

'So the Portingall is here tonight,' he said, flicking my cheek with his fingernail, as he had done when we first met. 'Don't you know better than to invade the privacy of your betters, Jew boy?'

'I am here at Sir Walter's invitation,' I said, wondering whether he could hear the grinding of the words between my teeth. 'As no doubt you are yourself.'

'Of course.' His tone was condescending. 'I am here for my wit and my discourse. You,' he looked me up and down insolently, 'you are one of his curiosities. He likes to collect strange species, barbarians. He has brought some of the natives of the New World to London, to exhibit. As similar freaks.'

There was something in his tone that made my heart pound. Had he seen through my disguise? Why else would he call me a freak? His hostility to Jews was extreme, though not unknown in London, but he seemed to reserve a special dislike for me. I clenched my fists.

'Do you call me a freak, you mincing monkey?' I said.

At that he raised his hand to strike me, but Harriot, who must have sensed trouble from the way we confronted each other, had crossed the room in a few swift strides and drew me away to speak to Dr Dee. I could not ignore the vicious look Marlowe flashed at me.

On the evening of the Durham House meeting at which Harriot had promised a surprise, Simon and I set out together. I mentioned my unpleasant encounter with Marlowe on the last occasion.

'Why do you dislike Marlowe?' Simon asked me. We had taken a boat from Paris Gardens straight across the river to the steps by Durham House. We were in the chinks that day, for usually we walked over the Bridge. It was pleasant on the river, for it had not yet developed the sewer smell of summer.

'Better to ask him why he dislikes me,' I said abruptly, staring down river through the arches of the Bridge at a fat merchant vessel making its way slowly up against the tide to the Customs House. 'The first time we met, he mocked and insulted me. As he mocked you, and still mocks you, had you wit enough to see it.'

'Oh, that is just his way.' Simon shrugged. 'He mocks everyone and everything, himself no less than any other. You should not take offence at it.'

'Besides.' I could not look at him directly, for I was shamed by what I had to say, and I lowered my voice so the boatman might not catch my words. 'I have heard that he beds men and boys.'

The ready colour flooded from Simon's neck up to his cheeks, until his whole face was reddened. Even at twenty, he blushed as easily as a girl.

'Well, he has not bedded *me!*' he said, much too loudly for my comfort. 'Don't think that of me, Kit. My tastes are not that way inclined.' He gave me a sharp look I could not read.

'I am glad to hear it,' I said, and climbed out of the wherry at Durham Stairs in a remarkably cheerful state of mind.

Harriot was already in the turret room with Raleigh, Dee, and the wizard Earl of Northumberland when we arrived, a little earlier than usual, through having crossed the river by wherry. Harriot beckoned me over eagerly.

'Come now, Kit, and see what you think of this.' He had laid on the table a long bundle, about a yard in length and about the thickness of a bedpost. It was wrapped in green silk, which he unwound carefully, exposing a wooden tube, which did indeed resemble a length of bedpost. Unlike a bedpost, however, it was hollow and had a lens of domed glass at each end.

'What is it?' I asked, as Simon craned over my shoulder to see.

'It is a perspective trunk,' said Harriot, which left me as ignorant as before.

Gently, cradling it in his arms like a newborn infant, he carried it over to one of the windows that looked out over the Thames.

'You know that I have been devoting much of my time lately to the study of optics? And that I have been in correspondence with fellow scholars in Europe?'

I nodded.

'This is the fruit of our ideas. I have made it up in my laboratory, with the assistance of a carpenter and a spectacle maker.'

It seemed an odd combination to me, but I saw that Raleigh, Dee, and Northumberland were grinning, as though they already knew the purpose of the perspective trunk. Dee reached across and opened the casement, so that a chilly wind blew in and swept a sheaf of papers off the table. Simon stooped to retrieve them, while Harriot balanced the instrument on the window sill, pointing it across the river towards Lambeth Palace, and beckoned to me.

'Now, Kit, close one eye, put the other to this inner end of the trunk, and tell me what you can see.'

I looked at him dubiously, but I had never known him make a fool of me, so I did as I was told. And leapt backwards so suddenly I collided with the Earl. I was too astonished even to apologise.

Cautiously, I lowered my head and put my eye to the lens again. This time I felt blindly about in the air beside the instrument, but there was nothing there but Harriot's arm supporting it.

'Is it magic?' I asked. 'I can see Lambeth Palace as close as if I were standing on the south bank of the river. Yet I am here, in Durham House. And the palace . . .' I took my eye from the instrument and looked out of the window, '. . . the palace is still there, in Southwark.'

'Let me see!' cried Simon, elbowing me aside. When he put his eye to the lens, he gasped and did as I had done, feeling about in the empty air, to touch what was not there.

'Magic!' he breathed.

'Not magic,' said Harriot briskly, laying the instrument tenderly back on the table. 'Natural Philosophy. Optics. We have long known that glass lenses can help poor or ageing eyesight, by means of spectacles, and for some time those of us with an interest in optics have been experimenting with different uses of lenses and mirrors, individually and in pairs. Have you ever seen a *camera obscura*?'

Simon shook his head.

'A pretty instrument, that artists use sometimes when they need great detail in a painting. I will make one and bring it another time. With this instrument,' he tapped it with his finger, 'we find we can make far away things appear near. You will discover, if you reverse it, that it makes them appear even further away. Our results are mostly experimental at the moment, but we are hard at work on the mathematics. You would enjoy that, Kit.'

He looked at me a little severely, for I knew he believed I should devote my life to scholarship. My work as a physician he regarded as a hindrance to my true vocation, although I had explained to him that I must eat, and clothe myself, and rent a roof for my head. We cannot all be so fortunate as to have Sir Walter Raleigh and the Earl of Northumberland for our patrons.

Our happy discussion of the new invention, and its wondrous possibilities for studying the stars or aiding mariners, was interrupted by the arrival of several more members of the group, including Marlowe. At once he bearded Dr Dee and began a long and provocative discuss of theology. It seemed that Dee was to be the victim of his baiting tonight. Harriot drew me aside.

'Well, Kit, what do you think of my perspective trunk?'

He looked as eager as a small boy hoping for praise.

'It is truly wonderful,' I said in all honesty. 'I could not have believed it, had I not looked through it myself. It will be a great help in your drawings of the moon.'

'Oh, I believe I have been able to complete those quite satisfactorily with the naked eye. I hope to use the new instrument to study the more distant stars. I should like to be able to provide more precise celestial charts for our mariners.'

'I can see that such instruments could be of great use to mariners,' I said, 'enabling them to recognise enemy vessels in the distance, or study a strange coast where no rutter chart exists. It is heavy, though. It would be difficult to hold it up while trying to keep one's balance on a heaving deck in a high wind. I have seen how seamen struggle to use an astrolabe, even the simple mariners' astrolabe.'

'You put your finger on it,' he said. 'That must be the next step, to produce a version lighter in weight. If you go on this next Muscovy voyage, I shall try to have one ready for you.'

I stared at him in astonishment.

'What do you mean? Who told you I was to go to Muscovy? I have heard no such tale.'

He looked apologetic. 'I am sorry if I have spoken out of turn. As you know, I supply the Muscovy Company with charts and calculations of tides and celestial forecasts. And John Dee was an important adviser during the very earliest expeditions, when he was just a young man.'

This was a surprise to me. I could not imagine the mystic Dee occupying himself in anything so practical, but perhaps he had changed with the years.

Harriot cast a somewhat disapproving glance in Dee's direction. 'That was before he neglected his serious scholarly pursuits for all this nonsense about messages from angels.' He lowered his voice. 'I believe Edward Kelley to be a fraud and a charlatan who has gained Dee's trust and exploited it. He has found himself a very comfortable living in Dee's employ.'

I believed the same, but I brought him back to what he had said that had alarmed me.

'The Muscovy Company?' I said. 'Why should you think I have anything to do with them?'

'They held their monthly Court of Assistants yesterday and I was present, to hand over my latest calculations before this year's fleet sails. You were recommended as a suitable person to search for the missing stipendiary, Gregory Rocksley.'

'Surely that is a task for one of their own men.' I tried to speak calmly, but I felt a wave of panic coming over me. Was Ambrose's casual remark at the Lopez dinner table being taken seriously?

He glanced at me out of the corner of his eyes, then looked away.

'Rocksley was referred to as a stipendiary, but of course many of us know that story is no more than an invention, to cover up his real purpose. He is – he was – an experienced agent of Walsingham's. As of course you know. So your name was not unexpected. Though Dr Nuñez protested that you are too young for such a mission.'

'And I have my work at St Thomas's,' I said, feeling my stomach tighten in apprehension. 'They should send someone who is now without employment. Nicholas Berden would be an excellent choice. He is much more experienced than I am.'

'Ah, but it seems that English physicians have been particularly requested by the Tsar and his advisers. Indeed, even in the late Tsar's time they were asking for English physicians. Now it seems they are anxious above all for a physician who is skilled in the problems of children. There are two children in question. The Tsar has a young half-brother, Dmitri Ivanovich, whose mother is concerned about him. On what grounds, we do not know. And there is another child in the court who has a troublesome rash that none of their physicians can cure. So you can see why your name was being discussed.'

He smiled apologetically. 'I am sorry if I have taken you by surprise. I thought you must have been approached already.'

I shook my head.

'I have heard nothing. I am sure it was merely idle talk. I am too young and too inexperienced for such a mission. Besides, I cannot leave St Thomas's.'

It was clear Harriot wanted to discuss other things, realising perhaps that he had caused me considerable alarm. Soon afterwards, Raleigh's servants brought in refreshments. I had a lively discussion with Dr Dee about optics over the cheese and wine. He seemed relieved to be rid of Marlowe, who had now attached himself to the young Earl of Oxford, here for the first time. As soon as I could, I persuaded Simon to leave, and we made our way back to Southwark. Simon chattered enthusiastically about the wonders of the perspective trunk, but I responded in little more than monosyllables.

Ambrose's casual remark at that dinner when I was half asleep seemed to have taken on a life of its own. First there had been Dr Nuñez's warning that it might be regarded seriously. Then Master Harriot's assumption that it was already a settled matter that I would be travelling to Muscovy. Now, less than a week later, I received a letter from Master Rowland Heyward, governor of the Muscovy Company and a man of considerable wealth and distinction in the City of London, requesting me to call on him in the forenoon of the following day.

I considered the possibility of refusing, but realised that it would be unmannerly. It would be the act of a coward to shy away from meeting the gentleman in person. Warned in advance by Harriot's indiscreet remarks, I could go armed with irrefutable arguments. Face-to-face with Heyward, I could explain my unsuitability for the mission and my many commitments to my patients at St Thomas's. I penned a brief note and despatched it with one of the hospital's lads, stating that I would be pleased to call on him at ten o' the clock the next day at the Company's London headquarters.

In the morning I arrived early at St Thomas's, in order to visit both the lying-in and children's wards in good time. Fortunately there were no serious cases or emergencies on hand. The mother who had caused concern earlier had recovered well and returned home the previous day. The Whittington ward had been set up specifically for unmarried mothers, but not all of them were the local Southwark prostitutes. There were usually a few victims of rape, and also some women – or more often young girls – who had been promised marriage and then abandoned.

This recent case was a sad one. The father of the child had been on the point of marriage to the mother, the banns had been read, and then he had fallen ill of a pleurisy and perished the very day of the planned wedding. The woman had now returned from hospital to her parents, and the baby would be cherished, as a living reminder of his lost father. This was one child I would not need to take to Christ's Hospital.

In good time I set off across the Bridge, wearing my physician's cap and gown to emphasise my true profession to Master Heyward. Recently, with my increased salary as a fully licensed physician, I had had a new gown made, so I hoped my appearance would go some way to convincing the governor that I was not a suitable person to be sent on some wildgoose chase across the remote lands of Muscovy, in search of a man who had disappeared weeks before. I could feel some compassion for Rocksley, adrift in such a barbarous country – that is, if he was still alive – but I was convinced Nicholas Berden would be a far better agent to send. Besides, Nick would no doubt be glad of the employment.

The Muscovy Company occupied a handsome building not far from the Customs House and the Legal Quays. I had passed it many a time on my way to and from Seething Lane. Indeed I believe they had once occupied a property in Seething Lane itself, but as the Company had grown larger and richer they had bought this large house, not more than ten years old and better suited to their needs.

I was shown promptly into the governor's office and Master Heyward came forward politely to greet me.

'I thank you for coming, Dr Alvarez,' he said, smiling and bowing me to a large cushioned chair. 'I believe you will have some idea of why I wished to speak to you.'

I shook my head, feigning ignorance.

'I am afraid I do not. Your letter made no mention of why you invited me to meet you.'

As calmly as I could, I sat back in the chair and waited to see how he would broach the subject. His eyes were shrewd and I suspected he did not believe my protestations. He resumed his seat behind a massive desk which would have looked out of place in a smaller room, but was in proportion to this impressive chamber. There were windows facing in two directions, those on the south side no doubt providing a view of St Botolph's wharf, which was leased by the Company from the City. The walls of the room were hung with tapestries which would not have disgraced a royal palace, and there were Persian rugs on the floor, no doubt imported by the Company along their eastern trading route. A side table against one wall was carved of some exotic timber and bore jugs and glasses that certainly came from Venice.

Heyward leaned forward, resting his elbows on his desk and his chin on his clasped hands. He looked relaxed but determined, a man accustomed to conducting business briskly and commanding obedience.

'I understand from Dr Nuñez, who is a shareholder and a member of our Court of Assistants, that you are familiar with the case of Gregory Rocksley, one of Sir Francis's men, who has gone missing in Muscovy.

I nodded. I could hardly deny it.

'He was engaged on a most vital mission, one about which Sir Francis, God rest his soul, was deeply concerned. We have evidence that information of vital importance to England and Her Majesty has been leaking out through Narva, almost certainly through the actions of a traitor or traitors who were once in the Company's employ.'

25

'May I ask what kind of evidence?'

He gave a quick nod, as if he approved of the question.

'A Spanish merchantman was captured off the coast of Denmark by one of our own ships, when it was travelling from Narva to the Spanish Netherlands. This was in the spring of last year. Documents were found on board which contained secret information, dangerous to England's safety.' He drew a deep breath. 'They were not even in cipher.'

He shook his head at such carelessness – or was it a kind of arrogance? – on the part of the sender. And I raised my eyebrows. It suggested an amateur to me.

'There was nothing in these documents to reveal the source?' I said.

'Nay. But one was written on a piece of paper with the Company crest. It was old and somewhat grubby, as though it had been kept for some time, but that was one of the details that pointed us toward a possible former employee. That, and the fact that it came from Narva, where several former Company men have set themselves up as independent merchants on their own account.'

His expression showed his disgust at such disloyalty.

'I understand that Rocksley was sent to investigate,' I said, 'but the war between Muscovy and Sweden may have prevented him from reaching Narva.'

'That is correct. Why he then headed for Astrakhan, we cannot know. Perhaps someone he suspected had travelled that way.'

'If it was one of these independent merchants,' I said slowly, 'I suppose he might have had legitimate reasons for travelling to Astrakhan and thence to Persia.'

'Aye, although the area beyond the Caspian Sea can be as dangerous as the Swedish war. Perhaps more so. Trouble is forever breaking out amongst the Tatar tribes and the other barbarians in those parts. We have had disasters there in the past.'

He paused, as a manservant came in with wine, which he poured for us. When he had gone, Heyward resumed.

'It is essential that we discover what has become of Rocksley. To rescue him, if he still lives. Not merely for the man's own sake, but also because he may have discovered information vital for the safety of this nation.'

He raised his glass to his lips and gave me a piercing glance over it. I felt my heart sinking. I had been far too confident, thinking I could withstand this man.

'Her Majesty has always protected the interests of the Company,' he said, 'and the safety of our people, from the moment she came to the throne. There have been times when our men have been held prisoner, for no reason, by the ruthless rulers of that country, merely to use as pawns in political negotiations with Her Majesty. She has never, *never* abandoned them. It is therefore our duty as loyal subjects to do everything in our power to root out this devilment before it goes any further.'

I opened my mouth to speak, but he raised a hand to silence me.

'I know how highly Sir Francis valued both your skill and your discretion. The Earl of Leicester himself was grateful for what you achieved in the Low Countries. On the Portuguese expedition you showed great resourcefulness in extracting Titus Allanby from Coruña under the very noses of the Spanish.'

'A series of lucky accidents,' I protested. I could see perfectly clearly where this was leading, but I would not go down without a fight.

He smiled. 'Perhaps. But it is those who contrive and make use of such lucky accidents who are most useful in situations like these. You will understand that we want you to go to Muscovy and find Rocksley.'

No small order, then.

'Do you even believe he is still alive?' I said.

'That we cannot know. We can only hope.'

'Surely someone more experienced than I would serve you better. Nicholas Berden–'

'Nicholas Berden has recently entered Lord Burghley's service. Besides, the Russians have specifically asked for an English physician to be sent, especially one with particular skills in the treatment of children. You will understand how perfectly you fill all the requirements.'

It crossed my mind to argue that I was Portuguese, not English, but I thought he would not like such a quibble. Besides, my vanity was a little touched by the fact that he regarded me as English. There was, however, one sound argument he could hardly refute.

'But, Master Heyward, I am no longer employed in Sir Francis's service. I serve full-time as a licensed physician at St Thomas's hospital. I have charge of two wards.'

'Ah, I anticipated that you might regard that as a problem.' He gave what I could only describe as a self-satisfied smile. 'More wine?'

27

I shook my head. I sensed that I would not like what was coming next and I needed to keep my wits clear.

'One of my deputies, William Armstrong, has a nephew who has just completed his studies in medicine at Oxford. Early next year he is to take up a position as senior physician in the household of the Archbishop of York, when the present incumbent retires. In the meantime, he is anxious to gain some practical experience in a hospital. Your superintendant at St Thomas's, Master Ailmer, has agreed that he should take over your duties while you are away.'

I half started from my chair in horror, so that wine slopped over the rim of my glass on to my hand.

'A student, fresh from university? With no practical experience?' I swallowed. A vision of maimed and dying patients danced before my eyes. 'He could not possibly take over my duties.'

It may have sounded arrogant, but I was too distressed to care. I set down my glass on a nearby table, for my hand was trembling too much to hold it safely.

'And how could experience in the care of children and pregnant women benefit a man who is to work in an archbishop's household?'

'I daresay both women and children are not unknown in such a household,' he said mildly. 'But your concern for your patients does you credit. Your predecessor at St Thomas's, Dr Colet, has agreed to return for the period of your absence, to supervise young Armstrong. He is experienced and reliable, and will see that no harm is done. His eyesight was beginning to fail and his hands are no longer steady, but there is nothing wrong with his experience or his intellect. It is all arranged.'

All arranged! I gaped at him. This had all been arranged behind my back. Master Ailmer must have known, but had said nothing to me. As if he read my thoughts, Heyward continued.

'I asked Master Ailmer not to mention these arrangements until I had the opportunity to speak to you myself. I know, as a loyal subject of Her Majesty, that you will be glad to undertake this mission which is of such vital importance to the nation. Your possess all the necessary qualities. You are a discreet, resourceful and experienced agent from Sir Francis's service. You can be spared from your work here in London. You are a physician with the essential skills. Moreover, I believe you speak several languages.'

'Not Russian,' I said weakly, acknowledging that I had lost the battle before I had even begun.

He waved a hand dismissively. 'You will have time to learn the essentials on the voyage. I am sending an interpreter with you, but he has also been instructed to teach you as much as possible before you reached Muscovy.'

I put my head in my hands. It was decided, then. I was to travel to that barbarous land ruled by insane tyrants.

'When do we leave?' I asked.

'The end of May.'

I paid a final visit to Sara Lopez before we left for Muscovy. Whenever I saw her, which was not so often now that I lived south of the river, she seemed nervous and afraid. In recent months her hair had grown quite grey, and Ruy's beard and long locks were nearly white. I had not seen either of them since that dinner at which this whole crazed venture had first been mooted, though I heard of Ruy's activities from time to time. How was he faring in this changed world, now that Walsingham was gone? Still attending his noble patients – the Queen, Dom Antonio (failed claimant to the Portuguese throne), and, ironically, the leaders of both the bitter factions, Essex and the Cecils.

After the disaster of the Portuguese expedition, I had thought he would content himself with his profession as a physician and rebuild his fortune patiently through the spice trade, as Dr Nuñez was doing, but Ruy continued doggedly to pursue his financial claims against the Dom, who still owed him thousands of pounds, until the Privy Council, in exasperation, tied them together in such legal knots that I did not suppose he would ever be able to free himself. Sara admitted to me now that he was involved in some other dangerous business. We were sitting in her pretty parlour, where a serving maid had brought us small ale and an assortment of bite-size cakes.

'He has not told me what it is, Kit,' she said, 'but it involves some projection that Ruy and Walsingham had plotted between them, using a Spanish agent called Andrada.'

'Andrada?' I asked, surprised. 'I thought he was one of Dom Antonio's followers, not a spy for Spain.'

'He was. But he grew disillusioned because he had sacrificed so much – family, property, high position in Portugal – all for the Dom. He turned traitor and offered to the Spanish that he would kidnap the Dom and hand him over to King Philip. He reported to the Spanish king under the code name David.'

I looked at her in horror. I had no love of the Dom myself, after what we had endured in Portugal and on the return journey, but this

29

was cruel treachery indeed. And I had deciphered some of those David letters myself. I had not realised that David was the Dom's man, Andrada. I was surprised Sara knew as much as she did, but I suppose, despite all Ruy's cunning, he sometimes felt the need to confide in someone.

'Andrada was seized by Walsingham's men,' Sara went on, 'then released into Ruy's custody, because Ruy said he could turn him again, to work for England. Andrada was told he was in my husband's debt for his very life, and he was kept safe for a while in that house Ruy owns in St Katharine Creechurch.'

I nodded. I knew about the house, a discreet place near the warehouse, where Ruy and Dr Nuñez sometimes lodged Marrano refugees, newly arrived penniless from Portugal. Walsingham had also used it when he needed to keep one of his agents hidden and safe for a time.

'I do not know what they were planning,' said Sara, 'but I have the feeling it was some very dangerous projection, something at the highest level, involving Spain. Andrada went to the Continent on this affair, but then he disappeared. Now that Walsingham is dead, I am so afraid, Kit! If the plot is discovered, Ruy himself might be taken for a Spanish agent, without Walsingham to speak for him and explain that the plan was intended for the benefit of England.'

She sobbed suddenly, and I put my arms around her.

'He is too old for these dangerous games!' she cried angrily. 'Let younger men indulge in them. All I want is for our family to remain safe, but always he seems to seek out danger by choice. He is like a moth who cannot resist the candle, although it will perish in the flame.'

The following day I left my lodgings soon after dawn, handing the key of my room to Goodwife Atkins.

'Master Shakespeare will be here later today,' I said, 'but I shall want the room again when I return.'

She nodded. She had inspected and approved Will as a temporary lodger during my time away. There had been some difficulty between Will and his own landlady, so he was eager to take over my lodgings as soon as possible. What the difficulty was had not been specified, but Simon believed that the lady in question was young, widowed, and somewhat over fond of Will, who did not reciprocate her feelings, though I suspected he was not averse to a little dalliance when the mood took him, as long as it did not tie him in chains. I was grateful that he would keep my room tenanted for me, and he had promised to

30

move on when I returned. He seemed to have shifted about a good deal since coming to London.

I shouldered my knapsack and picked up my satchel of medicines, turning away to walk slowly toward St Thomas's, letting Rikki roam about to his heart's content, for the next parting would be much more difficult.

'Eh, lad,' Tom Read said, when I tapped on the door of the porter's lodge. 'Come to keep company with Swifty and me, have you?'

He crouched down and scratched Rikki behind his ear. Rikki, all innocent of what was happening, went happily to the cushion in the corner where he usually settled.

'I've brought the bowls he eats from,' I said, setting them on the table. 'And he is supposed to sleep on this bit of old blanket, but I am afraid he usually sleeps on my bed. You will need to break him of that.'

I tried to keep my voice steady, but the lump in my throat made it difficult. I knelt down beside Rikki and buried my face in his fur for a moment in the hope that I could take the memory of his warm familiar smell with me.

'God go with you,' I whispered. I would certainly not see him for months, even if I was able to return with this year's fleet. If my task kept me in Muscovy beyond the end of August, I would not return for more than a year, perhaps never. Would he still know me, after so long?

I got slowly to my feet and felt in my purse for coins.

'I must leave you money for his food, Tom,' I said.

'Nay.' He shook his head. 'I get plenty of scraps from the hospital kitchen for Swifty, and they'll give me enough for Rikki, too, knowing he's your dog.'

I could not linger, fearing I would begin to weep, so I turned briskly away, but Tom was not so easily fooled. He patted my arm.

'Do not fret, Dr Alvarez. He'll do fine with us. He'll miss you, but he'll be safe and well fed until you are home again.'

I nodded, not trusting myself to speak.

Out in the courtyard, I found Master Ailmer and Goodwife Maynard, governess of the nursing sisters.

'We could not let you set off without wishing you God speed,' Ailmer said, shaking my hand and bowing.

Goodwife Maynard was tearful. 'That's a fearful place, they say, Dr Alvarez, that Muscovy. Full of heathens and wolves and I dunno

31

what monsters.' She sniffed and passed the back of her hand across her eyes.

'I'm told the whole country is nothing but ice and snow, so I've knitted this for you, to wear over your shirt.'

She handed me a sleeveless garment, knitted in soft natural wool, which would reach nearly to my knees. I could hardly imagine myself appearing in such a shapeless thing, but I thanked her for her kindness.

'And they are not heathens, you know,' I said. 'They are Christians, but they belong to the Eastern Orthodox faith, like the Greeks of Constantinople.'

She shook her head disbelievingly. 'It amounts to the same thing.'

I bade them farewell and strode through the gate, not allowing myself to glance behind me.

By the time I reached the Bridge, I could hold back the tears no longer, so I made a great business of blowing my nose, as if I had a rheum. I knew I could trust Tom with Rikki, but memories of finding my dog neglected and starving in the street on my return from Portugal kept passing through my mind. Besides, how would I fare, without his loving companionship?

Once I reached the quays that lay between the Bridge and the Tower, I was forced to think of other things. There were dozens of ocean-going ships moored at the quays or anchored a short way offshore, so that it would have been difficult to locate the vessels of the Muscovy fleet, had they not all flown the standard of the Company. There were eight of them, all large merchant vessels of considerable tonnage, but unlike many merchant vessels they also bristled with a respectable provision of cannon. I knew I was to travel on one called the *Bona Esperanza* (not an uncommon name for a ship), but at the moment I could not see which one she was.

A hail from behind brought me round from studying the ships. It was the group of Burbage's Men who had chosen to make the journey to Wardhouse. Cuthbert Burbage, Master Burbage's elder son, strode at their head. He was no actor like his younger brother Dick, but an excellent man of business, following in the footsteps of his father. He was already giving directions to a boatman and seeing to the loading of a remarkable amount of baggage into one of the lighters that ploughed back and forth between the quays and the larger ships out at anchor.

Simon was there, and several of the younger players, including three of the boys. He broke away from the company and came over to where I was standing on the quay.

32

'Which ship do you travel on, Kit?'

'The *Bona Esperanza.*'

'That's as well. So do we. Otherwise I should have demanded that you be moved to our ship. Guy would never have forgiven us if he could not have the enjoyment of your lute duets on the long voyage.'

'Guy is coming?' I was astonished. Guy Bingham was the chief musician and comic actor of the company, and I could not believe that Master Burbage would have agreed to manage without him for what would be at least four months, perhaps more.

'Guy has had a little problem with creditors,' Simon said with a laugh. 'London was becoming somewhat uncomfortable for him. Master Burbage agreed to allow him to come, on the understanding that his earnings should be used to pay his debts on his return. In the meantime, Master Burbage will satisfy Guy's creditors, even if it means paying them off himself.'

I raised my eyebrows, but said nothing. The actors were notoriously careless with money, but Guy was usually better than the rest. I was surprised he had entangled himself in such a knot.

'Good morrow, Dr Alvarez.' The voice came from somewhere a little above my elbow. I turned round.

'Davy!'

The boy acrobat had filled out a good deal since I had first seen him brought into St Thomas's, gaunt and near death, but he was still wiry and small. Early malnutrition meant that he would never grow tall, but that would probably prove an advantage in his profession.

'You are going to Wardhouse?' I said.

'Of course. I am apprenticed to Master Bingham. Where he goes, I must go.'

He gave us a wicked grin, then skipped off to where I saw Guy talking to Cuthbert. For good measure, he turned a couple of cartwheels as he went.

'Trouble,' I said. 'Trouble always follows in Davy's wake. I shudder to think what mischief he may get up to on board ship.'

Simon laughed. 'Well, we must hope he does not fall overboard. Guy has spent many hours training him, and would think it a great loss.'

'I had as well brought Rikki,' I said. 'He is considerably more obedient than Davy.'

'From what I hear of Muscovy, he would not have cared for it. Nothing but snow and ice.'

'You sound like Goodwife Maynard. She has knitted me an extraordinary garment against the cold. Master Harriot tells me Muscovy is quite agreeable in summer.'

'Then let us hope you can return when we do, before the bad weather sets in. I suppose you must leave your horse behind, as well as your dog. And your orphan children. And all your other waifs and strays.'

I frowned. Simon was forever teasing me.

'My horse Hector remains at Seething Lane,' I said stiffly, 'and the stable lad Harry has promised to keep him exercised.'

'Well, then, you must rest easy. Both your horse and your dog are in safe hands. Come, let's find our ship.'

He was right. I had been entrusted with a serious mission, where a man's life might be at stake. I must lay aside my private concerns and think only about what I needed to do to carry out that mission. The better I prepared for it, the sooner I might hope to come home.

I followed Simon back along the quay to join the rest of Burbage's men. Guy grinned a welcome, while Cuthbert gave me a somewhat distracted nod. After that, matters moved swiftly. The players' baggage was borne away to the largest of the Muscovy ships anchored in the deeper water and we all followed soon after in three wherries. A rope ladder had been thrown over the side of the *Bona Esperanza* and I was one of the first to swarm up it and jump down from the railing on to the deck. For a moment I felt a pang of apprehension. The last time I had stood on the deck of a ship, we were returning from Portugal with crew and passengers dead and dying around us. And there before us at anchor in Plymouth harbour had been the treacherous Drake, who had made off with all our provisions.

But I must not dwell on the past. Davy and the other boy actors were racing about, getting in the way of the seamen, who shouted at them and cuffed them whenever they could catch them. Cuthbert was overseeing the loading and stowing of the baggage, while the rest of the players were hunting for their quarters.

As the Muscovy ships regularly carried ambassadors, senior members of the Company, and gentlemen travellers, they were well appointed, and provided with comfortable cabins. Dr Nuñez had told me that he had insisted that I should have a cabin to myself, as a distinguished emissary of the Company. The players were distributed between four much larger cabins, and I came in for some good-natured ragging at my privileged state. I did not care. It would make my journey much safer and more comfortable if I was on my own.

Once I had deposited my knapsack and satchel in my cabin, I came back up on deck. The lighter and wherries had rowed back to the shore and the seamen were busy about the rigging, while six men stood ready by the capstan to hoist the anchor. Simon came to stand beside me at the rail. I pointed down at the river, where fragments of straw were spinning in lazy circles.

'The tide is turning,' I said. 'We will sail on the ebb tide.'

'I had forgotten that you are an experienced sailor.' He grinned at me. 'We shall have you swarming up the masts before we know it.'

I shuddered, leaning back and screwing up my eyes to watch one of the sailor boys, as young as Davy, climbing up to the masthead, swift as a squirrel, while other mariners walked along the yardarms as casually as along a London street.

'I haven't the head for it. A tree, that I do not mind. But not . . .that!' I waved my hand at the masts towering above us. They seemed even higher than those on the ships I had known before. The Muscovy ships needed to be fast as well as capacious, to outrun pirates and to make the long return journey to northern waters as speedily as possible.

There was a shrill whistle and shouted orders. The men at the capstan seized the handles and began to tread round it, as the anchor chain tightened, slackened, then tightened again when the anchor began to rise. I noticed that towlines had been thrown across from two of the ship's pinnaces and secured to our bows. Their crews bent to their oars and began to row as the anchor rose, dripping with weed, and was secured in place. As first there was no movement, then the *Bona Esperanza* swung round like a stately lady in full skirts, and began to follow the pinnaces downriver.

Simon gave a sigh of pure excitement and turned to me, his eyes alight.

'We are on our way!'

Chapter Three

*A*lthough the tide was flowing in our favour, there was little wind, so it was clear that the pinnaces would be needed to tow us at least down the first few miles of the river. Although the Thames is a busy thoroughfare for ships and boats of every size and description, it is strewn with muddy shallows and sandbanks, constantly shifting with wind and tide, so that a large ship under sail, with little wind for steerage way, is in constant danger of going aground. To find ourselves in such an embarrassing situation would mean waiting out the time until the next high tide floated us off again. I was aware that a ship's officer was standing in the stern of one of the pinnaces, shouting directions to guide the tow-boats along the deepest channel.

The remaining ships of the fleet took up their positions behind us, the larger vessels towed by two pinnaces, the smaller by a single one. As we moved into the centre of the river, other craft hastened to draw out of our way. The departure of the Muscovy fleet was an important annual event, for everyone in London knew that the Company brought both wealth and fame to England. Spain might plunder the riches of the New World, but our mariners and merchants braved more tempestuous seas and stranger lands to bring home their exotic cargoes. Though to be sure, the cordage and canvas that they imported were just as vital, having equipped our ships which fought against the Spanish invasion fleet, as I had learned during my time with Walsingham.

On our port side, beyond the Tower, lay the shipyards of Ratcliffe, where I could see the wooden skeletons of three unfinished ships. Behind, on the muddy ground and dwarfed by the ships that were a-building, huddled the poor cottages of the craftsmen. On the starboard bank of the river, where Southwark dwindled into Bermondsey and then into fields of green corn, crowds were gathered here and there to watch the Muscovy fleet set out on the long voyage to the frozen north.

Simon had joined the players grouped in the bows of the ship, but I turned in the other direction and climbed the companionway to the poop deck. To my surprise, Guy was leaning on the stern railing. I joined him, resting my arms on the polished wood of the rail and watching the spires and towers of London, wreathed in a summer mist, slipping away behind us.

'I wonder when we shall see it again,' Guy said.

'London? For you it will not be long. You will be home with the fleet by the end of the summer. It must leave Muscovy before the ice and fogs set in, and I am told that can be as early as late August or the beginning of September. I may not be so fortunate.'

'I have never been more than fifty miles from London,' he said. 'It is like being ripped from some umbilical cord.'

I glanced sideways at him in surprise. It was rare for Guy to speak thus sorrowfully. And I had never supposed that he was so little travelled.

He must have caught my look, for he gave a rueful smile.

'I expect that seems very odd to you. In your young life you have been tossed hither and yon. My feelings must sound pathetic.'

'Nay,' I said slowly. 'I remember how strange it felt to leave Portugal, even though we were terrified and were fleeing for our lives. But since I have lived in London . . . well, I suppose it has come to seem home to me. I have no wish to leave either.'

'Following orders, are you?'

'Aye.' I hesitated. 'And you? Simon said London was becoming awkward for you.'

He grimaced. 'I've no one to blame but myself and I ought to know better.'

He turned and leaned his back against the rail. 'There was a time in my life when things became very difficult. I was on my own after I lost my wife and children, and I suppose I turned a little mad. Then I lost my employment as well, and stupidly thought to better my fortunes by gambling at the dice. For a while I was lucky, so I grew over-confident, only to sacrifice everything, all the little that I owned. I swore I'd never gamble for the rest of my life.'

'Have you been at the dice again, Guy?'

He sighed and shrugged. 'More fool that I am. Do you remember Henry Allinger, from the Twelfth Night Revels at Whitehall Palace?'

37

'Aye, the "Turkish" sword swallower from Bermondsey. Who could forget him?'

'We've known each other since we were no more than lads. Took to drinking at an inn down Billingsgate way earlier this year, where there were regular gambling nights two or three times a week. Henry had the sense to give it up after a few weeks, but not me. Oh, no. Once it gets in your blood . . . it's like a drunkard who thinks he'll have just one more drink, it won't do any harm. Just one more throw of the dice and you know this time you'll win.'

His mouth twisted in a self-mocking smile. 'By the time I realised that the fellows there were rogues, using weighted dice, I'd borrowed money to keep on playing. Now I'm in debt to one Ingram Frizer, who is not above beating the life out of anyone who does not repay promptly.'

'That is bad news indeed, Guy.' I was sorry to hear the tale, for I had always respected him.

'Never fear. I'll not be such a fool again. Master Burbage has taken matters in hand and sent me off to Wardhouse while he settles with Frizer. By the time we return, I should have earned enough to pay him back. If not, he'll stop it out of my wages.'

'You may enjoy your time in Wardhouse,' I said, attempting to console him. 'And you will be away from London during the time of year the plague can strike.'

'Aye, there's that.' He did not sound convinced.

We stood in silence as the brown water swirled behind us, stirred up by the tide and our passage. The fleet was strung out now in a long line. Two of the ships had hoisted their mizzen sails, but they hung slack, for the little wind that had been with us as we set out had fallen away to nothing.

The long Limehouse Reach was bordered by flat muddy banks on both sides of the river. Attempts to build here from time to time over the centuries had proved doomed to failure, for in the end the Thames would always flood, carrying down storm water from far inland augmented by high tides swept in from the sea, a sudden devouring monster, leaving behind nothing but ruins and drowned men and beasts. The land here had returned to its primaeval state, a haunt of herons and other wading birds, who made their homes amongst the fallen stones of those abandoned settlements.

'At this rate,' Guy said, 'we shall be fortunate to reach Greenwich before nightfall. I am told that the seamen will not sail down to the estuary and the ocean except by daylight. It is too treacherous.'

We did seem to be making very slow progress. Already the crews of the pinnaces had been changed twice as they grew exhausted.

'I think I will go and inspect my cabin,' I said. As I turned away, Simon climbed up to join us on the poop deck.

'We wondered where you had gone,' he said. 'Did you see that small ship's boat that came alongside?'

Guy nodded. 'We did not pay it much mind.'

'It was from one of the other ships. It seems a problem has developed with her rudder, so we must all put in to the shipyard at Deptford that it may be repaired. They cannot embark on our long voyage with defective steering.'

Guy raised his eyebrows. 'Not even as far as Greenwich by nightfall, it seems.'

'The ebb tide is growing slack,' I said, pointing to the movement of the reeds and grasses along the shore. 'We would have been obliged to drop anchor soon anyway. There is no wind, and the pinnaces cannot tow us against an in-coming tide.'

'Well,' said Simon, 'at least it means the ship will be at rest while we eat our dinner, not tossing about as it has been. I have eaten nothing since I broke my fast this morning, and we are well into the afternoon by now.'

'Aye,' said Guy. 'My stomach agrees. 'Sbones! I had forgotten about Davy! Where is the scamp?'

'Never fear,' said Simon. 'At least for the moment. One of the sailors is teaching him and the other lads how to tie complicated knots. It is keeping him out of trouble.'

'For how long?' I wondered. 'And to what use will he put this new skill? I foresee trouble ahead.'

I said nothing to contradict Simon's description of our passage down the river. If he regarded this slow and stately progress as tossing about, he must have had an exceptionally calm crossing to the Low Countries last year. I wondered how he would fare in the rough weather we would encounter once we were away from land, out in the German Ocean. As for Guy, I suspected he had little idea of what lay ahead.

We were held up at Deptford that night and the whole of the following day and night, while the shipwrights worked to repair the rudder of the *Tudor Rose*. It appeared that the original rudder had been replaced after the previous year's voyage, but made of inferior timber which had already warped, so it was fortunate that the trouble had been discovered before we were fully under way.

I took the opportunity of the delay to start my lessons in Russian. Before leaving, I had received instructions for my mission from Anthony Marler, the Company's chief agent in London. While Rowland Heyward and the Court of Assistants decided on Company policy and managed the finances, it was Marler who oversaw the purchase and loading of the goods to be traded in Muscovy when the fleet departed, and then directed the evaluation and sale of the cargo carried home by the returning fleet. Marler had explained to me the workings of the Company in Muscovy, how I was to travel about, and how to conduct myself in encounters with Russian merchants and officials. It seemed there were very precise rules of behaviour and etiquette that I must observe, if I was to avoid causing grave offense. While I was with him, he also introduced me to the man who was to be my interpreter in Muscovy, one Peter Aubery.

While the shipwrights of Deptford swarmed over the *Tudor Rose*, Aubery and I found a quiet corner on the poop deck, and seated ourselves on coils of rope.

'You seem like an ordinary Englishman to me, Peter,' I said bluntly. 'How is it that you are to be my interpreter?'

He was a slightly plump young man, a little older than I, with a round guileless face. Anyone less like a barbarian from a strange land it was difficult to imagine.

'My name is really Pyotr,' he said mildly. 'My father was a Company stipendiary and my mother Russian, a merchant's daughter, living in Kolmogory, where my father was stationed. They were married in the Orthodox faith, but when my mother was with child my father was recalled to England and the Company would not allow him to bring my mother, not recognising the marriage as legal.'

'That seems very cruel,' I said.

He shrugged. 'She returned to her father's house, which was one of the finest in the town and I grew up there until I was fifteen. She made sure that I was taught English, in case I should ever have the chance to come here. I managed to obtain a clerking post at the Company house in Kolmogory, though my mother died soon after.'

'And what had become of your father?'

'I wrote to him after my mother's death, and he was able to arrange for me to come to London. I have lived with him and his English family ever since, and continue to work for the Company, mostly as an interpreter, since on the whole Englishmen find it difficult to learn Russian.'

He gave me a questioning look.

'And now I am supposed to teach you during the course of a single voyage.'

I sensed the underlying question and laughed.

'I do not expect to become fluent. I think you are only supposed to teach me some simple vocabulary. And I had better learn the Cyrillic characters too.'

He nodded. 'It would help me to know what languages you are already familiar with.'

I pondered. 'English. Portuguese. Spanish. Italian. French. Latin. Greek. Hebrew. No German. Only a few words of Dutch.'

He laughed. 'Well, that gives us a starting point. Greek will help you with the alphabet, which has some similarities. You do not know any Slavic languages?'

I shook my head. 'I have never had the opportunity.'

'Well, we shall make a start by learning the Russian names for simple things like man, woman, father, mother – will that be acceptable?'

I nodded. I do not know whether Pyotr had ever taught the rudiments of Russian before, but he proved a good teacher, concentrating on basic words and correcting my pronunciation carefully and patiently until he was satisfied. Fortunately I have always had a good ear for languages, and I believe that the more languages you learn, the better you understand how any language works. By the end of the day I had memorised about twenty useful phrases and Pyotr had written out the Cyrillic alphabet for me.

As we walked toward the cabin where our meals were served, Pyotr cleared his throat and looked at me nervously.

'I believe you come from a Marrano background, Dr Alvarez?'

'Please call me Kit,' I said, wondering where this was leading. 'Aye, there is no secret about it.'

'I thought I should warn you . . . Muscovy is intransigent in this . . . No Jew is permitted to enter the country.'

'I am a baptised Christian,' I said, 'as I suppose you are. I have nothing to fear on that score.'

'Good,' he said, and never mentioned the subject again.

Yet I shuddered inwardly. One more secret to be kept, if I valued my life.

The next morning the fleet was readied for the onward journey. Coming up from the dining cabin where we had broken our fast, I was surprised to see all the crew very grandly clothed in Company livery.

'What is this?' I asked Pyotr, who was standing with Cuthbert and Guy on the foredeck. 'Why are the men wearing this finery?'

'We will be passing Greenwich Palace soon,' Pyotr explained, 'and Her Majesty is in residence. She likes to watch the Muscovy fleet set out. She has always taken a great interest in the Company's affairs.'

It was what Rowland Heyward had told me. I suppose our Muscovy trading fleet was the Queen's riposte to Spain's treasure ships which loot the New World.

'A salute will be fired on our cannon,' Cuthbert warned, 'so be prepared to cover your ears.'

'I have never understood why that should be regarded as a way to please monarchs,' I said.

Guy grinned. 'Because they like a lot of noise, and the louder the better. And seeing how well armed are our ships must be a way of thumbing our nose at our enemies. Gloriana has never despised a little pageantry whenever possible.'

Fortunately for the dignity of our departure from Deptford and our ceremonial parade past Greenwich Palace, there was now a moderate breeze from the south west. As we began to move away from the shipyard, there was much blowing of whistles and trumpets, the sailors broke out the full canvas, and the *Bona Esperanza* began to make her stately way downriver, followed in strict order of tonnage by the other seven ships.

As we drew level with the palace, the captain himself raised a trumpet to his lips and blew a signal I had not heard before. Immediately there was the crack and roar of all our cannon being fired at once. I had my hands over my ears, but even so my head rang with the noise, while I could feel the ship buck and shiver under my feet. I had been involved in the edges of the battle with the Spanish two years before, and the noise had been almost unbearable then, but the guns had not all been fired at the same time. Now the air was filled with a choking cloud of smoke. The breeze was not strong enough to disperse it, so we were all soon coughing. These ceremonial firings use all the usual gunpowder, though happily they omit the shot, otherwise the palace would have been peppered with cannonballs, as first the *Bona Esperanza* and then each of the ships in turn saluted Her Majesty.

The royal standard was flying from a flagpole above the palace and all the sailors not engaged in manning the rigging stood to attention in their livery, facing the shore. I could see no sign of the Queen, but I am sure she was watching discreetly from a window. She could hardly have failed to be aware of our passing.

Once past Greenwich and clear of the drifting cloud of smoke from the cannon, we moved out into the middle of the river, where we had the benefit of another ebb tide as well as the favourable wind, though it barely filled the sails. A long, slow, and meandering sail lay ahead of us. Pyotr pointed out to Guy the dark banks at the place they call Blackwall, but there is little to recommend it other than the slippery foreshore of black mud. Some smaller ships were hauled up on the shore, where they were being scraped clean of barnacles by workmen themselves blackened by the mud they waded through. There was a small shipyard here as well. The whole of these lower reaches of the Thames were dotted with them, established at the time when the Queen's father had first taken an interest in building up a navy.

Then it was on past the flat marshy country stretching out on either side as the river widened, drawing nearer to the sea – Kent to the south of us, Essex to the north. The ebb was slackening now, so that we moved more and more slowly through this dull, sluggish country. I felt I should be more usefully occupied, perhaps studying my Russian, but there is something hypnotic about standing on the deck of a moving ship and watching the land slip by.

'Woolwich,' said Cuthbert, pointing to a busy shipyard, larger even than Deptford. 'Please God none of our ships need further repairs. If we continue to travel at this pace we shall not reach Wardhouse before next year.'

Guy shuddered, but Pyotr only grinned.

'You will find everything will change, once we are at sea.'

Cuthbert shook his head in disbelief. Like Simon, he had travelled to the Low Countries last year. From Simon's remarks they must have had a most unremarkable voyage.

We were all relieved when we passed Woolwich without stopping. It was late afternoon when we came to Gravesend. The sailors, who had laid aside their finery and donned their everyday slops, began to climb the rigging and haul in the sails, tying them loosely to the spars, until we were driven only by the foresail and mizzen. The captain had retired to his cabin in the stern-castle and his pilot officer was now in charge. The ship came slowly about until she was heading into the wind. At a signal the anchor was released and the remaining sails struck. The *Bona Esperanza* came quietly to a stop.

Cuthbert strode over to the pilot officer.

'There are several hours of daylight left,' he said. 'Surely we can go further today.'

The officer gave him the kind of polite but pitying look mariners are apt to bestow on landsmen.

'The estuary is very dangerous. The shoals and sandbanks will have shifted even in the last few weeks. Only a fool would attempt a passage at the end of the day. We will lie at anchor until full light tomorrow.' He turned away to his duties.

Cuthbert shrugged and came over to where Guy had persuaded me to join him in some music making, to the amusement – but I think also pleasure – of the sailors.

'It is no use,' Cuthbert said. 'Here we stay until tomorrow.'

'Be glad of the rest while you may,' Pyotr said. He had brought out an odd stringed instrument unlike any I had seen before and had formed a trio with us. 'You see those clouds building up over the German Sea? There will be stormy weather ahead. You will be looking back with regret at our peaceful journey down the Thames, however frustrating you may have thought it.'

Before dusk the next day, Pyotr was proved right. After we had carefully picked our way through the complex maze of sand, mud, and water that forms the mouth of the Thames, we had perhaps two or three hours of moderate wind, blowing first from the south west, then veering round to the south. We were all cheered by the brisk pace of the fleet, and a fine sight we made, creaming along under full sail northwards up the Essex coast.

It was almost possible to ignore the increasingly black clouds building up out to the east over the German Sea. After all, the wind was not blowing them towards us. Or so we reassured ourselves. Nevertheless, I could not help but notice the worried looks exchanged by the officers and the older sailors. It was about then that the order was given to furl the topsails.

'What is this?' Cuthbert said.

He had found Pyotr and me in our usual place, where I was being drilled on the words and phrases I had learned.

'Why are they taking in some of the sails? Surely we want to move at the best possible speed.'

Pyotr gave him a wry glance.

'The captain expects the wind to veer round to the east. That will blow the storm our way. It also risks driving us onshore. He needs to keep enough sail on to give him steerage way, but to reduce our speed, so that we cannot rush out of control and wreck ourselves on the shore.'

Cuthbert snorted. 'I do not believe that storm will come anywhere near us. It will blow away to the Low Countries.' He stamped off, where I soon saw him arguing with one of the officers.

'You seem to know a great deal about ships and sailing,' I said to Pyotr.

He shrugged and smiled. 'I cannot tell you how many times I have made this journey. I am no mariner, but I have eyes and ears. I have seen this kind of operation before. If the wind grows too strong, blowing us onshore, they will run for a harbour. Probably Harwich will be the most likely.'

He paused and looked at me sideways, as if judging my courage. 'On the return from the second Company voyage to Muscovy, back in '56, Richard Chancellor was drowned when his ship was hit by just such an onshore wind off Scotland.'

'I believe I have heard of him,' I said slowly. 'Wasn't he–'

'He was a brilliant mariner and scientist, who discovered the route through the arctic seas to Muscovy and so began the whole of this.' He waved his arm to take in the fleet. 'Despite all his skill, he could not save his ship, though he saved the life of the first Russian ambassador. Both he and his young son were drowned.'

'In weather conditions like these?' I asked.

'Probably a worse storm. But Captain Turnbull is an experienced and sensible man. He will not take unnecessary risks. See, we are beginning to head more westerly. I think we are indeed making for Harwich.'

By late afternoon we had dropped anchor in the harbour at Harwich, and even Cuthbert was forced to concede that it was the right course of action, for during the last hour we had been driven in from the sea by a rising gale, while the sky grew almost as black as night and lashing rain had sent all of us passengers below decks. We cast our anchor in a spot partially protected by a spit of land but still in deep water and well clear of other ships. Even so, the *Bona Esperanza* flailed about in the wind, fighting against the anchor chain, bucking from side to side like an unbroken horse, while the wind howled in the rigging. From time to time a crash up on deck warned us that something had broken loose.

Almost all of the crew were also below decks, apart from two on watch, one in the bows, one in the stern, who had lashed themselves to the railings, lest they be thrown overboard. Before the worst of the

45

storm had broken, the men had fixed a network of ropes along the decks to provide handholds for the men who would relieve the watch. I was grateful I would not be called upon to brave the violence breaking over our heads, but even below decks it felt far from safe, for the timbers of the ship creaked and groaned as she was assaulted. I began to fear her sides might spring apart and open a way for the sea to swamp us.

When I made my way along to the dining cabin after the bell had clanged to call us to dinner, I could barely keep on my feet, as I was tossed first one way and then the other, bruising my shoulder hard against the doorframe as I entered the cabin. We were a much reduced company. Most of the officers were about their duties elsewhere. Simon and Cuthbert were not to be seen.

'Seasick,' said Guy. He looked somewhat green about the mouth himself. 'If it is this bad in harbour, what must it be like out at sea?'

'Unpleasant.' It was Christopher Holme, travelling out to Muscovy to take up the position of chief agent. He gripped the edge of the table as the ship tried to throw him flat on his back.

'And this is just on the coast of England.' He gave a rueful smile. 'I have heard that the conditions are much, much worse off Norway and round the North Cape this year. I am already beginning to question whether I wise to accept my new post.'

Guy was beginning to look very pale indeed.

'Sit down,' I said to him. 'Trying to stand is making you dizzy. Do not eat much. Or if you like, eat nothing, but go and lie down. You will not feel the movement so much then.'

Guy shook his head. 'I will not be overcome by this. If I can walk a tightrope without losing my nerve, why should I be alarmed by a little tossing aboard ship?'

At that moment we were hit by a wave driven athwart the ship, so that she heeled over alarmingly. Like Master Holme, Guy grabbed the edge of the table for support and lowered himself hastily into one of the benches screwed in place to the cabin floor.

Having survived a worse storm in the Bay of Biscay on the return journey from Portugal, I knew I was unlikely to suffer from seasickness, but it was still possible to receive a battering from the movement of the ship. And I did not feel particularly hungry either, which was as well, for we were served a skimpy meal, all of it cold.

'The cook dare not light a fire,' the cabin boy explained. 'The wood could be thrown off the fire if another wave like that one hit us. Then the whole ship would take fire.'

'So we have a pretty prospect before us,' said Guy, pulling one of his long clown faces. 'Either we shall drown or perish by fire.'

Fortunately, neither fate befell us. However, we spent three miserable days storm-tossed in Harwich harbour. On the fourth day we tottered up on deck, those of us still on our feet, to survey the damage. Some of the smaller spars were broken and hung haphazard in a cat's-cradle of tangled rigging. The damage did not seem too serious, but there would be further delays while repairs were made. Peering out across the rest of the fleet, through the fine drizzle that still fell in the aftermath of the storm, we could see that the other vessels in our fleet had suffered too.

'God's bones,' Simon said, joining me on the poop deck and drawing deep breaths of the damp but clean air. 'I hope it will not be like this all the way to Wardhouse.'

'You look terrible.' I said.

'That is very reassuring. Could you not, as a physician, have come to our aid? Given us some sort of potion?'

'There is no cure for seasickness but time,' I said. 'Eat nothing, drink nothing but clean water or small ale, and lie down until it passes. Eventually it *will* pass. I have heard of sailors who are sick every time they go to sea, until they get what they call their "sea legs". After that they are not troubled.'

He gave a disbelieving snort. 'So why do they continue as sailors? It sounds like madness to me.'

'Perhaps they enjoy the life.' I knew I did not sound very convincing, for I was aware many sailors had been pressed into service, and I could not imagine the appeal of such a life myself. Perhaps some of them had no other choice.

Cuthbert bustled toward us.

'I am going with the shore party so that I can send a letter to my father, explaining how we have been delayed. The officer in charge of supplies will also be purchasing fresh meat and vegetables. Do you wish to come?'

We both shook our heads, but Guy, coming up behind Cuthbert, said he would be glad to set foot on dry land for a while. We watched them board one of the pinnaces, which had been lowered into the water, and they were soon rowed away to the port.

'I am beginning to wish I had not volunteered for this voyage,' Simon said. 'Let us hope that we have now suffered the worst of it.'

'Oh, I think not,' I said. 'I am sure it will be *much* worse as we sail further north.'

With that he chased me the full length of the ship, until we both collapsed, laughing. At least he looked the better for it, his face no longer grey.

With the repairs in Harwich and more delays due to unfavourable winds, it was the last week of June by the time we found ourselves off the Firth of Forth, the wide estuary which has Edinburgh and Leith on its southern shores. Once again there was a storm brewing, but this time Captain Turnbull hoped to outrun it. The clouds were boiling up in the south, but the wind was also blowing from that direction, and he planned to run ahead of the storm, further up the east coast of Scotland and then heading north-east toward Norway.

'He has told me there will not be much time now to reach St Nicholas, unload the cargo, load the Muscovy goods, and escape before the ice closes the seas,' Christopher Holme said. 'It is a risk, but he has chosen to take it. If the storm overtakes us, we can seek shelter in the estuary of the Tay, not far north of here.'

We were under full sail now, scudding over the choppy grey waters of the German Ocean at an alarming speed. With our greater spread of canvas, we began to pull away from the rest of the fleet. It was strict Company policy that the Muscovy fleet should stay together, ever since the disasters of the very first voyage of exploration. Then, two of the three ships had failed to reduce sail in a high wind and vanished into storm and fog. The remaining ship, Richard Chancellor's ship, had gone on to discover the port of St Nicholas, where we were now bound. The other ships were only found the following year, with their crews mysteriously dead, seemingly frozen while eating or writing or playing cards, with plenty of food still left on board. It was a tale to frighten naughty children – or nervous voyagers aboard the Muscovy fleet.

It seemed that our own captain was afraid of losing contact with the rest of the ships, for once again the topsails were tied down, and our headlong speed reduced a little, allowing the other ships to catch up, though by now the wind was so strong that I think we would have been blown along with no canvas hoisted at all. The sailors were raising a signal flag which meant nothing to me, but Pyotr, coming up from below decks and squinting at the yardarm, gave a quick nod.

'He's signalling that we are to take shelter. That will mean the estuary of the Tay, and it is as tricky as the mouth of the Thames. I hope the pilot officer has an up-to-date rutter.'

'What is a rutter?' Simon muttered in my ear. I think he was a little resentful of Pyotr's familiarity with these mysteries of the sea.

'It's a written description of a piece of coastline,' I said. 'Harriot told me about them. When a chart does not give enough detail, mariners record rocks and shoals wherever they observe them, and useful sights on land for guiding a ship's course. These "rutters" are copied and shared between ship's officers. I suppose Pyotr means someone who has sailed up here to trade with the Scots may have given one to Captain Turnbull.'

'Do people ever come here?' Simon looked about disparagingly as we began to make our way into a vast stretch of water. It looked more like an arm of the sea than a river. There were low hills on either side, but in the distance ahead of us the land rose much higher. There was no sign of habitation.

'About six miles upriver there is a town called Dundee.' Pyotr had overheard Simon. 'It is a busy port, trading with Danzig and the Low Countries and Narva. Second city after Edinburgh for trade amongst the Scotchmen. Further along is Perth, and Scone, where they crown the Scotch kings, like Her Majesty's cousin Jamie.'

'We are not going all that way, are we?' Simon sounded horrified.

Pyotr laughed. 'I do not think so. We'll probably anchor off Bruach Tatha. See? That fishing village, there. Beside the castle on the north shore.'

We looked where he pointed. A formidable old castle stood on a spit of land, with cannon pointing out over the water, clearly intended to deter any unfriendly ships from proceeding upriver. Beside it clustered a huddle of fishermen's cottages. Their boats could be clearly seen pulled up on the shingle, their nets were draped over long lines strung between the boats and the cottages.

'That's a poor-looking place,' Simon said. 'And what are those people doing, clambering about on the rocks below the castle? They're half naked.'

'They seem to be gathering seaweed,' I said.

'Are they so poor they must eat seaweed?' Simon was shocked.

One of the sailors, busy coiling down a rope nearby, heard him and laughed. 'Nay, they sell it to farmers to fertilise their fields. Or so I've been told. They claim to speak English in these parts, but it's no English I've ever heard.'

One of the officers shouted at him, and he ran off, his bare feet slapping on the boards of the deck. It seemed the captain judged we

49

were sheltered enough by the hills on either side of the river, although the river must have been two miles wide. The last of the canvas was furled, the anchor rattled down, and the *Bona Esperanza* came to rest. The remainder of the fleet soon joined us, anchoring at a safe distance just as the clouds rolled in and our second storm overtook us.

'It seems that some unkind Fate is determined to put a stop to our voyage,' Simon said, as we lowered our heads and ran for the companionway. 'I do not believe we shall ever reach Muscovy.'

This second storm passed more quickly than the first. By the afternoon of the next day the storm clouds had blown away to the north and a watery sun lit up the shores of this wide river. Seen properly now, the Tay was magnificent. By comparison, the Thames and the Tejo, and the rivers I had encountered in the Low Countries, were but streams. The countryside seemed fertile too, so that it was strange to find it so sparsely populated, despite Pyotr's claims of a busy port further upstream.

There was no sign of life on the south bank. The seaweed harvesters on the north bank had disappeared from the castle rock when we ourselves had gone below to avoid the storm. As the sun began to dry the decks and the bundled canvas, creating a small cloud of steam over each ship, I stood with Simon and Pyotr studying the only people and houses to be seen. There were guards patrolling at the castle. Otherwise I could make out no one except a small group of women and children on the foreshore below the cottages. The women appeared to be gutting fish and packing them into barrels, while a cloud of gulls swooped and screamed about them, snatching up the fish guts as they were thrown away, before ever they touched the ground.

'Are they salting the fish?' Simon asked, screwing up his eyes.

'Probably,' Pyotr said. 'This is a famous salmon river and they export hundreds of barrels of salmon. "Lax" they call them.' He laughed. 'A Scotchman told me the apprentices in Dundee managed to have a law passed that they should not be fed salmon by their masters more than three times a week, they were so heartily sick of it!'

'Many a pauper in London would be glad of it,' I said, thinking of my Southwark patients. 'If we had Master Harriot's perspective trunk, Simon, we should be able to see whether the fish are salmon, and if they are salting them.'

'Did he not intend to make you a smaller one, to bring on the voyage?' Simon said.

'He did, but one of the workmen knocked the box of lenses on to the floor and they were smashed. Master Harriot has sent to Venice for more, but they did not come in time.'

'What is a perspective trunk?' Pyotr asked.

I could see that Simon was pleased that for once he was able to do the explaining.

On the ebb tide mid morning the next day, we set out again. Almost immediately, Captain Turnbull set our course to the north east. The wind, blowing steadily from the south west could not have suited us better. Before long we had left the estuary behind and were out in the open sea, passing a small rocky island where a bell clanged mournfully, tossed by the waves.

'How did the bell come there?' I asked, throwing out my question to anyone who might answer. 'It looks a treacherous place. Sharp rocks awash with the waves.'

'Monks,' said Guy. 'I wondered myself, and asked the pilot officer. So many ships were wrecked there that the monks of Arbroath Abbey, further up the coast from here, made attempt after attempt, until at last they were able to secure the bell there, where the waves would sound it and give warning to passing ships, even in the dark. He says he has heard that several monks died before they succeeded at last. Even then the bell was stolen by pirates and had to be replaced.'

We all regarded the vicious looking rock soberly, as breakers creamed around its jagged fangs. I thought of the courage of those monks and of the terrible deaths of those who had gone down there with their ships. But it was soon left behind us, as we made for the open sea.

'The next land we will see will be Norway.'

I think Guy was beginning to enjoy the voyage, now that the storms had passed and we were moving briskly on our way.

'How are you feeling now, Simon?' he said. 'No more sickness?'

'Not at the moment,' Simon said bravely, although he looked a little queasy. 'I feel better up on deck.'

'Well, if you decide to be sick,' Pyotr said, 'make sure you head for the lee rail.'

The next few days were a pleasant change after all we had endured along the coasts of England and Scotland. The winds remained favourable, blowing from the best quarter and continuing steady – strong but not dangerously so. We saw a school of dolphins, who

51

frisked about us and followed us for some miles. It was the height of summer now, but the wind meant that it was pleasant on deck, although below it became hot and airless. My small cabin was stuffy at night, but I loved the privacy it provided. Mostly I slept with no covers at all over me.

On the second day out from Scotland we caught sight of a single ship flying the Danish flag away on our starboard side. For a time she seemed to be shadowing us, but finally she turned away and vanished to the east.

'The Kings of Denmark think they own these waters,' Captain Turnbull muttered to Cuthbert. 'The present king is just a boy, but the regency keeps up an old tradition.'

Like Simon, Cuthbert seemed to have recovered from the worst of his seasickness, although he still looked pale.

'Could he cause us trouble?' he asked.

The captain shrugged. 'Not with a single ship. He is more concerned to protect the route through the Straits to the Baltic, and to charge tolls for the privilege of sailing through it, but now that we no longer go to Narva, that is no concern of ours. We should catch sight of the coast of Norway before the day is out.'

His words proved true. About halfway through the afternoon there was a shout from the boy on watch at the masthead. He was pointing to the east. Where the rest of us were, down on the deck, the land was not yet visible, but after a while it came in sight. Norway had a coast unlike any I had seen before, as fretted and pleated as a courtier's ruff, with inlets running deep into the land between towering cliffs covered with dense forests of pine. Here and there small villages clung to the steep slopes or lay at the waterside, their wooden houses painted in a rainbow of colours, bright reds and greens predominating. Small fields had been hacked out of the forest, where herds of diminutive cattle, sheep, and goats grazed, but it was clear, from the number of boats we saw, out on the water with their fishing nets, or pulled up on shore, that most men lived by harvesting the sea. It looked a pretty country, somehow miniature, such as you might see in a painting, through a window behind the sitter's chair. Perhaps this was an illusion caused by the towering cliffs, which dwarfed both houses and people.

Captain Turnbull, however, was not venturing close to land.

'The whole coast along here is strewn with islands,' he said. 'Some are pleasant and inhabited. We shall stop at the Lofoten Islands for fresh water and food, but many of the islands are nothing but rocks, sharp as a razor and hidden at high tide. No monks' bells here to give us warning.'

As a result, we stayed well offshore, so with little to distract us, Pyotr and I continued with our lessons. He declared himself satisfied with my progress, even when Simon sat with us and tried to distract me from my studies.

'It is important that I learn as much as I can,' I pointed out, with some asperity. 'I may find myself somewhere without Pyotr's help and I must know enough of the language to extricate myself from trouble.'

Pyotr nodded. 'We must hope that will not happen, but it is wise to be prepared.'

Simon opened his mouth, clearly intending to say something to annoy Pyotr, but we never discovered what it was, for at that moment there was a shout from one of the sailors who had climbed up to clear a tangle in the rigging.

'You fool boy,' he yelled. 'Are you sleeping? Why a'nt you keeping a lookout?'

A tousled head appeared above the lip of the crow's nest. The boy clearly had been sleeping. He gave a startled yelp, but before he could call out, the sailor was scrambling down the rigging, shouting.

'Four ships off the port beam, sir! Heading our way and coming fast. No standards flying.'

Simon and I looked at each other blankly.

'More Danish ships?' I asked. 'Alerted by the one we saw before?'

'No standards,' Pyotr said grimly. 'Pirates.'

Chapter Four

'Get below!' Captain Turnbull bellowed, no longer the courteous gentleman but an angry despot. 'All you landsmen, get below decks and stay there, out of our way!'

We scrambled to obey. I ran first to my cabin to fetch my satchel of medicines, for I was certain they would soon be needed, then I made my way to the dining cabin, where I found the players, mostly huddled together with horrified looks on their faces. Simon was trying to brave it out, but he looked pale. Master Holme and Pyotr seemed calmer, so I joined them, hoping they could offer reassurance.

'There are often pirates off the coast of Norway,' Master Holme said. 'That is why our ships are always fully armed now. In the early days we were not so well provided. We lost cargoes, and even ships and men, to pirates. It was a lesson soon learned. Unless these pirates are exceptionally well armed, we should be able to withstand them.'

I was a little concerned by the tentative nature of that 'should be able', but he sounded convinced by his own words.

Pyotr nodded. 'Last year we were attacked by six ships and beat them off without too much damage. Three men injured and one dead. Some rigging torn away and one topsail in tatters, but the ships always carry spare cordage and canvas.' He grinned suddenly. 'The best cordage in the world, made in the Company's rope-walk in my native town of Kolmogory.'

I did not trouble to tell him I cared not a fig where the cordage came from. I was more interested in the quality of our cannon. I had a sudden memory of the cannon foundry I had seen four years before in the Wealden Forest, where half-naked men had moved in silhouette against a hellish cascade of fiery red molten metal. On the skill of such men our very lives now depended.

The cabin where we had gathered was directly under the captain's cabin, which itself lay immediately below the poop deck. These modern fast ships had much lower fore and aft castles than the older ships we sometimes saw in the Thames. They were not as top heavy, so would surely be more stable in the fast manoeuvres of battle. Directly below us lay the gun deck, where we could hear the running feet of the gunners and their powder monkeys. There came a loud clatter as the hatches over the gun ports on our port side were raised, followed by the rumble of the cannon being rolled out.

Then there was a deathly hush, as if the very ship held her breath.

I strained to see over the shoulders of Pyotr and Master Holme, who were blocking the view through the cabin window. The glass of the window was thick, as I suppose it must be on board, for strength, and it was slightly distorted, so the approaching ships appeared twisted. They were already much nearer.

Cuthbert wiped his face with a handkerchief, then – noticing that I had seen him stuffing it into the breast of his doublet – assumed a falsely cheerful air. Indeed, it was hot in the cabin, but he was sweating with more than heat.

'Why do they not fire?' he demanded. 'Are they waiting for those rogues to board us?' He voice rose several tones above normal.

'I believe they are waiting until they are sure of a clean shot,' Master Holme said. He sounded calm, but I saw that the hand he rested on the sill of the window was trembling slightly.

I had more to fear than the rest of them. For if the pirates boarded, they might discover my sex. Better to die in a clean fight than that.

The nearest pirate ship was turning broadside on to us. She had run out her own cannon. Behind me I could hear one of the player boys sobbing and another whispering frantic prayers. My elbow was jostled and I looked aside to see Davy on tiptoe, also straining to see through the window. His face was alight with excitement. He was fearless, the madcap imp – or merely foolish – but I hoped his fearlessness would communicate itself to the other boys.

There was a puff of smoke from one of the pirate's gun ports, followed almost at once by a splash as a fountain of water shot into the air directly outside our window. The flash and boom of the enemy cannon.

'Why do we not fire!' Cuthbert cried angrily.

Guy patted his arm. 'Any moment now.'

He had hardly spoken when the roar of the cannon beneath nearly deafened us, the floor boards shaking under our feet. Three of our own cannon balls fell short, but one scored a direct hit against the side of the nearest ship, another struck their mainmast. It was not broken, but I saw a great splinter fly off it and land amongst the crew, who were lined up along the rail, armed with muskets.

'I think we were better away from the window,' Master Holme said, taking Davy by the arm and drawing him to the far side of the cabin.

Pyotr and I followed, and Simon joined us as we sat at the table. I found that my knees were trembling. I did not know whether it was from the vibration of the cannon below, or from fear. My heart was racing, and yet I felt oddly calm. Every detail of the faces about me seemed sharper than usual. I have noticed this strange effect before when I have been in danger. It is only afterwards that I have begun to shake.

'There is so much smoke now, Davy,' I explained, 'that you will find it difficult to see anything. And if the glass of the window shatters, we could be cut by flying fragments.'

He shrugged, and pulled a handful of small balls out of his pockets. As he began to juggle, whistling cheerfully, one boy stopped sobbing, the other stopped praying. Davy was not as skilled as Guy yet, but they began to toss balls between them, as if nothing else was happening on board. I grinned across at Simon.

'He's not a bad lad, that Davy,' he said.

I nodded. Anything else we might have said was drowned by the crash of more cannon fire. I looked over my shoulder and caught a brief glimpse of the nearest pirate ship through the window. It was closer, but part of the mainmast was now sheered off and hung from a tangle of rigging. Our gunners must have found their aim.

'We're doing them some damage!' I shouted over the noise, but just as the others smiled and nodded, there was a crash overhead and a scream.

'We've been hit!' Several people cried out at once.

I grabbed my medicine satchel.

'Someone is hurt,' I said. 'I have to go. I may be able to help.'

Simon grabbed my arm. 'There is a surgeon in the crew,' he said. 'There's no need for you to risk your life up there.'

I shook his hand off. 'I've seen him,' I said. 'I would not place high hopes in his skill.'

Master Holme looked angry. 'The Company would never employ a man who was incompetent.'

'He may be competent,' I said, 'when he is sober, but I have observed that he is a little too fond of his beer. There is no need for anyone else to come. I am only going to see if I am needed. That was the cry of a man badly injured.'

Before they could stop me, I was through the door and shut it behind me. I leaned back against it, my eyes closed, and drew a deep breath. In front of the others I could pretend to calmness, but my heart was pounding so hard I though I should see it fluttering my doublet, and the palms of my hands were sweating. I rubbed them on my breeches. I could not hold my instruments or open a jar of salve if my hands were damp.

I climbed the few steps up to the deck, for the cabin was sunk about four feet below it, while another shallow flight led up to the captain's cabin above.

'What are you doing?' The pilot officer grabbed me by the shoulders and was about to throw me back down the steps.

'I am a physician,' I gasped, twisting away from him. 'I've come to see if I am needed.'

'Oh, in that case . . .' He pointed to where two men were carrying another to the far side of the deck and laying him down in the shelter of the pinnace that was lodged there.

'Jos Needler is hit,' he said. 'Those bastards are firing scrap shot, not balls. They aim to kill us, but keep the ship intact, so they can seize it. Jos stopped a fistful of broken iron. I doubt there's much you can do for him.'

'Your own surgeon?' I said. 'I would not trespass where I'm not wanted.'

He gave a sharp bark of laughter. 'Nothing but a b'yer lady coward. Locked himself in his cabin. Never been to sea before. Never seen fighting. You go right ahead, Master Alvarez, and welcome.'

I wasted no time, but scrambled across the deck to where the injured man had been laid. Some of our own rigging had been brought down, and the deck was strewn with debris. Instinctively I ducked as a cannon ball shot over my head and landed in the sea beyond the ship. It seemed the pirates were using balls as well as scrap.

The sailor Jos was bleeding badly when I reached him. His left side and thigh were a mass of torn cloth, blood, and fragments of metal embedded in his flesh. The two men who had laid him here were gazing at him helplessly.

'Here, you,' I said, 'dip me up a bucket of sea water and fetch a mug of small ale. And you,' I pointed to the other man, 'lift his head and shoulders.'

I unbuckled my satchel and took out my flask of poppy syrup. When the first sailor returned, I reached out my hand for the ale without looking up, then added a generous dose of poppy syrup.

Jos was wild-eyed and moaning, but I slipped my own arm under his shoulders, while the sailor held him up.

'Now, Jos,' I said, 'this will ease the pain a little, then I am going to remove these bits of metal those bastards have peppered you with. Do you understand?'

He nodded, and made a valiant effort to hold back his moans. As he drank the dose from the cup I held, his teeth clattered again the rim.

The whole ship shuddered as another volley was fired. The bucket slopped over and I found I was kneeling in water, but there was no time to worry about that.

I fumbled in my satchel until my hand closed over my larger tweezers.

'I'm going to start removing the metal now,' I said. 'It will hurt, but remember, each time you feel it hurt, it's one more piece gone. Right?'

He did his best to give me a smile. 'Right, doctor.'

'I need you both to hold him still,' I told the sailors. 'He's bound to flinch. He can't help it.'

I began at once. Each piece I pulled out, I set aside in a small pile. It would give Jos some satisfaction to see it all. If he recovered. About ten pieces came out easily, then I moved on to those more deeply embedded. In some cases I had to enlarge the lesion with a surgical knife in order to catch hold of the piece with my tweezers. One of the sailors found it too difficult to watch and fled to vomit over the side of the ship, but by now Jos had swooned away with pain and shock, helped by the poppy juice.

Finally there was only one fragment left. It was long and thin, and had penetrated deeply into the man's side. I wiped my face with the back of my hand, and realised I had smeared myself with blood. Both my hands were covered with it.

'It looks like a dagger blade,' the remaining sailor whispered. 'Has it killed him?'

'Not yet,' I said grimly, though I did not like Jos's pallor and the ragged sound of his breathing. 'Pray that it has not penetrated his lung.'

He took me at my word and closed his eyes, his lips moving in a silent prayer. I drew the bucket of sea water close and laid a fist full of clean bandage beside it, for when I drew this vicious spike out, a rush of blood would follow. I eased the opening a little wider, then gripped with my tweezers and pulled. At first it resisted me, then it came out smoothly, like the dagger blade it resembled. Blood poured out over my hands and on to the deck. At once I swabbed the place with cloths soaked in sea water, for sea water has curiously curative properties.

'I shall need to stitch this,' I said.

'Here.' The voice came from behind me.

I twisted round and saw Simon kneeling on the deck, holding out my suturing needle, ready threaded.

I nodded my thanks. I did not know how long he had been there, or when he had taken the needle and thread from my satchel, but he had saved me precious moments. I wiped the blood away again from the wound, then began to stitch it as swiftly as I could, but carefully. When I was finished, I laid my ear on Jos's chest, to listen to his lungs. As I did so, I realised that the noise of cannon fire had ceased, but I had no time to think of that.

There were still the remaining wounds to clean, though no others needed stitching. Then I salved the whole area liberally, and wound bandages first round Jos's chest and side, then round his upper leg. The sailor who had been sick had returned and helped the other two lift and turn the injured man until I was satisfied that the dressings were firm and would stay in place.

'Can you carry him to somewhere clean and quiet?' I said. 'What he needs now is rest. He should recover, provided that filthy metal carried no infection.'

'Our quarters a'nt too bad, doctor.' It was the sailor who had helped me throughout. He looked a little green about the mouth, and he was clearly relieved it was over.

'I'll come and see him in an hour or two, when the poppy syrup has worn off. Here.' I bundled up the pieces of metal in a cloth. 'He might like to see these, to know just how much of the enemy's shot he stopped.'

I got to my feet with a groan. My knees were numb with kneeling so long, my hose and breeches were soaking. I looked around in surprise. 'Where are the pirates?'

'One sunk, the rest fled,' Simon said. 'And our men are repairing the small amount of damage they did to us.'

We watched the two sailors carry the injured man away, then I plunged my bloody hands into the bucket and rubbed them hard until they were clean.

'Why did you keep the fragments of metal for him?'

'It was something I learned when my father and I treated the wounded soldiers after the siege of Sluys,' I said. 'Strange as it seems, they liked to keep the pieces of metal or shot that wounded them.'

Simon shook his head. Like me, he clearly found it strange.

'Will he live?'

I tipped the blood-stained water into the sea. 'I think so. It was a nasty injury and he'll have scars all down his side, but I think he will survive.'

'No thanks to the ship's surgeon,' he said.

There was some damage to the *Bona Esperanza*, but it was not serious, nor any impediment to our continuing.

'We will sail on at once for the Lofoten Islands,' Captain Turnbull said. 'We can carry out our repairs there. I want to be well away from this part of the sea, in case those devils have more friends nearby.'

The sailors were soon scurrying to replace a shredded foresail and to make a jury rig where the yard of one of the topsails was broken. Within less than an hour we were making our way swiftly northward again. The cannon were withdrawn, the gun ports fastened, and down on the gun deck the gunners and their boys were setting up fresh powder kegs and crates of shot, in case we should be attacked again.

My fellow passengers were loquacious in their relief, chattering and grinning, as if the frightening encounter had been a game, but I remembered the same almost hysterical reaction after the battle off Gravelines two years before. For myself, I found I had begun to tremble, so I took myself off to my cabin to wait quietly until I needed to visit Jos.

By the time I made my way to the sailors' quarters, we were speeding north again under full sail, as if nothing had happened. Jos was the only man seriously injured. Two had been struck when pieces of the topsail yard feel on the deck, but they were merely bruised. Another said he had been grazed by a musket ball, but he had wrapped a rag around the place himself and declared he needed no physician's help. The pirates had never come near enough to make accurate use of their muskets, so he had simply been the unlucky victim of a random shot. Their cannon had also been of inferior quality and shorter range than ours. The other ships in our fleet had fired on the two smaller pirate vessels, which had fled as soon as they realised how well armed we were. The leading ship, which had attacked us, had been sunk by two of our cannon balls which had struck it below the waterline, but I had been so absorbed in physicking Jos that I had been unaware of what was happening.

As I made my way along the gun deck to the far end where Jos lay in a hammock, I heard the pilot officer speaking to the master gunner.

'Brutes,' he said. 'The two remaining ships never stopped to pick up their own men from the water.'

'All drowned, then?'

'We saved three. We'll keep them in chains till we return to London. They can face trial there. Two are Danish, but one is a damned rogue Englishman.'

'If I was them,' the gunner said, 'I'd rather have drowned at once out here than gone back to that.'

I walked on, feeling sick. I knew what would happen to the men. They would be chained to posts driven into the river at Wapping and left till they had been covered by high tide three times. I agreed with the gunner. Better to have drowned at once, and swiftly.

Jos was awake, but still drowsy from the poppy syrup.

'This is all looking clean,' I said, 'but I will keep an eye on it for the next few days, until I can take the stitches out. You are to stay here and not work until I give you leave.'

'Stitches?' He looked fuddled.

'I had to stitch up the worst injury, but it has come together cleanly. You were lucky. That shard of metal just missed your lung.'

'Would that have killed me, doctor?'

'Aye,' I said briskly, 'but it did not. You will be whole and fit for work in a week.'

He gave a rueful grin. 'Officer won't let me lie abed till then.'

'I'll tell him. Better to have you a fit man than a dead one.'

'Aye.' He laughed then. 'Mebbe he'll see the sense in that.'

Like all the sailors, he slept in a hammock slung from the beams that supported the deck overhead. It was hardly a luxurious bed for a wounded man, but he was used to it, so I supposed it would do him no harm. I went in search of the sailor who had physicked himself.

'Let me see what lies under that dirty rag,' I said, pointing at his right arm.

He was a surly fellow and snarled at me. 'I don't need no doctor. Keep your hands off me.'

'Do you want to lose that arm? Because from the filth on that rag you have tied round it, you'll be infected by tomorrow and dead in three days' time.'

That shocked him (though I may have exaggerated somewhat) and he held out his arm reluctantly. I unwound the torn piece of cloth, which looked as though it might have been used to wipe out a gun barrel or something worse. I handed it to a passing boy.

'Take this to the cook and tell him to put it on the fire.'

He was so surprised that he ran off to do what he was told without a word.

The arm was already inflamed from elbow to shoulder.

'You're a fool,' I said. 'That musket ball did not just graze you. It's embedded in your flesh.'

A guilty look flashed in his eyes and I realised he was one of those who will do anything, even pretend they are not injured, for fear of falling into the hands of a physician or (more often) a surgeon.

'Don't you take a saw to me!' He snatched his arm away. 'I seen that before. And seen a man die of it, after. I can get it out with my knife.'

'Are you left-handed?' I demanded. 'I thought not. And if you start poking about in that wound with your filthy knife, which I don't suppose has been washed for the last ten years, you'll give yourself gangrene for sure.'

'You doctors. You're all the same. Nothing but butchers. You'll say I have gangrene and get out your saws.' He cupped his hand protectively over the wound.

So that was the problem.

'Of course I am not going to amputate.'

I was tired and I knew I sounded exasperated. 'Sit down on that keg over there and I'll remove the musket ball. You are lucky. It hasn't gone deep, so it should not have done any damage to the muscle, but it will soon go bad if it is left there.'

Glowering at me suspiciously, he sat down on the powder keg and I got out my forceps. The musket ball was too large for the smaller tweezers.

'Now, are you brave enough to keep still for me, or shall I call a couple of your fellows to hold you down?'

'I a'nt no coward!'

He held out his arm, but I noticed he closed his eyes and gritted his teeth. I smiled to myself. I reckoned I had taken his measure fairly accurately. Fortunately, the ball had not gone deep and I was able to seize hold of it without too much probing. It slithered out and fell to the floor, rolling away into a dark corner. He gave one involuntary grunt, but that was all. I cleaned and salved the wound, and decided it did not need stitching.

When I had bound it with a clean bandage, I said, 'You can open your eyes now. I have done.'

His eyelids flicked up, and he gave me a sheepish look. 'Is that all?'

'That's all. Keep it clean and it should heal in a few days. If it troubles you, come and find me.'

'Where's the devil that did it?'

'The musket ball? It rolled away over there.' I pointed.

As I made my way from the gun deck, I saw that he was on his hands and knees, searching the dark corner.

It took us four more days to reach the Lofoten Islands. The wind was steady, the weather fair, and we sighted no more pirates, though we did see one Scottish merchant vessel sailing south. The *Bona Esperanza* and the Scotch ship hove to, and her captain came aboard our ship. He and Captain Turnbull were in conference for nearly an hour, dining in the captain's cabin. As he left, the Scottish captain bowed and shook Turnbull's hand.

'I thank ye for the warning about yon pirates,' he said. 'I'll be on the lookout. Forbye, I'll head further west instead of keeping to the Norway coast. I can make for Shetland instead. Better to fetch into home waters as soon as possible.'

'Aye,' Captain Turnbull said. 'Though if only their two smaller ships are left, you may not need to worry.'

'Those Danes – getting above themselves, they are.'

'We do not know if they were all Danes. That kind of rabble tends to hail from the scum of every country.'

I noticed he did not mention that one of the prisoners was an Englishman.

The Scotchman paused as he was about to climb down the rope ladder to his pinnace.

'Mind how ye go near the Lofoten Islands,' he said. 'The Mokstraumen is the worst I've ever seen it this year.'

'It is usually bad in July and August,' Captain Turnbull said.

'Aye, but not like this. We kept well out to sea, but I swear it must have been five miles across. God go with ye, then.'

'And with you.'

The Scotchman disappeared from sight as he climbed down the ladder, and soon we could see him being rowed back to his ship. The *Bona Esperanza* came about and began to head north again. The last we saw of the other ship, she was setting a new course to the west.

'What is this Moskstraumen they were speaking of?' I asked one of the sailors. He was the man who had helped me with Jos.

'It is a terrible thing, master. A place in the sea between a headland in the Lofotens and a small offshore island called Mosken. They say there is a monster hides in the deeps of the sea there, and stirs it up into great cross currents and whirlpools, so big they can catch a ship and suck it down to the very bottom of the ocean.' He shuddered, and he raised his hand as if to cross himself, then thought the better of it. 'They also call it the Maelstrom. It can be five miles across, like the Scotchman said.'

'Five miles!' Guy had overheard and looked out across the sea in horror. 'But I thought we were heading for these Lofoten Islands.'

'We are. The Moskstraumen is at the southern end of the group. Reckon the captain'll swing right out to the west and then make landfall much further north. The rest of the place is fair enough,' the sailor conceded. 'And we can buy fresh food. The Norways are decent enough people. Not like those Danes.'

He ran off and Guy looked at me with raised eyebrows. 'I do not like the sound of this Moskstraumen or Maelstrom, or whatever it is called. It can suck down whole ships!' He wrapped his arms around himself and shivered. 'I did not agree to come on this voyage merely to end up in a watery grave.'

'I am sure the captain will take care to avoid it,' I said, and hoped I could trust my own confident words.

We did see the Moskstraumen. Although the ship steered well clear of it, standing high on the poop deck Simon and I could see the great turbulence in the sea off to starboard. I could never have imagined anything like it. The very sea seemed to boil, waves coming from every direction, haphazardly crashing against each other, the surface foaming like a boiling pot. There was not one single whirlpool but a chain of them, running through the centre of the chaos. It was the very stuff of nightmares. I think I held my breath until I was certain the *Bona Esperanza* was safely out of reach of whatever monstrous force created such horror.

When we made landfall at a small port on the largest of the islands, Løføt, it was hard to believe that it lay so near those dangerous seas. Løføt was about halfway up the western side of the chain of islands, islands so spectacular that they took my breath away. Towering, jagged mountains, sharp as a wolf's teeth, rose straight up from the depths of the ocean. They appeared to be less forested than the mainland of Norway, although below the vertical cliffs there were woodlands of birch and rowan. Here and there patches of arable land could be seen, though it was clear that here too men made their living primarily from the sea.

The island of Løføt was precipitous on its south-eastern side, but we had sailed round to the northwest, where there were tranquil beaches of silver sand and a safe harbour large enough to accommodate our whole fleet. The people welcomed us warmly, and although no one onboard spoke their language – except perhaps the Danish pirates held in chains below – the Norways all spoke at least a little English. The Company's ships had been calling here for fresh food and water for more than thirty years, so good relations had long been established with the people of the islands. The water brought on board to refill our water casks was pure and sweet, straight from the streams that tumbled down their mountains, fed by snow melt. The food, however, was mostly fish in one form or other, for it seemed these people not only lived but also fed almost entirely from the sea. They had a few grazing animals, but the sheep were kept primarily for their wool and the cattle to provide milk, cheese and butter. We were glad of these to augment the fishy diet, for they ate little meat. They had some fields of wheat and barley, too, so we were able to obtain bread and beer.

While the officer in charge of stores negotiated for supplies and the minor damage to all the ships was repaired, some of us went ashore. I found myself staggering a little on dry land, as one is wont to do, after a long time at sea. The players found this disconcerting, for none of them had travelled so far by ship before. Our stumbling steps ashore caused some hilarity amongst the sailors. Even the company men, stipendiaries and apprentices going out to Muscovy, had mostly some experience of sea voyages.

Simon, Guy, Pyotr and I strolled about the little town together and explored their market place. There were the usual foodstuffs, and tools, and baskets, but there were also some beautiful pieces of embroidery.

'The local women make them to sell to the merchants and Company ships that put in here,' Pyotr said. 'Lonely men send presents home to their wives and daughters.'

'I shall buy something for Sara,' I said to Simon. 'A set of embroidered sleeves, or a pair of gloves.'

'Is Sara your sweetheart, then?' Pyotr gave me a knowing look.

I laughed. 'Sara has a son five years older than I. She is a friend who took my father and me into her home when we first came to London from Portugal. I was twelve years old and very afraid. Sara became a second mother to me.'

Pyotr looked abashed. 'I crave your pardon,' he said.

'Pardon granted,' I said. 'Look, these are beautiful, these gloves embroidered in blue silk with silver thread. I shall buy them for her.' Then a thought struck me. 'That is, if they will take English money.'

'Aye, that is never a problem,' Pyotr said. 'They know the value of the Queen's coins. Not debased like the coins of some countries.'

I purchased the gloves for far less than I would have paid in London, and was well satisfied with my purchase when I examined them closely.

'I will give them to you to take back for Sara,' I said to Simon. 'We have been delayed so long on this voyage, I cannot see how I can possibly carry out my mission before the fleet returns to London.'

Simon looked grave. He knew very little of my mission, only that I was to try to find a man who had gone missing.

'Do you truly think you must stay until *next year's* fleet returns? You will have been away more than a twelve month.'

'It is either that, or try to return overland.'

Pyotr shook his head. 'With the war between Muscovy and Sweden, that would be dangerous. The only other way would be to travel far to the south, but that would mean crossing the territory of the Tatars, which would be just as dangerous. Nay, it must be next year's fleet.'

Simon wore that resentful look again. He did not like Pyotr laying down the law.

I shrugged. 'If it must be, then I have no choice.'

I strove to make my voice sound indifferent, but I dreaded the thought of spending so long in the alien land of Muscovy. Already I missed Rikki, and my work at the hospital, and even my little room in the Southwark lodgings. I was also worried that if I was absent so long, St Thomas's might not want me to return. The new graduate from Oxford might worm his way into my place. Or he might leave for his new post in the spring, leaving Master Ailmer and the governors with no option but to appoint a permanent replacement. Had Walsingham still lived, he would have had the power to protect my interests, but I did not believe that the governor of the Muscovy Company, for all his confidence, had anything like the same power and influence.

I tried not to dwell on these thoughts, but they often kept me awake in the watches of the night.

Once our stores were replenished and the damage to all eight ships repaired, we set off again to travel further north. It had become evident, the further we travelled, how much longer the daylight lasted, and how much shorter were the hours of darkness. By the time we reached the Lofoten Islands, the sun stayed above the horizon all night long. My studies with Master Harriot had introduced me to the theories of the changing patterns of the sun in relation to the seasons and to latitude, but it was intriguing to experience them finally myself.

When the last of the Lofoten Islands had dropped behind us, our course took us a little more to the east of north. When I came up on deck one midday, I saw the pilot officer taking a reading from the sun with a mariner's astrolabe.

'I have always wanted to use one of those,' I said, when he had finished and jotted down his reading in the ship's log.'

'Do you know how to use it? he asked.

'In theory.' I smiled. 'I have never had one in my hands before.'

He handed it to me.

'There you are. See how you fare.'

I could tell from his smile that he did not believe I should be able to take a reading. Indeed, I wondered whether he would warn me not to look along the movable rod called the adilade directly at the sun, but I knew better than to risk blinding myself. I stood where I could shine the beam of light on to a vertical surface, in this case the wall of the cabins lying under the foredeck. The officer had taken care to return the alidade to the upright position, so I would have no help from his reading. It was not easy to hold the instrument steady on the pitching deck of a ship at sea, so I braced myself in the angle between the deck railing and the wall I was using for the reflection. I held the astrolabe up so that it hung straight down, although it continued to sway a little with the movement of the ship, and I moved the outer end of the alidade in the direction of the noonday sun. Carefully I pushed the alidade around the dial, glancing over my shoulder to see whether the tiny disk of light had fallen on the wall.

It appeared for a moment, then disappeared. Was that the movement of the ship, or had I moved it too far? Very gently I eased the alidade a tiny fraction back. The light appeared again on the wall and held steady. I lowered my arm, which was shaking with the effort of holding the weight of the instrument steady. It should now be possible to read off our latitude from the scale on the body of the astrolabe.

'Seventy degrees and two minutes north,' I said, hoping that I was not too wildly astray.

'Very good,' he said. 'Only one minute out. We will make a mariner of you yet, doctor.'

The last days before we reached the North Cape and Wardhouse passed too quickly. My patient Jos had returned to his duties. I had removed his stitches, although his wounds were still covered with scabs, which he complained were rubbed by his clothes. His complaints were mild indeed, considering the seriousness of his injuries. The surly fellow who had stopped the musket ball allowed me to inspect his arm once, but thereafter refused further treatment, and I could only hope the damage was healing cleanly.

My Russian lessons with Pyotr continued, and I was becoming quite fluent. I made no attempt to read or write the language, but I have a good ear, so that I could hold my own in simple conversations. Pyotr now insisted we speak only Russian during meals, which was a further cause of annoyance for Simon, although Guy found it entertaining and was beginning to learn a little of the language himself.

'You can never know,' he said as we sat around the table after dining one night, 'when it might prove useful. Perhaps some Muscovite prince will employ me as his court fool.'

'Then I would not accept the post.' Pyotr did not know Guy, even after these weeks aboard the *Bona Esperanza*, and took him seriously. 'From what I know of Russian princes, they are best avoided.'

'That does not augur well for me, then,' I said. 'One reason I am being sent to Muscovy is because the Russian Court is desirous of an English physician with some skill in the treatment of children.'

We had dropped into English as our meal ended. Simon gave me a troubled look.

'You have not mentioned that before,' he said. 'For once, I agree with Pyotr. Surely all the royal family of Russia are insane and violent.

They behead people who disagree with them. Or whose clothes or table manners they do not like.'

Pyotr looked puzzled for a moment. I believe he had failed to notice Simon's jealousy, but he agreed now. 'There is a strain of madness in the family. Or else they are simple-minded. The last Tsar was mad. The present one has the brain of a chicken. No one knows the truth about his young brother, Dmitri Ivanovich. There are tales that he is mad and violent too, but as Boris Godunov has kept him out of sight together with his mother, he is hardly known.'

This was one of the children I was meant to examine, but I kept that to myself.

'How old is he, this Dmitri?' I asked.

'About seven or eight years, I believe,' Pyotr said.

'At that age, tales of madness may be no more than stories born out of a child's mischief. He may be no more mad than Davy.'

Confinement to the ship had begun to tell on Davy. Earlier that day he had been caught with two of the ship's hens, kept to provide fresh eggs. He was about to shut them in the master gunner's cabin, in revenge for a clout on the ear he had received for trying to create an explosion with some filched gunpowder – fortunately without success. He had been locked in one of the players' cabins for the rest of the day.

'Perhaps you are right,' Pyotr said, but he did not sound convinced.

The following day we rounded the North Cape. This was the furthest north that we would sail, and although we had passed the summer solstice, the daylight lingered on, so that the sky barely grew dark before dawn came again. I had stayed on deck all night, for I had promised Master Harriot that I would observe it, so that I could describe it to him when I came home again, although he had hoped we would reach this point around the time of the solstice. I found it eerie. Guy had joined me, and we watched in companionable silence as the sky barely darkened to grey before growing light again.

'We shall be going our separate ways soon, Kit,' he said, as we went below in search of some hot ale, for there had been a cold wind up on deck. 'I fear somewhat for your safety in the land of those barbarians. Can you not stay in Wardhouse and come home with us?'

For a moment the idea seemed almost unbearably tempting, but I shook my head.

'I must at least try to discover what has happened to Gregory Rocksley,' I said. 'It is clear that little effort has been made to search for him. If I were lost in such a land, I would hope that someone would care enough to search for me.'

I had told the players that I was to search for the missing man. I had not told them why he had been sent to Muscovy, or that Walsingham had feared a traitor was passing vital information to England's enemy, Spain. There was every likelihood that Rocksley was dead. In which case, I must try to find some evidence as to the traitor myself.

Guy sighed. 'That fellow Pyotr is a little too pleased with his own abilities, but he is probably competent and experienced enough to be of some use to you. He is to travel with you?'

'Aye. As my interpreter. I know I am beginning to have a little knowledge of the language, but only a little. Besides, their ways and manners are strange. I must take great care not to give offense, or I could jeopardise everything.'

'Well, do take great care. For who else will play lute duets with me?'

'I promise you, I shall take care.'

After that, the time until we reached Wardhouse seemed to pass very quickly. It is a curious place – an island off the coast of Norway, long disputed between Norway, Sweden, Finmark, and Muscovy, boasting a fortress which might have meant it was hostile to us, yet it was an international trading post of growing importance. Since the Company had opened up the route to the Muscovy trade, other countries had grown interested. England had insisted on exclusive rights to trade, free of taxes, with the state of Russe, and the old Tsar, Ivan, had agreed to that, for he wanted our Queen as an ally against his many enemies, a role she had never quite promised. The new Tsar, Fyodor Ivanovich, or more accurately his brother-in-law, Boris Godunov, tended to play one country off against the other in these trade wars. The result was that Wardhouse – or more properly Vardøhus – was a-buzz with ships and merchants of many nations, circling like wolves around a carcass.

The Netherlanders had become particularly active of late, although the Nordic lands had far more experience of these northern waters than any of the countries in mainland Europe. The Dutch, however, were much more skilled merchants than the Norways.

I went ashore at Wardhouse with the players, wanting to make the most of my final hours in their company. Cuthbert was first to land and hurried off to make arrangements for the players' lodgings in the town of Vardø which lay outside the walls of the fortress. After that, he planned to seek out the governor, to ensure that the players would be allowed to perform here for the month or six weeks while they waited for the fleet to return. His father, James Burbage, had applied for permission by letter the previous year, but matters might have changed during the intervening months.

Guy was left to supervise the loaded of the company's costumes and props into a pinnace, to be taken ashore if Cuthbert returned with the necessary permission. Simon and I joined the second party to go ashore.

'It is a formidable fortress,' Simon said, as we made our way around the huge walls.

Originally, I believe, the place was nothing but a fortress, but soldiers acquire wives and families. Fortresses need supplies and so do the satellite families. A safe harbour in this barren northern ocean provides workshops for the repair of ships battered by these hostile seas. The shipwrights have families. As trade routes open, various nations establish their own premises in such a promising spot. Inns are needed. And shops. So Wardhouse had grown from a single grim fortress to a small town. The one thing they lacked, as James Burbage had shrewdly discovered, was any form of entertainment for the many inhabitants, permanent and transitory.

Cuthbert joined us where we were trying out the local ale, sitting on benches outside the inn where he had booked lodgings.

'Everything is settled,' he said, rubbing his hands together and beaming. 'Here, lad!' He crooked a finger at a passing pot boy. 'We'll have another flagon of that ale here.'

The boy nodded and ran off. It seemed that English was understood here, as it had been on the Lofoten Islands.

When the fresh flagon arrived, Cuthbert drank deeply and stretched out his legs contentedly in the sun. It was bright, though not very warm.

'We begin in two days' time, Simon lad. There is a merchants' hall which is used for trading by day, but we are to have the use of it every evening while we are here.'

'Will it not be very expensive to light in the evening?' Simon said. 'Candles will surely be costly here.'

Cuthbert tapped his nose and grinned. 'You forget how light the evenings are. And when we have need of candles, they will be provided as part of the arrangement I have made. A very favourable arrangement, I may say.'

'What do you want to play first? One of Will's pieces? Or Kit Marlowe's?' Simon asked.

'Nay, we will start them off with a simple old-fashioned comic piece, like *Friar Burgay.*'

Simon groaned.

'Don't pull faces at me. The groundlings love it. And you'll find there are more groundlings than gentlemen here. Once we have drawn them in, we'll lead them on to something a little cleverer, but still funny. *Two Gentlemen*, I think. Then after we have their appetite awakened, we might try something darker, *Tamburlaine* or *Jew.*'

'Will you let me play Tamburlaine?' Simon was eager. I knew how much he wanted to try the roles that usually fell to Cuthbert's brother Dick.

'We shall see. Do not let your excitement run away with you. It might prove meat too strong for the audience here. At the moment it is difficult to judge.'

They plunged into a technical discussion full of theatrical jargon, so that I began to feel left out.

'I shall see whether I can find an apothecary. I need to replace the medicines I used on the journey,' I said, getting up and setting down my empty ale pot.

They smiled and nodded, but I doubt they heard a word I said.

For a while I strolled around the town. Most of it was quite new, probably built in the last thirty or forty years, since the English ships had first begun to venture past the North Cape. I found a pleasant, clean apothecary's shop, where I was able to purchase everything I needed and pay with English coins. Rowland Heyward had given me a purse of Russian coins before I left, and Pyotr had explained their meaning and values to me, but I was saving them until I reached Muscovy. I also carried a letter for the agents in charge of the various Company houses, directing them to supply me with more coin, clothes, and anything else I might need.

'Clothes?' I had asked, puzzled.

'If you stay beyond the start of autumn,' Heyward said, 'you will need the kind of clothes the Muscovites wear – furs, mainly. Thick boots. Do not refuse them. It is common in that place to die of the cold.'

I hoped I should not need to make use of this offer, but I kept the letter safe nonetheless. After I had made my purchases, I walked back to the inn, where I found that the remaining players had joined Simon and Cuthbert. Some were drinking ale, others were carrying their belongings and the costumes into the inn. Davy was impressing a crowd of small children with his acrobatic tricks.

It was clear that they had all turned their minds to what lay ahead and how they might spend the next weeks plying their trade in the town. More than ever I felt shut out.

'Stay and dine with us tonight,' Guy said. 'The fleet does not move on until tomorrow. We are told that the food is good here. The cook on the *Bona Esperanza* is somewhat lacking in imagination.'

For a moment I hesitated, then I shook my head. It would only add to my sense of being an outsider. I was fond of the players, but when they became absorbed in their craft I knew I was not part of their world. Oddly, I had felt more at home with the affairs in Seething Lane, discussing how to break a difficult code with Thomas Phelippes, although I had gone there unwillingly at first. Still, there was no use dwelling on that. The world of Seething Lane, Walsingham, Phelippes, and the others was gone for ever.

'Nay,' I said, 'I had best return to the ship. You will drink and talk late, while I know we are to leave at dawn tomorrow. I will wish you God speed.'

They slapped me on the back, wished me a successful mission, warned me to be careful amongst the barbarians, but I could see that their minds were elsewhere. At the last moment Simon decided to walk to the quay with me.

We stood together on the stone-built quay, waiting for the pinnace to come and carry me out to where the *Bona Esperanza* lay at anchor.

'I cannot believe we may not meet again for a year,' Simon said.

I felt an embarrassing urge to weep, but I turned my back to him and stared out to sea. It was still almost as light as midday, although at home the evening would have been drawing in by now.

'Perhaps I shall find Gregory Rocksley snug at St Nicholas,' I said, 'waiting to travel home on this year's fleet. Or hear that he has sent a letter from Astrakhan, saying that he is on his way to Greece and will be returning via the Mediterranean.'

'You do not believe that.'

'Nay.'

We were silent, watching the pinnace drawing nearer.

'You have the gloves for Sara?' I said.

'Aye.' He paused. 'I wish I were coming with you.'

'No you do not. You are going to persuade Cuthbert to allow you to play Tamburlaine.'

He grinned. 'Perhaps.'

The pinnace bumped gently against the side of the quay, where thick ropes were slung to save the paint of mooring vessels.

'God go with you, Simon.'

'And you, Kit.' As I turned to jump down into the pinnace, he grabbed me in a rough, boyish hug, as he had done many times before. But then I felt his lips brush my cheek. Before I could turn or speak, he was running back along the quay. I tumbled into the pinnace, my mind in confusion.

I remembered Simon's emphatic words all those weeks ago on the way to Durham House: 'My tastes are not that way inclined.' Did that mean he had guessed my real identity? We had known each other for more than four years, spent much time in each other's company, lived in the same lodging house. Somehow Walsingham had discovered I was a girl. Had Simon done so as well?

The sailors rowing the pinnace asked some questions about my time in Wardhouse – what did I think of the place? I answered abstractedly. My face was burning. I scooped up a handful of cold sea water and splashed my cheeks. If the sailors noticed, they probably thought I had been imbibing too much of the Wardhouse ale.

Did Simon know I was a girl? Had he really kissed me? I was tormented by the thought, and I could not hope for an answer before my year in Muscovy was over.

Chapter Five

*T*he fleet sailed east from Wardhouse along a barren coastline which showed almost no sign of habitation. Low rounded hills were clothed in thin grass dotted with occasional bushes, the sort of terrain I have heard described as tundra. Near the shore there were patches of bog. Here and there rocky inlets or the mouths of streams and rivers opened a view deeper into a land that was sparsely wooded with pine forests, interspersed with occasional patches of scrubby moorland. The whole place had a desolate, despairing air. We saw no permanent buildings, though there were a few clusters of tent-like dwellings, not unlike those Harriot had sketched for me of the native peoples he had seen on his Chesapeake expedition. Twice we saw groups of men fishing from small coracles. These, Pyotr explained, were the Laplanders, or the Sami as they called themselves, whose tents were erected near the coast in summer during the fishing season.

A few days after our departure from Wardhouse, we sailed past one of the wider estuaries. There seemed to me to be nothing notable about it, but the pilot officer called my attention to it as I stood on deck watching the land slide by, breathing in the sharp clean air, and wishing myself back in the dirt and bustle of London.

'Do you see that, Dr Alvarez?' he said. 'That is the mouth of the Varzina River. It was there that some Muscovite fishermen found the two missing ships from the first expedition into these waters. The *Bona Confidentia* and the *Bona Esperanza*. It was the spring of the year after they disappeared. All the men were on board, they had taken shelter, the ships were sound, the supplies remained in plenty. But every soul was dead, in the very act of eating, or writing, or playing cards.'

I had heard the story before, though I had not known where the ships had been found.

'Did you say one of the ships was called the *Bona Esperanza*?' I shivered.

'Aye. But she was not the first ship to be called that, nor will this ship be the last.'

'I hope it may not be a bad omen.'

'Captain Turnbull has sailed this route for years, man and boy. You will not find him wandering off into the arctic, to the place the Russes call Novaya Zemlya, as those men did. Their commander was a fine soldier, it seems, Sir Hugh Willoughby, but knew nothing at all of the sea.'

He spoke with all the scorn of the professional mariner.

'Why was he the commander, then?'

He shrugged. 'A gentleman courtier? I do not know. It was back in the days when the boy king was dying, it seems. Her Majesty's brother. A long time ago. Things are managed differently now.'

'But if all those men died, how do we know they went to this place – Novaya Zemlya, did you say?'

'Willoughby had kept an account of where they had gone, all written out carefully, but not a true log, as we should keep one now. It just stopped, with the words "Haven of Death".'

He seemed to take a ghoulish relish from repeating the words.

'Poor creatures,' I said. 'Yet it sounds as if they did not suffer for long, all dying suddenly, and together.'

'Froze to death,' he said with authority.

I did not contradict him, but it seemed strange to me. If the men had been so cold, surely they would have huddled in their bunks, under piles of blankets. They would not have been sitting playing cards. It was an unpleasant mystery, and did not make me feel any more eager to visit this forbidding land.

Pyotr joined us by the rail.

'Disputed territory, that,' he said waving his hand towards the coastline. 'Sweden claims it. Norway claims it. Muscovy claims it. The Finlanders claim it. And the people who live there are mainly the Sami people.'

'People *live* there?' I said. 'I thought those men we saw in the coracles came only to fish.'

'They are nomads. They live in tents and follow their reindeer herds. They move further south in the winter, which is why Willoughby's scouts could find no people in the area when they sheltered here. You may see the Sami sometimes in Muscovy. But they are a different people from the Muscovites, with a different language.'

I welcomed a diversion from the fate of Willoughby and his men.

'Do not tell me. You speak Laplandish as well?'

He laughed. 'Nay. I have heard tell it is a strange tongue, very difficult. Besides, what would be the need? A few of them come into Muscovy from time to time, to trade furs, or to hire out as sleigh drivers in the winter, when the ground is frozen and everyone travels by sleigh. They speak enough Russian.'

'They have horses? It would be a hard life for horses in such a place.'

'The Muscovites have tough little horses who can endure the bitter winters. But nay, the Sami use reindeer to draw their sleighs. You may see some this winter.'

It was clear he was already certain that I would be here in Muscovy when winter came. It was not a prospect I relished.

Eventually, after some days' sailing with changeable winds, we left that barren coastline behind and entered a wide channel leading to a vast bay of the sea, which the captain told us was some four hundred miles across at its widest, though very irregular in shape.

'It is also the outlet into the sea of the river Dvina,' he said, 'the major river which flows from south to north in Muscovy. We keep a fleet of boats and barges on the river, to carry our goods into the interior and to bring out the furs, wax and tallow which we buy from the Muscovites.'

'You do not carry them by road?' I asked.

He smiled at my ignorance. 'Nay, Dr Alvarez, we do not. And you will not spend a day here before you realise why. During the months of summer, which are short enough, God knows, most of the land is soggy with melted snow. The roads are channels of mud, used by peasants on foot, for the most part, to go from village to village. Anything on wheels is apt to find itself sunk to the hubs in mud.'

Christopher Holme was standing with us and nodded his agreement.

'I haven't been here for fifteen years, when I was a stipendiary in Yaroslavl, but I remember the difficulties of transport. You can move about on horseback. Their ponies are hardy little creatures. But moving goods has always been a problem. Water transport in summer, travel by sleigh once land and water are frozen solid.'

'Does that mean I shall have to travel by water to reach Moscow?' I asked. I had decided I must make a start on my enquiries in the capital, after I had discovered all I good from the Company's men in St Nicholas.

'We should travel together,' Master Holme said. 'It would be unwise for you to travel alone, at least until you hold an official pass from the government. I shall make my way from St Nicholas to Moscow by stages, stopping at our main Company houses, once I have permission to travel. I need to acquaint myself with the state of affairs at each of them.'

It sounded as though I would be obliged to make slow progress, but I comforted myself with the thought that at each of these Company houses – or 'factories' as they were often called – I could make enquiries about Gregory Rocksley. Any information I could glean would benefit my search. I was not quite sure what Master Holme meant by 'permission', but I did not like to show my ignorance by asking.

It took us some time to cross to the far south-eastern end of the great bay, which Pyotr told me was called the White Sea. At first we sailed along the wide channel, about as wide, I should say, as the sea between Kent and France. The wind was spasmodic, so our speed dropped sometimes to almost nothing; then it would pick up, only to drop again. At length the two shores drew away and the full extent of the White Sea was revealed. The ship changed course to a more easterly direction, but hove to as the short summer night approached.

The nights were now not as brief as they had been, for it was early August and the sun dropped below the horizon for a short time. I knew that the fleet did not stay in these northern waters later than early September. It seemed impossible that they could be trapped by fog and ice so soon, but every mariner assured me it was so. The White Sea itself froze solid.

As we took up our position for the night, I noticed the sailor Jos coiling down a rope on the main deck, so I climbed down the companionway from the poop to speak to him.

'Will the fleet really stay here no more than a month?' I asked.

He nodded, sitting down on the coil and pulling a clay pipe out of his pocket. I had been surprised to see the sailors smoking, for I thought tobacco might be too expensive for men on their low wages, but it seemed the Company supplied it to them cheap. The reason I learned from the ship's surgeon, in one of the very few conversations I had with him.

'Aye, tobacco keeps them calm in times of danger. It also helps to stave off the pangs of hunger when supplies run low. The Muscovy Company does not provide it out of kindness.'

78

He gave a twisted smile, showing yellowed teeth, which suggested he made use of the same supply himself.

'Would you like me to get you some?' he offered.

'I thank you,' I said, somewhat coldly. 'But I do not smoke the weed.'

I thought it an odd and slightly unpleasant habit, though Harriot had often spoken of the aborigines he had seen smoking when he had gone on the Chesapeake expedition. He gathered it was some kind of ritual denoting friendship.

Once Jos had his pipe fairly alight, he took it out of his mouth, peered at the bowl with a grin of satisfaction, then clamped it between his teeth again.

'It's dangerous to bide here more than a month,' he said. 'Into September. Once – it must be five years ago, or six, I reckon – we was held up. One of the barges bringing wax up the river from Kolmogory got itself stuck on a mud bank, and we had to wait. Orders from the Palace. We *must* bring the full quota of wax. Desperate for candles, they are, see? A'nt enough wax in the whole of England to light up the Queen's palaces. And wax for all the lawyers' seals.'

He puffed reminiscently on his pipe, blew out a cloud of smoke, and coughed. There was one benefit from his smoking. Whenever we were near the land, we were troubled by clouds of tiny biting flies, but the smoke seemed to keep them away.

'So we waited until the wax was loaded on to another barge and brought down the Dvina to Rose Island.'

'Rose Island?' I said.

'Island offshore from St Nicholas. That's where our buildings are. Rose Island because the whole place is covered with wild roses. Tear you to bits, they would, if you was to go wandering around in the dark. Smell fine, though,' he conceded.

'So what happened when the wax finally arrived?' I said. Jos was inclined to wander off the subject.

'It was all hands to loading it. I sailed with Captain Turnbull that year too. Captain and agent, they was frantic to have all loaded and the ships away, but we didn't leave till the first week of October. 'Sblood, I never want to sail through that again!'

'Through what?'

'Great floating islands of ice. Ice mountains, they call them, or icebergs, but I call them floating ice islands, for they don't stay put on land, they float about on the sea, and they can smash a full man o' war to splinters. The worst thing is, what you see is only the least of it. You may think the ice island is a hundred feet away, but all the time it will have a prow or a shelf underwater, sticking out ready to hole you below the waterline, and you none the wiser.' He shuddered.

'That year there was thick fog everywhere. We crept out of the White Sea without harm. Thought we was safe. Started to head up toward the North Cape, feeling our way through the fog, when this great ice island come looming out of the fog. Twice as high as the mainmast, it was, big across as London Guildhall, what you could see above the surface. God knows what lay below the surface, for we didn't. Captain, he grabbed the tiller – no time to shout orders to the helmsman – and we heeled over as we changed course, heading much too close to land. I was by the seaward rail, and I swear that ice island was coming directly for me,'

He crossed himself, oblivious of the Romish character of the gesture. 'It began to slide astern, but then there came this terribly scraping, all along the side of the ship. She'd hit us.'

I gasped. 'Did you sink?'

It did not seem likely, for here he was, alive, and so was Captain Turnbull. If they had fallen into that sea in October, they would surely have died of the cold, if they had not drowned.

'Nay, but the caulking was torn away in a great strip along our starboard side. Two men had to go over on ropes into the sea to caulk it, or we'd have split.'

I looked down into the darkening waters and trembled at the thought of what those waters must have been like, full of ice and shrouded in fog.

'The two men,' I said, 'what happened to them?'

'Both died afterwards of the cold. But the rest of us lived. And the ship was saved. And the wax for the royal candles.'

The following morning we weighed anchor and headed toward the Muscovy shore, where I could see one large building topped by a curious pointed dome, which must be the monastery of St Nicholas. A small town of low wooden houses huddled around it, as if for shelter, like chicks around a mother hen. It was the monastery which gave the place its name, and before the Company had been set up to trade here, there had been nothing but the monastery, a few fishermen, and the houses of the small community that served the monks.

As we drew nearer, the sound of bells carried across the water, followed by a deep-voiced melodic chanting. It sounded like nothing I had ever heard before, neither Jewish nor Catholic nor Protestant, yet perhaps the music was closer to Jewish than anything else. It had a strange quality, that I can only describe as eastern. I knew that the Muscovites followed the Orthodox faith, like the Greeks, but since the rulers of Byzantium had been destroyed by the forces of Islam, the Greek church was in disarray. It was said that the Muscovite Church held itself to be the guardian of the only true Christian faith, regarding Rome as merely a recent and arrogant upstart, while Protestants were seen as nothing more than godless barbarians. Yet despite these claims, I had been told that in many ways Muscovy was ignorant and backward, ruled by a tyrannical and despotic system, which kept the nobles or boyars in a constant state of fear and the common people as little better than slaves. Well, it would not be long before I discovered the truth behind all these tales.

'We will put in at the St Nicholas quay first,' Christopher Holme said, coming to stand beside me to watch the land draw nearer. 'Out of courtesy. And report to the abbot. Then we will cross to our own premises on Rose Island, where we have modern docks, with warehouses and cranes for loading and unloading the cargo.' He shaded his eyes with his hand. 'I see that we have built extensively since I was last here. Excellent. It is testimony to the Company's success, despite our sometimes tricky relations with the government of the country.'

'You said you had not been here for fifteen years,' I said. 'Is that not strange?'

'For some of that time I was based in Narva. You knew that we had a trading post with the Russians there? When Muscovy lost Narva to the Swedes, I travelled on one unsuccessful voyage to the New Found Land. Since then I have worked in the London offices.'

He smiled suddenly. 'It is good to be back.'

'You like it here?' I was incredulous.

'I like the challenge. I like pitting my wits against the Muscovites. And the trade is rich and profitable, as long as we can keep their prices down and curtail the sharp practices of the Court, which tries to claim our best goods for next to nothing. Mark me, though, Dr Alvarez. It is a dangerous country. Put a foot wrong, cause offence to someone in power, and you could end in prison. They do not hesitate to use torture. Englishmen have been imprisoned and tortured here before now, for imagined offenses or merely in a game of diplomacy. The present Tsar has a weak mind and is unpredictable, while his brother-in-law Godunov can seem most charming, but he is ruthless.'

'I was worried before,' I said, with a poor attempt at a laugh, 'now I am truly alarmed.'

81

'I am sorry. I did not mean to frighten you, merely to warn you to be careful. Did you say you are required to physic two of the royal children?'

I nodded.

'Then that is when you will need to be most careful. Better to stay away from those in power all the rest of the while you are here.'

I had been so absorbed in our conversation, that my attention had been drawn away from our progress toward land, so that I was startled by the jarring as the *Bona Esperanza* was laid alongside the quay at St Nicholas. A gangplank was run out and a few minutes later I would set foot for the first time on the soil of Muscovy.

I had left my small cabin on the ship with some regret. It held nothing but a bunk screwed to the floor, a chair, a shelf and a small coffer for my clothes, but it had provided me with a private retreat where I could escape when I did not feel like sharing the company of my fellow travellers. Since the players had been left behind at Wardhouse, I had spent more time there. Pyotr and Holme were pleasant enough, but I felt no particularly close friendship for them, and once we were in Muscovy I would hardly be able to avoid their constant company.

So I had packed up my few belongings in my knapsack with some reluctance, as much out of dread because of what lay ahead as regret at leaving the *Bona Esperanza*. Apart from the medical supplies in my satchel, stuffed as full as it would hold, I had a couple of changes of clothes, the odd knitted garment Goodwife Maynard had made for me, and my two books, which were growing rather battered from much travel – the volume of poetry Simon had given me for my seventeenth birthday and the small New Testament pressed on me by our old rector at St Bartholomew the Great. I had not much cared for it at the time, but it had brought me consolation in times of trouble, although I was uncertain what my father would have thought of it. Despite being a Christian convert, his roots had been deep in the Jewish faith. My own beliefs were confused. I must remember Pyotr's warning about the banning of Jews from Muscovy and give no hint of my ambiguous heritage.

The gangplank seemed to ripple as I took my first few steps across it, so that I feared for a moment that I might topple into the uninviting waters of the White Sea, but it was probably no more than a sensation produced by my sea legs. Even on shore, the ground felt unstable. The monastery quay was an old structure, built of wood, slimy with ancient rotted seaweed. It looked to me as though it might collapse soon. I wondered that they did not rebuild it, now that the place had become an important port. There seemed to be money enough here, if the monastery was anything to go by, although the houses which lay outside the monastery's fortified walls were poor hovels made of undressed logs, with roofs of yellowing turf or blackened reed thatch. Country houses in England are often poor, but I had never encountered any as wretched as these. I have seen better pigsties.

However, there was little time to study our surroundings, for I found myself being escorted, along with Holme, Pyotr and the ship's officers, through a massive gateway into the monastery. The courtyard was crowded, and I fear my mouth fell open in surprise. If the appearance of the monastery dome was strange and the music alien, the crowd of monks which awaited us left me gasping.

They were very richly dressed, in black robes woven with gold and silver thread, and every man wore a heavy pectoral cross adorned with great uncut jewels which I took to be rubies, emeralds, pearls and turquoise. Each monk seemed bent on growing a longer beard than the next man – many had black beards down to their waists, a few to their knees. Their hair was long as well, sometimes hanging loose to their shoulders, sometimes braided. And they wore the most extraordinary hats, like tall black chimney pots.

Like some small, colourful, but alien bird amongst these native ravens, a fair-haired Englishman stepped forward and began to make introductions in Russian to the most imposing of the monks, a hawk-nosed man, elderly but fiercely upright, whose beard was turning white, as though it had been sprinkled with snow. This, I thought, must be the abbot. The Englishman would be William Holbeche, the Company's agent in St Nicholas.

Whereas the Russians were robed to the ground, William Holbeche's clothes were a mixture of European and Russian. He wore bright green hose, so that his lower legs were visible, elegantly shaped, like those of any gentleman at home, but instead of short padded breeches and a doublet above them, he wore a loose robe of scarlet wool, reaching just to the knee and drawn in at the waist with a belt of gold cords. The sleeves of the robe were loose and revealed a shirt which was certainly not English, for it had voluminous sleeves, gathered into cuffs embroidered with red and green thread. Around his neck there was a ruff, but a ruff so badly starched and pleated that it was clear that Company employees were forced to use local laundresses, who had not mastered the art of dressing a ruff. It flashed through my mind, irrelevantly, that I was glad I wore nothing grander than a simple gathered and unstiffened ruff. I could afford nothing finer. Besides, it would have interfered with my work. Looking at William Holbeche's bedraggled affair, I thought it would be wiser if he left it off.

Christopher Holme was drawing me forward by the elbow, after he had been presented by William Holbeche.

'My lord abbot, Father Sevastyan,' he said in Russian, 'may I present the physician, Dr Christoval Alvarez?'

'My lord Abbot,' I said.

Taking my clue from the others, I knelt and kissed the ring on the hand the abbot held out to me.

'You are welcome, Englishmen,' he said. His voice was deep and his pronunciation a little different from Pyotr's, but I found I could understand him. 'We invite you to dine with us.'

I had thought we would be leaving at once for Rose Island, but it seemed it was a great honour to be invited to a meal at the abbey, so we obediently followed Father Sevastyan into a large building lying to the right of the church, and up wooden stairs to a refectory, where we were seated at a high table on a dais with the abbot and several of the older and more distinguished-looking monks, while the remainder filed in behind us and took their seats on benches at the lower tables. I noticed that there was a sprinkling of youngsters amongst them, some no more than twelve or thirteen. They too wore black, but no finery, merely plain robes tied in at the waist with a rope belt, like monks I had seen in Portugal when I was a child.

Food will always vary from nation to nation, and I was not sure what to expect here. It was with some nervousness that I watched the servants carry in platters of food. Clearly they were men from the houses outside the walls, dressed in rough woollen tunics which reached to their knees, below which they wore the sort of loose trousers I had seen on shepherds and other countrymen, both in England and the Low Countries. Their hands, I noticed, were not very clean and I wondered whether they prepared the food as well. Indeed, the monks' hands were also not very clean. And now that I was seated between two of them, I was aware that, despite the gorgeous nature of their habits, they had not bathed for some months. Their breath, too, had the stink of rottenness, while they belched frequently and unashamedly.

More and more platters arrived on the table. It seemed the monks did not stint themselves in the matter of food either, although I noticed that beneath their bulky tunics the serving men were rake thin. To my relief, I saw that the food placed before the English guests was mostly recognisable: roast meats of the usual sorts – beef, mutton, pork – together with fish, some of which were unfamiliar. Platters containing only fish were put before the monks, and there were bowls of common vegetables – onions, garlic, carrots, beets, cucumbers, and cabbage. Wine, beer, and mead appeared (and quickly disappeared) in abundance. I was uncertain whether I was supposed to converse with my neighbours, but they were applying themselves with such enthusiasm (not to say greed) to the meal that it hardly seemed necessary. It was clear that the platters of meat were not intended for the monks, since I had been told that they were forbidden to touch the flesh of animals, though that did not prevent them reaching across to help themselves to choice morsels from the guests' platters, if something took their fancy. Their long sleeves dragged in the grease and once my neighbour to the left knocked over his goblet of wine. He made no attempt to mop it up, so that I was obliged to lean sideways as the spilled wine poured over the edge of the table.

Most of the monks seemed at best boorish, although I noticed a few, including the abbot himself, who were abstemious, restricting themselves to vegetables, together with a small amount of fish, crossing themselves and murmuring prayers over each portion. Even these men drank freely.

The dinner was of excellent quality, though I ate little through nervousness. The meal ended with bowls of the new season's apples and pears, and a selection of nuts – walnuts, hazels and almonds. There were no nutcrackers. The monks smashed the shells with a well aimed wine flagon, or cracked them between their teeth. I had more care for my own teeth, though I managed to shell a few hazelnuts.

We rose to listen to a grace in a curious language which sounded to me something like Russian, but was quite incomprehensible. The monk on my right bestowed a smile on me, and when it finished, essayed in English: 'You like our food, English?'

'Thank you,' I responded in my simple Russian. 'It was very good.'

To my relief, we were at last able to leave the refectory.

Despite the obvious wealth of the monastery, the buildings were of wood – very fine, nevertheless, with elaborate carvings on lintels and window frames. The curious dome resembled an onion, with its root end pointing to the sky, and appeared to have been given a twist. It struck me as strange, almost barbaric for a Christian church. It was painted blue, with the joints between the timbers overlaid with gold leaf. Before we could finally leave the monastery, we were conducted into the church, which was so bright with colour that it almost hurt the eye. After coming to England I had grown accustomed to the sobriety of Protestant churches, although I had known wall paintings and brightly coloured statues in Portugal. The St Nicholas church was flamboyant beyond belief. Every vertical surface which could hold paint was painted; every horizontal surface was draped with cloths stiff with gold thread and crowded with candles and holy vessels.

The strangest things were the small paintings on wood of the Holy Family and of saints, magnificently framed in gold and jewels, grouped together in side chapels and niches, spilling out into the body of the church. The faces were curiously flat, with large almond-shaped eyes, the painted clothes ornate and oriental, the haloes thickly layered with pure gold leaf. These 'icons', as they called them, were venerated beyond belief. According to a whisper from William Holbeche, the Muscovites believed that these stiff painted images were in fact the living saints themselves. I saw one man, a poor fisherman, prostrate before an image of St Nicholas, weeping and beating his head against the floor until the blood ran.

We all made polite comments about the splendour of the church, even William Holbeche and Captain Turnbull, who must have seen it many times before.

'It is much changed since I was last here,' Christopher Holme murmured in my ear as we escaped at last into the open air from a stifling fog of incense. 'Clearly trade with the Company has brought great riches to St Nicholas. The church is even more . . .' he sought for the right word, '. . . more *embellished* than it used to be. I remember speaking many years ago to one of the sailors who had served on Richard Chancellor's first voyage, when they discovered St Nicholas. He said it was a wretched little place, a few monks living in hovels like these outside the walls.'

He gestured at the fishermen's huts.

'The few local people lived by fishing and making salt, which they carried south into the country, or traded into Norway. And they killed seals for their oil. The monks were as poor as the common people, living simple, devout lives.'

'Then things have indeed changed,' I said. 'They eat like princes, and dress like them in fine cloth, even if their garb is black. Did you notice the gems on their crosses?'

He nodded. 'How the Puritan preachers back in London would love to cite such flamboyant greed and worldliness!'

'They would probably die from shock at the sight,' I said.

And he laughed.

When we reached the wooden quay, we found that the eight ships of the fleet had already sailed across to Rose Island, but two pinnaces remained to convey the shore party after them. It was a sensible arrangement, to site the Company's premises a little apart from the monastery. As we approached the island, I saw that the 'factory' had the form of a fortified manor, surrounded by a wooden palisade, which enclosed the main house and all the subsidiary buildings. There were two stone-built quays, running out into deep water and long enough for several large merchant ships to moor at each. The cranes for moving cargo must have been imported from England, for I could not imagine they had been built here.

William Holbeche showed us around while Captain Turnbull went to supervise the unloading of the English cargo, which had already begun. Pyotr wandered away on his own. No doubt he already knew the Rose Island establishment well.

'This is our central building, as you can see,' William Holbeche said, indicating a substantial house of three storeys. 'Offices on the ground floor. Living accommodation on the first floor. Apprentices and servants on the second floor. There is also a locked cellar, for wine and valuable goods. Over on the right are the three warehouses.'

These were impressive. I think I had not truly grasped until then the vast scale on which the Muscovy Company operated. They were larger than any warehouses I had seen by the Legal Quays in London.

'Over to the left,' William Holbeche went on, 'the usual outbuildings – bakehouse, brewery, laundry, blacksmith, carpenter. We have two skilled shipwrights as well as a jobbing carpenter. Now, if you will follow me, I will show you your quarters.'

He led the way inside and up a curved staircase of some pale wood. Given the abundance of pine forests which crowded down to the shores of the White Sea on all sides, it was probably pine.

'Do you know how long you will be staying, sir?' He turned to Christopher Holme as we reached the landing.

'Only a night or two,' Master Holme said. 'Dr Alvarez and I are both anxious to reach Moscow. It will depend on the availability of a boat to take us up river to Kolmogory. And of course, permission.'

There is was again. Permission.

'Forgive me for interrupting,' I said. 'But what is this "permission" I keep hearing about?'

'My apologies,' Christopher Holme said. 'I thought you knew. Perhaps I should have explained. The Tsar takes a very *personal* interest in everything that happens in Muscovy. No foreigner is permitted to move about the country without documents from the Tsar himself, authorising it. A kind of internal passport, as you might say.'

'But I thought the Muscovy Company had a charter from the Tsar,' I said, puzzled. 'Permitting travel and trade and exemption from taxes.'

'Oh, we have. However, the Tsar still exercises his right to control the movement of every foreign citizen in his vast domain.'

'But, as you say, it is vast. Would he even know if we were moving about?'

'He would know,' Holme said flatly. 'Or at any rate, Godunov's spies would soon find out. You may be accustomed to the secret services of England and Spain, Dr Alvarez, but I assure you they are but as children's games compared with the hold the Tsar has over the people of Muscovy.'

'It would take a vast army–' I began.

He shook his head. 'He rules by fear. The people are kept down by terror. Where a populace is so cowed, you do not need a vast army. Every man will betray his neighbour to save his own skin. He will not hesitate a moment to betray a foreigner. My advice is: Trust no one.'

'I understand that the country was in such a state under the last Tsar. He was not known as Ivan the Terrible for nothing, but is not his son a much less dangerous man?'

Holme exchanged a look with William Holbeche and shrugged. The St Nicholas agent replied.

'He is weak, and useless as a leader, but he is also spiteful, arrogant and dangerous. It is his brother-in-law who rules the country, though he lets Tsar Fyodor believe he himself is emperor, just because he wears the great crown and sits on the throne. Godunov is every bit as dangerous as Ivan Vasilyevich. He merely disguises it under a smiling exterior. Master Holme is right. Trust no one.'

'Not even Pyotr Aubery?'

They exchanged another glance.

'He has been a reliable Company man for some years,' Holme said, 'but remember, he is half Russian. He still has family here. Trust him, but cautiously.'

This warning troubled me. At first I would be able to travel in company with Christopher Holme, when I reckoned I would be reasonably safe, but eventually we must part company, for he would not be going beyond Moscow, while I must follow wherever the trail led. Gregory Rocksley had been heading for Astrakhan when last seen. I might have to go even as far as that. It must surely be a thousand miles or more to the south. And I would be travelling with Pyotr Aubery. He seemed harmless enough, but Holme was right. He was half Russian and if he had family here, threats might be made to them, to force him to betray me and my mission.

William Holbeche showed me my room on the first floor and the two men walked on down the corridor. It was a pleasant room – large and airy, with white-washed walls and a large window looking over the Company compound to the sea. I threw it open and leaned out. Beyond the narrow stretch of water I could see the dome of the St Nicholas monastery rising above the huddle of poor huts. The wind was blowing from that direction, bringing with it the sound of the monks' chanting. Carried thus softly over the water, it had an almost magical quality. I longed to remain here while the ships were loaded with the Russian goods, then board again and travel home.

I sat down on the bed and wrapped my arms around myself, suddenly shaking with fear. The mission I had been cajoled or tricked into back in London had seemed unpleasant, but possible, but now I found myself here in this terrible, alien land, alone. Trust no one, Holme said. How could I hope to travel across a country which was largely unknown even to the experienced Company men, speaking very little of the language, trusting no one? I must work hard to improve my Russian, so that I would feel less helpless. And what of my mission itself? Find Gregory Rocksley and bring him back. If you cannot, find out what he discovered about the treason afoot amongst English merchants, believed to be passing secret information to the Spanish. It was absurd. It was impossible. I could not succeed. It was madness ever to have embarked on such an enterprise.

That night I slept badly. In truth, I hardly slept at all, but spent much of the night staring at the patterns of moonlight playing on the ceiling from the uncurtained window, during the short hours of darkness. I tried to tell myself that it was the change from the constant movement of a ship at sea to this land-locked bed that kept me awake, but I knew it was because my mind refused to let go of the worries that had plagued me by day. Could I return with the fleet and tell Rowland

Heyward and the others that it was impossible even to embark on the task they had set me? One part of my mind argued that it was the only sensible course of action. But then a small voice whispered to me, 'But what of Gregory Rocksley? What if he is in danger or in need of help, and you abandon him to the cruelties of this most cruel land?' For, to be honest with myself, I did not care much for discovering the traitors who were passing information to the Spanish. If dangerous intelligence was channelled through Narva (as it seemed to be from the evidence), then let them – Lord Burghley, or whoever now managed these affairs – let them send someone to Narva. The only thing which could persuade me to continue here was the man in trouble, as I might one day be in trouble and in need of help. When morning came, my mind was still divided.

The Company men, both on the ships and here at Rose Island, worked efficiently and fast. By the end of two days they had unloaded all the cargo from the ships. By far the largest part of the cargo was fine woollen cloth, for it seemed that the Muscovites loved the quality of our worsteds. We had brought says and kerseys, Bristol friezes, bright red frizadoes, and rashes – all the finest of our great variety of English cloth, which is the best in the world. There was a parcel of delicate knitted silk garters, and all manner of extravagant hats. I was to learn how much the Muscovites adored extraordinary headgear.

There were other goods too, some of them not produced in England, but imported by our merchants and then carried to Muscovy, the main ones being large quantities of sugar, and smaller shipments of spices and gems. Merchants like Dr Nuñez imported exotic goods through their trade with Venice and Constantinople, and made a considerable profit in selling on to the Muscovites. Although it would have been a much shorter route for the Muscovites to bring such goods into their country overland from the southeast, all those lands were full of hostile Tatars or warring Khanates. No merchant could safely pass through their territories. So the jewels I had seen on the monks' crosses and the spices used in the imperial kitchens had made their way along many, many thousands of miles and passed through many hands before they were unloaded at Rose Island.

I had been shown the Russian goods waiting in the warehouses to be exported to England. There were rich and costly furs, including sables, which only royalty and the greatest nobles were permitted to wear, but there were also many mundane goods, far more than I had expected. There was the wax Jos had talked about, and barrels of train oil culled from seals and whales. There were vast coils of rope, made in the Company's own factory at Kolmogory, together with bales of ship's canvas.

However, I was not to see these goods loaded aboard the *Bona Esperanza* and the other ships of the fleet. As we were breaking our fast on the third day of our stay on Rose Island, Christopher Holme smiled across the table as he passed me a basket of fresh rolls baked that morning in the Company's bakehouse.

'You will be glad to hear, Dr Alvarez, that I have secured transport for the first part of our journey. The barges carrying the goods we have landed will be heading up river toward Kolmogory. One has been made suitable for carrying passengers, so that we will be able to leave with them first thing tomorrow morning – the two of us, together with Pyotr Aubery, and two of the stipendiaries from here. One is being transferred to Yaroslavl and one is coming to serve on my staff in Moscow. So you will not need to kick your heels here much longer. As Company men, we may travel to the first Company house along the Dvina while we wait for permission to travel further.'

I nodded and did my best to smile. It seemed I had left it too late to retreat now.

'We shall also visit Yaroslavl as we move onwards,' he said. 'I understand that the Tsarevich Dmitri is now living at Uglich, which is not far from Yaroslavl. At least not far in Russian terms, perhaps sixty miles. Is he not one of your intended patients?'

'That is the Tsar's younger brother? Aye. I have been told that his mother has worries about his health, but not exactly what they are. Does he not live in Moscow?'

William Holbeche leaned toward me. 'There are rumours that he has fits and falls on the floor, foaming at the mouth. Would that be *petit mal*?'

I was startled. I had no idea that it might be something so serious. Yet his father's behaviour had been very strange. Perhaps this child had been cursed with an inherited madness or disease. It was beyond the range of my skills and I felt a sinking in my stomach. If I was expected to cure a permanent condition like *petit mal*, the falling sickness, I was doomed from the outset.

The next morning we bade farewell to William Holbeche and our other hosts, and walked down to the quays. A flock of river boats was moored there, wide flat-bottomed vessels, more barge than boat. Each had a single stumpy mast fitted with a clumsy square sail, to take advantage of the wind when it was favourable, and they were also equipped with oars. They reminded me a little of the river barges I had seen in the Low Countries, but these were much more crude. Amongst the barges there were even some rafts, nothing more than floating platforms of rough pine logs lashed together. I hoped that none of our valuable goods would be entrusted to such primitive transport.

One of the largest boats was fitted with a cabin where the cargo would normally be loaded. It was more like one of the fishermen's huts than a ship's cabin, and it was clear that this was our intended accommodation. It was made, like them, of undressed logs, with a roof of birch bark shingles and moss stuffed between the cracks to keep out the worst of the wind. We climbed aboard and inspected our quarters. The cabin was divided into two rooms, one (I supposed) for living and one for sleeping, although they were identical. Narrow benches lined the walls, apparently intended for either sitting or sleeping, and there was a pile of coarse blankets and undressed furs for warmth. A barrel of mead stood in one corner, with a collection of dirty pewter cups on top, for your Muscovite takes his drinking more seriously than eating. Mead is a cheap and popular drink, for there is an abundance of bees in the country. Bees which also provide that all-important wax for the Queen's candles. I saw no sign of food.

We deposited our luggage in the cabin. Pyotr and I carried very little, but Christopher Holme and the two stipendiaries were heavily laden, for I supposed their homes would be in Muscovy for the present. Christopher wrinkled his nose as he looked around.

'I had forgotten how primitive these boats are. They do not seem to have improved in the last fifteen years. And it is not very clean.'

'Are we not supposed to eat on the journey?' I said. 'Only drink?'

'We will tie up to the bank and eat on shore,' Pyotr said. 'The boatmen will light a fire and cook over that. They do not carry a firebox onboard. These boats made of raw pine are full of sap, which can burst into flames from a single careless spark.'

'Turpentine,' I said absently. 'I suppose that shows sense.'

We all made our way out on to the small deck of rough boards. Our boatmen, of whom there were six oarsmen and a steersman, had hoisted the sail, a poor patched thing, but we were being towed across to the river Dvina by one of the pinnaces from the fleet, so it was hardly needed. I had not noticed before just how many mouths there were to the river Dvina, which spilt into a maze of waterways before flowing into the White Sea. The pinnace headed for the largest of these and as the tow rope tightened our barge bumped along behind, followed by the cargo barges, each given a tow by a pinnace. Once we were fairly in the river, the tow rope was cast off, our pinnace drew away to the left-hand bank, and we crawled past, propelled by that inadequate little sail.

I sat down on the deck out of the way of the boatmen, as there was nowhere else, and wrapped my arms about my knees. Pyotr and the stipendiaries joined me, but Master Holme declined, saying at his age his joints were growing too stiff. I put him at about his middle to late forties, and he did not look overly stiff too me, but perhaps he valued his dignity. One of the stipendiaries jumped up at once, and fetched one of the luggage chests from the cabin. Seated on this, Holme lost no dignity and also gained a better view of our progress than the rest of us.

The wind and sail proving useless, the boatmen took in the sail by the simple expedient of tying it to the yard, which was no more than arm's length above their heads. They ran out the oars and began to row. We were passing through a featureless country, a patchwork of pine and birch forests, interspersed with bog. Hardly a human habitation was to be seen, save for an occasional woodcutter's cottage, and in one spot four cottages where women sat outside, weaving baskets from osiers, while men fished from the river bank and barefoot children poked about in the mud.

The river current was strong, so that the oarsmen could make only slow headway against it. And as the river twisted and turned, we sometimes found the wind in our faces, so that both current and wind were against us. The steersman headed the barge toward the right bank and my hopes rose that they were planning to cook a meal, for it was past midday and my stomach was aching for food.

'Are we stopping to cook? I asked generally.

'Nay, I do not think so.' It was Christopher Holme who replied. 'We are driven to our last mode of propulsion.'

I frowned, not understanding him. Three of the boatmen, but not the steersman, were donning some kind of harness, which was strapped around their chests, with an additional leather strap across the forehead. Once they were satisfied that all was in place, they climbed out of the barge on to the rough grass of the bank. I saw now that long ropes trailed from their harnesses to the bow of the barge. There was a kind of path along the bank, where the grass had been trodden down, which I had not noticed before.

The steersman shouted something I did not understand, the three men leaned forward, then began to walk, The ropes tightened and the barge jerked. The men stopped, still leaning forward, then heaved again. This time the barge began to move. The steersman put the tiller over to starboard, so that the barge moved away from the bank, though it tended to keep heading back toward the towing men, causing an unpleasant zigzag motion.

I could see that, proceeding thus, we were going to make very slow progress. I knelt up and looked over the side of the barge. Although judging by our movement through the fast flowing river, we seemed to be making reasonable headway, our movement relative to the bank was painfully slow, as the men placed one foot in front of the other, slowly, slowly.

Sitting down again and leaning my back against the side of the barge, I squinted up at Christopher Holme.

'How far is it from St Nicholas to Kolmogory?' I said.

'Overland?' he said. 'About a hundred English miles.'

'And by river?'

He paused, then shrugged. 'About six hundred.'

Chapter Six

*I*t sounded impossible and at first I thought Christopher Holme was teasing me. How could a journey that was a hundred miles by land possibly stretch to six hundred miles by river? And if it was true, surely it would be better to travel by land? Even if wheeled vehicles did become bogged down in the mud from time to time, it could not multiply the journey time by six. As it was, it seemed that for most of the river journey we would be proceeding at the very slow pace of the men hauling the barge. I was not so unfeeling as to expect them to go faster, but could the Muscovites not have devised some better way to move about their country? Six hundred miles! I did not know for sure, but I thought that must be about the same distance as travelling from the south coast of England all the way to the north of Scotland. And this journey was merely to reach the *nearest* town to St Nicholas.

Christopher Holme must have seen the doubt in my expression.

'It is quite true,' he said. 'When we are in Muscovy we must resign ourselves to the way the Russians live, and travel, and do business. Their sense of time is very different from ours. Thomas Randolph, when he came as ambassador back in '68, took all of five weeks to travel up the Dvina from St Nicholas.'

I groaned, and bowed my head to my drawn up knees. It was at that moment, I think, that I first began to get a real sense of the sheer impossible size of Muscovy. I felt as if I were drowning in some vast ocean of land, which could engulf pitiful small humans as easily as the sea.

'Why do they not use horses to drag the barges?' I said crossly. 'They would be stronger than men and would move faster.'

Robert Farindon, the stipendiary who was travelling all the way to Moscow with Christopher Holme, pointed to the river bank.

'That was what I thought when I first came to this country. But look. What horse could navigate that?'

I looked where he pointed, and realised he was right. The bank here was broken by a treacherous tumble of rock, over which our human draught beasts scrambled with great difficulty, stopping from time to time to jerk free the tow ropes when they caught on rough outcrops.

'I suppose you are right,' I conceded. 'But could they not construct a path suitable for horses?'

'For six hundred miles? In this desolate area? Even with the forced labour of peasants? Nay, the Tsar would never think it worth his while. The merchants are not in a hurry. No one is in a hurry in this country, except when the army goes to war, and that is never in this district. It is either in the west, against Sweden or Livonia, or in the south against the Tatars.'

His reasoning was irrefutable. I sighed. I would just have to resign myself to days and days of boredom.

'After Kolmogory,' I said, 'do we go on by river?'

'That will depend on the weather,' Robert said. 'The main towns, and hence the Company's trading stations, tend to be built along the rivers, as they provide the best means of travel. If the Dvina is still not frozen, we follow it to the junction with the river Sukhona. That will take us up river to Vologda, the next Company factory that Master Holme wishes to visit.

'Up river again?' I asked. 'With these poor men still struggling to tow the barge against the current?'

Robert was literal minded. 'Probably not the same men. They will return to St Nicholas. We will have a different crew after Kolmogory.'

'You said, "If the Dvina is still not frozen". Is it likely to freeze soon?'

'It will not be long now,' Pyotr said. 'Remember, I spent my first fifteen years in this region. Frost comes earlier inland than at St Nicholas, even though we are a little further south. It may be that after Master Holme finishes his business in Kolmogory the river will be frozen, and the ground too.'

'So we will travel by land?' I asked, full of hope.

He nodded. 'Much faster. By sleigh. Robert may say that no one in Muscovy is in a hurry. It is merely that we have adapted ourselves to live according to the climate and the seasons of the year.'

I sensed that he was offended by what Robert had said. Moreover, by using 'we', consciously or not, he was regarding himself as Russian, whereas before we reached the country he had striven to give the impression that he was a loyal Englishman. I had thought him a simple soul at first. Now I was not so sure. His loyalties might be more complex that I had supposed.

It was fortunate that Robert and the other stipendiary, John Upton, were accustomed to the long, unrewarding hours of travel in Muscovy. They had come provided with means of entertainment – playing cards, a set of chess and a backgammon board. Without them, I think we might have gone mad on that journey. I also took advantage of the long, slow hours to urge Pyotr to more and more lessons in Russian. If there was to be no other profit from this time aboard the barge, I was determined to become as fluent as possible in the language. I made no attempt to read or write it, but as the days passed I found I could express myself reasonably well.

It must have been about the beginning of the second week that we woke to a fine crust of frost lying on the surface of the deck and sparkling on every blade of grass. When we clambered ashore for the morning ritual of lighting a fire and preparing a meal, our boots crunched on the frozen turf. I had brought one of the furs with me and kept it wrapped round my shoulders, despite its somewhat rancid smell. Although I had the hood of my cloak up, my head ached with the cold, filling me with dread, for if this was just the beginning of the cold weather, what would the true depths of winter be like?

When we had tied up here the previous night, the boatmen had dragged some fallen tree trunks for us the sit on, so I perched on one now, taking care to ensure there was a layer of the fur between me and the icy bark. Bear skin, I think it was, that fur. At least it was the shape and colour of a brown bear, only roughly dressed, which was probably why it smelled rancid. Other furs provided in the cabin were wolf, and several types I could not identify. I had been told about white bear skins, but had seen none. It seemed they were particularly prized.

Despite the fur, I could not stop my teeth chattering, even after the men managed to get a fire going. The flames seemed pitiful in that vast uninhabited wilderness. We were surrounded on three sides by dark forests of pine and birch. On the fourth side the Dvina was flowing fast, a wide grey snake of a river. I think I have never been anywhere so desolate.

The boatmen were cooking up a kind of thick porridge they made every morning. Sweetened with honey, it was bearable and sustained us until we stopped again in the evening for a meal of fish caught in the river and fried over the fire, but after the first week I was heartily sick of it. During the day we did not stop, but nibbled at dried rounds of a kind of flat rye bread, which was almost black, topped with lumps of hard cheese. So hard, you could break a tooth on it. There was always plenty to drink, of course. The Muscovites had an enormous capacity for strong drink. In the long, dark winters I supposed they probably had nothing better to do than drink themselves senseless.

'Here, take this.' Pyotr was holding out a wooden cup from which steam rose, mingling with the cloud of steam from his breath.

'What is it?'

'Hot mead. It will warm you.'

As soon as it had cooled enough not to burn my mouth, I sipped it gladly. I would have preferred it spiced, like the spiced ale I prepared over my own little fire at home, but I was grateful for the heat in my stomach, though I found mead over sweet. I even ate the mess of porridge with some enthusiasm, thinking its warmth might also help to disperse the dreadful cold.

All the others were now wearing fur hats, with flaps which hung down to protect their ears from frostbite. Even Christopher Holme had one of these hats, although his looked a little tattered and moth-eaten. He must have kept it from the time when he had lived in Muscovy before. I realised the hood of my cloak was poor protection against the cold and wondered whether I would be able to purchase one of these hats in Kolmogory.

As if he could read my thoughts, Master Holme said, 'We must find you better clothes for the Muscovy climate, Dr Alvarez. Your English garments will not do.'

I nodded, and remembered Rowland Heyward's promise that the Company would provide me with clothes. I had not taken him seriously at the time.

'I certainly need a hat,' I said. 'And my legs are cold too. I cannot always walk about clutching a bear skin.'

Like every well-dressed Englishman, I wore knitted hose that covered my legs and were laced to my doublet, with short padded breeches reaching about halfway down my thighs. From thigh to ankle my legs were beginning to grow numb. I would have been much colder had my hose been of silk, like a courtier's, but mine were of fine wool. On this freezing morning, however, they gave no protection at all from the cutting wind. The other passengers had donned long tunics which came to their ankles. The boatmen, who wore knee-length tunics, protected their legs with baggy woollen trousers.

None of use wanted to linger on shore. The men put out the fire, heaping shovelled earth over it until it was quite smothered, for an unattended fire so close to a pine forest could cause a disaster. They had some difficulty digging up the earth. Clearly the ground was beginning to freeze, which I took as a good omen. However, there was no hope that we could transfer to sleighs until we reached Kolmogory, for where would we find a sleigh in this uninhabited land?

Once we were back on board and underway, I rummaged in my knapsack for the peculiar garment Goodwife Maynard had knitted for me. Confronted by the first inkling of a Russian winter, I did not find it quite so ridiculous. How to wear it? It was too bulky to wear under my shirt. If I wore it over my shirt but under my doublet, I doubted I would be able to button my doublet. In the end, I simply pulled it on over my doublet, then slung my cloak over my shoulders. I probably looked like something fit to scare the birds from the cornfield, but I was past caring. I felt the increased warmth at once.

I regarded my fellow passengers defiantly when I joined them in the outer cabin, daring them to mock me, but Master Holme merely said, 'Good, that will keep you a little warmer. When we reach the Company station at Kolmogory, we will fit you out with appropriate clothes for winter. I should have remembered when we were at Rose Island. You could not be expected to come fully prepared for the weather here.'

Altogether, the river journey took us over three weeks. I did not believe Christopher Holme's assertion that it was six hundred miles, but it was a considerable distance. As we neared the end of the journey, we woke each morning to find ice had enclosed the barge, holding us fast against the land, so that the bargemen were forced to smash us free with their oars. All along the river, ice was forming, especially by the banks, and this tended to impede our progress. Lumps of ice also came swimming down the river toward us. Not large enough to do us harm. Not yet. But I began to be anxious. What if the river should freeze over before we reached Kolmogory?

When I mentioned this fear to Pyotr, he laughed.

'There is no need to worry. If the river should freeze that hard – and I do not expect it will – then the men will simply drag the barge along on the ice. It will slow us down, but will not stop us. We call the frozen rivers "winter roads".'

We had lost sight of the other barges long since, the ones carrying the cargo brought from England by the Company fleet, but I supposed they were still following doggedly behind. They were more likely than we to be forced to move over the ice. I commented on this to Pyotr, who nodded.

'They will arrive eventually. We are making faster progress than the cargo barges. We have more men to tow us. Master Holme is an important man, the new chief agent. It would not do for him to be delayed by a slow journey.'

I kept my tongue behind my teeth. My sharp comment about the slowness of the journey would not have been welcome.

Some days later, as the evening was drawing it – which it did more noticeably with every passing day – we could see that the men towing us were looking for a suitable place to moor for the night. This stretch of the river bank was not very promising, for it rose in a rocky cliff, over which the bargemen had difficulty scrambling. Suddenly there was a sound of slithering rock, a scream and a loud splash. We had been huddling inside the cabin, but rushed out to the deck.

'What is it?' Christopher Holme shaded his eyes from the low lying sun which almost blinded us.

'It's one of the men,' Pyotr shouted, 'he's fallen in the river.'

'His harness is still attached to the barge,' I cried. 'We can pull him in.'

I ran forward along the side of the cabin to the point where the tow ropes were tethered to the bow. The steersman, abandoning the tiller, was there before me, a large dagger in his hand. He began to saw at the fallen man's tow rope, to cut him away from the boat.

'Nay!' I shouted. 'Nyet! We must pull him in! Stop!.'

He paid me no heed, but went on slicing through the rope. It was severed halfway.

I struck his hand from the rope and the dagger flew away, sliding along the deck, which was already beginning to glaze over with the night-time frost.

Leaning over the gunwale, I seized hold of the rope below the point where it was half severed, and tried to haul it in, but the drag of the man borne away by the current nearly pulled me overboard.

'Help me!' I shouted. 'Pyotr! Robert! John! I can't . . .' I gasped, my breath forced from my lungs by the edge of gunwale. 'He's too heavy for me.'

But it was Christopher Holme whose hand grabbed the rope next to mine, then the others were there, hauling the man over the gunwale to lie in a pool of icy water at our feet. The steersman shrugged and picked up his dagger, before returning to the tiller.

'He will die anyway,' he shouted over his shoulder.

'Oh, God help us,' Pyotr said. 'He is probably right.'

'Get him into the cabin,' Holme said curtly.

The men were not normally permitted to enter the cabin. At night they erected a sort of tent in the stern of the barge and sheltered there, but this was no time for the niceties.

'Strip his wet clothes off first,' I said to Robert and John. 'We need to get him warm and dry as quickly as possible, or he *will* die. And we don't want that cold water in the cabin. I have something that will stimulate his heart. The danger is that the cold and shock will stop it. Pyotr, bring some of the mead. I wish we could heat it.'

'We could warm it a little over our candle lamp,' Holme said. 'It won't be much, but–'

'Aye, a good idea.'

The two stipendiaries worked quickly and carried the naked man into the cabin. As we wrapped him in layer upon layer of furs, I saw that his chest was covered with bruises from the cruel pressure of the towing harness. He was unconscious and flaccid with the cold. I might be too late to save him. I rummaged in my satchel for my phial containing tincture of digitalis, though my hands were shaking so much I nearly dropped it.

Christopher Holme had lit the candle lamp and was attempting to warm some of the mead Pyotr had brought, which he had poured into a pewter cup.

'Don't burn yourself,' I said absently, and he held up a handkerchief to show that he had thought of that.

Digitalis is a tricky drug. It can be effective in treatment of the heart, but too much will kill a man. I knew nothing of the bargeman's state of health, so I would simply need to guess. Already his pulse was faint and his breathing shallow. I must act now or lose him.

'Robert, prop him up. I need to give him this. John, can you force his mouth open, so I can get a spoon between his lips? Squeeze his jaw between your fingers. Have you ever given medicine to a dog? Aye, like that.'

I had taken a spoon from my satchel. Now I pulled the cork from the phial with my teeth and poured the tincture of digitalis into the spoon. How much? In the end I decided to give him a full spoonful and pray that I had made the right decision.

John managed to force the man's mouth open, though I could see his jaw was rigid with the cold. I slipped the spoon in and the throat muscles moved automatically as he swallowed.

'Now the mead,' I said, reaching out for the cup. Holme passed it to me.

'It is not too hot,' he said. 'I have only warmed it a little and put it in a wooden cup. Perhaps I should–'

'It will be fine, if we can just get him to drink it.'

I forced a little of the mead between the man's lips while John held his mouth open, though some of it dribbled away down his chin. I sat back on my heels. I did not want to risk making him choke.

We all watched him in silence. Would the steersman be proved right? Perhaps it would have been kinder to let him drown at once. I pushed the thought away. Even if he died now, he was warm and surrounded by people who wished him well. Surely that was better than a lonely death in a half-frozen river.

As I was forcing more of the mead into his mouth, there was a jarring as the barge hit the bank. The remaining men must have found a place to moor for the night. That meant hot food.

The bargeman moaned and muttered something. I could not understand his guttural accent. 'What does he say?' I asked Pyotr.

'He thinks he has died.'

Pyotr reached down and squeezed the man's shoulder, then said something in the same thick accent. The man made a choking noise which sounded almost like a laugh.

'What did you tell him?' Christopher Howe asked.

'I told him he wasn't ready for Heaven yet. He'd more time to spend on this shitty earth.'

We all laughed at that.

'If we can keep him warm,' I said, 'if we can feed him some hot food, if he is allowed to rest for a day or two, then I think we may keep him from Heaven yet awhile.'

That night we took it in turn to keep a watch on the bargeman, whose name was Sergei. He had eaten a little fish in the evening, but remained very weak and shaken. I did not allow him to go ashore, but insisted he should stay in the cabin, wrapped in furs. His clothes were still sodden, and like all the bargemen he had no others, wearing the same things day and night. It would be a long time before they were dry, for it had now grown bitterly cold. They would probably freeze first. It was not yet the dry cold of full winter, which Pyotr said would come soon. Instead a layer of freezing fog hung over the river, which is probably the nastiest weather ever known to man. Even the rest of us, who had not taken that near fatal plunge into the river, began to feel the insidious damp cold creeping into our very bones.

The cabin contained a small brazier, which the bargemen were very reluctant to light, for fear of fire. Apparently it was intended to be used only in extreme emergencies, but Master Holme now asserted his authority and said that we would light it. There was an abundance of firewood lying about in the edges of the forest, so we soon had a plentiful supply. Pyotr – who was inclined to take the bargemen's part in the argument over the brazier – insisted that we should keep two buckets of water always ready next to the brazier, in case of accidents.

'At least,' I remarked dryly, 'that means we will have water instead of ice to wash with in the mornings.'

For the previous few days the water on board had frozen during the night. All the men had abandoned any attempt to shave, and were growing beards like the Muscovites. I feared it might draw attention to my beardless state, although I knew several men of my age in London who remained beardless. Simon was one. John, the younger of the two stipendiaries, had no more than a soft down on his chin. I threw out a casual remark that the men in my family had never grown much facial hair, and hoped my story would be believed. Fortunately, we had other matters on our minds.

I took the first watch over our patient that night, and was relieved by Christopher Holme around midnight.

'How does he fare?' he whispered, as he came through from the sleeping room to where I sat on one of the benches, trying to read by the flickering flames of the brazier. I feared if I did not read I might fall asleep myself.

'Well enough,' I said. 'His breathing is regular and his heart beat is stronger than it was. It was fortunate that he fell into the Dvina and not the Thames. This river is clean, while the Thames is an open sewer, tainted with God only knows what filth. Anyone who gulps down a dose of Thames water has a choice of several diseases from which he may die.'

'If he is resting well and recovering,' he said, standing near the brazier and rubbing his hands together to warm them, 'you should try to get some rest.'

I stood up and stretched, cramped from sitting still on the hard bench so long.

'Aye. I will so.' I tucked my book of poetry under my arm. 'They are a brutal people, these Muscovites. The steersman was going to send Sergei to his death without a qualm. He made no attempt to save him.'

Holme sat down on the bench I had vacated and picked up a fur to wrap round himself.

'Do not judge him too harshly, Dr Alvarez. He would have thought that the extra weight might have pulled the other men into the river, then we should all have been lost. Stranded here, without the means to move forward, we would have perished in the cold.'

'Perhaps,' I conceded. 'But he could have called to us for help. We had no great difficulty in hauling Sergei aboard.'

'It is the way the people here are apt to view the world,' he said. 'For men like the steersman and the others, like the peasants you will see in the villages, we are almost a different species. They are so cowed into submission, so forced into a condition almost of slavery, that it would simply never cross their minds to ask for help from us. They would not believe they had the right to ask.'

'That is a sad state of affairs.'

'It is. There is another thing.' He paused, and glanced toward the sleeping cabin. 'In this country, all foreigners are viewed with the deepest suspicion. We will not be allowed to move beyond Kolmogory until written permission arrives from Moscow. Should we try to do so, we would be stopped, by local officials of the government, and possibly thrown into prison. Moreover, we are constantly watched. Never allowed to move about the country without some "guide" or "interpreter" to aid us – but really to report back on everything we do.'

'But there is no one like that here,' I objected.

'Do not be too sure. I have kept an eye on the steersman. I suspect he is not merely a bargeman, but is also here to keep a watch on us. Or possibly . . .'

He broke off, but I saw his eyes flicker briefly again towards the sleeping cabin.

I lowered my voice to a whisper. 'You spoke of interpreters. Do you think Pyotr . . .?'

He shrugged. 'I cannot tell where his loyalties lie. Although he works for the Company, do not forget that the Company refused to recognise his parents' marriage. That must have left a legacy of bitterness. All I can do is warn you to be cautious.'

I shivered, but nodded my agreement.

'Now go and get some rest, Dr Alvarez,' he said.

I turned aside, but paused at the door to the inner cabin. 'My friends call me Kit.'

He smiled. 'And I am Christopher.'

In the morning, Sergei was a little stronger and we tried to dry his clothes by the cooking fire onshore. A great deal of steam rose from them into the cold morning air, but they remained thoroughly sodden. In some ways this was a boon, for it meant he could not possibly be forced to resume his place amongst the towers. For the most part, he slept.

From the time we went ashore to break our fast, I noticed that the bargemen seemed wary of me, giving me furtive looks from the corners of their eyes and taking care to stay well away from me. I had thought they might have been grateful that I had saved their companion's life, but instead they seemed afraid of me, or even hostile. I commented on this once we were back in the boat and on our way again, along a river more thickly scattered with ice floes than before.

'There is little knowledge of medicine in Muscovy,' Pyotr said, 'at any rate amongst the common people. We have no locally trained physicians. The only physicians in this country are foreigners, mostly from Germany, a few from Italy and England. They practise in the court and amongst the nobles.'

'Someone must treat the common people,' I protested. 'They cannot be totally ignorant. Simple cures – the kind of knowledge every mother of a family possesses.'

He shrugged. 'There are wise women who practise herbal cures, though it involves a good deal of superstition and magic too. The sort of women who would be suspected of being witches in England. Here, well, they are regarded as a kind of witch too. A dangerous kind. The sort that the whole village will turn against, when things go wrong.'

'They surely do not think me a witch!' I laughed, but without much conviction. Here was more danger. If my sex was discovered, I was aptly suited to the role of witch.

'I have heard them muttering amongst themselves,' Pyotr said. 'They believed Sergei was dead when we hauled him out of the river. Therefore they believe you raised him from the dead. Consequently, you must be a saint, a witch, or a devil.'

'It is absurd,' I said briskly. 'He was *not* dead, you all saw that. I would take it kindly if you make that quite clear to them, Pyotr.'

This uncomfortable atmosphere persisted. I do not know whether Pyotr said anything to the men. If he did, it seemed to make no difference, so I was relieved when, two days later, he pointed out how the endless pine forest was giving way ahead of us to cultivated fields, though there was little to see at this time of year but frosted stubble. No beasts were visible, but I could make out some buildings crouched at the edges of the fields, which might have been cottages, or barns, or served as accommodation for both animals and men.

'Those are the farms that lie around Kolmogory,' he said. 'We will reach the town tomorrow.'

'At last!' I said. 'And we seem to have beaten the ice, just in time.'

That very morning it had been almost impossible for the men to break the barge free from the encroaching ice. Now, alerted by the bargemen shouting to the peasants on shore, Sergei threw off the furs and insisted on donning his clothes, although they were still damp. There was nothing I could do to prevent it, although I feared the effect of damp clothing on his still weakened state. Perhaps once in Kolmogory he would be able to get warm and dry in some tavern. I was sure every Muscovite town would be well provided with drinking spots.

Our first sight of Kolmogory was the imposing fort, rearing up round a bend in the river. It was timber built, like almost every structure in a country which was almost entirely covered by forests, but it was large and intimidating. The vast perimeter walls were three times the height of a man, studded at regular intervals with watchtowers. Within the ramparts we could glimpse a number of large buildings, including a tower as high as an English castle keep, which would provide extensive views of the surrounding countryside. It was clearly placed here to protect access to the interior of the country along the Dvina, a secure defence against foreigners, whom the Muscovites seemed to fear so obsessively. I commented on this to Christopher.

'Aye,' he said, 'they do fear us, the English. Even Company men who have worked here for years. But they also fear the Sami and the Samoyeds from the north, the Swedes from the west.'

'Surely Sweden is a long way from here.'

'Not as a Muscovite thinks of distance. And the country is yet again at war with Sweden, which is a modern country with a well organised and disciplined army. The Muscovites will never defeat the Swedes. All they can hope is to keep them at bay. And the Poles. And the Livonians. And especially the Tatars.'

He sat down on one of the chests which held the belongings of the Company men.

'I first came here just over twenty years ago, with the '69 fleet. Three years later, I was sent with two senior men to Moscow. It was only the year after the destruction of the city in '71and I shall never forget the sight of the burnt-out houses.'

'There had been a fire?' I said. 'I can imagine, a careless spark, where everything is built of wood–'

'It was no accident. Tatars from the Crimea had invaded again, and that time they reached Moscow. Murder, rape, and pillage. Then they deliberately burned the city to the ground. The walls of the Company's house were badly damaged, but that was the least of it. Twenty-five men, women and children had taken refuge in our cellar, and they all perished. I went with the others to make arrangements for the repairing of the Company House. It was terrible. The smell! Still in the air. Not only the smell of burnt timber, but burnt bodies. They were still being found, as the ruins were cleared. You cannot imagine.'

'Oh, I think I can,' I said. I did not speak my thoughts aloud, but if you have witnessed an auto-da-fé, you live with the memory of the smell for ever.

'So you can see why the Muscovite government is nervous,' he said. 'They were nervous before, constantly under attack from the Golden Horde, from the Tatars, and from Europe, but after the Tatars managed to reach Moscow, all the way from the Crimea, their fear of foreigners has grown all the stronger. Whatever one may say about Ivan Vasilyevich, he was a strong leader. Now they have a ruler who is all but simple-minded, and they have his chief adviser, his brother-in-law, who is intelligent, capable, and ruthless, but who has no right to rule the people. It is a situation of great delicacy and danger, which is why I continue to warn you to be careful.'

'I did not choose to come,' I said, growing ever more alarmed at his words. 'It seems hardly surprising that Gregory Rocksley should disappear in such a place at such a time. It is clear that I have been set an impossible task. I cannot believe that the Company shareholders, sitting safe in London, have any idea of what they have asked me to do.'

'I did warn them,' he said, 'before we left. But they brushed my objections aside.'

'No one told me of that. You have not mentioned it.'

'There seemed little point. Here you are. However,' he smiled suddenly, 'it may be that you will not be granted permission to travel any further than Kolmogory. You will be safe here. The town is virtually controlled by the Company.'

'And wait here until next year's fleet arrives?'

'That would be wisest. Of course, there are other ways out of the country. Not through Sweden, certainly, at the moment. Perhaps through Poland.'

Our discussion was brought to an abrupt end as the barge nosed in towards the quays – sturdy and newly built, clearly Company property. For this final approach to the town, the bargemen had abandoned their harnesses and run out the oars, which they had scarcely used since we had left St Nicholas, for we made better progress when towed. However, they clearly favoured oars within the confines of the town harbour.

'Later,' I said hastily to Christopher, 'you must tell me of these other ways out of Muscovy.'

He rose to his feet and regarded me gravely. 'They are all dangerous. The Tsar is as unwilling to allow foreigners to leave his country as to enter it. More so. They believe that every foreigner is here to spy on them and steal their secrets. What secrets I am not sure. Perhaps something that might help the King of Sweden overrun their western lands. I was not seriously recommending that you make your own way home. If it should happen that you are refused permission to voyage further into Muscovy, then stay secure within one of our Company houses and travel home with our fleet. While you are under the Company aegis, you are reasonably safe.'

'I am sure I shall have no need to wander unlawfully about the country,' I said with a laugh. 'I should be lost in a few hours in one of these great pine forests.'

Still, I intended to find out more. I had no wish to be trapped in this dreadful place at the whim of a half-mad Tsar. It might have wide skies, broad rivers, and vast forests, but nonetheless it reminded me powerfully of the Inquisition prison.

Kolmogory proved to be a pleasant little town, and after the interminable voyage by barge, cold and comfortless, it seemed a haven. Warmth, food, a bed of English design. The Company factory lay within the outer defences of the fort, for security, but had its own compound within the greater one. It was of some considerable size, for the rope factory had been established here, close to a good source of hemp, grown on the surrounding farms. The Muscovite knowledge of rope making had initially been poor, but labour was cheap, so instead of importing raw hemp to be spun into naval cordage at home, the

Company had sent out skilled English rope-makers to teach the Muscovite labourers.

The result was highly successful – an abundant source of inexpensively produced rope of every dimension needed by our ships. The whole enterprise was so thriving that English merchants were now able to export the surplus to other nations at a healthy profit, for the Company's rope was recognised as the best in the world. The first merchants had invested in the Muscovy Company expecting to import luxury goods – furs, above all, and rare items from Persia and the Orient. Yet now, a generation later, their real profits lay in rope, canvas, wax, tallow, and oil. Mundane, but a sound investment.

The Company house in Kolmogory was timber built, but unlike the local houses, even those of the merchant classes, it was constructed of properly dressed timbers, and the roof was of neatly trimmed shingles, not the turf or bark which served the Muscovites. I had seen no window glass in any house, for I suppose this was too costly in such a remote country. Instead, the windows were glazed with thin sheets of horn, like ancient cottages of rural paupers at home in England. They let in a diffuse yellowish light, which was an improvement on nothing but wooden shutters, but the view through them was poor. Heavy shutters were also provided, for I could imagine that they were needed to keep out the severe cold of winter.

To my relief, I had a room to myself, and indeed I was always treated with great courtesy by the men who worked for the Company. It seemed that word had gone ahead that I was in the country on a special mission for their governor. I hoped it would not inhibit their answers when I began to ask questions about Gregory Rocksley, for he had travelled this way before me. It was the accepted route to Moscow – St Nicholas, Kolmogory, Vologda, Yaroslavl, Moscow.

Not that I expected to learn anything of importance here, I thought, as I unpacked my few possessions. Gregory's movements as far as Moscow were clearly known. He had then travelled west toward Narva, but the war with Sweden had broken out. Either that, or some other reason, had caused him to change course and head southeast. He had passed through Moscow again and was last seen with his interpreter in a small town some eighty or a hundred miles south of the capital, where he had apparently told a fellow traveller quite openly that he was heading for Astrakhan. That was the last time he was seen.

It had always seem strange to me that he should have headed for Astrakhan. If the intelligence leak was through Narva, and if the way to Narva was closed to him, why had he not rejoined the Company in

Moscow? He could then have been waiting in St Nicholas when our fleet arrived this summer and returned with it to England. The expected despatches explaining his actions had never been received. Or so the Company believed, though it was possible something might have been amongst the papers stolen from Walsingham's office.

However, now I had some experience of Muscovy myself, it was not surprising that letters from Rocksley had not arrived. It was always difficult for Walsingham's agents to send reports from hostile or even neutral countries. Many were lost or intercepted. Even if he had attempted to send something, I thought the chances of its going astray were very high indeed in this remote, dangerous, and vast country.

After my various conversations with Christopher Holme, I was beginning to see the matter of Gregory Rocksley in a different light. His despatches might not have been lost, but rather stolen, quite possibly on the orders of the government. And although the purpose of his mission had been to catch a spy, this suspicious regime might have taken him for a spy himself. For all we knew, the Muscovite government might have been behind the passing of secret information about England to Spain. Muscovy sent ambassadors regularly to England and would have seen much of our ports, castles, and navy, all of which would be of interest to our enemies. As far as I knew, Spain was no friend of Muscovy, but Godunov might be involved in some covert diplomacy with that country.

If everyone who travelled here was constantly watched by government spies, they must gather many fragments of knowledge about England, which an intelligent man like Godunov could piece together, along with the information brought back by ambassadors. He probably ran a network similar to Walsingham's, but even more widespread within his own country, and set to entrap every unwary foreigner.

I paused in shaking out my physician's gown, which was sorely crumpled after weeks rolled up in my knapsack.

'So, that may have been why he was heading for Astrakhan!'

I spoke the words aloud, then looked around anxiously, hoping that my voice could not be heard outside my room.

Perhaps when Rocksley returned to Moscow after trying to reach Narva something happened. Something to put him on his guard. Could he have been heading south in order to escape a ruthless Muscovite government? Christopher had said that the Tsar was usually reluctant to allow foreigners to leave the country. For whatever reason, that might have happened to Rocksley.

I closed my eyes and tried to envisage the map I had been shown of Muscovy back in London. Astrakhan was a town on the Caspian sea. From there one could take a boat – but to where? I was vague about the geography in that part of the world, and the map had been sketchy at best, the lands beyond the Caspian falling off the edge of the paper. Persia was somewhere there, and various khanates, conquered by Ivan the Terrible, but now restless under the weak rule of his son. The Crimea was down there as well, somewhere to the south and inhabited by the Tatars who had wreaked such destruction on Moscow less than twenty years ago. Would Rocksley really have tried to escape through those territories? Perhaps he had no choice. To travel east would have been pointless. The way north was held in an iron grip by the Tsar, any peasant might betray him. To the west there was a war. South would seem the only way. Eventually one would reach the Mediterranean and civilisation. It would be easy to take ship for home in Venice or Constantinople.

I shook my head in annoyance. I was inventing a story for Rocksley based on pure speculation. It was equally probable that he was following some lead connected with his original investigation of treasonous information being passed by a former Company employee. I knew that the Company traded through Astrakhan from time to time. And it was more than likely that he had simply perished of exposure or illness during the winter weather.

Or he might be languishing in one of the Tsar's prisons. Or dead after being tortured. I had heard the tales of what happened here.

I went down to join the others for the evening meal, determined to push such speculation to the back of my mind.

It was a good meal – English food cooked in the English fashion by an English cook employed by the Company. It was a relief to eat something other than porridge and fish. However, I was tired and excused myself soon afterwards and retired to bed. Here was luxury indeed, after weeks of sleeping on what passed for a bed in this country, nothing more than a narrow wooden shelf. A tester bed with heavy woollen curtains. An English bedstead – or if it was made here, it was made to an English design – strung with ropes, with a flock and a feather mattress. There were even sheets of good quality linen, surely brought from England, topped with blankets, a further feather bed and some clean, well dressed furs. I would not perish of the cold here.

Despite the comfort of the bed, I was restive and could not sleep. My new thoughts about what might lie behind Rocksley's disappearance went round and round in my mind. They made the prospect of finding him even more unlikely. My nerves were strung tight at the prospect of what I must do, so when I heard a noise at the window, I sat up abruptly in alarm. I parted the bed curtains cautiously and peered toward the window. I had not closed the shutters and a weak moonlight shone through the horn. There was movement against the light. I saw that it was snowing heavily, great clusters of flakes thrown at the window by a rising wind. A blizzard was rising.

While we were taking breakfast the next morning, I noticed the Pyotr was nowhere to be seen. He had not eaten with us the previous evening either.

'What has become of Pyotr?' I asked generally, reaching out for more bread. It was made from some sort of mixed grain, but it was not unpalatable.

'He has gone to visit his family,' John said. 'He left while you were upstairs before dinner yesterday. I expect he has been kept away by the storm.'

'He has family here then?' I said cautiously. It had been mentioned before, but I remembered Pyotr telling me that his mother had died when he was fifteen and he had subsequently lived with his father's new family in England. I supposed there might be cousins or other distant kin still in the town.

'His grandfather is still alive,' Christopher said. 'I spoke to Edmond Leget here about the family this morning.' He nodded toward our host, the agent in charge of the Kolmogory house.

'Aye,' Edmond Leget said. 'It seems his mother was very young when Pyotr was born, around sixteen, so his grandfather is not an ancient even now, a man perhaps in his sixties. He was a leading merchant in this town before we came here, and we have traded with him ever since. His is one of the important families in this part of Muscovy. Relations were strained for a time when the Company refused to recognise his daughter's marriage, but he is a practical man and knew it would do his business no favour to quarrel with us permanently.'

'I am not surprised that the family should be deeply offended,' I said. 'It was an insult both to the family and to their faith.'

'Very true,' Christopher said. 'Though I suspect John Aubery was not greatly troubled. He married again soon after returning to England. A woman he had formerly been betrothed to.'

'He does not sound very honourable.'

'Probably not,' Christopher said. 'But these marriages across nations and faiths can often be troublesome.'

'Cruel to Pyotr's mother,' I said. 'She was the one left with the baby and the shame.'

'It did not end so badly,' Edmond Leget said. 'The church absolved her of any guilt, and annulled the Orthodox marriage, so that she was free to marry again. Which she did.'

I was astonished. The impression Pyotr had given me was that he was left without family after his mother died.

'So he has a Muscovite step father?' I said cautiously.

'Aye, and three brothers and a sister from this second marriage. Some of them married, with children.'

I suppose I should have been glad for Pyotr, but I found it oddly disturbing that he had been at pains to give me a quite different impression.

'This is no weather to show you the town,' Edmond Leget said when we had finished eating, 'but perhaps you would like to see our rope-works? It is but a step across the courtyard, and we are proud of it.'

I must confess I was not much enamoured of venturing out in a blizzard in order to see rope being made, but there was little else to occupy us here, and the invitation was clearly meant as a courtesy.

In fact it proved more interesting than I had expected. Rope must be made in a very long building, called a 'rope walk', in order to stretch out the full length of the cordage. I had never seriously examined rope before, and did not realise that it was built up of strands which were twisted in alternate directions, layer upon layer, until the desired thickness was reached. The men used a simple winding mechanism, but there was clearly skill in ensuring that the twist was kept even and there was no weakness at any stage in the process. The workers moved back and forth along the rope walk in a kind of coordinated dance which was quite mesmerising.

We returned to the house after about an hour, stamping the snow from our boots on the threshold, our cheeks and noses red from the cold. I was curious to see a sleigh in the courtyard, draw by creatures quite unknown to me. They resembled a large, heavy type of deer, with thick coats of wavy hair, and their antlers were very different from those of any deer I had ever seen, ending in splayed-out formations, like spread hands. Their heads also were large and bony. The breath of these beasts made great clouds as they stood in the cold air of the courtyard, but they seemed untroubled by the snow which fell inexorably, settling on their backs. These must be the so-called reindeer I had heard of, used by the Sami people. I wondered what they were doing here.

When I asked, Master Leget nodded. 'Aye, there is a Sami settlement over in that direction.' He waved vaguely toward the north west, though nothing could be made out beyond the perimeter wall through the curtain of driven snow. 'In better weather we can see it from the upper windows. Hardly a village, in truth. Just a crude settlement which they set up here in winter. In summer they will move on again. If the snow clears you will be able to see their pagan images.'

He led the way indoors.

'Images?' I said.

'Carved figures of wood. Crude, naked, humanlike totems. I do not know whether they are gods or devils or memorials to the dead. It is best not to ask.'

'They are not Christian?'

'Nay.' He laughed. 'They are not.'

'Why is the sleigh here, then?'

'Oh, they will be looking for work. They hire themselves out as sleigh drivers. Or they may be selling their carvings. They make very fine carving of morse ivory. Little boxes, ornaments. To tell the truth, it is very fine work.'

'I have never heard of morse ivory. I thought ivory came from Africa, the teeth of oliphants.'

'The morse is a sea creature, somewhat like a seal, but much larger. Very fierce, I am told. They have these great tusks of ivory. The Muscovites hunt them and so do the Sami, for their hides and their oil, and for their ivory tusks.'

We found the rest of the company in the hall, where two men bundled in furs from their boots to the tops of their heads were setting out some delicate objects on the table. I thought it astonishing that men who worshipped wooden totems, and looked clumsy as bears in their crude clothing, could make anything so exquisite.

The two stipendiaries had heard of the ivory carvings but never seen them. Christopher remembered them from his former time in Muscovy. And I believe we were all entranced by the work. The haggling began. The two Sami men spoke a little thickly accented Russian. I could barely understand it, and all the others apart from Master Leget were little better than I, but he acted as our go-between. In the end, I secured a lidded box about three inches in diameter and

114

two inches high, carved all over with twining leaves and flowers. In the centre of the lid there was a tiny bird, his beak open to sing.

I looked up from my purchase, which had cost no more than a handful of ribbons in Cheapside, to see Pyotr standing in the doorway, with a curious smile on his face. When the Sami men had gone, he said, 'You could have bought those things cheaper from people here in Kolmogory. There was no need to buy from those heathens.'

'They make these ivory carvings too?' I said.

'They do.'

'But surely there are none of these creatures, these morse, around here? Do the Sami not hunt for them in the north? They are found in the sea, I understand, not here in the Dvina.'

'Anyone may buy the tusks from the Sami. There are poor craftsmen here in Kolmogory who would be glad to sell you their carvings.'

I could sense that he was angry with us.

'You shall tell us where to find these craftsmen,' Christopher said calmly, 'or send them here. I should be glad to buy more of this fine work. Now, tell us, how did you find your family?'

'Well enough.' Pyotr seemed to relax after that and peace was restored.

We waited two weeks in Kolmogory, and I spent my time improving my Russian, with growing confidence in my ability to speak on simple matters. It seemed that a messenger had been despatched from St Nicholas before we had left the port, to ride to Moscow and request permission for us to travel on to the capital via Vologda and Yaroslavl. How long the journey would take him, no one could be sure, for much would depend on the state of the roads.

'The first part of his journey would be slow,' Christopher said. 'The roads south of St Nicholas were deep in mire when we set out, but as the ground has hardened, he would make better progress. Then he would certainly be kept kicking his heels in Moscow until the right official agreed to see him. Who would it be now, Master Leget?'

'Probably Vasilii Shchelkalov. Unless he was required to go to Boris Godunov himself. Then he would be held up by the blizzard coming north again.'

Eventually the blizzard abated and finally the Company messenger returned and presented a leather satchel to Christopher, who opened it and drew out several rolled parchments, from which dangled enormous seals.

'They look like the sort of documents which seal treaties between nations,' I said.

He laughed. 'The Muscovites take these matters seriously. You might say that this amounts to a treaty between nations.'

He unrolled the parchments on the table. They were written both in the Cyrillic script of Russian and in English in a neat secretary hand. Someone in the Russian court was learned in both English language and handwriting. There was one permit each for our travel from Kolmogory to Vologda, from Vologda to Yaroslavl, and from Yaroslavl to Moscow. Christopher Holme, Robert Farindon and I were all named individually, so that the permits could not be used for anyone else. John had already taken up his duties in Kolmogory. We were also permitted a retinue of eight Company men for our protection on the journey. It seemed that after several years of bad harvests and the imposition of cruel taxation, there were bands of landless men roaming the country, preying on travellers.

'Excellent,' Christopher said, rolling up the permits and returning them for safety to the satchel. 'Tomorrow we will arrange the hiring of sleighs and drivers. The day after, we leave for Vologda.'

Chapter Seven

*T*wo days later, we were ready to leave, by land, for Vologda. While we had been restricted to Kolmogory, the cargo had arrived from St Nicholas and been despatched onwards in huge transport sleds along the same route as we would follow. There was no restriction on the movement of the Company's goods. Indeed, it was essential that they should reach the capital as quickly as possible, for it was the Tsar's prerogative to choose whatever he wanted from each shipment, and likewise to pay whatever he chose for them, payment which might be made months or even years in arrears, and was generally inadequate.

'It is the penalty of trading with this country,' Christopher said, with a grim smile. 'At any moment the Tsar could withdraw all our privileges on a whim – force us to pay monstrous taxes, allow other countries to compete with us, or ban us from Muscovy altogether. We must bow to his demands and pretend to like it.'

'I thought this Tsar was not very powerful.' I was still finding the politics of Muscovy confusing.

'When it comes to personal greed, he is as powerful as any other ruler. When it comes to the skills of kingship, he is sadly lacking. And that is why we must also bow to the demands of Godunov. He too will make his selection from amongst our goods. After him, the most eminent nobles in the court. Who those nobles may be alters with every shift in the political wind. Only after all the men in power are satisfied can we begin our normal trading with the Muscovy merchants.'

'It seems the cargo will surely reach Moscow before us,' I said.

'Aye. And no bad thing. Austin Foulkes will remain in Moscow until I arrive, so he will oversee the unloading of the merchandise and the viewing by the court. I hope all that may be finished by the time we arrive.'

'He will leave with next summer's fleet?'

'Aye. It is best if he waits for us to reach Moscow, so that he can explain everything I need to know before I take his place. We will make a brief stop in Vologda, a longer one in Yaroslavl, and should reach Moscow in time for Christmas.'

It was hard to believe so much of the year had already wasted away while we travelled by barge and then lingered in Kolmogory. We had seen nothing of the bargemen since we had reached the town, for they had vanished at once into the poorer district around the docks, with never a backward glance. If Christopher was right, that the steersman had been set to watch us, then someone else would take over from him as we journeyed further. When I mentioned this to Christopher, he nodded,

'Probably one of the drivers. We merely have to pretend that we suspect no one of spying, and at the same time do nothing that might appear suspicious.'

Master Leget had arranged for me to be fitted out with clothes suitable for travel in a Russian winter, and I now donned these before joining the others in the courtyard. There was a pair of baggy trousers, similar to those worn by the bargemen, but made of fine English broadcloth, which is close woven, then fulled to render it partly resistant to the wet as well as windproof. I pulled these trousers on over my hose, and tucked them into my boots. These were my normal outdoor boots brought from England, but one of the Company servants had coated them with bear grease, rubbing it well in. The treatment had given them a certain aroma, but I was assured it would make them more waterproof.

I still wore Goodwife Maynard's knitted garment over my doublet, but Master Leget had also provided me with a long robe to wear over all, which reached my ankles. My cloak was declared too thin, so I bundled it up into my knapsack. In its place I had a cloak far grander than I would have been permitted to wear in England, for it would have flouted the sumptuary laws. Again made of broadcloth, it was lined with the pieced skins of martens, and around the neck it was trimmed with that precious fur, beloved of royalty, sable. Probably the garment most essential to survival was my fur hat with its double brim and ear flaps. As soon as I put it on I could feel the warmth of my whole body increasing. The whole was finished off with mittens of wolf skin.

Thus clad, and doubtless looking twice my normal size, I descended the stairs and walked – or rather waddled – out to the courtyard, which was crowded with men, animals, and sleighs. Three of the sleighs were driven by Sami and drawn by reindeer, the remaining ones, seven in all, were horse drawn. The six sleighs for passengers were much more elaborate than the one I had seen in the courtyard before. Although the driver was exposed to the weather, except for a kind of wooden apron which curved up to his waist, the part for the passengers was enclosed like a small cabin, all but the front. There was a deep padded seat with cushions and fur rugs, and behind the seat a space for our personal luggage. The roof overhead would protect us from most of the snow, though it was still possible for it to fly in our faces.

I was relieved to see that I was to travel with Christopher in one of the Sami sleighs, while Robert and Pyotr occupied another, for the Sami sleighs looked more robust than the Muscovite ones. The men acting as our guards were allotted two to each of another four sleighs, while the remaining sleighs had no seats but were piled up with luggage, over which covers of oiled canvas had been roped. I was glad that I had learned to travel with little luggage, for my knapsack and medicine satchel stayed with me, fitting easily into the back of our sleigh, along with a satchel of Christopher's, in which he carried the permits, for we would be required to show them if we were stopped by government officials.

Servants from the Company house brought out hot stones to place at our feet, then buckled a leather sheet across the front of the passenger seat, protecting us from the waist down. Master Leget himself saw to the distribution of earthenware flagons of spiced wine and cups to each sleigh.

'Best drink some now,' he said, 'while it is hot. It will stay warm for a while if you keep the flagon well wrapped in fur.'

I drank the wine Christopher poured out, although I had to remove one of my fur mittens in order to grasp the cup. To tell the truth, in my thick clothes, bundled in furs, and with my feet on a hot stone, I was beginning to sweat, even though it was barely past dawn on a freezing winter morning. These Russian winter days were so short, it was essential that we should make the most of the limited hours of daylight and set out early. One of the guards' sleighs led the way out of the compound followed by a second one. We were next, calling our farewells and thanks to Master Leget. The other sleighs filed in behind us, with the last two guards' sleighs at the rear, after the luggage.

I had never ridden in a sleigh before, nor been drawn by reindeer, and through the streets of the town, where the snow had frozen into hard-packed ridges, the ride was bumpy and uncomfortable.

'You should put your mitten on again,' Christopher said.

'I'm quite *hot*,' I said, taking off my hat and wiping my forehead with the glove.

He shook his head. 'Put them on. You will soon see why.'

I did as I was told, for he knew more about this country than I could ever hope to do. Once we were outside the town we were running over soft snow that had fallen during the night and the ride was much smoother.

'This is remarkably comfortable,' I said, leaning back into the nest of cushions.

'Better than the barge?'

I laughed. 'Much better.'

However, now that we were out in the countryside there were no buildings or walls to protect us from the wind. The pace also increased, so that the sleigh skimmed along at the speed of a cantering horse. Inevitably, the bitter wind found its way into the sleigh. Christopher had been right to warn me. I drew one of the furs up over my face, so that only my eyes were exposed. It was cold. Bitterly cold. But I loved the speed and the excitement of dashing over the glittering snow along an invisible road lined with birch trees. This was surely the finest way to travel.

I am not sure what the distance was to Vologda, but we covered it in eight days, with breaks to rest the horses and reindeer. One striking aspect of the countryside we passed through was the number of abandoned villages. Robert explained the reason.

'There have been several desperately poor harvests in the last few years, but at the same time Godunov has introduced vastly increased taxes. The government is short of money, for legitimate reasons, like maintaining an army, and others not so legitimate, like extravagance and corruption. But the common people simply could not pay. With the threat of government tax inspectors coming, the peasants have fled their homes.'

We were spending the night in the largest house in one of these deserted villages, sitting around an open central hearth after a meal of bread and dried reindeer meat. These houses had no chimneys.

'But where have they gone?' I asked. Snow was falling again and we could hear it thrown softly against the window shutters. I wondered where anyone could go in this desolate land.

'Some in despair have sold themselves into debt slavery. Others have tried to escape over the border into Poland. Those have mostly been caught and brought back.'

He broke off and glanced uneasily to where the drivers were sitting a little apart, the three Sami together, the Muscovites separately. I realised that his comments could be taken as critical of the government and he had suddenly remembered that one of the drivers might be a government spy.

Vologda was smaller than Kolmogory, and clearly less important. No special goods were manufactured here, and it was not a place of great political significance, although it possessed a fortress, like all the towns a little too close to Sweden. The fortress was enclosed by a wall built of stone and brick, unlike the usual wooden palisades, and there were numerous churches. As far as the Company was concerned, Vologda served mainly as a staging post for men and goods, although Christopher mentioned that it was an important centre for Muscovite merchants.

We stayed there just four days, while Christopher examined the accounts and discussed business with the local staff. It also meant that the beasts were given a longer chance to rest. I asked once again about Gregory Rocksley, but heard only what I already knew. He had reached Vologda the previous year, a little earlier in the season than we had, and stayed one night before carrying on to Yaroslavl.

It was no more than I expected. There would be nothing new to learn until we reached Moscow. There I must try to uncover what had happened during Gregory's second visit to the capital, whether he told anyone why, after returning from Narva, he had decided to head south to Astrakhan.

The distance from Vologda to Yaroslavl was much shorter than that from Kolmogory to Vologda, probably about a quarter of the distance, and only took us three days, despite the fact that we had to cross several frozen rivers and innumerable frozen streams. At one point we travelled along the surface of the frozen Sukhona, one of Muscovy's 'winter roads', where we skimmed faster than ever, an exhilarating but somewhat frightening experience, for it seemed the sleigh might tip over at any moment.

Yaroslavl was a considerable town, standing on the great river Volga and of a similar size to Kolmogory, or so I judged, for I did not venture outside the compound, confined indoors by yet another blizzard. Here too the Company house was large and comfortable, with substantial warehouses but no rope factory. I had enjoyed the journey by sleigh, but we had been hit by storms twice on the way, so it was pleasant to sit by a fire, burning in a proper fireplace, and relax for a few days.

Once again I received the same uninformative answers about Rocksley's visit last year, but I had expected nothing better, so I settled in for a quiet time while Christopher and Robert were busy about Company business with the agent at Yaroslavl, Walter Deynes. Pyotr disappeared again, saying that he had a married cousin living in the town, one he had not seen for several years. I paid little attention to this, for I had accepted that Pyotr's family might be spread throughout Muscovy, for all I knew. Instead I discovered that the Company house possessed a small library of books, half a dozen or so, left here over the years by employees going back to England.

On our third day I settled by the fire with a book, enjoying the sensation of remaining still for a time. The book I had picked up was a small, square volume, rather battered: Thomas Tusser's *Five Hundreth Pointes of Good Husbandrie*. It seemed a strange book to find in a snowbound house of the Muscovy Company. Having no knowledge of farming, and no experience of agriculture other than my childhood visits to my grandfather's estate in Portugal, I had never read the book, though (like most people, I suppose) I knew of it. Why was it here? Had some past employee of the Company carried it with him to this place in the heart of a Russian forest, pining for the gentle fields and familiar hearth of his father's country manor? And why had it been left behind? When I asked, no one could tell me.

It was no great work of literature, but its simple rhyming couplets, setting forth the inherited wisdom that comes with generations of working the land, provided a soothing picture of the English countryside, which I found comforting.

> *In Cambridge shire forward to Lincolne shire way,*
> *the champion maketh his fallow in May.*
> *Then thinking so dooing one tillage woorth twaine,*
> *by forcing of weede, by that meanes to refraine.*

I turned over the pages idly.

> *Get downe with thy brakes, er an showers doo come,*
> *that cattle the better may pasture have some.*

In June and in August, as well doth appeere,
is best to mowe brakes, of all times in the yeere.

To be honest, it was fairly baffling. Aristotle in the original Greek made more sense. I turned over more pages. It seemed that Tusser included advice for the farmer's wife, as well as the farmer – husbandrie and huswiferie, hand in hand.

Call servants to breakefast by day starre appere,
A snatch and to worke, fellowes tarrie not here.
Let huswife be carver, let pottage be heate,
A messe to eche one, with a morsell of meate.
    No more tittle tattle,
    Go serve your cattle.
What tacke in a pudding, saith greedie gut wringer,
give such ye wote what, ere a pudding he finger.
Let servants once served, thy cattle go serve,
lest often ill serving make cattle to sterve.

That made more sense. I could picture that hasty farmhouse breakfast, with no idle chatter, and was smiling over the farm servants being hustled through it and chased off to tend the cattle, when the door was thrust open and one of the servants hurried in. He looked pale and frightened.

'What's to do, man?' I said, starting from my chair in alarm.

'Oh, Dr Alvarez!' He was shaking. It must be serious.

'Aye, out with it!' I set down Thomas Tusser and strode across the room to him.

'A man has ridden in from Uglich, sir. You are sent for, by the Tsarina Maria Nagaya. That is, we are not meant to call her the Tsarina.'

This made almost less sense than Thomas Tusser.

'I am sent for? Why am I sent for?'

He gulped and drew a deep breath.

'The Tsarina was the late Tsar Ivan's last wife. His fifth wife, I think, or was it his seventh? I misremember. Their peculiar church here does not recognise marriages after the third as being legal, but Tsar claimed it was legal and he had every right to have as many wives as he chose, as long as he had them one at a time. I think he murdered some of them.'

He gave me a conspiratorial grin. 'Not like our Henry, eh, sir? He used the law to rid himself of the ones he tired of.'

'Better not say that back in England,' I said grimly. 'Start again. This Maria Nagaya who was or was not a lawful wife of Ivan the Terrible is somewhere called – did you say Uglich? Is there a place called Uglich?'

'There is, sir. About seventy miles from here. That's nearby as the Russes reckon.'

'She has sent for me? Is she in need of me as a physician?'

'Aye, that's it, sir. Only not for herself. For her son. The Tsarevich Dmitri Ivanovich.'

Suddenly it made sense. This was the younger half brother of the ruling Tsar Fyodor Ivanovich. But I had expected to find him with the court in Moscow. Not out here in the remote countryside of northern Muscovy.

'I understand now who the child is, but why is he not in Moscow?'

Another voice came from the doorway.

'He was sent away into exile with his mother and her brothers a long time ago. The present Tsar's wife is childless, and likely to remain so. The Tsar Fyodor – he's a poor weakling.'

It was Pyotr taking up the story. He had come in unnoticed behind the servant.

'Uglich is the boy's own manor,' he went on. 'His appanage city, as it is called. Godunov had them all exiled there because there is a danger some of the boyars may try to overthrow Tsar Fyodor and put the little boy on the throne. According to church law, he is illegitimate, with no claim to the throne, but Godunov cannot risk it, since he intends to make a bid for the throne himself.'

'Has he any claim?' I had picked up my satchel of medicines and walked toward the door. I was not greatly interested in the shifts of Muscovite politics, unless they should prove dangerous to me.

'Nay. No claim at all. Except that he rules the country. And any who oppose him must keep a watch over their shoulders.'

We walked together toward the door.

'I knew that the services of an English physician were requested for the child, but I understood that it was the Tsar himself who made the request, for his half brother.'

Pyotr shrugged. 'Who knows? He may have done. And forgotten it afterwards. Or it might have been Maria Nagaya who sent, passing off the request as coming from her stepson, the Tsar.'

'You will come with me?' I said. 'I am likely to need an interpreter.' I paused. '*Seventy miles!* Are we to go by sleigh?'

'The messenger came on horseback, and we could ride, but you are likely to be too exhausted at the end of it to be much good in physicking the child.'

It seemed he accepted that he must accompany me.

I nodded. 'You are right. A sleigh it is, then. It will take us about two days, will it not?'

'If we start now, we can be there by tomorrow evening. We can make a stop for the night at one of the villages where post horses are kept. Or we can sleep in the sleigh.'

'And travel in the dark?' I thought of the rough countryside and the dark forests through which we had passed on the way to Yaroslavl.

'We will have a local driver. The road from here to Uglich is better than most,' he said. 'He will be able to drive by night. Nay, best with two drivers, who can take it turn about. Go and don your thick clothes. I will see about the sleigh. And you.' He cricked a finger at the servant. 'Go to the kitchen and tell them to pack us a hamper of food.'

I started up the stairs to my room as Pyotr went off whistling. He seemed excited at the prospect of a drive over the snow by night to Uglich, but I remembered Christopher Holme's warning, to stay away from the royal family if possible. Well, it was not possible. One of the reasons for sending me here had been the request for an English physician. But if it were true that the child had the falling sickness, there was no cure.

Master Holme was not happy at the prospect of our starting off at once for Uglich, but I felt bound to answer the summons.

'I have questioned the messenger,' I told him.

I had found the man in the kitchen, eating a hasty meal before setting off back to Uglich on horseback.

'It seems there have been several attempts to poison the little prince,' I said. 'He has fallen mysteriously ill on four different occasions, so that his mother has now insisted that every dish put before him must be tasted by one of the servants first. Three days ago, the maidservant who tasted his food died in terrible agony a few hours later.'

Christopher looked shocked. 'I know there is talk that Godunov wants him out of the way. First the exile. Afterwards, rumours began to circulate, which could be traced back to the Kremlin, that the child was violent and unstable, torturing and killing animals, having inherited his father's madness. Edmond Leget spoke of it. But he says that anyone who has seen the boy declares that he is a bright lad and kindly, nothing like the monster the palace portrays him to be.'

'There is this question of the falling sickness,' I said.

'Aye. I do not know if there is any truth in that.'

'The servant from Uglich told me that the child has indeed had moments of seizure, foaming at the mouth, but they have all happened recently. Now, the falling sickness usually manifests itself early in a child's life, though it can be brought on later in life as a result of some fearful shock. We think it may be an inherent inbalance in the humours which can be set off by some such a shock.'

'Could that be the case here?'

'Unlikely,' I said. 'It seems the household lives very quietly, for fear of attracting worse treatment from Godunov. I am wondering whether the seizures may be the after-effects of the attempts as poisoning. If so, I am not sure what poison may have been used, but I will see the child and try to investigate the cause. It seems his mother does not believe it is the falling sickness, and it is often worth listening to mothers. They know their children better than anyone else.'

'It would be convenient for Godunov,' Christopher said slowly, 'if the child were shown incapable of ruling through suffering from the falling sickness. Therefore, if you show that there *is* no such sickness, I think you may be in danger. It is a diagnosis which would not be appreciated.'

'If his enemies really believed the child to be afflicted, why should they take the trouble to poison him?'

'Because that way they can make doubly sure of him. Mad like his father and brother, and conveniently dead.'

'The falling sickness is not madness,' I objected. 'It is an illness. It is said that Julius Caesar had the falling sickness. It did not prevent him from becoming Rome's greatest general.'

'Nevertheless,' Christopher said, 'I think I should come with you.'

'Nay. That would give the wrong impression. I am simply a physician called in to see a patient. Let us not involve the chief agent of the Muscovy Company. That would draw far too much attention to a simple visit.'

'Very well,' he said reluctantly. 'But if you have not returned within a week, I am coming after you. I feel that I, and the Company, must take some responsibility for your safety.'

I inclined my head. 'Very well. It is agreed.'

Privately, I thought that if I had not returned within a week I would probably be beyond his or anyone else's help.

By the time I had donned my heavy Muscovite clothes, Pyotr had arranged for a horse-drawn sleigh with two drivers to be made ready for us. It was already mid morning, with much of the daylight already gone, but he assured me that the drivers would be able to carry on through the hours of darkness. They had loaded a supply of lamps, and would change horses at staging posts along the way.

'The government maintains a system of staging posts where post horses are always kept available,' Robert said, standing with us and watching the sleigh being prepared. 'It is advantageous for a village to keep post horses, for they are then excused a large proportion of their taxes.'

I eyed the horses which were being backed into the harness of the sleigh. They were small, nondescript creatures, hardly more than ponies, but they looked sturdy, with their thick necks, bony heads, and heavy coats.

'Are they as sure-footed as the reindeer?' I asked. On our previous journeys I had been impressed by the deer, swift and seemingly untiring.

'They are shod with special spiked horse shoes in winter,' Robert said. 'To give them a better grip on ice. Mostly, you will be travelling over snow, but the icy banks of the streams you will need to cross can be treacherous.'

That was a comforting remark, considering that we might have to negotiate those slippery banks in the pitch dark.

'There is a moon tonight,' Christopher said, as if he anticipated my worries about travelling by night. 'The darkness will not be so very dense.'

'And the moonlight will be reflected by the snow.' I was cheered, remembering that the previous night had also be lit by a near full moon.

Two more sleighs, with the pairs of horses ready harnessed were led into the courtyard from the stables.

'I thought you were not coming with us,' I said.

'I am not,' Christopher said, 'but it would not be safe for the two of you, unarmed civilians, to travel seventy miles alone in this part of the country. It may appear deserted, but some of those masterless men from the abandoned villages have taken to banditry and live in the forests. There is nothing to say there may not be some between here and Uglich. I am sending four of our guards with you. They are armed with muskets and cross bows. Their presence should deter any likely attackers.'

'I am sure that is not necessary,' I protested. 'No need for so many of us to endure a long, cold journey through the night.' I did not draw attention to the fact that I was indeed armed, for my sword was hidden by my heavy cloak, and I had slipped my dagger into my boot.

'Master Holme has the right of it,' Pyotr said firmly. 'We will be safer with an armed guard. Besides, if you arrive at the palace of Uglich without attendants, you will be treated with contempt. A man of any standing will always travel attended. Four is a modest number indeed for a distinguished English physician.'

So the decision was taken out of my hands. I was accustomed to making my way through the world alone, or with at most one companion, but these men knew best the customs of the country, and it was wise to pay heed to them.

Without any further delay, we were packed into our sleigh with cushions, rugs and furs, and once again had hot stones for our feet. One of the servants loaded a large hamper into the foot well between us, and I stowed my satchel and knapsack behind the seat. I had brought my knapsack as well as my medicines, for I felt I should wear my physician's gown – however rumpled – when treating a prince of the blood royal, and not come to him in my Muscovite clothes or Goodwife Maynard's curious tunic.

I felt somewhat uncomfortable, sharing the close confines of the sleigh with Pyotr. With Christopher I had felt no qualms, for I trusted him, and besides we had travelled only by day. I was not sure I would be able to sleep during the night, crowded into this small space with Pyotr. Some of the things I had learned about him, both from the Company men and his curious deceptions about his family, meant that I was not sure that I could altogether trust him. And I always had the fear that I might talk in my sleep, giving myself away. Perhaps it was foolish. After all, he had never really done anything to cause me to distrust him.

The four guards climbed into their sleighs, the gates to the compound were thrown open, and the horses were urged into a fast trot, out into the streets of Yaroslavl. At least, I thought, it is not snowing at the moment. In fact, the sky was a clear pale blue, with no sign of cloud, but the lack of cloud cover meant that it was very cold indeed. The sun lay low in the sky, as it had done ever since winter had begun, casting long shadows from the buildings as we sped through the town.

In no time, it seemed, we passed out through the town gatehouse into the open country, where the drivers whipped up the horses to a canter. Despite their rough appearance, these Muscovite horses had a smooth gait over the snow, and it was not long before we were travelling through the surrounding forest along a wide, cleared strip, which I took to be the line of the road to Uglich. My experience of the country so far had not led me to expect much of what were designated roads, but the way seemed clear enough by day. Whether it would be as easy to follow at night, I was not so sure. From the position of the sun, I reckoned that we were heading almost due west. Its orange glow caused the shadows of the pine trees to flick past us – black, gold, black, gold – in a way that was almost dizzying.

'What I do not understand,' I said to Pyotr, 'is how the Tsarina knew that I was at Yaroslavl. We have only been there just over two days. Uglich is seventy miles away. How could she have heard that I was there?'

He looked at me slantwise over the muffling of fur he had pulled up around his neck and face.

'It is not only the government which has spies everywhere. The Tsarina and her family must guard their own safety. Her uncle was sent into exile. Her father was languishing in prison before her marriage. Tsar Ivan then freed him, presumably as a favour to his new wife. But then, in the last months of his life, Ivan Vasilyevich set her aside, because he wanted to marry an English woman, Lady Mary Hastings.'

He gave a short bark of laughter.

'Fortunately Lady Mary was able to put him off through Her Majesty's intervention until he gave up the idea, or he died. I am not sure which happened first. Now that Boris Godunov rules the country, the whole of Maria Nagaya's family is under suspicion. I am certain they have their own spies. They could not hope to survive otherwise. And the movement of the new chief agent of the Muscovy Company across the country will not have gone unnoticed.'

'You mean they have been following our progress?' I said, horrified. I thought we had been travelling through the empty wastes of this alien country, unnoticed except when we stayed in the towns.

'Almost certainly. Remember how long we waited in Kolmogory? Plenty of time for word to reach Uglich that the new chief agent was accompanied by the requested English physician. You made no secret of your profession when we were aboard the barge. The first evening in a Kolmogory ale house probably saw the bargemen boasting about the English doctor who could raise the dead.'

I shivered. 'I hope not. I have no wish to be credited with magical powers. If I am expected to cure the child of the falling sickness, their hopes will be raised only to be crushed, and I fear the consequences.'

'Did you not say that you thought he did not have the sickness?'

'I cannot be sure until I have examined him, and talked to those who have witnessed his fits or seizures. It may or may not be epilepsy.'

After a while we fell silent, for the endless flickering of the trees was hypnotic. For the most part the forest consisted of pine, stretching away for miles in all directions, but from time to time we passed through areas of birch. These lovely trees with their silver bark stood out vividly against the sombre dark green of the pines. Every leaf was shed, now, in winter time, so we could see the delicate shape of each branch and twig. Until now I had found the Muscovy countryside unrelievedly dull, except perhaps for the wide reaches of the Dvina near its mouth and its wilder reaches upstream, but those birch trees were truly beautiful.

Sometime around the middle of the day we investigated the food hamper. There was the inevitable dried meat – I believe they dry it in the wind, as I used to see it prepared in Portugal. It required a good deal of chewing, but there was fresh bread, which must have been baked that morning in Yaroslavl, and some of that autumn's apples. There was dried fish as well, but I avoided it, for I knew by now that it would be very salty and would make me thirsty. There was the usual mead in a flask, and a bottle of a clear liquid. I had seen it before, but not tasted it.

'Is that vodka?' I asked.

'Aye. Would you like some?'

I shook my head.

He grinned. 'Good for emergencies, like brandy. Don't let the drivers have it. We don't want them wandering off the road.'

'Should we give them some of the food?'

'They have their own. Besides, one man is sleeping, so he can stay awake tonight.'

I realised that he was right. One of the drivers had curled up, so that we could just make out the top of his fur hat above the back of his seat, and he was snoring gently. In front of us I could see one of the guards' sleighs skimming along in the lead. I hoped the other was still behind. There was a small window set in the rear of our cabin, fitted with horn, like the windows in the houses. Twisting round I saw the blurred shape of the other sleigh, close behind. The guards were taking no chances with our safety.

A while after we had eaten our frugal meal, we reached a small village, which occupied a cleared area in the forest. It consisted of nothing but one double row of cottages with some scrappy, snow-covered fields beyond, and a church no bigger than the smallest cottage. The drivers pulled up at the largest of the buildings, which Pyotr assured me was the post station, though I do not know how he could tell. Certainly there was a stable behind it, more sturdily built than most of the hovels.

While the drivers changed the horses over, two of our guards kept a watch on them, in case, as they said, the bastards abandoned us here in the forest. Pyotr and I, together with the other two guards, went into the house to see whether they could provide us with anything hot to eat or drink.

The place was far from clean, but the master of the post station and his wife were clearly anxious to please, especially after Pyotr had spoken to them sharply in Russian almost too fast for me to follow. I was not sure that I wanted to risk anything that might be served here, but the smell of the pottage which was brought to us in wooden bowls was tempting, and the taste was good. It was mostly vegetables – cabbage and turnips – but there was a little meat, mutton by the taste of it, and it did not seem to be tainted. They also warmed a drink for us.

'What is it?' I asked Pyotr, after sniffing it. It smelled woody, like fresh cut logs.

'It is a kind of beer, made of birch. It's not a bad drink. Try it. It will warm you. One day you must try kvass.'

'Kvass?'

'Made from fermented rye bread.'

'Ugh!' I thought he was teasing me, but he looked quite serious.

The birch beer was somewhat bitter and tasted much as it smelled, but what is the use of travelling to foreign lands if you do not sample the foods and the way of life? I swallowed it while trying not to pull a face, then managed a smile for the bobbing wife, who seemed gratified. I also contrived to make her understand that I needed a piss pot. She directed me to a ramshackle shed at the back of the building, covering a hole in the ground that was their primitive privy.

When I emerged, I found the other two guards and the drivers finishing bowls of the pottage, everyone stamping their feet to stop them freezing in the snow. Pyotr paid the man what seemed a very small amount of money, and we were on our way again.

131

'I expect we have eaten their dinner for the next three days,' Pyotr said, 'but they will be glad of the money. Even the peasants here in the forest will sometimes need coin for goods they cannot make, or to pay the Tsar's taxes.'

'I thought the taxes were remitted if they kept post horses.'

'Not all of them. Not by any means.'

We had stopped only briefly, but already the sun was sinking towards the rim of the earth and the brief daylight would soon be coming to an end. It was about three weeks until the winter solstice and the turn of the seasons. I wondered how brief the daylight would be at that darkest time of the year.

The darkness seemed to come on even faster once we were underway. The drivers of the three sleighs shouted back and forth to each other, then by agreement, all three stopped. They unpacked the lanterns they had brought, and set about filling and lighting them. I had expected candle lanterns, but these had a receptacle for the train oil which the Muscovites derived, so I had been told, by rendering down the blubber of the seals and whales they killed in the seas north of St Nicholas. They secured wicks of string with a clip, one end dipped in the top of the chamber which held the oil, the other raised well above it. When the wick was saturated, they lit the free end with a strike-a-light, and closed up the lamp, which had transparent panes in the sides, like the candle lamps I was familiar with. Unlike candle lamps with their panes of horn, however, these were fitted with some sort of clear material which permitted a much brighter light to shine out.

'What is this?' I asked one of the drivers, tapping it with my finger.

'Sliuda,' he said, leaving me none the wiser.

I looked at it more closely. I believed it was mica. Thomas Harriot had once showed me some small pieces of mica, pointing out that it would make excellent window panes, were it available in larger sheets.

The light these lamps gave did not reach far, but it was certainly better than the light of candle lamps. Two were hung at the corners of the drivers' seats, two at the front corners of the cabin roofs, and two more at the rear. With eighteen lamps glowing, we made quite a festive sight, like a band of wassailers on Twelfth Night.

'If any outlaws should be hiding in these woods,' I said to Pyotr, as we set off again, 'they will have no difficulty finding us.'

'Oh, I think you need not worry. With our lamps and the boldness of our intention to travel by night, we send a clear message

132

that we are a strong party, and certainly armed. Outlaws are more likely to attack a lone horseman or a pair of travellers. It was wise of Master Holme to give us an escort.'

'I hope that messenger from Uglich will be safe. He was not long ahead of us, and he was on his own.'

'He would travel faster, but will certainly stop for the night, not risk riding in the dark. We shall probably overtake him.'

In truth, I believed him, and began to enjoy the mysterious ride through the dark forest, which seemed all the darker now, beyond our moving circle of light. The horses probably did not move so fast, for although they were fresh, the drivers needed to exercise some caution at night. Yet the dark trees seemed to slip swiftly past, as though our cavalcade was still and the forest itself fleeing away behind us.

Before long, the moon rose to the rear, casting a magical silver light over the surrounding half-seen forest. Glimpses of the sky away from the moon's brilliance showed it sprinkled with the glitter of stars, a multitude of gems, such as I had never seen before on land. Sometimes I had caught snatches of star-studded sky when at sea, but my voyages had nearly always been accompanied by cloudy skies. I gasped in wonder that there should be so many stars crowding the heavens. As we cantered through the moonlight, we seemed always to be trying to overtake our own shadows, and always failing, while the moving trees whispered an answering refrain to the swish of the runners over the snow and the muted jingle of the harness. The silver light, the soft sounds, and the trees, black and silver, turned the world into something other, some landscape of fairy tale or myth.

I had expected to fear this ride by night through a dangerous forest. Instead I found my heart lifting with a pure physical thrill at the beauty of it. For a long time I stayed awake. Even when I felt sleep beginning to come over me I fought against it, not wanting to lose a moment of this beauty and mystery, but finally I could resist no longer. I propped a cushion to support my head, turned my back on Pyotr, who was already asleep, and abandoned my resistance.

Once or twice I woke briefly during the night. The first time was when the sleigh hit something under the snow – a stone or a fallen log – and jerked violently sideways. It righted itself at once, but it had been enough to wake me. Through heavy eyelids I watched the forest skim past. The moon was overhead now, our shadows foreshortened, The second time I woke, the sleigh had stopped at another staging post, and the drivers were busy unharnessing the horses. Pyotr was no longer on the seat beside me. He soon reappeared.

'Ah, you are awake. I've brought a jug of hot mead and some sweet rolls.'

He handed them to me before climbing back into the sleigh. We drank the mead from the wooden cups in the hamper, and tore the rolls apart with our fingers. They were also sweetened with honey, and still warm from someone's oven.

'These are new baked,' I said, with my mouth full. I was not accustomed to so much honey, but they were fresh and good. 'Has some housewife been baking in the middle of the night?'

'No longer the middle,' he said. 'It will be morning, though not dawn, in a couple of hours. They work a long day, these peasant women.'

The fresh horses were soon harnessed and we were on our way again. I thought I should find it difficult to sleep after being so thoroughly wakened, but to my surprise I slept soundly until it began to grow light. The moon was gone, the trees were merely trees once more, and the magic of the night had vanished.

During the second day I found that the cramped quarters of the sleigh began to be trying. I would have tried walking, could I have kept pace with the horses, but that was a foolish thought. I even contemplated suggesting I might ride one of the horses, to ease the growing stiffness from sitting too long, but I did not entertain the thought for more than a moment. I must remember that I was on my way to a royal establishment, even if it was a royal establishment in exile, and it was essential to maintain my dignity.

As we drew nearer to Uglich by Pyotr's reckoning, I grew more and more apprehensive. I had spoken to Christopher of the child and his illness quite dispassionately, simply as a theoretical case. But in a short time I would be confronted by the reality in the form of a flesh and blood boy who might indeed be violent and cruel, who might suffer from the falling sickness, but who might also someday – perhaps someday soon – occupy the throne of all the Russias. Even in exile, he was the acknowledged son of Ivan the Terrible, whose name provoked terror throughout Europe. He probably had the power to condemn me to torture or to death if I displeased him, or merely on a whim, like his father before him. And what of his mother, the Tsarina Maria Nagaya, clearly a formidable woman who had been married to that same Ivan the Terrible and now controlled a band of spies to rival those of Walsingham? I imagined her as cruel and witch-like, prepared to do anything to protect her son, and perhaps one day see him as Tsar, even if it meant forcing her servants to eat poisoned food intended for him.

These grim thoughts made the final stage of our journey alarming and unpleasant. However, the task had been undertaken and must be seen through to the end. The forest began to thin out. The tiny villages were closer together. Finally we emerged from the fringes of the forest into open, snow-covered fields and more houses.

'Is this Uglich?' I asked Pyotr, and he nodded.

I felt grubby and unkempt after so long in the sleigh, and in no fit state to approach members of the royal family. I voiced my concerns.

Pyotr nodded. 'I am sure we will be shown the courtesy of being allocated our quarters before we need to appear before the Tsarina and the Tsarevich. We are not all barbarians, you know.'

I accepted that in silence, feeling I had been reprimanded.

Ahead of us, massive walls appeared, not a palisade of wood, as I had seen around most of the fortresses on our journey from St Nicholas. These walls were built of brick. There was a formidable gateway, manned by several guards wielding crossbows. Our three sleighs drew up, our own guards' sleighs protectively on either side of us. Pyotr climbed slowly out of the sleigh, his empty hands held out in the classic gesture of peace. He was speaking even as he moved, in the face of the raised weapons. I caught the words 'English physician' and 'Tsarevich Dmitri Ivanovich'.

The Uglich guards consulted amongst themselves, then someone was sent off, clearly to fetch an officer with greater authority. Pyotr climbed back into the sleigh.

'Now we wait,' he said.

I felt that, since I had been summoned, surely word should have been left that I was to be admitted when I arrived. As we waited, it grew darker, and the horses began to steam in the cold air.

'This is dangerous for the horses,' I said. 'They should be walked till they cool down, or else covered with rugs. The shock of the cold could kill them.'

Pyotr gave me an odd look. 'Why should you care?'

I have no patience with this attitude, but merely pointed out tartly that we might need our horses if we were ever to leave Uglich. There was nothing I could do, however, until eventually a man who was clearly a captain of the guard emerged from the gatehouse and indicated that the wide gates were to be opened and our sleigh was to be allowed to pass through. Our guards, however, were not permitted beyond the gatehouse.

We set off again through the last of the daylight along a drive which had been partially cleared, some of the snow thrown up into

135

banks on either side, although fresh snow had fallen since, probably earlier that day. The drive swept round in a curve and ahead of us I saw an extraordinary house. Nay, I should say 'palace', for this was the palace of Uglich.

The dark red brick of the walls stood out in stark contrast to the snow that lay all around and to the deep green of the pines, some of which grew quite close to the house. There was a vaulted undercroft, while a wide outside staircase led up to the first floor, making one sharp right-angled turn. The stair was roofed and at three points it was capped with curious conical turrets, like the hats you may see upon the heads of witches in the illustrated ha'penny sheets of dreadful tales, hawked about the streets of London. I was becoming accustomed to the onion domes of the churches in Muscovy, but I had never seen turrets like these. Two great pillars supported the lower end of the stairway roof, turned in a spiral like crude bed posts. The whole building seemed very strange, a mixture of sophistication and naïveté.

'Have you ever seen this place before?' I whispered to Pyotr as we climbed out of the sleigh.

He shook his head, but did not speak. A man, very tall and imposing, was descending the stairway toward us. A steward or majordomo, I guessed. No minor servant, for he wore a gown of red velvet threaded with gold. On his head was a tall headdress, built up in layers, and he carried a gilded staff of office.

All three of us bowed.

'Be welcome to the Kremlin of Uglich,' the man said. 'The Tsarina awaits your coming with gladness. Be pleased to follow me.'

He spoke slowly, and I was able to understand what he said. I opened my mouth to answer, but he did not wait for me to speak, instead turning on his heel and beginning to ascend the stairs again. Pyotr and I caught up our bags while the drivers and sleigh were hustled away to an outbuilding which I could just make out in the failing light. I hoped that it was a stable and that both men and horses would be well treated.

The house was beginning to blaze with light. We followed the steward – if that was what he was – past torches lodged in iron sconces at the side of the outside staircase, then entered the main door of the palace. Servants were moving from room to room, lighting candelabra, until the whole house was nearly as bright as day.

The first thing I saw was a large icon, clearly of great antiquity and glowing with gold leaf, which I thought might have come from Byzantium. I had been instructed what to do, though in my heart I

136

rebelled against it. Pyotr and I both knelt before the icon, and pressed our foreheads to the floor. To have ignored the icon would have been to insult the Tsarina, and I knew I must proceed cautiously.

When we stood, the man led us along a passageway and up an inside staircase to an upper floor.

He opened a door and stood back.

'These rooms are for the English physician. Your servant,' he gave Pyotr a cursory glance, 'will be given lodging in the servants' quarters.'

I knew with absolute certainty that I did not want to be separated from Pyotr now, whatever my earlier reservations.

'Pyotr Ivanovich is no servant,' I said in my slow and careful Russian. 'He is a gentleman and my interpreter. He will share my quarters.'

If the man was surprised at my Russian or my presumption, he showed no sign of it. He merely inclined his head. 'Very well. A maidservant will bring you water to wash. I will return in an hour to escort you to the Tsarina.'

With that, he left us.

I closed the door behind him and exchanged a glance with Pyotr, then let out my held breath in a gust of relief.

'If the steward is that formidable, what will the Tsarina be like?'

He gave me a weak smile, but raised his finger to his lips and stood close, so that his whisper barely stirred the air.

'These houses have peepholes and listening tubes. Be careful what you say and do.' Then he went on in a normal tone, 'There are two rooms. This parlour and a bed chamber beyond. I will sleep on the couch here, so that if anyone comes, I can speak to them. You managed very well with your Russian, but in an emergency–'

I nodded. The arrangement suited me, and I was already feeling sick with fear. I knew I would feel safer in the inner room, however illusory the idea might be.

The outer room had no windows, but the inner room had one which looked out at the side of the house. To my surprise there was a large sheet of mica in the window, surely an expensive feature. It seemed as clear as glass, though it was too dark to make out much of what lay beyond. I gestured Pyotr over.

'A possible escape route, should we need one,' I whispered.

'We would not get far.'

'How old is the palace?' I said, in a normal tone of voice. 'Do you know?'

'I think about a hundred years.'

We continued to discuss the history of the palace for the benefit of anyone who might be listening, while I shook out my physician's gown and Pyotr removed his outdoor clothes. When the maid arrived with the water, Pyotr asked directions to the privy.

I seized the opportunity while he was gone to strip off several layers of my own clothes and wash, then I donned my gown and cap, and checked that the contents of my medicine satchel had survived the journey intact. Pyotr returned, followed closely by the steward and we were led back down the stairs to the main floor of the palace.

There was an enfilade of grand rooms leading one into the other on this floor. Each was like a jewel casket. The wall hangings were tapestries from France, the rugs were Turkish, which surprised me, for I thought the Muscovites and Turks were constantly at war. The furniture looked heavy and clumsy to my eye, accustomed to English furniture which was more delicate and finely carved, but every horizontal surface was crowded with Venetian crystal and heaped with gold plates and goblets and vessels of every kind. There seemed to be little eye for beauty here, merely for vulgar ostentation, however valuable this treasure house of riches.

When we reached the third room, the steward spoke at last.

'You will wait here.'

With that he left, shutting the door behind him. We glanced at each other, but said nothing. There would certainly be eyes watching us here. We did not dare to sit or even move, so we remained standing where we were, in the centre of the room, until we heard footsteps approaching.

I looked at Pyotr and raised my eyebrows. He gave me what I suppose he thought was an encouraging smile, but it looked more like a grimace. I drew a deep breath, awaiting the fearsome wife of Ivan the Terrible, herself the declared enemy of Boris Godunov, the most powerful man in Muscovy. The door opened.

And the most beautiful woman I had ever seen walked in.

Chapter Eight

She was dressed in cloth of gold from head to toe, and every inch of her robe was embroidered with a riot of foliage and flowers picked out in silks of intense hues – azure and ruby and emerald. Tiny pearls outlined the leaves and adorned the stamens of the flowers, while larger gems were sewn in garlands that ran between the flowers. On her head was a gold crown encrusted with more precious jewels, from which a veil of transparent silk floated down over her shoulders and back. I had seen our Queen in formal processions in London, and once face-to-face at Greenwich palace, but even she had not dazzled the eye like Tsarina Maria Nagaya.

I knew I was expected to prostrate myself, even though her claim to the title was denied to her, but before I fell to the ground I realised that the sumptuous clothes meant nothing in comparison to the woman beneath. Her physical beauty was breathtaking. Yet it was not simply the beauty of perfect features. There was great strength in that face. Intelligent eyes, a strong chin, a generous mouth. As I fell to the floor and fixed my eyes on the tips of the golden shoes which just showed beneath the hem of her robe, I knew that, in another life, in another place, I would have wanted to befriend such a woman.

'You may rise,' she said. Her voice was low pitched and musical. She spoke slowly, for the benefit of my foreign understanding.

I scrambled somewhat inelegantly to my feet, for I caught my knee in a fold of my gown. How dull my English black looked beside such splendour! I saw a flash of humour in her eyes at my dilemma, but she kept her face grave.

'I am grateful to you for coming so swiftly, Dr Alvarez,' she said, 'through this winter weather. I trust the journey was not too disagreeable.'

'It was not, Your Majesty.' I answered carefully, and hoped I had chosen the correct form of address. Pyotr drew back a few steps, realising that his services as interpreter would not be needed unless we encountered difficulties.

'Please.' She took a seat and gestured to us to do likewise. Two ladies-in-waiting and an armed guard had followed her into the room and took up positions behind her chair.

'I am sorry to hear of the misfortunes to the Tsarevich,' I said slowly, hoping I was making the right approach and wishing I had had time to discuss it with Christopher Holme, or even Pyotr. I was not sure whether one was expected to come at the matter of the prince's health in a roundabout way.

It seemed I had not made a mistake, for she did not look affronted. Instead, a spasm of pain crossed her face and was quickly suppressed. This was a woman who had learned to control her feelings. I could sense a rigid self-discipline under that lovely exterior. One must remember, of course, that she had been married to the monstrous Ivan for several years. Married against her will, if the tales were true. She would have learned rigid control then. Ivan was reputed always to have chosen the most beautiful women to be found, whether they were willing, or even whether they were already married. One could not fault his judgement in this instance.

'I believe that there have been four attempts on his life,' she said, keeping her voice steady. 'Five, including this latest one.'

I noticed that her ladies in waiting and the guard were watching us closely, and had stiffened at my mention of the Tsarevich. The Tsarina did not bother to turn her head, but raised her hand and pointed imperiously at the door.

'Out,' she said.

The women looked at each other nervously, while the guard leaned forward and murmured something in the Tsarina's ear.

'Out!' she repeated.

Reluctantly, they withdrew, probably no further than the other side of the door, I suspected. I understood why she had dismissed them. Even here in her own home, she could not feel safe. There would be spies owing allegiance to Godunov amongst her staff. I would be careful to keep my voice down.

'Can you tell me more about this latest attempt?' I said. 'Poison in your son's food? A maidservant was ordered to taste it – describe the food and her symptoms before she died.'

I was aware that I was giving her brisk directions, like any other patient, but she seemed to welcome my straightforward approach.

'There was more than one dish,' she said, also speaking quietly. 'A soup of wild celery and cream. Beef cooked with onions, beetroot, mushrooms, chestnuts and dried plums. A comfiture of candied peaches and almonds. There was a sugar confection to follow, but she did not taste that, for she had already begun to feel ill. Another maid tasted the confection and was unharmed.'

'I do not suppose you have kept samples of the food,' I said, without much hope. This must all have happened some time ago and I knew from dealing with cases of food poisoning that people usually threw the bad food away immediately.

'It has all been preserved in a locked pantry,' she said calmly. 'Only I have the key.'

This was a woman in a million.

'Can you tell me about the effects on the girl who died? An unhappy fate.'

There was a flash of anger in her eyes. 'She was set to spy on us. That was why I chose her to taste my son's food. She was very reluctant. I suspect she was complicit.'

I pitied the girl. She might have been equally reluctant to spy, but it was too late to help her now.

'Her symptoms?'

'To begin with, she complained of stomach pains. I watched her, you may be sure. I could not judge at first whether it was pretence. Then she began to stumble about the room, saying that she was dizzy. And she vomited.'

She made a face, and I had a vivid impression of the scene. The Tsarina with perhaps a few trusted men, the food laid out on the table, the wretched girl. Had the little boy been present, aware of what would have happened to him, had he eaten the food? I realised I was not sure how old he was. The previous Tsar had been dead for six years, and the child was born before he died, so I supposed he must be at least six. Pyotr had guessed seven or eight.

'Did she die then?' I asked.

'Oh, no,' she said grimly. 'This is my principal reason for sending for you. She next began to thrash about wildly, flailing with her arms and legs, as though she could not control them, then she fell on the floor in a kind of seizure, her body writhing, her hands stretched out rigid.' She paused. 'Later, she died.'

There was something cold in her, which I found less attractive, but before I could question her further, she went on.

'You see, Dr Alvarez, these are the same symptoms my son has shown on four other occasions. Writhing helplessly, unable to control his limbs, moments of blackness. Not as severe as the girl. And the Blessed Virgin was kind.' Her eyes flicked to a corner of the room, where I noticed for the first time that there was an icon of the Virgin and Child. 'My son did not die.'

'I see,' I said. Things were now becoming very clear. 'Your son, has he been examined by other physicians?'

'Naturally.' Her lips curled slightly. 'On the first occasion – it was a remarkable coincidence, was it not? – one of the court physicians had made a stay here for a few days, so he was able to examine my son when he was so afflicted.'

'And he diagnosed the falling sickness.' I said.

She nodded.

'Of course,' I said, 'these are the characteristic symptoms. But your son had shown no signs of the illness before?'

'Never. He is eight years old and has always been strong and healthy. He is a beautiful boy.' There was both pride and sorrow in her voice. 'Not,' she said firmly, 'like his half brother.'

'So you believe that the same poison was administered before and produced the same effect which later killed the maidservant.' It was not a question.

'It must have been given to him in a small quantity, not enough to kill, though I am sure that was the intention. I do not know *how* it was given to him, but children can be tempted by sweetmeats, and do not always listen to their mothers.'

I smiled at her. 'Nay, they do not. But after it happened more than once, you persuaded him to be more careful?'

'He understands now. He eats nothing that has not been tasted. But of course Godunov has made sure that the story is spread widely throughout the country that my son is a victim of the falling sickness and therefore unfit to be heir to his brother.'

'From what you have told me,' I said, 'it seems unlikely that he has the falling sickness, but that these episodes have occurred as a result of his swallowing the same poison that killed the maid. I think I should first examine what is left of the suspected food, and afterwards examine your son, to make sure that no harm has been done to him.'

'Come with me,' she said, rising, with a sudden rustle from her cloth of gold skirts.

She walked swiftly toward the door, but before she reached it, she stopped.

'I think you have a suspicion what the poison may be, Doctor Alvarez.'

Both an intelligent woman and a shrewd one. She must have read my thoughts in my face.

'I can think of a possibility,' I said cautiously. 'I have no direct experience of it myself, but have read of this particular poison in a book once owned by my father. The effects suffered both by your son and by the maidservant are consistent with the description.'

'What is the source of the poison?' she demanded.

'Let me see the food,' I said, 'and I will show you.'

She accepted this and threw open the door. The women and the guard shrank away, but she ignored them, leading me along a corridor to the back of the palace, then down a narrow staircase, clearly meant for servants, for her wide skirts brushed the rough walls on either side. Her attendants followed us and I saw the women exchange a look. There was something patronising in it, as if they believed we were on a fool's errand. In seemed that they were convinced by the court doctor's diagnosis and believed that the Tsarina's summoning of me was folly. I felt angry on her behalf. Why did they suppose the maid had died, in that case? Pyotr followed behind, stealing glances from side to side, as if he suspected a trap. Or perhaps he was assessing escape routes, as I had done, almost instinctively, in the bed chamber.

At the bottom of the stairs we reached what must be the back premises of the undercroft, where the kitchens, laundry, bakehouse and store rooms were located. The Tsarina stopped before a small door and drew a long, fine chain up from round her neck. Hidden under the golden finery of her gown had lain a small bunch of keys. One of these she selected and unlocked the door.

It was a small windowless room, with shelves on three sides. Bitterly cold, so I judged that any food kept here would be fairly well preserved, even after a week or so. The Tsarina turned and said something sharply in Russian. I did not catch the words, but the meaning was clear. Everyone else was to wait outside. The armed guard objected, as I suppose it was his duty to do, for I might have been an armed assassin. I had left my sword in the bed chamber, but I still had my dagger in my boot. It was surprising that I had not been searched.

Maria Nagaya waved him away impatiently and closed the door in his face. Then locked it.

'The food is here.' She pointed.

I hardly needed to be told, for there was nothing else in the room.

'We may set aside the sugar confection,' I said, moving it to a different shelf, 'since another servant tasted it and was unharmed.'

Three dishes remained. The soup, pale green, with congealed cream risen to the surface. The beef stew with its vegetables, chestnuts, and plums, now with a greasy layer of fat from the meat, also risen to the top. The fruit comfiture, looking clean and healthy beside them. Dried peaches which had been poached in a honey syrup, scattered with flakes of almonds. It would be difficult to conceal anything there, particularly the poison source I suspected. I set the comfiture beside the sugar confection, which had drawn moisture from the air and drooped sadly. It had once been spun in the likeness of a horse, now missing its tail, presumably the portion which had been eaten by the second servant.

'I think we must look for the culprit either in the soup or in the beef dish,' I said.

I took one of the surgical knives out of my satchel and stirred the sluggish soup with it, breaking up the layer of soured cream on top. With the point of my knife I fished out some small pieces of leek, clearly identifiable. There was nothing else. I set the bowl of soup aside, absent mindedly noticing how heavy all the dishes were. They were made of solid gold. Something twisted inside me, as an image rose before my mind's eye of Matthew's little group of beggar children I had befriended. I remembered how they had devoured every crumb of the stale bread trenchers, on which the cook of the Golden Keys had doled out leftovers beside his kitchen door the previous winter. This unseen little boy might eat from dishes of gold, but he was as vulnerable as they, more vulnerable.

The Tsarina was watching me closely. 'I too suspect the beef,' she said.

I nodded. I wiped the knife on a scrap of bandage cloth and drew the dish of beef toward me. There were many ingredients here, as I poked about with the tip of my knife. Pieces of meat, unmistakable. Softened chestnuts. Dried plums which had plumped up in the cooking. Half rings of union. Some dull reddish grey lumps which were almost certainly the beetroot. All swimming about in a thick brown gravy. The caps of ordinary field mushrooms. No sign of the ingredient I suspected.

At last I found what I was looking for. It had been roughly chopped, but not very fine. I was able to spear a sizeable chunk with the point of my knife and lay it on the shelf, where the gravy drained away, leaving it exposed.

The Tsarina leaned forward for a closer look. 'Is that it? What is it?'

'It is a type of mushroom, no doubt mixed in with the other, harmless mushrooms, although you can see that it is very different.'

'It is hideous, like a ball of worms, knotted together.'

That was a good description of the fungus, though when I had seen it in my father's book, which pictured and described the plants and herbs of Europe, I had thought it most resembled one of the illustrations in his precious volume on anatomy by the Italian Vesalius. It looked like the packed and coiled matter which make up the human brain. I agreed with the Tsarina. It was hideous.

'What is it?' she asked again, impatiently.

'Some people call it the false morel. It is certainly false, and I cannot see how anyone could confuse it with a true morel.' I cut the lump in half with my knife. 'Its correct name is *gyromitra esculenta*. Anyone who ingests it will suffer stomach pains and vomiting, followed by delirium, cramps, loss of muscle coordination, uncontrollable shaking and seizure. Very similar to an epileptic fit. If consumed in more than a tiny quantity, it is invariably fatal.' I paused. 'It grows in the pine forests of northern countries.'

We looked at each other steadily.

'So I was right,' she said.

'Aye, you were right. Your son was extremely lucky. The previous amounts must have been very small.'

She raised her hand to her throat, as if she found it difficult to breathe.

'I will have every cook, scullion, and kitchen maid torn apart and fed to the wolves!' She said with sudden, passionate venom.

'Wait!' I reached out my hand to stop her, but remembered in time that I must not touch the sacred person of royalty.

'If you do so, you will only alert your enemies to the fact that you know exactly what they have done. Probably most of the people who work in your kitchen knew nothing of this. Someone, perhaps just one person, added that fungus to the dish of beef. It might even have been the maidservant who died. You said she was reluctant to taste it.'

She stopped, but she gripped her hands tightly together, so that the joints showed white under the smooth skin.

'You seem very knowledgeable about such matters, for a physician.'

145

I hesitated, then decided to be honest with her. 'I used to work for the secret service of the late Sir Francis Walsingham, our Queen Elizabeth's chief secretary. I do have some knowledge of these dark and wicked matters.' I paused. 'If you will take my advice . . . do not show that you know what was intended for your son. Continue with your practice of requiring all your son's food to be tasted, but tell no one that you have discovered the false morels. Once it is clear that all the prince's food is tasted, I doubt whether they will try to poison him again. If there is anyone you can trust, he should try to find out, discreetly, who delivered the fungus to the palace kitchen. If you can be sure of that, he is your culprit, along with the maidservant, as I should guess.'

She gave a sharp nod.

'Of course,' I added, 'whoever gathered the fungus and brought it here is unlikely to be your real enemy, but merely a hireling.'

'Never fear,' she said grimly. 'I know who is my real enemy.'

'Now, this food should be destroyed,' I said. 'Thoroughly destroyed, not left where any dogs or other domestic animals may find it and eat it. It will be equally fatal to them.'

She smiled suddenly, looking younger and less strained. 'My Dmitri has an English wolfhound, which is his dearest playmate. I would never let any harm come to him.'

'They are fine dogs.' I smiled back at her. 'I know an elderly wolfhound who is the companion of a friend of mine. A friend who is caring for my own dog, while I am from home.'

'You must talk to Dmitri of your dog. He will like that.'

'I think I should see your son now, and examine him, in case the previous attempts at poisoning have done him any harm.'

She frowned. 'I have not noticed anything, apart from the seizures at the time. And he bruised himself with the thrashing about. The servants were helpless. But it is late now. His nurse will have put him to bed. We must leave your examination until the morning. I shall be glad of it, for you English physicians are well known for your skill. I do not trust the man who came from the court.'

'He is Russian?'

'German.'

'Their doctors are well trained.'

'Perhaps. It is not his training I distrust, but his honesty.'

She heaved a sudden involuntary sigh. 'Come, we have done enough for tonight.'

'The food,' I said, gesturing toward it as she unlocked the door. 'It should be thrown on the fire. Except the soup, of course. That may be tipped down a privy.'

'One of my women will do it, and I shall stand over her myself, to see that she destroys every scrap.'

Pyotr and I were escorted back to our quarters by the majordomo, who had appeared while the Tsarina and I had been examining the food.

'A meal will be brought to your rooms here,' he said austerely, leaving us at our door.

Once he was gone and the door closed, Pyotr said softly, 'Well?'

'Poison in the beef,' I murmured. 'A deadly mushroom. It could not have been added by accident. Too distinctive.'

He looked worried, glancing toward the door. 'Do you think the food they give us will be safe?' he whispered. 'I have brought what was left of our food from the sleigh.'

I shook my head. 'The Tsarina is anxious for me to examine the child tomorrow. I am sure we will be safe tonight at least.'

'When can we leave? Tomorrow?'

'Perhaps. I have promised to examine the child. There were certainly several attempts to poison him with the same mushroom, but fortunately the quantity was not enough to kill him. It may have done him some damage.'

'If it has, can you cure him?'

'Probably not. The fact that he has always been in good health before must have been in his favour.'

I removed my physician's gown and cap and sat in my doublet and breeches, relieved to be still and quiet for a while. I was exhausted after my long discussion in Russian with the Tsarina. At least I could not have made many mistakes, for she had understood me well enough. The rooms were warm, with large stoves well stocked with firewood, which had been lit while we were with the Tsarina. They reminded me a little of the pretty tiled stoves I had seen in the Low Countries, though these Muscovy stoves, furnishing the rooms in a palace, were huge, filling half a wall in each of the rooms, compared with those found in a simple Amsterdam inn.

Pyotr, however, could not relax, but prowled about our rooms. I was not sure whether he was looking for spy holes, or whether he was simply restless. He had had little to do since we had arrived, after it proved the Tsarina and I could speak together without needing his help.

147

When our meal arrived, carried in on trays by two menservants, he regarded it with suspicion. I think he was not reassured by my belief that we were in no danger for the moment. Finally he sat down opposite me at the table provided and glowered at the dishes. I poured us both a glass of wine. It made a pleasant change after the endless mead, which I found a little too sweet for my taste. The bottle was still sealed when it arrived, so Pyotr must have decided it was safe to drink.

'Your health,' I said.

'And yours,' he responded, but gloomily. 'I am truly hungry, but I am not sure whether I want to eat any of this.'

'Well, as you have said, there is some of the food from Yaroslavl left. Dried meat. Salted fish. I think there was some bread, but it may be stale by now. Perhaps not. It was only baked yesterday morning. It seems much longer ago than that.'

'It feels like a lifetime. I do not like this place.'

I laid my finger to my lips, but he merely shrugged.

There was a collection of lidded dishes on the trays. I began lifting the lids so that tantalising aromas escaped.

'There's a pair of roasted game birds here,' I said. 'Some kind of partridge, I would say. Also a piece of roasted meat.' I sniffed. 'Mutton. No dangerous sauce.'

I lifted another lid. 'Fish. A fillet taken from a very large fish. In a sauce with parsley and what could be tarragon. I don't know what the fish is.'

Unable to resist any longer, he drew the knife from his belt and poked at it.

'Sturgeon. We are honoured. Only served to the nobility. I wonder . . .'

He found a small pot tucked behind a basket of warm flatbread and beamed.

'As I hoped. Caviar.'

I looked at a mess of small black balls, like large garden seeds, glistening with oil, and wrinkled my nose.

'What is it?'

'The eggs of the sturgeon. A special delicacy. We are greatly honoured indeed.'

At that he seized one of the rounds of flatbread, heaped it with the black stuff, using a small mother-of-pearl spoon, and took an enormous bite.

'Try it,' he said, with his mouth full. 'Food of the gods.'

Somewhat doubtfully, I spooned some of the fish eggs on to flatbread and took a small bite. I was quite pleasant. Very fishy. But not more exceptional than the fresh-caught sardines we used to eat in Portugal. Still, I was glad Pyotr had lost his fears of the meal, for I was reluctant to eat on my own. We made a good supper, finishing with some kind of sticky cake, sweetened – over sweetened – of course, with honey.

Soon after that, I retired to the bed in the inner chamber, but removed nothing but my boots. And I slept with my dagger under the bolster and my sword lying beside me on the fur covering. I had told Pyotr I was sure we would be safe until I had seen the Tsarevich, but I was taking no chances.

Food was brought for us in the morning, to break our fast, some sort of porridge, but made with wheat rather than oats, and served with a kind of partially soured and thickened milk. I was not very hungry after our large supper the previous evening, and besides I was feeling somewhat sick with apprehension. My encounter with the Tsarina had been courteous enough, but I had detected a woman of steel and unrelenting will beneath the beauty and the cloth of gold. She would be as fierce as any she-bear in protecting her cub, so I could only hope that the reports claiming that the Tsarevich was cruel, violent, and unpredictable, like his father, were no more than malicious rumours spread to discredit the boy.

It had not been explained to me what I was to do this morning, whether I should go in search of the Tsarina or her son, or whether I should wait to be summoned, but I donned my cap and gown in readiness. Nervously I checked my satchel again. I am not sure what I expected to find there. Certainly not a cure for the falling sickness, if my diagnosis of the poisoning had been wrong. I did have extract of willow bark, if he suffered any pain. And poppy syrup, which could be used in a very small dose to calm him, should he prove to be violent. I prefer not to give it to children, but the son of Ivan the Terrible might indeed be a monster. I found it a little strange that I had still seen nothing of the boy. I suppose, being a royal child, he must have his own suite of rooms and his own army of attendant servants.

When I had finally reached the point where I thought I should wait no longer, but go in search of someone – while Pyotr was urging me to keep to our quarters until I was sent for – there came a rap on the door with a heavy object and the majordomo entered, without waiting for a response. As before he carried his rod of office. I realised, from

149

the weight of it when he knocked, that it was very nearly a club. I wondered whether he struck out with it, at the heads of careless or impertinent servants. Not that I could imagine any servant being impertinent in this man's presence.

He jerked his head. 'You are to come with me to the Tsarevich's quarters.'

Without waiting to see whether we followed, he strode away along the corridor toward the main staircase.

He moved swiftly, so that we almost needed to trot to keep pace with him. I did not like his manner. We were invited guests of the Tsarina and should have been treated with more respect. I wondered how he behaved toward her, and toward the Tsarevich. It was difficult to believe he could have been personally chosen by her. Perhaps he was an official wished on her by her stepson, or by Godunov. Could he have been implicated in the poisoning? I thought not. He was too arrogant, thought too well of himself, to take part in some plot that involved grubbing about in the forest, searching for those hideous mushrooms.

Once more we descended one flight to the main floor which held the royal apartments and were led further back towards the end of the building, beyond the servants' stair. As we passed it, two maidservants carrying brooms flattened themselves against the wall as if they wished they could disappear into it, and remained motionless, eyes cast down, until we were out of sight. I was not sure whether they feared us, the foreign strangers, or the majordomo. I suspected that it was the latter.

When we reached an ornate door, the man tapped on it, subserviently this time, and with his knuckles, not his staff. A voice called from within, and we were shown into the apartments of the little boy who might some day – if he lived – become the Tsar of all the Russias.

At first I could not see him and my impression was that this was no place for a young boy. In every respect it was as extravagant and flamboyant as the room where we had been taken the previous day to meet the Tsarina. Tapestries, priceless rugs, too much furniture, too much Oriental porcelain and too many gold vessels. Somehow it resembled an aristocratic pawn shop, everything jumbled together. And quite unsuitable for a boy of an age to kick a ball about or play rough games with other children. I had been shocked by the stories of the attempted poisonings, but now I pitied him for the surroundings of his normal life.

'Majesty,' the majordomo said in a reproving tone, 'you have visitors.'

Where was the child?

Then there was a disturbance at the far end of the large room, as a rug was pushed forward, and a tousled head appeared from under a large cupboard on legs. A boy crawled out, followed by the lean, lithe form of a wolfhound, which licked his master's face in a reassuring way.

The boy stood up, looking defiantly at the majordomo, though I thought there was a trace of fear there too. Then his glance fell on us. I felt Pyotr tug at my sleeve and realised that we were expected to prostrate ourselves. While I was at floor level, I saw that the maids had not been very thorough in their sweeping of this room, however ostentatious it was at normal eye height. There were balls of fluff and a layer of dust under the grand furniture. There was also fluff clinging to the child's clothes when I raised my eyes slightly.

'You may rise.' The voice was young, but dignified. He spoke slowly, perhaps forewarned by his mother.

We rose to our feet, and I took good care not to trip this time. I had no wish to make a fool of myself before my young patient.

'You are the doctor from England?'

'I am, Your Majesty. My name is Christoval Alvarez, and this is my friend and interpreter, Pyotr Ivanovich Aubery.'

'Do you not have a patronymic?'

'Where I come from,' I said gravely, 'we do not use patronymics, but if we did I should be known as Christoval Balthazarovich Alvarez.'

'Your father has a strange name.'

'Aye, he did, Majesty.'

He grew thoughtful at that. 'He is dead, your father?'

'He is, God rest his soul.'

'My father too is dead.'

I noticed that he did not bless his father and wondered what had been the relationship between that terrible man and his small son. A man who had murdered his own eldest surviving son, heir to his kingdom, and then wept at his own deed. What a dreadful inheritance this child had been born to.

The dog bounded across the room to me and I held out my hand to him. After giving it a thorough inspection, he licked it. I crouched down and rubbed him behind the ears, something Rikki always enjoyed. The dog responded by rolling on his back and looking up at me with frank friendliness, his tongue slightly protruding from his mouth. I laughed and rubbed the stomach thus presented.

151

Dmitri Ivanovich, Tsarevich of Muscovy, drew nearer. Then squatted down on the other side of the wolfhound.

'He *never* does that. Not even with people he knows. Never with strangers.'

'What is his name, this fine dog?'

'I call him Volk.'

It was one of the first words Pyotr had taught me. Wolf. He thought it might be useful in the wilderness of Muscovy.

'My dog is called Rikki,' I said.

The boy looked behind me, his eyes lighting up hopefully, but I shook my head.

'I had to leave him behind in England. The journey would have been too long. He would not have been happy. I miss him very much.'

His hand joined mine, rubbing Volk's stomach, and he gave me a sympathetic smile. 'I would be very sad without Volk. Is he a wolfhound, your Rikki?'

'Nay, he is a Dutch carriage dog.' This was a breed I invented on the spur of the moment. I wanted to invest my nondescript Rikki with some dignity. 'He is about as tall as Volk, but much heavier, built for strength rather than speed. He is a golden brown. He saved my life once, when I was attacked by three men with swords.'

His eyes widened. 'Was he hurt?'

'Aye, a sword slash in his side, but he was very brave when I stitched it up. I think Volk can smell Rikki on my gown, and that is why he came to me. Dogs understand these things.'

'I think Volk would save my life, if I was in danger.' A bleak look passed over his face, and I knew at that moment that, young as he was, Dmitri understood very well the nature of his own danger.

'I am sure he would,' I said gently.

'Dimitka moi,' a voice spoke over our heads, 'why are you and the doctor on the floor?'

The prince and I both stood up hastily. I shook out my gown and made a hurried obeisance, Dmitri bowed, and the dog sat up, alert, his head on one side.

'I was introducing Volk to Dr Christoval Balfazarovich, Mamochka.' His tone was polite, but not in any way apologetic. I think he took some pride in remembering my peculiar patronymic.

She smiled, and I realised that she had not minded my playing with the dog. She was not quite so formally dressed today, having laid aside the crown. Her hair, which had been bundled tightly into a head cloth before, though a head cloth of silver tissue, was less rigidly controlled this morning, for a small strand had escaped over her cheek. It was the same red gold colour as her son's untidy curls, which still bore traces of the fluff from his private cave under the furniture. She noticed this, and brushed it away, with that click of the tongue which is a universal language amongst mothers. With a pang, I remembered my mother making the same sound when I came in dirty after playing outside on my grandfather's *solar*.

'My son, the doctor is a busy man and needs to examine you. Show him to your bed chamber.'

The three of us crossed to a door at the other end of the room, while Pyotr remained behind with the majordomo. This room was almost as alien to a young boy's needs as the other, although there were a few carved wooden toys here, some dancing bears on a stick, a set of soldiers, a red leather ball with tooth marks. There was an elaborate dog's bed in pristine condition, with never a sign of hair on it. I suspected this was not due to any particular attention on the part of the servants, but because Volk shared his master's bed, an enormous affair, in which he would have been lost without the dog's company.

Fortunately the room was well heated with another of the huge stoves, so I did not feel too cruel in asking Dmitri to strip. He shivered a little, his skin white as a girl's, his limbs still childishly delicate. Clearly he had not yet been set to any training in the manly sports, as a boy of his age and class would have been in England. Perhaps the Tsarina was too fearful for his safety.

Despite this, he was perfectly healthy and answered my questions about his bodily functions shyly but without prevarication. There did not seem to be any lasting damage done by the incidents of attempted poisoning. He had undressed without the help of a servant, and dressed again unaided, spurning his mother's help. I hid my surprise. Such a child in England would not expect to dress himself. Perhaps again his mother wished to avoid too much contact with unreliable servants, though a nurse had been mentioned yesterday.

'Now, Majesty,' I said, 'I need you to tell me what happened on these occasions when you ate something which disagreed with you.'

'You mean, when I was poisoned?'

I had hoped to avoid the word, but he looked at me with bleak knowledge in his eyes.

'Aye. Tell me how you felt.'

'I was dizzy and I fell over. And my arms and legs flew about, like this.'

He performed a grotesque mimicry of someone having a seizure, ending with throwing himself on the floor. The Tsarina went pale, and pressed her clasped hands to her breast, but Dmitri hopped up again, clearly rather pleased with his performance.

'And afterwards? How long did this last?'

'I forgot to say. I was also very sick.' He made a realistic vomiting noise, loud enough to bring the majordomo rushing into the room, but the Tsarina waved him away irritably.

'I don't remember how long. How long did I faint, Mamochka?'

'Perhaps half an hour.' She spoke with difficulty.

'Well,' I said, 'it was good you were sick. It got rid of the nastiness.'

Volk had come over to me, as if for reassurance in view of this disturbing performance. I ran his ears through my fingers without really noticing what I was doing, and he leaned against my leg.

'Majesty,' I said, 'will you promise me something, so that Volk is not frightened by that happening again?'

The boy knelt down and put his arm around the dog, pressing his face into the silky coat. I realised that the performance was nothing but bravado. He was trembling.

'What should I promise?' he mumbled against the dog's side.

'Promise that you will never, ever, accept food from strangers. Nor even from people you know, not until it has been tasted by someone else first.'

He nodded, not lifting his face from the dog's coat.

'I promise.' He gulped, then whispered, 'It was horrible when Natalya Petrovna died.'

He was the first to mention the girl's name. I laid my hand for a moment on the back of the thin neck, so childlike and vulnerable under the red gold hair. Never mind that this was a prince of the blood royal. He was also a small boy, living in daily fear.

'If you are careful,' I whispered back, 'it will not happen to you.'

After we left Dmitri's quarters, I was conducted back to the room where I had met the Tsarina the previous day. My mind was haunted by the image of the lonely little boy, hiding under the furniture with his dog. I had to hold back my anger that men greedy for power should treat a child like so much rubbish, to be swept carelessly out of the way.

'So, Dr Alvarez,' the Tsarina said, gesturing me to a chair beside an ornate table. Both were heavy with ormolu work. 'He is perfectly healthy, my son?'

I nodded. 'Perfectly healthy.'

'No sign of the falling sickness?'

'None. I think we may take it as certain that what he suffered was purely the effects of the *gyromitra esculenta*.'

'Good.'

Out of the corner of my eye, I could see Pyotr standing near the door, shifting restlessly from foot to foot.

'Forgive me, Your Majesty, but the rest of my party is awaiting our return in Yaroslavl and we are expected in Moscow. Will it be convenient for us to leave today? We have been received most courteously here in Uglich, but I do not wish to inconvenience Master Christopher Holme, who is anxious to take up his post as chief agent of the Muscovy Company. He needs to reach the Moscow house as soon as possible.'

'I understand, but there is one more thing I should like you to do for me, Dr Alvarez, and after that it will be too late to set out today. You may leave tomorrow morning.'

I could see there would be no arguing with her. Whatever her position in the rest of Muscovy, Maria Nagaya ruled absolutely in Uglich.

'And what would you have me do, Majesty?'

'I want you to write out a certificate for the Tsarevich, stating that he is not suffering from the falling sickness. The symptoms he exhibited before were the result of attempted poisoning by unknown persons by means of a deadly mushroom. Name it, specifically, so that they will know their schemes have been uncovered and you were able to identify the source of the poison.'

I noticed that Pyotr had frozen, with an expression of horror on his face. I was seized with a moment of sheer terror. Then I tried to speak calmly.

'Majesty, if I write such a certificate, and sign it, then I sign my own death warrant. If you show this document to those who would kill your son, then they will not hesitate to kill me, for I will have thwarted their plans to depict the Tsarevich as incapable, even if they have failed to poison him. You are asking me to lay a knife to my own throat.'

She looked straight into my eyes and gave a sharp nod. She knew as well as I what the consequences would be and had anticipated my reaction. Could she keep me here by force until I complied? Almost certainly.

'I will make a bargain with you, Dr Alvarez,' she said. 'Write out the certificate and I will keep it locked away until you leave the country. With the next English fleet, will it be?'

'Aye. In August.'

At least that was what I hoped. Surely by then I would either have discovered what had happened to Gregory Rocksley or been forced to abandon my search.

'Then it cannot be used against you while you are in this country. Once you return to England, there will be no danger to you.'

She walked to the door and opened it. The majordomo was standing immediately beyond and she gave him some rapid instructions. He looked surprised, but bowed and left. As he did so, the two women attendants and the armed guard entered. They must also have been waiting just outside. I shivered. The Tsarina lived always under the eyes of people who could not be trusted. A short time later, the majordomo returned and laid a book on the table with a bow. He withdrew a few steps, but watched us intently.

The Tsarina laid her right hand on the book.

'This is a Bible. I belong to the Orthodox faith. I know that you are one of these Protestants whom our own Church regards as heretics, but I think I have seen enough of you to judge that you will accept my oath on the Bible.' She gave a sad little smile. 'There are not many that Dmitri would allow to caress his Volk. Nor many strangers the dog would not attack.'

'Of course I will accept your oath, Majesty.' I did not burden her with an explanation of my dubious faith, in which Jewish, Catholic, and Protestant swirled in confusion.

'Very well. Here, you, Pyotr Ivanovich!' She gestured to him to come nearer. 'You shall bear witness. I swear on the Holy Word that I will keep locked away the certificate that Dr Alvarez is to write, concerning the Tsarevich's health. I shall show it to no one, until he has left the country. Amen.'

'Amen,' we both said.

I would have to trust her.

The Tsarina shared a midday meal with us there, then she sent away her attendants and retired to a window-seat while paper, ink, quill, and wax were brought for me to use. I suppose we were not exactly prisoners in that room, but there seemed to be no possibility of leaving it until she had got what she wanted.

156

I wrote out in some detail how I had examined the Tsarevich and my conclusions that he clearly showed no signs of the falling sickness. I then repeated all the information I had received about the four occasions on which he had been taken ill, the effects on him, and the more severe attacks of the same symptoms which had resulted in the death of the maidservant, Natalya Petrovna. Next I set out precisely the discovery of *gyromitra esculenta* in the remains of the food she had consumed, the known effects of this poisonous fungus, and my unqualified conclusion that the same poison had caused the death of the servant and the earlier illness of the Tsarevich.

I read it through when I had finished, then read it aloud to the Tsarina, translating as I went, for I had written it in Latin. She agreed that it covered every point that she wanted explained. I then dictated it in English to Pyotr, who wrote the whole certificate out again in Russian, for I expected the learned men of Muscovy would not be familiar with Latin, which they probably regarded as a despicable modern tongue.

By the time we had finished, it was dark outside. I melted some of the sealing wax over a candle, then dropped a puddle of it at the bottom of the certificate. I still wore the seal Arthur Gregory had made for me on a chain around my neck. I lifted the chain over my head and pressed the seal firmly into the soft wax, leaving a clear imprint that linked me irrevocably to the document. When the wax was hard, I rose from my chair, stiff from remaining seated so long. The Tsarina was still in the window seat, sitting in near darkness, as I handed her the closely written sheet.

'Very good,' she said, rising. 'Rest now. I will see that your sleighs are ready at dawn tomorrow.'

I think Pyotr and I both held our breath until we were back again in our own quarters. Shutting the door behind him, Pyotr leaned against it, and let his out in a long sigh.

'She fairly had you by the balls, lad.'

He had never addressed me so familiarly before, but it had been a trying day. I agreed that she had.

'Thank the good Lord, we leave tomorrow. Is that food I see? Do you think it is safe? She's got what she wants now.'

The same thought had crossed my mind, but I found I was ravenous. The food which had been left in our room was far more modest than the previous night's supper, but we had dined well with the Tsarina earlier. We both examined the food carefully, but it seemed safe. There was another sealed bottle of wine, bread, a hard white cheese, dried fruits, and some of Pyotr's beloved caviar. The caviar was the only thing which might have held poison, and I declined it, but assured Pyotr that I would have a vomitive to hand, should he show signs of poisoning.

At that he regarded the caviar dubiously, but yielded to temptation, eating it by tiny spoonfuls and showing no untoward effects. The remaining food was clearly harmless. After satisfying my hunger, I packed away all my belongings except my thick travelling clothes and fell asleep again fully dressed.

I was woken by the sound of Pyotr speaking to someone in the outer room. It was still dark, but I supposed that it might already be time to get ready to leave. I pulled on my boots and went through to the other room. Pyotr was speaking to an elderly woman too swiftly for me to understand. On seeing me, she dropped to the ground and kissed my boot, to my intense embarrassment.

'What is it?' I said to Pyotr. 'What is the matter?'

'This is the Tsarevich's nurse. He wants to see you before we leave.'

'Is he ill?' I asked in alarm, turning aside to fetch my satchel.

'Nay, not at all. He wants you to take something to Moscow for him.'

This was mystifying, but Pyotr and I followed the old woman back to the prince's apartments, where she entered without knocking and led us into the bed chamber.

Dmitri had laid aside his stiff embroidered gown of the previous day and was wearing nothing but a simple night shift. Simple, except that it was made of silk. His hair was tousled from sleep and his feet were bare. The sight of him made my throat tighten with pity, he looked so small and vulnerable.

'Christoval Balfazarovich,' he said formally, 'would you be kind enough to carry a package to Moscow for me?'

I knelt down, to bring myself nearer to his height, but I resisted the urge to hug him.

'I should be happy to do so, Majesty. And that it far too big a mouthful for a name. My friends call me Kit.'

His whole face lit up, and I realised with a pang that it was possible no one had ever offered him simple friendship before.'

'Then you must call me Dmitri.' He glanced over his shoulder at his nurse, but clearly he trusted her. 'Only,' he whispered, 'not in front of my mother.'

'It shall be our secret,' I promised. 'Now, where is this package?'

He held out a thick package of vellum, inexpertly tied together with a piece of ribbon woven with gold thread. It looked as though it had been ripped from a garment and I hoped it would not bring trouble down on the child or the nurse.

'And to whom am I to deliver this package?' I saw that it bore no address as I tucked it into the breast of my doublet. I doubted that it was intended for his half-brother the Tsar. From all I had gathered they had no affection for each other.

He glanced around again, as if he feared that the walls had ears. Which, I thought, they might well do.

'It is for me cousin Xenia, I have drawn her a picture of Volk and written a story for her. She tries to write to me, but it is . . . difficult.'

'I am afraid I did not know that you have a cousin Xenia. Is she the daughter of one of your mother's brothers?'

This was awkward. As far as I knew, all of his mother's family was here in Uglich or else exiled to the recently acquired western part of the Khanate of Sibir. None were in Moscow.

'She is the daughter of the brother of my sister-in-law,' he said, as if that explained everything.

I tried to work it out. The wife of his half brother Fyodor was Irina Fyodorovna, surely . . . Irina Fyodorovna Godunova. Whose brother was . . . Boris Godunov, the man Maria Nagaya believed (with some reason) to be behind the attempts on her son's life.

'Your cousin is Xenia Borisovna Godunova?' I said cautiously.

He nodded unhappily. 'They used to let her come here for the summer. She is my *cousin*, we *like* each other. But they do not let her come any more.'

His voice echoed with loneliness.

I got to my feet. 'I promise you, Dmitri, I will do everything in my power to see her, if they will permit it, and I will give her your packet.' I smiled at him reassuringly. 'I will also tell her how well and strong you are, and I will tell her about Volk, how he befriended me.'

'Thank you,' he whispered. Then he drew himself up, regal even in his night shift. 'We give you our thanks, Christoval Balfazarovich.'

'God go with you, Dmitri,' I said.

'And with you.' He hesitated, then smiled. 'And with you, Kit.'

As we left, I glanced back and saw him standing straight and valiant, his hand resting on the head of his wolfhound.

There was no time then to discuss this turn of events with Pyotr. The old nurse hurried us back to our quarters, which we reached just in time to seem to be rising from our beds when a servant arrived with more of the wheat porridge and news that our sleighs were packed and awaiting us in the courtyard below. We ate the food hastily. Although I found it glutinous and tasteless, I finished my share, for I was not sure whether we would have been provided with food for the journey.

The servant waited for us, watching us closely, as though he thought we might help ourselves to some of the gold ornaments, then he escorted us down the main staircase to the outside steps as the front of the house. It was still dark, though torches had been lit in the sconces along the wall.

With a muted jingle of harness, our three sleighs emerged from the back of the house. Our drivers and the guards Christopher Holme had provided all seemed safe, if sleepy with this early start. As Pyotr and I climbed into our sleigh – where I noticed that our food hamper had been refilled – the majordomo descended the steps, taking his time, as if he did not much care for his task. He handed me a leather purse, which clinked and weighed heavy in my hand.

'The Tsarina Maria Fyodorovna Nagaya says that you have not named your fee. She therefore sends you this, in the hope that it will be sufficient.'

I had no intention of examining the contents of the purse in front of this man.

'Please convey my thanks to the Tsarina,' I said. 'May God go with her. And with you,' I added somewhat tardily.

He turned and strode away without further speech, the drivers chirruped to the horses, and we began to speed away down the long drive. As it rounded a slight bend I looked back. Apart from the torches beside the steps, the palace was in almost total darkness, but near the back of the house, on the royal floor, light shone from window where the shutters had been thrown open. It was Dmitri's room. I wondered whether he was watching us leave, and raised my hand in farewell.

160

Chapter Nine

*D*espite our early start, it took us nearly four days to make the return journey to Yaroslavl. We spent most of the second day sheltering from a blizzard at one of the post stations, and we were buffeted by storms all the rest of the way. Even the tough little Muscovy horses could do nothing but plod along at walking pace, their heads down against the wind. Despite the furs and the heated stones which we renewed at every stop, I thought I should die, frozen into a block of ice, I was so cold. I even suggested to Pyotr that we should get out and walk part of the way, to warm ourselves with the exercise. We were travelling so slowly I was sure we could keep pace with the horses.

'That is pure folly!' he snapped at me. The cold was affecting his temper. 'You would be dead in half an hour. Less. In the sleigh we are at least sheltered from the wind. And before you died, your fingers and toes, and your nose, would drop off from frostbite. Do you want me to describe it for you?'

'I thank you,' I said sourly, 'but I am perfectly aware of the effects of frostbite.'

The cold and the confinement for so long within the cramped space of the sleigh were undermining my own temper. I turned my back on him and huddled down until I was almost buried under the furs. I would try to sleep. That would at least help the dragging hours to pass. But it was useless. My body would not stop shaking from the cold and would not let me sleep.

At last, near the early dusk of the fourth day, the roof and church domes of Yaroslavl came into sight. Even the horses seemed to sense that we were near journey's end and managed to rise to a trot and then a canter. Surely they sensed warm stables and a good feed awaiting them.

Pyotr and I became more cheerful and spoke politely to each other, both, I expect, ashamed of our ill temper of the last few days.

As the sleighs bowled through the gates of the Company compound and drew up in front of the main house, it was a relief to see windows cheerfully illuminated and flaming torches lit on either side of the door, as if we were expected. It turned out that indeed we were. Christopher Holme and Robert Farindon came out to greet us, clutching bearskins around their shoulders, over their cloaks. Even here, behind the sheltering walls, the wind was fierce, throwing snow in our faces with an almost human malice.

'Your sleighs were spotted from the town watch tower,' Robert explained, 'so we knew you would be here shortly.'

I started to climb out of the sleigh, but my limbs were almost locked in place, stiffened with the bitter cold. Robert and Christopher grabbed an arm each and steadied me until I was able to put one foot in front of the other. I was relieved to see that Pyotr was in just as bad a state. Two of the other stipendiaries were helping him toward the door.

Once inside, we were marched into the parlour, where a fire was blazing with a pot heating beside it. A familiar aroma met us.

'Can that possibly be spiced beer?' I asked in wonder.

'It is.' Christopher smiled. 'When the remainder of the cargo came through Yaroslavl, I insisted that two barrels of good English beer should be left here, and several more ear-marked for the Company house in Moscow. It is no loss to the Tsar and his court. The Muscovites have no taste for it. With apologies to you, Pyotr Aubery.'

Pyotr had regained his cheerfulness at the sight of the fire and the scent of the spiced beer. 'I may have come to it late, but I love English beer as much as any Englishman, and ale too.'

'Ale would not keep.'

'I know that.' There was a touch of irritation in Pyotr's voice. I judged he could not decide to which nation he belonged, England or Muscovy. It was a dilemma I could understand. But I had come to England at a younger age, and now felt no longer that I belonged to Portugal – a nation that had driven me out, and would execute me if I returned in my own person. For Pyotr, I sensed, it was different.

If Christopher noticed Pyotr's irritation, he showed no sign of it, but busied himself with pouring us large mugs of the steaming drink, while Robert went to call for our meal to be brought. By the time he returned, Pyotr and I had both cautiously shed some of the outer layers of our travelling clothes and had accepted a second mug of the beer which, in my case at least, was beginning to thaw me from the inside.

'The food will be here shortly,' Robert said, as he poked the fire and threw on more logs. 'I thought we should have it here. The two of us waited for you, but Master Deynes and the rest of the staff have eaten.'

'Aye,' said Christopher, settling back against the cushion in his chair. 'We have done a good deal of waiting and worrying while you have been gone. Tomorrow morning would have seen the promised week run out, and we should have come in search of you.'

'I do not think we could have managed to come back any sooner,' I said. 'I had hoped to leave Uglich one day earlier, but we were–' I glanced across at Pyotr. 'Prevented. And then the weather has been so bad on the return journey, it has taken twice as long.'

Christopher had guessed the significance of that glance of mine. 'I think you should tell us everything that happened,' he said. 'From the beginning.'

So while we waited for the food to be brought, and then while we ate, I did tell them everything that had happened during the last week, with Pyotr contributing when he thought I had forgotten something significant.

It was difficult not to talk with my mouth full, for it was a relief to eat good English food. The provisions on both journeys had been Spartan, while the food at Uglich had varied from the tasteless to the exotic. Now we tucked into a good white onion soup, followed by beef which had been slowly roasted before a steady fire and – oh, joy! – alternately basted and dredged, so that it had a crisp herb-flavoured crust and a rich gravy, in which whole onions had been roasted underneath the turning meat. It was followed by a creamy custard and an apple tart. I hope I may not be thought a glutton, but that meal did much to restore my health and my temper.

When both the meal and the account of our visit to Uglich were concluded, Christopher sat looking into the fire for a long time before commenting.

'It is excellent that you were able to reassure the Tsarina and to tend the Tsarevich,' he said at last, 'and to know that the stories of the falling sickness are fabrications, but clearly they live in the shadow of murder. If the child's enemies are bent on assassination, and if they find that their attempts at poisoning have been frustrated, will they not try some other way?'

'That too has been in my mind,' I said soberly, 'but the boy is well guarded. I am not sure whether he is ever allowed out of the palace. He is as pale as plant which receives no sunlight, poor mite.'

163

'You liked him.' Christopher smiled.

'He is a valiant little soul.' I said.

'And what of this certificate you were forced to write?' Robert spoke for the first time since I had finished telling our story.

'Aye,' Christopher said. 'I do not like the sound of that.'

'There was no help for it,' Pyotr said. 'It is certain the Tsarina would have kept us there by force until she had it in her hand.'

'She swore she would not reveal it while I am in the country,' I said. 'Swore on the Bible, and I believed her.'

'No doubt she did so in good faith,' Christopher said, 'and believed it herself, but what if circumstances change? What if the Tsar or Godunov were to try to take the child away, saying he must receive treatment? Or be confined, for his own good? I think, *in extremis*, the Tsarina would abandon her oath to you in order to save her son. I do not believe she would hesitate for a moment, or feel she did wrong. When a child's life is at stake, what is the value of a casual oath, even if it has been taken on the Bible?'

'I know you are right,' I said. 'I was aware of that even as I wrote the certificate, but, as Pyotr says, I do not think we would have been allowed to leave unless I did as the Tsarina asked.'

'Well, you must be cautious. We must keep an ear always open for any news from Uglich. If at any time the child is threatened, then you will be in danger too.'

I did not like the sound of this, spoken aloud, although it was what I had already acknowledged privately, to myself. I shrugged, and tried to appear unconcerned.

'What can I do?' I said. 'I have barely begun on the main mission I was sent here to undertake. I must go with you to Moscow, then travel on, perhaps as far as Astrakhan, or even further, in search of any trace of Gregory Rocksley.'

'The man may be dead, these many months.'

I acknowledged this. 'Nevertheless, I must try to discover his fate. The man has a wife and three children. They must be told what has become of him.'

Christopher shifted uneasily in his chair. 'A man with children had no business undertaking such a mission for Sir Francis.'

I knew that he had children of his own, although, judging from his age, they must be well grown. I said nothing in answer to this, but that night, despite being safely back in my room at Yaroslavl, I slept badly.

Christopher and Robert had waited only for our return before setting out for Moscow, but they allowed us two days' grace after our unpleasant trip from Uglich before we left for the next stage of the journey. I was sorry to see that the Sami drivers with their reindeer sleighs were gone.

'Back to the north,' Robert said. 'Mostly, they do not care to stray too far south. We will have our own Company drivers from here to Moscow. There is frequent traffic between the two towns as a regular part of our trade, so we maintain our own fleet of drivers, horses, and sleighs.'

'How far is it to the capital?' I asked. I was growing weary of these long journeys. Although Moscow would mean an end to travelling for the two Company men, Pyotr and I still had the journey to Astrakhan ahead of us. Somehow the way to this distant and mystical place seemed like something out of a dream, or one of those ancient romances, like the tales of King Arthur.

'The distance to Moscow? It is not so very much further than the distance from Vologda to Yaroslavl,' Robert said. 'Perhaps a hundred and fifty miles. Allowing for the weather – a week?'

Another week cooped up in a sleigh. Nevertheless, I was eager to be away. How many weeks and months had passed since I had set foot in this barbaric country? And I was no nearer discovering anything of Rocksley's whereabouts that I had not known before I left London. I felt frustrated and impotent.

We were off at last. This time I shared a sleigh again with Christopher, which was wise, for I felt that Pyotr and I had been too much in each other's company and were beginning to try each other's nerves, though I had been glad to have him with me in Uglich, despite the fact that his skills as an interpreter were required only occasionally.

The weather had improved slightly after our return from Uglich. There were two brief snow storms on our journey, but most of the time the sky was a cloudless ice blue and the firm snow provided good footing for the horses. On this route there were regular post stations, so that we were able to spend our nights there, instead of camping out in one of the deserted villages. Nevertheless, I slept in my clothes and kept my sword and dagger to hand.

My skills as a physician were called upon as well. At one post station a man had that very morning managed to bury an axe in his calf while chopping wood. His wife had spread it with bear grease and bound it up, but it was a nasty gaping wound, which I cleaned, stitched, and salved. I explain to the wife how she was to remove the stitches, and when, but had to trust that he would survive. Where we spent one night, word must have spread that there was a physician in the party, for the following morning there were three patients awaiting me before we could leave. One man with a chest congestion, a woman with a large boil that needed lancing, and a small child howling with the pain in his ear. In this cold winter, I suspected an ear infection, but on examining the child I discovered that he had lodged a dried pea in it. Or rather, I suspected that his anxious elder brother was the culprit, although he admitted nothing. I managed to extract the pea, and the patient received a cuffing from his mother, which I felt was undeserved.

As Robert had guessed, it took us about a week to reach Moscow, and for the first time I was impressed by a town in Muscovy. It seemed Moscow was a town within a town, for the central citadel, palace, and churches formed a self contained inner town, with many other royal buildings crowded together, hugger mugger, and surrounded by a vast wall.

The houses occupied by all the rest of the citizens lay outside this wall, on either side of the Moskva river. It was less than twenty years since the terrible sacking and burning of Moscow by the Tatars, that Christopher had spoken about. Parts of the town still contained ruined areas, but gradually it was being restored. Our sleighs took us directly to the Company's Moscow house, driving over roads where the snow had been packed down into hard ice by the passage of people, horses, and sleighs. I saw more than one person slip and fall, or else grab the corner of a building or the arm of a fellow pedestrian to avoid falling. I wondered what might be the incidence of broken bones in Moscow during the winter.

The Company house proved to be very fine indeed, repaired again in stone after the disaster when so many people had perished in the cellar of the old building given to the Company by Tsar Ivan. It was located in the merchants' quarter, standing out as one of the finest buildings in the street,

'Come in, come in!'

It was Austin Foulkes, the out-going chief agent. I sensed he was relieved to see us, for it meant that within a few weeks he could hand over Company affairs in the capital to Christopher and begin the long journey back to St Nicholas, to meet the next fleet for the voyage home. I hoped fervently I would be able to join him.

The house was large enough for us all to have separate rooms on the first floor, though they were small. As in the other houses, the apprentices and servants had dormitories in the attics, while the ground floor held the large rooms for conducting business with the merchants of Moscow, as well as a dining room and parlour for the Company staff. The kitchens were in an outbuilding. Despite the fact that all the new buildings in this quarter were now constructed of stone or brick, memories of the terrible fire lingered, so that kitchens were accommodated separately, at a distance from the houses. Below the main house there was apparently a labyrinth of cellars, used for storing the Company's merchandise. In the northern towns where we had stayed, the compounds had held warehouses, locked, barred, and guarded, but here in Moscow it seemed the Company felt its goods were only safe when stored under the very house itself. I did not visit the cellar. I feared it must be the same cellar in which so many people had died. I had no wish to enter it.

'We wait, now,' Christopher said, after we had eaten that first evening. 'When it suits the court to send for me, I shall go to the Kremlin and present my credentials as the incoming chief agent for the Company. Austin will introduce me.'

Master Foulkes nodded. He was an older man than Christopher, and I thought he showed the strain of his years in Muscovy. Difficult years, during which it had been impossible to know which way the political wind would blow. As I understood it, Tsar Fyodor was more interested in praying than ruling, in church building than overseeing foreign policy, but when he did take an interest in trade, he was fickle, sometimes playing one country off against the other, withdrawing the Company's long established rights and granting them to others, then changing his mind again. Godunov, on the other hand, had originally favoured England, but had been offended by a previous arrogant English ambassador. It had taken great patience and skill on the part of senior Company men to soothe his angry pride. No wonder Master Foulkes was glad to be going home.

'And you, Dr Alvarez,' Foulkes inclined his head toward me as we sat over supper that first evening, 'I understand you have been in Uglich, to attend the Tsarevich. Now your skills are required at Court. It seems they are dissatisfied with their German physicians. That is why they have been constantly requesting Englishmen, though I think, by your name, you are not English.'

Before I could answer, Christopher spoke.

'Dr Alvarez has lived in England since the age of twelve, and is the son of a distinguished professor of medicine at the University of Coimbra.'

Foulkes smiled. 'I have heard of that medical school. It is said to be one of the best in the world.'

'He has practised at both St Bartholomew's and St Thomas's, is licensed by the Royal College of Physicians, and is highly valued by Lord Burghley himself. As indeed he was by the late Sir Francis Walsingham, God rest his soul.'

I felt that Christopher exaggerated somewhat. I had met Lord Burghley, but I was not sure that he valued me highly. Still, this praise would do me no harm, if I was to penetrate the inner sanctum of the Court and deliver Dmitri's package to his cousin Xenia.

At the same time, what concerned me was the fear that the Court might demand my services for many patients, preventing me from continuing to Astrakhan. I had been warned repeatedly that the Tsars of Muscovy were reluctant to allow foreigners, once admitted to the country, to leave again. I had already had experience of their tight control over travel within the realm. Besides, I had no wish to fall out with their resident German physicians. A professional quarrel would mean nothing but trouble. And if I were required to treat a patient and failed? I feared what the consequences might be. I tried to play down Christopher's praise.

'It would be better if I could confine myself to the one patient I was asked to see,' I said. 'There was a child in the royal household with a skin rash no one could cure. If I am called upon for other work, I shall never be able to get away.'

They considered this.

'You are right,' Master Foulkes said. 'I will make some cautious enquiries.'

'In the meantime,' Christopher said, 'it is nearly Christmas.'

'Aye. We celebrate here, with all our English staff. Afterwards, we will be expected to attend the blessing of the river, on Twelfth Day.'

At the time, I took little note of this, but I was to learn more later.

A few days after our arrival, Christopher and Austin were summoned to attend the Tsar in the Kremlin. I had understood that 'kremlin' meant any town citadel, as it might be the castle in an English town, but when people spoke of The Kremlin in a particular tone of voice, they meant the whole of that walled inner city and everything that went on within those massive fortifications, including all of the government and the Court. Even far away at St Nicholas, washed by its icy northern seas, the people of Muscovy trembled at the mention of this Moscow Kremlin.

It was clear that the two chief agents of the Company were not immune to this same fear. They dressed with great care and had their hair cut by a Russian barber. Austin already sported a full beard; Christopher had left England with the neat pointed beard fashionable at that time, but ever since he had allowed it to grow. It was not as impressive as Austin's, but had changed his appearance.

'The Muscovites honour and respect a man with a full beard,' Christopher explained. 'One of our earliest explorers here possessed a beard down to his knees. Or so it is said. He was greatly honoured. I am afraid I do not offer any competition.'

Involuntarily, I ran my hand over my own, smooth, chin. Not for the first time, I wished that I was not marked out by my lack of facial hair. For the moment I could still be accepted as too young, but how much longer?

The two men set off for the Kremlin in their finery, attended by Company servants in ceremonial livery. Christopher's documents had been placed in an ornate gilded box and were carried on a red velvet cushion by Austin's senior stipendiary. Fortunately, it was not snowing.

We did not see them again until halfway through the following day. On leaving us, they had been unsure whether they would be entertained to dinner by the Tsar after their reception. It seemed this would depend on the whim of the moment. On this occasion he had apparently been in a jovial mood, although he normally shunned company.

'It is difficult to say which would be worse,' Christopher said, flinging himself into a chair on his return and clutching his head in his hands. 'To be dismissed abruptly is an insult. To endure a Court feast is a test of endurance. Have you any cure for a hangover, doctor?'

I looked at him with some sympathy. I had heard tales of Muscovite drinking bouts. The Russian men seemed to have an almost inexhaustible capacity for strong drink, and if the English guests had failed to keep pace, their position in the country would be seriously undermined.

'Could you not have used subterfuge? I asked. 'Tipped some of the drink away? Pretended to drink when you did not?'

He shook his head, then regretted it and groaned.

'Impossible. You are watched, hawk like, all the time. To fail to drink to the innumerable toasts would be counted an insult.'

I took pity on him and went to the kitchens to oversee the straining and boiling of water. When I returned, carrying a large jug, he had been joined by Austin, and both looked really ill.

'Here,' I said. 'You must drink as much of this clean water as you can. And only very simple food for the rest of the day and tomorrow. Bread is good. Eat plenty of it. I do not want to lose the two of you to alcohol poisoning.'

Austin paused in gulping down his first mug of water to look at me in surprise. 'Can alcohol truly poison you?'

'It can,' I said austerely. Despite their assurances, I did not quite believe that it would have been impossible for them to drink less.

We celebrated Christmas quietly in the Company house, with a simple Christian service and an excellent meal, centred on roast goose and ending with plum duff and nuts. Afterwards, we all gathered in one of the large trading rooms to sing carols. The apprentices, servants, and younger stipendiaries got up a few games like Snapdragon and Hoodman Blind, but compared to Christmases I had known in London, it was a subdued affair. The fact that we were not only outside the Orthodox faith, but belonged to the heretical Protestant sect, meant that we needed to be careful not to draw attention to ourselves. As we kept withindoors, we saw nothing of the Muscovites' Christmas services, though snatches of music were carried on the wind to us from the many churches. I was beginning to find it very beautiful, now that my ear was attuned to their curious scales and harmonies. Certain musical phrases reminded me of the Jewish music of my early childhood, before the Spanish had invaded Portugal and put an end to it. I suppose both traditions had their roots in the east.

The celebrations of Twelfth Day would be open to all, I was assured. Even foreigners might attend the blessing of the river.

'Curious,' I said to Christopher, as we broke our fast together very early that morning with bread and honey, washed down with small beer. I was glad to see he had lost the pallor brought on by the Tsar's feast.

'Curious?'

'Blessing the river. It does not sound to me like a Christian ceremony.'

'It is believed to be very holy,' Austin said. 'Could you pass the basket of bread, Master Farindon? Afterwards, the water is believed to possess almost magical powers.'

'That is exactly what I mean,' I said. 'I believe, if you could trace its beginnings, it would be seen to have started as a pagan ritual. A sort of appeasement of the local river deity. And the fact that it is held close to the winter solstice – perhaps it is somehow meant to persuade the river to abandon the dark and cold of winter, give up its frozen state and return to life and movement.'

'You may well be right,' Christopher said, 'but take care not to voice such thoughts in public. You would certainly be branded a heretic. Or worse. The ceremony is taken very, very seriously. You will see.'

We left the house before dawn on Twelfth Day, well wrapped up, for it felt colder than ever. I reflected that today was my twenty-first birthday, but I had decided not to speak of it to anyone. Their minds were on other things. Besides, it hardly seemed to have any meaning for me, here in this alien land. As we walked along the street, the steam of our breath froze in the air, and icicles formed in the men's beards, tinkling together like sad bells. Everyone in Moscow, it appeared, was heading for the river, so we simply followed the crowd, which was making for the frozen river immediately below the walls of the Kremlin.

The people standing about on the ice were silent, or speaking only in reverent whispers, and had gathered around a vast square hole in the ice, each side about the length of three tall men. It must have taken immense effort to cut through the ice, which was at least four feet thick. Wooden boards had been laid along each side, while centrally placed on one side was a raised dais on which stood an elaborate gilded throne.

'Is that for the Tsar?' I murmured to Austin.

'Nay, for the Patriarch. In religious matters, he takes precedence even over the Tsar. Job of Staritsa is an ally and protégé of Boris Godunov. He was Metropolitan of Moscow until recently, but he owes his elevation to Godunov.'

This did not surprise me. So this Russian churchman was indebted to the man who held the reins of secular power. 'Is a Metropolitan akin to a bishop?'

'More like an archbishop, but this former Metropolitan has become much more. He is the first Russian to be made a Patriarch. Just two years ago, under persuasion from Godunov, Patriarch Jeremias of Constantinople raised Job to the Patriarchy – that is something akin to a Pope. And considering that Constantinople is now ruled by Islam, Job's position is virtually that of ruler of the Orthodox Church. Quiet now, they are coming.'

I raised my eyes to the walls of the Kremlin on the slope above us and saw that one of the massive gates had been opened, armed guards standing on either side. First to emerge and start down the slope

171

to the frozen Moskva was a young man with an elaborate lantern, followed by more young men, two and two, each carrying aloft a great lighted candle, such as those you may see in Paul's or Westminster Abbey.

It was still dark, although a thin strip of pale grey showed in the eastern sky above the roofs of the town. The lantern and the candles were so bright that they seemed to banish the intrusion of the sun. Immediately behind the candles walked a monk carrying an enormous cross, whose jewels glittered in the light from the flames. It must have been immensely heavy, for it was solid gold, and although the monk who carried it had clearly been chosen for his size and strength, beads of sweat stood out on his forehead, despite the freezing air. Behind the cross, more sweating monks, carrying between them litters on which stood holy images. First, the Virgin, unmistakable with the Christ Child in her arms, dressed in cloth of gold studded with gems. The next saint I recognised as St Nicholas, dearly beloved by the Muscovites, then, one after the other, saints I could not name.

The images were followed by a solemn procession of Orthodox priests, strange to western eyes with their long beards, black or grey, and their odd black tubular hats. The last of the priests was the Patriarch of all the Russias, walking alone. He was an impressive figure, a large man made larger by the wide sweep of his rich robes. Hung from his neck, a jewel-studded pectoral cross of gold almost as long as my forearm. In his hand an ornate staff. Unlike the priests, he wore a white headdress embroidered with gold thread, which hung to his shoulders, somewhat like a lawyer's coif. By his very walk he conveyed power, unlike the shambling figure behind him, a disjointed manikin ill at ease in its stiff bejewelled robes.

I realised with a shock that this must be the Tsar, whose weak neck could barely sustain the weight of the pointed Monomakh's Cap of gold and jewels, the sacred crown of Russia. Behind him walked another, a much more impressive figure, only slightly less gorgeously clad. That, I was sure, must be Boris Godunov. The rest of the procession was made up of men, women, and children as brightly coloured as exotic birds. The Court.

The people of Moscow prostrated themselves there on the frozen river, and to avoid discourtesy, we were obliged to do likewise. When I regained my feet, I saw that the Patriarch was seated on the throne, the Tsar standing on one side, Godunov on the other, while the priests and the Court had arranged themselves on the wooden boards, leaving clear a path for a dozen priests who moved slowly around the hole in the ice, swinging censors and chanting psalms in their ancient form of Russian. The smoke from the censors rose in clouds, scenting the clear, cold air with the unmistakable perfume of burning frankincense. On the far edge of the opening in the ice, facing the Patriarch, the great cross and the litters holding the images had been arranged, surrounded by the candles, growing dim now as the sun crept slowly up the sky.

The Patriarch rose from his throne, stretched out his arms to the river and began to chant. I was too far away to hear the words, but it was clear that he was blessing the Moskva. When he had finished, he stepped down from the dais, leaned forward, and scooped a little of the now holy water in his cupped left hand. With the fingers of his right hand, he flicked a little of it over the Tsar, who had removed the Monomakh's Cap and stood bare headed. Even at this distance I could see that he was shivering, and he flinched as the water fell on him.

There was not enough of this precious water for the Patriarch to sprinkle many. Godunov was blessed, and one or two other grandly dressed men of the Court, and a woman I took to be the Tsarina Irina, sister of Godunov. To my surprise, I saw Godunov lead a little girl to the front, a child perhaps eight or nine years old, and exceptionally beautiful. The Patriarch sprinkled her with the last of the water in his hand. Then lesser priests moved amongst the rest of the Court, those outside the privileged inner circle, sprinkling them with the holy water.

This, it seemed, was the end of the ceremony. The procession formed up once again and made its solemn way back up the snowy bank of the river and disappeared inside the walled Kremlin. The last of the procession had barely passed out of sight when there was a surge of the crowd toward the hole in the ice. Everyone, it seemed, had come with a vessel of some sort which they dipped in the river, so that they might carry home some of this precious holy water, from elegant silver and gold buckets on chains, lowered by portly merchants and their wives, to battered wooden cups which the poor knelt to fill.

To my astonishment, I saw a woman stripping the clothes off a child, until he was stark naked. Then she stepped up to the hole in the ice, holding the naked child under the armpits. Naked, in a cold that would freeze water as it was poured from a jug. A little boy, about five years old. Then she dropped him through the hole into the freezing river.

I lunged forward in horror, but felt both my elbows grabbed from behind.

'Nay!' Pyotr hissed in my ear. 'Do not interfere.'

I tried to shake him off, but he held me fast.

'The child will die!' I spat at him.

'Look, they have him out already.'

He was right. A man, perhaps the child's father, had fished him out of that death trap. The child, too shocked at first to do more than gasp, was wrapped in a blanket and only then began to wail. The parents walked off with him, back towards the bank of the river.

'What are they thinking of? Are they mad?' I was so shocked myself I could hardly speak.

'The waters of the Moskva are holy,' Austin said, 'now that they have been blessed by the Patriarch. Every devout Muscovite believes that they will cure disease, promote health, and prolong life. See?'

He gestured toward the hole in the ice. In my agitation I had turned my back on it. Now I saw that other small children were being thrown into the water, while older children, men, and women were stripping naked and leaping into the water of their own free will. They climbed out quickly, their skin flushed with the sudden cold, their teeth chattering, and wrapped themselves in blankets and furs. One or two invalids were carefully lowered into the river and lifted out again. Down from the Kremlin a procession of grooms led horses from the royal stables to the river, bringing them forward to drink from the hole.

'Even the Tatars recognise the power of holy Moskva,' Pyotr said, pointing.

In front of the dais where the Patriarch's throne stood, a group of priests led naked men to the edge of the ice. The men lowered themselves into the water, and then were pushed down below the surface and held there for a few moments by one of the priests. When they emerged, another priest spoke words I could not hear, before making the sign of the cross over each man's head. Then a cloak was thrown round the shuddering victim's shoulders before the next man plunged in. I could only think of them as victims.

'Tatars?' I said. 'Is this some kind of ritual punishment?'

Pyotr gaped at me, then gave a strained smile. 'The Tatars are being baptised into the Christian faith. To undergo the ceremony at the blessing of the Moskva is the most reverent and auspicious time to choose for baptism.'

I could not find the words to answer him. I would never understand these people.

As when we had been at Uglich, I was uncertain of the protocol here. I consulted Austin Foulkes several days after the blessing ceremony.

'A request was sent for an English physician,' I said, 'with some expertise in the treatment of children. That was partly the reason I was chosen for this mission. Or at any rate that was used as an excuse, as cover for the real reason I was sent here. But I *must* pursue the main reason for my coming here. I do not know what I am supposed to do about the child patient at Court. I cannot simply walk into the Kremlin. Nor can I kick my heels here much longer. I am anxious to discover what has happened to Gregory Rocksley and return with you on board this summer's fleet. My enquiries here have proved fruitless. I must move on. What am I to do?'

'I am afraid you must await summons from the Court,' he said. 'And you will not be granted permission to leave Moscow until you have treated the child, if your attendance is still required. Much of our time in this country is spent waiting about for the wheels of officialdom to grind slowly on their way.'

'You still think my skills are required?'

'Christopher Holme mentioned to one of the Court officials that you had arrived in Moscow, accompanying him from St Nicholas. Word will have been passed along the chain of officials to whomsoever it concerns. Do you know who the child is?'

I shook my head. 'One time I was told a child of the Court, at another, a child of the royal family. But I know now that the only child of the royal family is the Tsarevich. Originally I expected to find him in Moscow also, not in Uglich.'

'A child of the royal family?' He rubbed his head. 'I wonder. The daughter of Boris Godunov might be described thus. The Tsar is, after all, her uncle by marriage. The little girl Xenia Borisovna Godunova. You saw her at the blessing of the Moskva.'

'The only child the Patriarch sprinkled with the river water?'

'With the *holy* river water.' He smiled. 'Aye, that is the child. She is lovely, is she not?'

'Very.' Like the mother of her *soi disant* cousin Dmitri, I thought. There were some true beauties in this ravaged and violent family. Dmitri himself had a fragile beauty. My spirits rose a little. If it was Xenia I was to physic, there should be no problem in passing to her the package entrusted to me.

'In the meantime,' he said, 'one of my stipendiaries who has been on a trading mission to Nizhnii Novgorod arrived back late last night. Alexander Wingrave. He travels regularly with goods to that town, and while Gregory Rocksley was here last year they became quite friendly. I believe they even travelled part of the way south

175

together, for a day or two, when Rocksley set out for Astrakhan. I think if you are to learn anything useful while you are here, it will be from Wingrave.'

Alexander Wingrave slept late, exhausted, it seemed from his journey, after a successful mission to this town whose name I had never heard before. I was impatient to speak to him, but of course he knew nothing of that. When he finally rose he was occupied with Austin Foulkes and Christopher Holme, going through the paperwork and checking the goods he had brought back with him – fine goods from the orient, it appeared, which had come through Persia during a rare period of settled peace between the constant flare ups of war in the southeast. Silks, spices, and gems, all goods of high value, which occupied little space, and so were doubly welcome.

The three of them emerged just in time for our midday dinner looking pleased with their accounting, so I was forced to wait in increasing impatience until the meal was finished. We had been introduced briefly at its start, but I judged from his manner that Wingrave had not been told of my interest in finding Rocksley.

'May I have a word with you, Master Wingrave?' I said, as we rose from the table. I felt we had been sitting over the remnants of the meal far too long. 'In private?'

He raised his eyebrows, looking a little put out. A man well into his thirties, he seemed somewhat old to be a stipendiary, but I suspected, from the way he had talked up the success of his trading trip, that he was hoping for promotion to agent soon.

Christopher Holme came to my support.

'Dr Alvarez is here not only in his capacity as a physician,' he explained. 'He has been sent by the governor himself to discover what happened to Gregory Rocksley.'

I saw the flash of surprise in Wingrave's eyes. He must be wondering why a young physician should be considered suitable for such a mission. I was accustomed to this reaction from men of his type – self assured, perhaps a little too pleased with their own superiority over others.

'Dr Alvarez also worked for the late Sir Francis Walsingham,' Christopher continued. I realised he had made the same assessment of the man Wingrave as I had. 'He has served on delicate missions not only in England but in the Low Countries and Portugal. It was at the Twelfth Night Revels in Whitehall Palace last year that he personally thwarted an attempt to assassinate the Queen. You would do well not to underestimate him.'

Wingrave flushed, and had the grace to look embarrassed. For myself, I was taken aback. I had never spoken to Christopher of the events at Whitehall. Perhaps he had been told more about me than I realised.

'Use the office,' Austin Foulkes said. 'We have finished with your documents for now, Wingrave.'

We walked back to the small office together. It was tucked between two of the larger rooms, which were used when goods like bolts of fine English cloth would be spread out to be inspected by Muscovy merchants wishing to purchase. There was a small fireplace in the office, of English design, with a comfortable fire burning in it, and the walls were covered with shelves and pigeonholes for account books – dozens of them – and scrolls containing sales and purchase documents, inventories of goods, trading agreements with local merchants, and all the other clutter which accumulates in a large mercantile concern.

Wingrave and I pulled up chairs to the fire.

'What is it you want to know?' he said.

'Everything you can tell me about Gregory Rocksley when he was here. Particularly anything he may have said when he returned unexpectedly from Narva, why he decided to go south to Astrakhan, what he spoke of when you travelled together. You may have been the last person to see him alive.'

He looked uncomfortable at this stark assessment.

'Hardly, I think. His interpreter was still with him.'

'His interpreter has also disappeared. Incidentally, no one has ever mentioned his name to me.'

'Ivan Petrovich . . . I can't recall his surname. John, son of Peter. That's the name of every second man in Muscovy.'

His tone was patronising, but it would be a waste of time and this single opportunity if I allowed my annoyance to show.

'Master Foulkes said you became quite friendly with Rocksley. Did he tell you why he was here?'

'Oh, I soon guessed that. He was posing as a stipendiary sent from London, and certainly he was a competent accountant, but I was not taken in.'

'What do you mean?'

'New stipendiaries do not travel about the country from one town to another, or go off into disputed lands, on their own except for an interpreter, without goods to buy or sell. A new stipendiary is allocated to one Company house, under one agent, until he has been trained up. Besides, he was too old, well past thirty.'

I knew that Rocksley was thirty five. It had not occurred to me that his age might make people suspicious of him.

'What do you suppose he was doing here, then?'

'What do men sent out from London usually do? Examine the books, look for fraud or private dealing on the part of some employee.'

'I was told, before I left London, that the shareholders turn a blind eye to petty trading. Do you suppose there might have been major fraud?'

He shook his head. 'Only by Jerome Horsey. He even tries to cheat the Tsar, but Godunov is after him. Everyone knows about Horsey.'

'So you thought he was here to investigate some other instance of fraud?'

'That was what I thought when he first arrived in Moscow. He stayed for some weeks and we got to know each other. Pleasant enough fellow, though a little dull. A little nondescript.'

He smoothed down his own doublet, which was made of plum coloured velvet with mustard satin slashings. I smiled inwardly. Gregory Rocksley would be like Nick Berden, one of Walsingham's agents of the same age and experience, a man I knew well. He would certainly be practised in blending with the background, never drawing attention to himself, the sort of man you would forget was near you in an inn parlour or a busy street.

'That was what you thought when he first arrived,' I prompted. 'But afterwards?'

'Well, for one thing, there was his trip to Narva. I mean, the town fell to Sweden nine or ten years ago, and Muscovy wants it back. War is always brewing along those borderlands, and at that moment it was about the break out. We all knew that. He had no business going there.'

I knew that a visit to Narva was exactly Rocksley's business. It was unfortunate that he was overtaken by other events. I was unsure whether he had returned from Narva before or after full scale war had overwhelmed the area, so I asked Wingrave.

'He was back in Moscow just in time, before the fighting started, but his whole manner had changed. I was quite curious about it.'

This man's manner was so indolent, I wondered what it would take to really rouse him to action.

'In what way had his manner changed? When he came back from Narva?'

He frowned, as though he had never tried to put it into words before. 'He was preoccupied. He was always reticent, but now he seemed . . . worried. Perhaps almost fearful. When he was here in Moscow before, that first visit, he talked about going north after his trip to Narva, to rejoin the fleet at St Nicholas and return to London. That was another thing that marked him out as *not* being a genuine stipendiary, who would have been here for at least three years.' He looked pleased with himself for working this out. 'We had not expected him to return to Moscow.'

'Did he say anything to you, or to Master Foulkes, to indicate why he was worried?'

'Master Foulkes was not here at the time. It is part of the chief agent's duties to make the rounds of the other Company houses every few months. Keep the provincial centres on their toes,' he added, with the superior air of the man at the centre of affairs.

It was the kind of remark you heard in London, about the remoter counties of England. It was proving tedious trying to extract information from this fellow. I did not think he was being deliberately obstructive, he simply did not care very much, and was not a very observant witness.

'So,' I said, hoping that by summing up I might focus his mind. 'Rocksley had travelled around the Company houses, looking at the accounts and asking questions. You thought he was not a normal stipendiary, but someone sent by the London office to investigate fraud. Such a person was not unknown, and you accepted that. Then, inexplicably, he went off to Narva, which is no longer in Russian hands and no longer has a Company house. He returned hastily and seemed worried, even afraid. You say Master Foulkes was not here. You did not say whether he confided in you.'

I knew I was becoming somewhat sharp with him, but I felt that at last I might be hearing a faint echo of what might have happened to Rocksley.

'I would not say he confided,' he admitted. 'But he said he did not want anyone in the Muscovy government to know that he was with us here. He never went out, but mostly stayed in his room, writing despatches.'

Ah, so he *had* written despatches.

'And?' I prompted.

'He did say one odd thing. He said that we should not trust too much to the belief that Godunov had made his peace with England. Godunov had "other irons in the fire", in his words. Rocksley was heading south to secure some clinching evidence. I remember him saying that: "clinching evidence". I thought it rather melodramatic.'

'How long did he stay on his second visit to Moscow?'

'Just two days. I was about to head south myself, to Nizhnii Novgorod. I have some excellent contacts there.' That patronising tone again. 'We decided to travel the first part of the way together. Then I headed further east, and he went south, in the direction of Astrakhan. I do not know if he ever reached it.'

'And those despatches he wrote?' A sudden hope flared in my mind that they might still be here, in which case I would be able to learn what it was that Rocksley had discovered in Narva, and what were his suspicions of Godunov. They would be in code, but that would not be a problem. He would use one of our regular ones, and I had them off by heart.

'Oh, the despatches went in the satchel with other business papers. We send them regularly up to St Nicholas to await the fleet. If there is some matter which is exceptionally urgent, we will sometimes send it overland, but that is risky and generally means that a messenger has to ride through Poland.'

'This batch of documents was not sent that way?' Confiscated, I thought, at the border.

'Nay, there was nothing urgent. Come to think of it, that might have been the satchel that met with an accident. I only heard about it went I arrived back from Nizhnii Novgorod. The clerks were complaining at having to copy all the business documents out again.'

'What kind of accident?' I felt a tightening in my stomach. I knew this was important.

'The messenger had a fall from his horse before he reached Yaroslavl,' he said. 'By the time our people recovered his body, the satchel was gone. These Muscovites will steal anything they can lay their hands on.'

'His *body*!'

'Nasty business. Someone had strung a rope across the road. Caught him right across the throat. Probably killed him even before he hit the ground. The whole country is swarming with outlaws – these peasants who won't pay their taxes. Steal anything, they will. Kill you for the shirt off your back.'

'Had they stolen anything else, besides the satchel?'

I held my breath.

'Nay,' he said thoughtfully. 'Come to think of it, they hadn't.'

At last! I thought. Despite the difficulty of extracting anything useful from Alexander Wingrave, a number of very important facts had emerged. Sitting on the bed in my room, I went through them in my mind, trying to put an ordered narrative together.

Rocksley had expected to track down in Narva the rogue former employee of the Company who had passed compromising information about England to the Spanish. He would then join the Company fleet and return to London, to report on his findings.

Instead, he had learned something there concerning Godunov. Treachery by Godunov. Which had sent him hurrying back to Moscow, where he was not expected.

While staying in Moscow for just two days, he had kept out of sight, writing long despatches for London.

He had then left for the south in company with Wingrave, parting with him when their routes diverged. He had not been seen since.

In the meantime, the despatches had been sent north, but before the messenger could even reach Yaroslavl, he had been ambushed and murdered. Not by outlaws, who would have stolen his clothes and money, but by someone who was only interested in the contents of the satchel. The ordinary business reports travelled safely all the time, therefore it was known that, on this occasion, the satchel contained incriminating documents by Rocksley. *Ergo*, Godunov knew that Rocksley suspected him of treachery to Muscovy's ally England and had sent someone to steal the despatches.

What was not clear was how Godunov had gained the information. Either an agent of his in Narva had sent word to the Kremlin, or else Rocksley had been followed back to Moscow. It would have been easy to deduce that the next posting of documents by messenger to the St Nicholas house would contain despatches from Rocksley.

However, what was abundantly clear was that Rocksley had been a marked man from that moment on. It was unlikely that he was still alive.

What should I do?

I could return north with Austin Foulkes and report my discoveries to the Company governor back in London. Once I was given permission to leave Moscow, of course. That was the safest course, the sensible one. But a nagging doubt troubled me. What if Rocksley were not dead?

And besides, I still did not know *why* he had set out for Astrakhan. The explanation would have been in those despatches. I fervently hoped that Godunov did not have any skilled code-breakers at his command. Thomas Phelippes's codes – which Rocksley would have used – were complex and sophisticated, difficult for anyone to break, particularly a foreigner with poor English. I had not encountered any English speakers amongst the Muscovites so far, but that did not mean that the Kremlin had none.

I hoped Rocksley had memorised the codes, and did not carry the keys with him. If he did, and he had been caught, even a Russian with poor English would be able to decipher the despatches.

The day grew dark as I sat there, chewing my thumb nail.

Astrakhan lay on the shores of the Caspian Sea. Did that mean that Godunov was sending out information via that route, and the papers captured on the Spanish ship out of Narva were the exception? Nay, I thought of something else. Perhaps Godunov had originally used Narva, a convenient direct route to the west and formerly Russian controlled, to send out messages before the latest outbreak of war with the Swedes. It was likely that some Muscovites had remained in Narva, just as some former Company men had done.

Once the war had started – and it had been foreseen – he had switched to a route via the Caspian. Further to go, a complicated route. *That* was why Rocksley had gone there, to root out this new source of harm to England.

I would have to follow him, whether he was dead or alive.

Chapter Ten

 $\mathcal{M}$ y meditations were interrupted by hurried footsteps in the corridor outside and a knock on the door.

'Come.' I said.

It was one of the menservants, breathless and alarmed.

'It is a summons from the Kremlin, Dr Alvarez,' he said. 'You are to go immediately. Konyushy Godunov has sent for you.'

I felt sick. The man was all powerful in Muscovy. Surely he could not also read my thoughts?

'Konyushy?' I said. 'What does that mean? I have not heard the word before.'

'It's a title newly given him,' the servant said. 'Last year. After he saw off a raiding army of Tatars. I don't rightly know what it means myself, but it's better than "boyar". Next best after "tsar", I'd say.'

'He wants me *now*? But it is dark. Do you know why?'

'The palace messenger didn't say, doctor. And we don't ask questions. If Godunov says, "Jump!" we jump. Don't matter if it's dark. Wouldn't matter if 'twas midnight, you'd still have to go.'

'He probably wants my services as a physician,' I said, trying to sound calm, to reassure myself as much as him. 'Can you tell Master Aubery? I shall need an interpreter.'

He nodded and scuttled off.

Of course I was merely needed as a physician, wasn't I? If the royal child who required medical care was indeed his daughter, it was not strange that Godunov himself should be the one to send for me. He clearly treasured his daughter. He had brought her to stand beside the Tsar and the Patriarch at the blessing of the river.

I began to check through my satchel of medicines, relieved that I had persuaded Pyotr to take me to the best apothecary in Moscow to replenish my supplies. I hoped I had everything I needed.

183

When I set off about a quarter of an hour later, I was accompanied not only by Pyotr and the messenger from the palace, but a Company servant with a flambeau and four armed guards. Master Foulkes would not allow us to walk unescorted through the dark streets to the palace.

'You and Pyotr must leave your weapons behind,' he told us. 'If you try to carry a concealed weapon into the Kremlin, you will be strung up by your heels.'

So Pyotr and I both handed over our swords and daggers to him.

'But what of my surgical knives?' I said. 'I may need them. I have not been told why I am summoned.'

Austin Foulkes turned to the messenger and spoke to him rapidly in Russian. He had told me he could not read the language, except for the terms used repeatedly in business contracts, but he was remarkably fluent in the spoken tongue.

'I have explained to the messenger that you must take your medical equipment with you,' he said. 'He says that he will carry your satchel for you, and make clear the need for it to the guards at the gates.'

I had understood the messenger's reply, so with great reluctance I handed over my satchel. In normal circumstances I never let anyone else touch it, but these were hardly normal circumstances. I would watch the man every step of the way, and if it looked as though he was going to make off with it, or damage it in any way, I would snatch it back and face the consequences.

Our walk through the frozen streets of Moscow was an eerie experience. It was very dark indeed. Even the stars and moon were hidden by heavy cloud, threatening more snow. In London, the better houses and merchants' premises place lanterns or torches at their doors during the hours of darkness, so that, if you keep to the main streets, there is always a little light. Here, no light was set to help the passerby. From time to time we glimpsed a thread of light showing between closed and barred shutters, but the people of Moscow turned their backs on the world at night. I suspected that there was a curfew, rigorously enforced. In London there is a nominal curfew, but honest citizens going openly and briskly about their business are at no risk from the parish constables, who take more interest in those up to no good skulking about the dark alleyways.

On our way to the Kremlin the only living souls we encountered were a few mangy dogs and cats, scavenging in the gutters, and a band of heavily armed soldiers, whom I took to be the Muscovite equivalent of our humble constables. Seeing the royal insignia on the messenger's robe, they bowed and withdrew to the side of the street to let us pass.

As we reached the great wall about the Kremlin, we passed the most beautiful building in Moscow, the church of St Basil, built not long since by the last Tsar. I thought that Ivan Vasilyevich must have been a man compounded of many contradictory elements. His reputation for violence, cruelty, and unpredictable rages was certainly deserved, yet he had a love of music and art, and he had commissioned the building of this church. To my eyes, accustomed to the classical symmetry of the churches of Europe, it was an astonishing jumble of styles and colours, like something a child might make from bits of coloured glass and broken pottery. Yet in spite of this, it was awe-inspiring, especially now, lit up against the night sky with lanterns and torches, whose flames flickered in the wind, awakening ever-moving reflections in the gold which adorned much of the church. From within, came chanting. Like the monks of old, now banished from England, it seemed the priests of the Orthodox church also kept the ecclesiastical hours even during the night.

At the great gate just beyond the church, the messenger spoke to the guards and handed over my satchel. I watched anxiously as they pawed through it, fearful that they would steal or break something. Pyotr stepped forward, ready to intervene, but he was pushed roughly away.

'What is this?' One of the guards held up a pot of wound balm.

I answered in English, and Pyotr translated.

'And this? And this?'

It seemed I was going to be required to account for every pot and phial. In exasperation, I spoke slowly in my careful Russian.

'The Konyushy Godunov has sent for me,' I said clearly. 'Do you wish to keep him waiting until dawn?'

They looked at each other in alarm, then bundled everything back into my satchel and thrust it at me.

Our own guards were required to remain in the gatehouse, so Pyotr and I went on alone with the messenger.

There was no time to linger, however, for the messenger was hurrying us along a narrow street which opened into a sort of square – except that it was not square – enclosed by several important buildings. Pyotr had confided in me before we set out that he had never been inside the Kremlin, but he understood that there were several royal palaces, together with private homes for the most distinguished courtiers. As we were led across the square to the largest house, I guessed that this must be the home of Boris Godunov and his family.

We were shown in at once and hurried up a staircase to the first floor. A door opened and a large man emerged, the man I had seen walking behind the Tsar on Twelfth Day. He was not quite so grandly dressed now, but the value of his garments would have fed a respectable English burgher's family for a lifetime.

I took my cue from Pyotr. We did not prostrate ourselves. This man was not Tsar. Yet. Whatever his ambitions. Instead we removed our caps and bowed low, as we would have done for one of the great courtiers at home. It seemed that this was acceptable, for he gave us a quick nod of acknowledgement, then spoke rapidly in Russian to Pyotr.

'The Konyushy Godunov says that his daughter is in great pain,' Pyotr translated into English, although I had understood what had been said. 'She suffers from a serious rash which none of the resident doctors have been able to cure.' Pyotr was speaking quickly. We could both see that the man was in a hurry.

'He begs that you do what you can for his little flower, to relieve her distress. Unfortunately he has been summoned by the Tsar, but he has left instructions that whatever you need shall be provided.'

There was a further hasty exchange of bows, then the Konyushy was hurrying, almost running, toward the staircase. Interesting, I thought. Everyone says he is the most powerful man in Russia, but even he fears that bent little manikin. I suppose the Tsar is so fickle he could even turn against the man who holds this vast, unwieldy country together. Have him executed, even. It happens, it happens. Did not our Queen's father destroy the man who held England together? His chief minister, Cromwell? And regretted it all his life after. Heaven spare me from the company of the world's tyrants. My present position was far too close for comfort.

We entered the room Godunov had just left, while the messenger waited outside. It was extremely hot, so hot that I began to sweat inside my heavy outdoor clothes. It was a large room, overly ornate in the same style as the royal rooms at Uglich. Clearly Godunov did not see the need to be any less ostentatious than the Tsar's family.

I could not see the child at first.

An elegantly dressed lady stood near the stove which was heating the room. Another vast stove tiled in the Dutch manner, like the ones I had seen at Uglich.

'Is that the mother?' I whispered to Pyotr, trying not to move my lips.

A barely perceptible shake of the head. 'Lady-in-waiting.'

The other woman, elderly, and neatly but plainly dressed, would be a body servant. Probably a former nurse, like the one who attended Dmitri. Both children were too old for a nurse, but perhaps they clung to them as a comforting presence in the turbulent waters of their intertwined families.

Then I realised that the crown of pale gold hair I could just see above the back of a low chair must be the child's. They had placed her very close to the stove. I walked toward the little group of three. The lady-in-waiting spoke to Pyotr in Russian, and he answered.

'She asks which of us is the physician,' he murmured to me, maintaining the pretence that I could not understand. 'I have explained. She says I am to stand behind that screen to translate for you. The lady is not to be seen naked by any but the physician.'

I nodded. It was not unreasonable. I walked round to the front of the chair as Pyotr stepped behind the screen, placed to protect the child from drafts which might slip through the doorway, though given the heat in the room they might have been welcome.

Nature had given the child great beauty, but it was marred now. Her face was fiery red, her eyes were swollen with weeping, and tears continue to roll down her cheeks, although she made no sound. Like Maria Nagaya, this was another who had learned stoicism. Only her hands gave her away, clenched in her lap. As I laid aside my heavy cloak, fur hat, and wolf skin mittens, she fixed on me eyes that were full of pleading, but she did not speak. I addressed her quietly in careful Russian.

'I am sorry to hear that you are ill, my lady.'

I was unsure what mode of address to use, whether I should address her as 'Majesty', though clearly she was not. It seemed, however, that 'my lady' was appropriate.

'I thank you for coming, doctor.' She spoke hesitantly, as if she was not sure whether I would understand her, but we would manage very well, without needing Pyotr to interpret, which was much more satisfactory.

I laid my hand, still cold from the walk through the dark streets, on her forehead. It was burning, but whether from the heat of the stove or from fever, I was not yet sure.

'That feels good.' She made a brave attempt at a smile. 'They make me sit by the stove, but I am so *hot*!. They say it will make me better, but it just makes me worse.'

It was unsurprising that she was hot. In this stuffy, claustrophobic room she was dressed in layers of wool, velvet, and stiff cloth of gold, with a tight, high collar, even fine woollen gloves on her hands.

'Tell me how you are ill,' I said, pulling out a stool and sitting on it uninvited, thus obliging the lady-in-waiting to move further away. I raised my voice and spoke to Pyotr in English.

'Order the women to wait at the far side of the room. I need privacy with my patient.'

The women went, slowly and grumbling, but they went.

'It is an old trouble,' the child said, in answer to my question. 'I think I have had it all my life. I have this rash, and it *itches*! And it *hurts*! Oh, doctor, it itches so much I can hardly bear it.'

'Where does it itch? Show me.'

She pointed to her elbows and wrists, and behind her knees.

'And here,' she said, tugging frantically at the tight collar.

'Ask them,' I called to Pyotr in English, 'why she is so heavily, so tightly dressed.'

There was a brief exchange with the waiting woman.

'They say that it is to keep the miasma of the bad air away from the child's skin. The woman says they have done their best. The child is thoroughly washed and scrubbed every morning before she is dressed.'

'Tell them she must be undressed, so that I can examine her.'

The nurse came and began removing the layers of clothing. There were even more than I had expected. I would have liked to move Xenia away from the fierce heat of the stove, but feared the shock of the drop in temperature.

Finally she stood before me in nothing but her fine woollen shift, her eyes cast down in shame. At the sight of her, I nearly rounded on the women in fury, but managed to bite back the words I would have liked to shout at them. The little girl's arms and legs were tightly bandaged. Another bandage was wrapped round her neck, but from below the edge of it an angry rash was creeping down to her chest.

'Remove the bandages,' I said.

The nurse looked from me across the room to the waiting woman, who shrugged, and then nodded. As the nurse began to unwind one of the leg bandages, Xenia closed her eyes and bit down on her lips.

'Wait!' I said, in English. Then, 'Nyet!' I laid my hand on the nurse's arm to stop her. 'Bring water,' I said in Russian.

188

For I had seen that blood and pus had soaked through the bandages and hardened to a crust. Unwinding the bandages would rip the scabbing off the raw flesh underneath.

'What have they been doing to you, my poor pet?' I muttered to myself, but in English.

It took a long time, soaking each bandage until it was wet enough to remove with as little pain to Xenia as possible, but she must have suffered terribly. All the while, she endured almost in silence, with just an occasional involuntary gasp. Like Dmitri, she too was a valiant soul. Did she endure this every morning? And they *scrubbed* her? The skin below the bandages was covered with a familiar rash, but one I had never seen in such a terrible state, so raw and bleeding.

I sent the nurse away again.

'The priests say I am afflicted because I am sinful,' she whispered. 'God has caused this so that I may suffer and my soul will be cleansed.'

'I think the priests should keep to their own affairs, in church,' I whispered back, which brought a wan smile. 'This is an affair for a doctor. Now, I am going to wash away all the unpleasant matter. There are threads of cloth stuck to you, and something brown and nasty.'

'That was something Herr Doktor Friedmann gave them, to put on my rash. But it only made it hurt more.' She paused. 'You will not scrub, will you?'

'I promise. I will not scrub.' I stood up. 'Pyotr,' I called, 'go with the nurse and make her bring me a bucket of boiled water. See to it that she does boil it. I want nothing dirty to touch this skin.'

I heard them leave the room, but I did not look up. Instead I sat down on the stool again, and Xenia took the chair.

'It already feels better, without the bandages,' she said.

'There will be no more bandages.'

'You do not think it is because I am sinful?'

'Not at all. It is not unusual, this rash. It is called eczema. Lots of children have it, and it will go away, but not if you are treated like this. It can be caused by different things. Some children cannot wear wool, which means they must always wear a linen undershift. Sometimes your body does not like something you eat, it unbalances your humours and forces the ill matter out through your skin. Many things can cause it.'

When Pyotr and the nurse returned with the bucket of water, he assured me that he had seen it boiled. The nurse rolled up her sleeves and knelt down beside Xenia's chair, clearly expecting to undertake the

189

washing herself. The waiting woman returned from the corner where she had been sitting ever since Xenia's clothes had been removed. She held something out to the nurse, a hard grey lump, but I intercepted it.

'What is this?' I asked Xenia.

She looked puzzled. 'It is soap.'

But what kind of soap? I wondered. It was rough to the touch. I held it close to a lamp and saw that sand had been incorporated into the mixture when it was made. No doubt excellent for scrubbing a filthy floor, but not for use on any child's skin, certainly not one in this state. The soap was harsh, as though there was a high proportion of lye in it. In irritation I flung the thing across the room, where it skidded to a halt at the feet of the waiting woman.

'Have you been using this on the child's skin?' I rounded on her. 'You would be better employed in a torture chamber than in a little's girl's care.'

She glared at me, and I realised I should have been more tactful, but I was very angry. I jerked my head to send the nurse away.

'See now,' I said to Xenia. I had dropped the 'my lady', for it seemed we were now allies against her tormenters. I reached into my satchel and searched until I found a tied bunch of a dried herb and drew a few sprigs from it.

'This is a herb called soapwort. Country people use it. Smell. It is dry now, but there is some scent left.'

She leaned forward and sniffed. 'It smells sweet.'

'It does. Watch.'

I dropped the herb into the water which was warm now, not too hot, and swished it about with my hand. A soapy froth formed on the surface.

'Now, this is what we will use to wash your rash, and you shall help me. Then you can stop if it hurts.'

She was fascinated. I do not suppose she had ever washed herself before. Between us we gradually washed first her legs, then her arms, and finally I sponged very gently round her neck. As each section was finished, I dried it gently with a linen towel.

'Oh,' she cried, the tears gone, gently wiped away, 'oh, I feel so much better already. Am I cured?'

'Not yet. Your skin must heal. Then you will be cured.'

I fervently hoped this was true. It was the worst case of eczema I had ever seen. Not even amongst the paupers of Southwark had a child's rash been treated like this. I blamed the appalling soap, the bandaging, and probably the tight, hot woollen clothing, but there might also be something in her diet, which would be more difficult to track down. In the places where the rash had broken into a raw wound I gently applied a little soothing cream, but elsewhere I left the skin simply open to the air.

When we were about halfway through the washing, I told Pyotr to order the nurse to find a linen shift for Xenia, which, after much grumbling, she did. Now I replaced the woollen shift with the linen.

'Now, my pet,' I said. 'This is what you must do. You are a clever girl, and you need to understand yourself what is best for you. From now on, you must wear no more wool. Only linen or silk. And no heavy, tight clothes at all until the rash is healed. You understand?'

She nodded.

'No more of that terrible grey soap. I will arrange for an apothecary to supply soapwort, and that is what you must use to wash. Do you think you can do that yourself?'

She nodded again. Her eyes were shining. 'But what of them?' She barely nodded in the direction of the waiting woman and the nurse, who had both retired to the far side of the room and were holding a muttered conversation.

'I will ask my friend Pyotr Ivanovich to write all my instructions down in Russian. They will be delivered to your father, and he will see that they are carried out.' I stretched and yawned. 'It must be nearly morning. We have been up all night!'

I glanced over my shoulder at the two women, then reached into the breast of my doublet and drew out Dmitri's packet, standing so that I blocked their view.

'This is for you,' I said, as I pressed it into her hands. 'From your cousin Dmitri.'

'You have seen Dmitri?' She almost jumped off her chair, but I laid my finger to my lips.

'I will come back the day after tomorrow, to see how well the rash is healing,' I said. 'We will talk then.'

Suddenly she threw her arms around me and clung. 'Thank you,' she whispered. 'Thank you for making me better, and bringing Dmitri's present.'

For a moment I was afraid I would weep. These children, these poor children.

'Till the day after tomorrow,' I said, giving her a quick hug. 'Let the air get to your skin. There is no miasma here that can hurt you.'

Only people, I thought. Only people.

The following day I wrote out a schedule for Xenia's care, explaining in precise detail exactly what was and what was not to be done in the treatment of the rash and in her clothing. She was also not to be exposed to excessive heat. Moreover, her diet was to be watched carefully. If eating any particular food caused the rash to flare up again, that food was to be omitted altogether in future. I recommended that she should be given *boiled* water to drink several times a day. I underlined 'boiled' twice. No one else was to touch the rash. The lady Xenia Borisovna herself understood how to wash the affected skin with boiled water and soapwort. I would arrange for soapwort to be supplied.

Pyotr read my instructions through with a barely suppressed smile. 'You sound very fierce. I hope the Konyushy may not be offended.'

I glared at him. 'You did not see what they had done to that child. She might have been flayed. It was an abomination. Besides,' I added, more mildly, 'I suspect the Konyushy will appreciate frank guidance. For all his faults, I think he loves the little maid. Is she his only child?'

'There is a small boy, not yet two.'

'Well, I pray that he may not suffer the same treatment. If he develops eczema, which he may, for it can occur in families, then I may have saved him similar agony before it can be inflicted on him. Xenia is so brave.'

'I will translate this into Russian,' he said, 'then write it out fair. Will you sign it?'

'Aye, and seal it. When you are done, we will visit the apothecary.'

The apothecary was only too pleased to receive the order for a regular supply of soapwort to be sent to the Godunov household. I saw no reason to spare the Konyushy's coin, so I made it a generous order. The apothecary beamed. It would be a lucrative source of income for him.

Pyotr translated, for I feared I might make a mistake in my instructions if I spoke Russian. 'He thanks you, and says he will supply the dried plant for now, but once the soapwort grows again in spring, he will provide the new growth.'

'Either will do,' I said. 'Remind him he can also make an extract from the roots. I do not know whether they make it here in Muscovy.'

Even without Pyotr's translation I could tell from the apothecary's bows and smiles and eager rubbing together of his hands that he would retire to his back room and his equipment before the day was out, with a pile of soapwort roots.

As we walked back to the Company house, it was beginning to snow again. Pyotr looked at me sideways and laughed.

'I suspect the fellow will be selling extract of soapwort for high prices in future, "recommended by the English physician to cure all manner of skin diseases". Your fame will be ensured.'

I grinned. 'Perhaps. As long as he does not claim it is a cure for the plague. It is nothing but a mild form of soap. I should be lynched if ever I returned to Moscow.'

We began to hurry, for the snow was falling more thickly.

'When do you think we will be able to leave for the south?' Pyotr's voice was muffled by the fur collar of his cloak, which he had pulled up to cover the lower part of his face.

'I hope that, once I can certify that Xenia's eczema is on the mend, they will let us go. I am anxious to pursue the search for Gregory Rocksley, now that I have a little more to go on.'

'Good. Further south it may not be quite so cold.'

I had lost track of the date. The winter here seemed to go on for ever. Was it about the middle of February?

'When does spring come in this country?

'Not for some time yet,' he said. 'April, perhaps, brings the first hint? It depends on how severe the winter has been. By May most of the snow will be gone.'

'Dear God! How can people live in such a country?'

'We are a sturdy people,' he said stiffly.

I must be careful. He was in one of his Russian moods.

The following day we returned to the Kremlin by daylight, and were admitted more courteously this time. Word must have been left at the gates. Once we reached the Godunov house, I insisted on seeing the Konyushy's private secretary. He proved to be a harassed man with a stoop and grey hair. I explained, through Pyotr, that these were the medical notes and instructions for the care of the lady Xenia Borisovna. They were to be given to the Konyushy, and *no one else*. I tapped his desk sharply with my fingernail, to make sure he paid heed.

He promised fervently to give the document into no one's hands but the Konyushy's, and rang a small bell on his desk for a servant to conduct us to Xenia's apartments.

I was glad to find that the stove had been damped down somewhat, so the room was warm but not unbearably hot. The shutters were open and the windows, I noticed, were glazed with mica, which allowed a thin winter sunshine to enter. It showed up the expensive clutter crowding the room. As I had seen at Uglich, there was much effort at rich, even vulgar, ostentation, but rather less effort was directed at combating the inevitable dust. This would not be good for my patient. I gave orders that many of the useless objects should be removed. The lady Xenia Borisovna should decide which ones, and then everything was to be given a thorough clean.

'You may make use of that grey soap,' I said, pointing, 'to scrub the floor.'

It still lay where I had thrown it two days before. Which spoke volumes about the cleaning carried out here.

There were more attendants present this time, putting an end to any hope of much frank conversation with Xenia, but I took her behind the screen, where I could examine her in private. She was wearing a loose gown of silk with full sleeves. The neck was low cut, so I was able to see that the rash on her neck was already beginning to dry up.

'And how are you feeling today, my lady?' I thought we should revert to the formal mode of address now, by day, with so many pricked ears on the other side of the screen.

'I am much, much better, thanks to you, Dr Alvarez.' She spoke in a clear, loud voice, intended to be heard by those listening ears.

Then she whispered, 'Dmitri says you are called Kit? May I call you Kit.'

'Certainly you may, Xenia.' We smiled at each other in shared conspiracy.

I examined the other areas of rash, and interspersed my running commentary with whispered information about what I had seen of Dmitri and the wolfhound Volk. The unpleasant lesions were beginning to heal, even on the back of her knees, where they were the worst, probably rubbed by folds in those accursed bandages whenever she bent her legs. Before I left, she drew a small package from the pocket of her gown where it lay over a chair. It was smaller but fatter than the one Dmitri had sent to her. She handed it to me.

'Will you see Dmitri again?' she whispered, as I helped her dress.

'I do not expect to.'

Her face fell.

'But on my way north to St Nicholas, perhaps I could call in at Uglich.' It would add several days to my journey, but I hated to disappoint these children, who seemed to have no other friends.

'It would be very kind,' she said. Her voice was polite, but there was hope in her voice.

'I will do my best,' I promised.

She nodded. 'If you cannot give it to Dmitri, I would like you to keep it for yourself. As a remembrance.'

Twice more, while I was in Moscow, I visited Xenia Borisovna, and by the last visit the rash was nearly gone. The lady-in-waiting who had been present at my first visit was not seen again, something which worried me a little. I was glad she had been dismissed from attending on Xenia, but I hoped that nothing worse had happened to her. No one spoke of these things. The old nurse had become less hostile when she saw that the child was recovering, and remained with her.

At last one of the servants from the Godunov household appeared with a sealed letter and a purse for me. The purse, too, was heavily sealed with wax, bearing Godunov's imprint. It seemed he did not trust his servants not to filch some of the contents. The letter was, naturally, written in Russian, which Pyotr translated.

'The Konyushy thanks you unreservedly for your care of his daughter, who has now been relieved of much suffering. He has received your instructions for the future care of the lady Xenia Borisovna, which he will see are carried out to the letter, and sends a purse in recompense for your services. He also understands that you are required to carry out a mission for the Muscovy Company in his southern territories, and is providing a passport to allow you to travel freely. You may leave as soon as you wish.'

I gave him a sharp look. 'Did you say *his* southern territories? Surely the Tsar's?'

He looked down at the letter, then up again with an enigmatic smile. 'It definitely says "his". He must have been distracted when he dictated the terms of the letter, or else the secretary who wrote it absently mindedly wrote the reality instead of the pretence we all subscribe to. Interesting.'

'It was written by a secretary?'

'Great men do not normally write their own letters. Besides, he is spoken of in the third person.'

He picked up a small sheet of vellum which had been enclosed in the letter and bore a seal at the bottom.

'This is the passport for you, with attendants. That will ease matters for us.'

'Good.'

I had very nearly decided to leave Moscow without permission, if it did not come soon. I picked up the purse and broke the heavy wax seal. There was a great deal of money inside, for which I was grateful. The Russian money provided by Rowland Heyward before I left London and the coins from Uglich were dwindling. I was not sure how much I would need on the further journey and this would be one less thing to worry me.

Now that I had permission at last, I wanted to depart the next day, but neither Austin Foulkes nor Christopher Holme would hear of it. Austin was about to leave Moscow himself, to make his way slowly north. It was March, and for the last part of his journey the snow and ice would have melted too much to allow travel by sleigh. He would either need to journey by boat or on horseback.

'Depending on the weather and the condition of the ground,' he said. 'By the time I reach Kolmogory, it will most probably be boggy again, but we shall see.'

'You need to think of this as well, Kit,' Christopher said. 'You could start out by sleigh, and then, since you will be further south, where the thaw comes earlier, find yourself unable to carry on.'

Pyotr agreed. 'Horseback would be better.'

'I am agreeable,' I said. 'Let us by all means go on horseback.'

'In any case,' Christopher said, tapping Godunov's letter and passport where they lay on the office table between us, 'in any case, you need a letter of authorisation to use the post horses. I will see to it that the government authorities provide one. It may take a few days.'

I groaned. I had learned to know what 'a few days' meant to the bureaucracy of Muscovy. 'Why do we not simply take Company horses and rest them at intervals?'

Once again Pyotr intervened. 'The journey will be made quicker by changing post horses, rather than constantly waiting while our horses recover. You forget how great the distances are in this country.'

'Very well,' I said in a resigned voice, 'tell me how far it is to Astrakhan.'

We all looked at Austin. He was accustomed to dealing with merchants in the south. He would have a better idea than any of us.

'I cannot be certain, not exactly. It will depend on river crossings and how directly you are able to travel, but it must be the best part of a thousand miles.'

I put my head in my hands. Even with fast horses, changing at the posts . . . it could take weeks. And just as long to travel back again.

'Perhaps we will not need to go all the way,' I said, but I said it without much hope.

It was another week before Pyotr and I were able to leave Moscow. By then Austin had started by sleigh on his way to Yaroslavl, taking armed guards with him, after Alexander Wingrave had reminded him of the ambush which had killed the letter carrier on that stretch of road the previous year. Before he left, he insisted that we should also take an armed escort. This was not my intention at all.

'We need to be unobtrusive,' I complained. 'How can we be unobtrusive with an armed guard?'

In the end, we compromised. One of the Company guards would attend us, and would do his best to appear a simple traveller like ourselves. When I met Thomas Edgewick, a huge Yorkshire man with fists like cannon balls and a sword to match, I found it hard to believe he could make himself unobtrusive. His whole appearance shouted 'English soldier!'. However, I had agreed, so I must make the best of it.

The weather was good when we started out from Moscow. The sun had gradually been rising a little sooner and setting a little later every day. Already I was conscious of more daylight, but I insisted we must set out at dawn. I had been growing more and more impatient to begin at long last on the first reasonable search for Gregory Rocksley. Looking back, I wonder whether something more than reason, some blind instinct, prompted me. To begin with, we followed the west bank of the Moskva river, which led us in a south-easterly direction, under a clear sky, and were troubled by very little wind. There had been no more snow since the brief fall on the day Pyotr and I had visited the apothecary. The path we followed was beaten down hard from frequent traffic, for villages and small towns were strung loosely along the bank of the river, like occasional beads on a string.

There was no real sign of spring yet. The river was still hard frozen, hard enough to be used as a winter road. We saw passenger and goods sleighs moving along it in both directions, but it wound a good deal, so we were able to save time over the river traffic by taking short cuts across the neck of some of the loops, where the ground and trees permitted it. For there were trees here too, interspersed between the settlements and the areas cleared for farming, although it was probably never so densely forested as the northern lands we had travelled through.

Our plan was to ride the good Company horses for most of the first day, then leave them at a post station, where they would be collected by the next Company men to pass this way. This was located at a major trading town, where river and road traffic crossed. Like all the Company horses, ours were branded on their left rumps. Woe betide any Muscovite who tried to steal one of them! The animals at the post stations would be a poorer form of horse flesh, but if they were like the other local horses I had seen, they would be sturdy and resilient, if not too fast on their feet. I fancied that our large Yorkshire man would look somewhat incongruous on a small Muscovite horse, but when it came time to change our mounts, he accepted it with equanimity. His feet did not quite touch the ground when he was mounted, but they came near.

We continued like this, changing horses four or five times a day. It was not the way I cared to ride, for how can you get to know your mount in such a short time? In difficult or dangerous circumstances, horse and rider need to understand one another, but there was never time to build up this trust. I could only hope that such difficult or dangerous circumstances would not arise.

At last we reached the confluence of the Moskva with the Oka river, where we were obliged to take a ferry across to the far side. We now left the water ways behind and headed across a thinly inhabited region. There was a clearly marked road – more of a track, in truth – which headed east, rather than south. It was still early morning after we had crossed the river, and the sun shone painfully into our eyes as it rose.

'Can this be right?' I said. 'Should we not turn more to the south?'

None of us had been this way before, but Pyotr had received directions from Alexander Wingrave before we left.

'Aye, this is the way,' Pyotr said. 'According to Wingrave, we carry on along this road for about a day's ride, then we come to a fork in the road at a large village. That was where he and Rocksley parted company, Wingrave continuing along this road, while Rocksley with his interpreter took the southern branch.'

The directions appeared to be correct, for we reached the village about nightfall and decided to spend the night at the post station, which had a room with benches where we could sleep. The village was not much of a place, but clearly the flow of travellers provided a good living for the post station.

Before we set off the next morning, Thomas Edgewick asked if he might have a word with me. Considering that he hardly ever opened his mouth, this was unusual. Pyotr had gone to see about horses for the next stage, and Thomas beckoned me outside, with one of his huge fingers. Mystified, I picked up my knapsack and satchel and followed him.

We strolled along the mean street, where the snow was already turning to filthy slush, until we were well away from the post station.

'We'm being followed,' he said bluntly.

'What?' I was so startled I forgot all my training and nearly looked round, but he grabbed me by the elbow and propelled me further along the street.

'Not now,' he muttered in irritation. 'Ever since we crossed the river.'

'Are you sure? There must be plenty of travellers along these roads, especially now that it isn't so cold.' I was ashamed that I had noticed nothing. What would Nick Berden have thought of me? I must be growing careless.

'Aye, I'm sure,' he said flatly. It was his very lack of emotion that convinced me. He was, after all, an experienced soldier and knew this country and its people tolerably well, for he had served here for five years.

'What are they like?'

'Two men I seen so far. Big men, carrying weapons. Swords and crossbows. Not footpads or outlaws. These lads are soldiers, they know how to track and keep out of sight, but some of this last way has been open and flat. Nowhere for them to dodge, see? That's when I seen 'em clear. Could be, they bin following us since Moscow.'

Involuntarily, I shivered.

'But why?'

'I a'nt asked any questions, master, but this fellow Rocksley you're trying to find, was he in trouble?'

'I don't know for sure. He may have been. He may have discovered something. Something someone was trying to hide.'

'Like someone from the Court?'

'Aye.'

'Like maybe that fellow Godunov?'

There was clearly more to Thomas than I had allowed for.

'It's a possibility,' I admitted. I might as well be honest with the man. I might need to depend on him. 'Rocksley was investigating the leaking of secret information about England through Narva, but he came back from Narva and hurried off this way, possibly suspecting information was now being channelled through Astrakhan and the Caspian Sea. Somewhere along this road, he seems to have disappeared. He was last seen in this village, when he and his interpreter parted from Master Wingrave.'

Thomas sucked his breath in. 'Sounds like a nasty business. How do you think you can do anything about it?'

I had to admit what had been in my mind from the start.

'I think it's likely Rocksley is dead. If so, I want to confirm it. Also, if I can, I want to discover what he had found out, but that is not hopeful, if he *is* dead. On the other hand, there is a very slim chance that he is alive.'

'If he's alive,' Thomas said reasonably, 'why a'nt he turned up?'

'Because he can't,' I said quietly.

'Because he's in prison somewhere.'

'Aye.'

'Well,' he said briskly, 'those lads following us think we know something, or they wouldn't be troubling us. If the man is dead, why would they bother?'

It was a good point.

'You think he's alive, and they believe we know where he is?' I said.

'Stands to reason.'

Suddenly, I felt a mixture of hope and fear. Thomas was right. Why would they bother? If they had been sent after us, they thought we knew where to find Rocksley and would try to stop us. It seemed more and more likely that he *was* alive. Why they would keep him alive, I was not sure, but time to think about that later.

'I wonder whether Godunov is behind this,' I said.

'Sly piece of work, he is, but more use than that freak of a Tsar. Still,' he looked at me thoughtfully, 'just cured his daughter, haven't you?'

'Aye.' I smiled grimly. 'I think that counts for little with a man like Godunov. He would use my skills, pay me off, then move on to the next thing. If the next thing means eliminating me, I do not think he would hesitate.'

'That's great men for you.'

'Aye. I'm sorry you have been caught up in this, Thomas.'

'Don't you worry, master. There's only two on them, and we're three.'

'The trouble is,' I said with a sigh of exasperation, 'I don't *know* where Rocksley went beyond this point. I am searching blind.'

'There's Pyotr waving at us,' he said. 'Must have the horses.'

In silence we walked back to the post station.

200

Once we were away from the village and riding three abreast, Pyotr demanded to know what was afoot. He had guessed from our manner that things had changed, so we explained what Thomas had observed, and what we had deduced from it.

'If they, whoever they are, had wanted to get rid of you – us – then why not do it in Moscow?' he said.

'Too difficult,' I said. 'Most of the time I was inside the Company House, except when I went to the Kremlin, well escorted. Besides, if it *is* Godunov who is behind it, he wanted his daughter cured first. Pat me on the back, issue a passport, send us on the way. Then when we are well away from the capital, in some remote area–'

I broke off. We were riding through a remote area now. When I glanced over my shoulder, I could not see our pursuers, but I knew by the prickling of my scalp that they were there. It was a relief to see a merchant's pack train approaching us from the south. As long as they were in sight of us, before or behind, I reckoned we were safe from attack.

'If we were to gallop ahead now,' I suggested, 'pass the pack train, get it between us and those men, it might impede them a little.'

Thomas nodded. 'Good plan. It won't shake them off, for this seems to be the only road hereabouts, but it might give us some breathing space.'

Without more to-do, he kicked up his horse and galloped ahead. We followed.

The pack ponies were startled to see us bearing down on them and began to mill about in distress, but we circled round them and rode past.

'Good,' Thomas said. 'That should slow 'un down.'

We rode fast for a few miles, then eased off again to rest the horses. We were nearing another village, not a post station, so we rode through without stopping.

To our surprise, our simple ruse must have caused our pursuers more trouble than we had expected. For the next two days we saw nothing of them. Instead, every time we stopped for food or to change horses, we made enquiries for Gregory Rocksley, or at any rate Pyotr did. No one here spoke anything but Russian or occasionally one of the Tatar languages. Pyotr described Rocksley, as far as I could give him details. A man in his mid thirties, about Pyotr's height, light brown hair, slim – above all, an Englishman. Travelling with him, a Russian interpreter. Predictably, no one in the Company had really noticed the man, Ivan Petrovich. As if in England you spoke of John Smith. A shadowy, anonymous figure.

The people who lived along this road saw the occasional Englishman from the Company, but far fewer in recent years. Lately, little Company trade flowed this way, for the southern areas beyond and to the east of the Caspian were hotbeds of war. Safer, if more expensive, to fetch eastern goods from Venice or Constantinople, as Dr Nuñez did, sail them from the Mediterranean to London, and then ship some onwards to Muscovy.

So I reasoned that an Englishman seen in recent months – or last year – might have been noticed. For the next day and a half, nothing. By now we had left the snow behind and bit by bit we were shedding our heavy winter clothing, tying it in bundles behind our saddles. We stopped in a small village, hardly more than a hamlet, to let the horses drink from a stream where three women were washing clothes, beating them against stones in the shallows, while they stood knee deep in the water with their skirts tucked up.

Pyotr asked his usual questions, leaning down from his saddle to speak to the women. Thomas had dismounted and was pouring water over his head and neck from his cupped hands. Indeed, it was beginning to grow quite hot. I was considering doing the same when I noticed the women exchanging looks and muttering to each other. The usual response to Pyotr's questions was a blank look and a shake of the head. This was different. The women were talking fast and Pyotr was asking more questions. I caught my breath. Was it something at last? One woman was pointing over to the east, beyond the stream, where a narrow path to the left led off the road we had been following.

Thomas mounted again, his eyes on the women. Pyotr was smiling, thanking them, then he leaned down to give the oldest a coin. We splashed over the stream and did not query it when Pyotr led the way on to the path. Once we were out of earshot of the women and amongst a clump of trees, he reined in.

'They were here,' he said. His voice rose excitedly. 'Last summer. It must have been about the time we were leaving London. An Englishman and a Muscovite. They were arguing a little, the women said. Not seriously, but disputing which way to go. The village women were doing the washing then, just like today. Then a party of Muscovites rode up. Four of them. Or maybe five. Northerns, they said. They were arguing about how many it was, but I told them it didn't matter. They persuaded the other two men, our two, to go with them up this track, and off they all went.'

'Was that all they said? Were they certain it was Gregory Rocksley?' I held my breath, waiting for the answer.

'It certainly sounded like him. And the Russian he was with was called Ivan, but that means nothing.'

'So they all disappeared up this track?'

'Not quite. The following day, the man called Ivan rode back through the village, by himself. He did not stop, but headed north.'

Thomas had said nothing until now. 'Sounds to me as though this Ivan was a traitor, or a paid informer. This country is crawling with them, like lice,' he growled.

Rule by fear, I thought, and this is what you breed. Men who will betray anyone for money. Or out of fear, to save their own skin. Ivan Petrovich was probably alive and well, living comfortably somewhere under a different name. A name like Pyotr Ivanovich. Stop! I told myself. That is folly.

I turned to Pyotr. My horse was shifting uneasily under me, for there were flies clustering here under the trees. In irritation, I brushed away some which were trying to land on my face.

'Did the women tell you what lies along this track?' I asked.

Pyotr was avoiding my eyes. 'They did. It is a country estate belonging to "the big man in Moscow", they said. "What big man?" I asked. "Him they call the Konyushy Godunov," they said.'

I sat very still in the saddle, looking up the track to where it bent through the trees. For the first time I realised there was a bird singing. A common thrush. It might have been a wood in England. There were early spring flowers starring the grass at the foot of the trees.

Dead or alive, we had found Gregory Rocksley.

Chapter Eleven

I do not know whether I had spoken the words aloud, but I could see the same thought passing through their minds. Dead or alive. We had come this far. We could not turn back now. Those men urging Rocksley down this track to a house owned by a man he suspected of treachery. The interpreter riding away, surely having betrayed him. I felt sick. He must be dead. Yet we had to know for sure. Pyotr and Thomas were looking at me, waiting.

'We need to make sure,' I said, and turned my horse to ride up the track.

Without a word, they followed me. At that moment I felt a rush of gratitude toward them. This search had been wished upon them and I was leading them toward danger and possible death, yet they had not questioned my decision.

The trees grew more dense as we rode on, the lovely delicate birches which are found everywhere in this country. It was a natural wood, untended. Fallen trunks lay haphazard on the ground, sinking into decay amongst undergrowth and brambles. I could hear the sound of running water, but could not see it, because of the tightly packed trees. It must be the continuation of the stream where we had watered the horses.

This place was very different from a country manor in England. There, the woodland would be as meticulously cared for as the formal gardens around the house, undergrowth cleared away, fallen trees not left to rot. The English landowner cared for his woods and kept them clear for hunting. He also knew the financial value of his timber. In this country timber was so abundant it must be almost worthless, certainly not worth the landowner's attention, though I knew the Muscovites enjoyed the hunt as much as any man. Perhaps they were indifferent to trees that could trip you or brain you when you pursued wolf or bear or boar.

It was a long track, and winding, and the longer it went on, the more apprehensive I grew. At last through the trees we caught our first glimpse of the building. Thomas put out his hand to stop me, but I was already reining in my horse. I moved a little to one side, so that I could get a better view of the house. It was not what I expected.

This was no fortified manor. There was no protective wall, no battlements. It was as open and accessible as a farmhouse, and not much bigger, although it was well built of brick, with a shingle roof and modest pillared portico. It was surrounded by a rather ragged lawn, which led down a slight slope to the stream, but there appeared to be no formal garden. Beyond the house I could just glimpse some lower buildings that might be stables.

'What is this place?' I asked Pyotr. 'It does not look like a house belonging to a boyar like Godunov.'

He was regarding the building with interest and did not turn round.

'It is a *dacha*. I had not realised there were any this far south.'

'A what?'

'A *dacha*. From time to time the Tsar will award a favourite or someone who has done him a service with a property in the country. It's a gift. That's what *dacha* means, a "gift house". I expect the last Tsar gave this to Godunov. He thought highly of him, raised him to be a boyar. After all, he married his son to Godunov's sister.'

'You mean Godunov lives here some of the time?'

'Possibly. Not often, I should think. He would not want to be away from the Court and the government, in case his enemies plotted behind his back. Not everyone is happy that he controls the Tsar. Besides, we are nearing the troubled part of the country here.'

'Place looks deserted to me,' Thomas said.

He was right. Most of the shutters were closed. There was no one to be seen, not even a guard dog. The house slumbered, peaceful and innocent under the spring sunshine. We must have been misled. Or else whatever had happened to Gregory Rocksley had happened months ago.

'I'll take a look.' Thomas slid off his horse, threw me the reins and was gone before I could stop him. For a big man he move remarkably silently. Nick Berden would have approved. In moment he had disappeared amongst the trees, circling round to the back of the house.

Pyotr and I waited. If Rocksley had been brought here, he might have been killed at once. On the other hand, they might have wanted to know just how much he had discovered, and would have questioned him. That probably meant they had waited for Godunov himself to come. With this remote and convenient place of concealment, they would not have risked carrying him back to Moscow. And Godunov could not often absent himself from Moscow, as Pyotr had pointed out. We had no way of knowing whether he had been away at all during the intervening months. I felt a faint flicker of hope. Rocksley might still be alive.

Thomas was back.

'Just an ordinary house,' he said. 'I saw one kitchen maid carrying a pail of milk in the door at the back, no one else. Shutters are open on that side of the house. Mebbe there's nothing but household servants here, main rooms shut up. Still think he might be here, doctor?'

'He might.' I was unsure what to do.

'Better decide soon,' Thomas said. 'Those buggers who're after us will be here before long.'

The shock set my heart pounding. Stupid, stupid! Thinking about what lay ahead, I had forgotten the men behind us. We would be trapped here, at the end of the track. It went no further. The woods were thick beyond the house.

'If they followed us here,' I said breathlessly, 'there must be something to find.'

'That's what I reckon,' Thomas said.

Pyotr nodded agreement.

'Do you think we can get into the house?' he said.

'Easy. But there may be more'n servants there. Wouldn't they leave a guard?'

'Probably.'

We looked at each other. Thomas was a fighting man. I could wield a blade, but I was no match for a skilled swordsman. Pyotr carried a sword, but I suspected it was mostly for show. I would not have put him down as a fighter.

'I think we should try to get in.' I said it without much conviction, but Thomas took it as a decision.

'Right. Got to secure our line of retreat first. There's a path on t'other side o' yon stream. Not much, but we could ride it single file. Take us back toward that village. Don't want to meet those bastards head on, going back by the main track. Leave the horses down by the stream, while we take a look.'

'Good.' I slipped down from my horse and began to lead him through the trees on our left, in the direction of the stream. We were hardly silent, crashing through the undergrowth, but there was no other way to reach it, out of sight of the house. All we could hope was that no one there was listening.

At the water's edge, we looped the horses' reins loosely over low branches, so that we could free them easily, then made our way, with rather less noise, back to the main track.

Thomas led the way round to the rear of the house and we crouched behind the unkempt bushes, examining it. There was a back door, probably leading to a kitchen and standing open to let in the welcome return of spring warmth. Somewhere a woman was singing, cheerfully if somewhat tunelessly. We might be making a terrible mistake. Perhaps this *was* no more than a farmhouse. Even if the house belonged to Godunov, there was surely nothing untoward happening here. I was opening my mouth to say we should retreat, and had turned to Pyotr, when he raised his finger to his lips and jerked his head toward the house.

Two men had just emerged from the door and leaned against a low wall surrounding what might be a well. They were relaxed, enjoying the sun. Both wore swords. They were not household servants. Where there were armed men, there must be something to guard. I could hear most of what they said, but they spoke in a thick accent, so I caught only a few words. One word I did catch, and I felt the sweat spring out on my palms. *Anglichanin.* Englishman.

I glanced at the others. They had heard it too.

'Take them now?' It was Thomas.

'You are in charge,' I whispered. I could trust him to know how best to act.

Quietly, he drew his sword, and so did we, then he nodded.

We burst from behind the bushes, yelling, as if we were part of a larger attack. The two men started forward, taken by surprise. Before they could even draw their swords, Thomas had punched one so hard in the face that he fell back against the wall, struck the back of his head, and slid to the ground. The other was coming for me. I met his sword with mine, a teeth-rattling screech of metal on metal. I am quick on my feet and well trained in sword play, but my wrist is not as strong as a man's. Master Scannard, who had trained me in the Tower, always said that it was skill which triumphed over strength and I tried to remember that. 'Read your opponent's eyes,' he said.

There was little doubt what was in this man's eyes. He wanted to kill me. But I could see how he was assessing me, his eyes flicking for a moment to one side, to see what had happened to his companion. I took my chance and chopped down with my sword on his right arm. A stronger swordsman might have taken his hand off, but I did enough damage for him to shriek. I thought he would drop his sword, but he clung to it, although it drooped toward the ground.

Then he raised it and was coming for me, with murder in his eyes.

I raised my sword. I would try to hold him off, but he was taller than I, with a longer reach, and twice my weight behind it. As he came within sword reach, he stumbled and fell forward. I leapt back just in time to avoid being struck by his head as he collapsed. There was a dagger sticking out of his back.

Thomas was on the other side of the yard, smiling complacently.

'Learned that trick off a Saracen prisoner,' he said.

'You threw from over there?' I was incredulous.

'Aye.'

Pyotr was tying up the unconscious man with a bit of rope he had cut from the well bucket.

'Not very strong,' he called, 'but 'twill serve for the moment. Is he dead?' He jerked his thumb toward the man lying at my feet.

I knelt down and took the man's wrist between my fingers. There was a faint pulse, but he was bleeding badly. The dagger could have punctured a lung or some other vital organ.

'He's alive.' Instinctively I looked round for my satchel, before I remembered that I had left it strapped to my saddle.

'Come *on*,' Thomas yelled. 'Bring my dagger. There may be more on 'em.'

'He needs help–'

'God's teeth, doctor, he would have killed you. Bring my dagger.'

'Fetch it yourself,' I said, running toward the door. I might have told Thomas to lead us, but I would not pull out the dagger. Almost certainly it would draw out the man's life blood with it.

Then we were all three inside the house. As I had guessed, this was the kitchen. At first I thought it was deserted, then I saw two women crouched under a table and pressed back against the wall. An

208

older woman and a girl, probably the girl Thomas had seen with the milk.

'Other men?' Pyotr shouted. 'Are there other men with swords?'

The woman was grey with shock, incapable of responding, but the girl, her eyes wide with terror, shook her head.

'The Englishman. *Anglichanin*. Where is the *Anglichanin*?'

Still the girl did not speak, but pointed with a trembling hand toward a place on the floor. I ran across the room to where a rough woven rug covered the stone flags and flung it aside. There was a trap door underneath.

'Cellar,' I said.

Of course this place was no castle or fort. They would have used the ordinary cellar, the place where households stored their dried, salted, and pickled winter food, anything which was not kept in the outside ice-house. The trap door was of wood, with hollowed depressions to serve as handles. I heaved, but it was heavy and Thomas came to help me. We pushed it to one side and peered down into the depths. Total blackness.

Pyotr was lighting a tallow candle he had found on a shelf. He handed it to me, then began tying up the women.

'Is that necessary?' I said.

'I won't make it too tight. They'll easily get free once we're gone.'

I forgot the women, leaning over the hole and moving the candle from side to side.

'Gregory!' I shouted. 'Gregory Rocksley! Are you there? We've come to get you out.'

There was no answer, but a kind of listening silence.

'I'm going down,' I said.

Thomas nodded, 'I'm after you. Pyotr, make sure those men in the yard a'nt able for to come after us.' Then, as I began to climb down the ladder, awkwardly because I was holding the candle, he added 'Best make haste. Those bastards following can't be far behind us.'

Dear God, I kept forgetting them. I scrambled to the bottom and raised the candle to look around.

In the far corner, his feet tied and his bound arms clutched over his head to protect it, was a man. He was the right age, as far as I could tell. The hair was the right colour. His face and hands were filthy, his hair matted and crawling with lice, his clothes tattered. And he stank. Peering at him in the flickering light cast by the candle, I could not judge whether he was the man I had met only briefly before. But he did not speak. I ran over to him and knelt on the earthen floor to saw through the rope around his legs and arms with my dagger. It must be Rocksley, but there was no time now to question him.

As soon as the ropes fell away, Thomas seized the man and threw him over his shoulder.

'You go first.' I nodded at the ladder. If I followed, I might be able to take some of the weight, but Thomas went up that ladder as if the man weighed nothing.

Pyotr had finished tying up the women and was standing half in and half out of the door.

'Is it him?'

'Must be,' I said, 'but he can't, or won't, speak.'

Thomas tried to set the man on his feet, but he simply crumpled.

'Been tied up too long,' I said. 'You take his shoulders, I'll take his feet.'

'I'll manage,' Thomas said, heaving the man over his shoulder again. 'Down this way, we can reach the stream.'

He led us along the back of the house, down to the bank. Pyotr and I started to run along it to the trees where we had left the horses, Thomas following in a kind of shambling trot. I hesitated, waiting for him.

'Go on. Free the horses.'

Of course he was right. I ran faster, reaching them at the same time as Pyotr and gasping for breath. Four of us now, and only three horses. And one who looked incapable of riding.

I swung myself into the saddle. 'Put him up behind me,' I said. 'I'm the lightest and this is a good horse. He can carry us both.'

Between them, Thomas and Pyotr managed to lift the man up behind me, so that he was sitting on the roll of my winter clothes.

'Can you hold me around the waist?'

I twisted round so that I could look at him. His eyes were empty, as though everything about him was concentrated and held inwardly, shutting out all the world around.

I had seen that look before. On my mother's face.

'We'll need to tie him, or he'll fall,' I said. 'Have we anything?'

'I have a spare belt,' Pyotr began to claw through his pack, 'as well as the one with my winter trousers. We can buckle them together.'

They both fumbled frantically with the belts. We needed to ride away from here as quickly as possible and their haste made them clumsy. At last they had the belts secured, passing round the man's

210

waist and then round mine. If the horse stumbled under our combined weight and we fell, one of us might be crushed.

The two men were mounted now. Pyotr walked his horse across the stream. It was fast flowing, but not too deep. As they scrambles up the opposite bank, I tried to follow, but my horse, alarmed by our panic and the increased weight on his back, baulked at the water. Thomas rode up beside me and grabbed my reins. Reassured by the other horse at his side, mine lost his fear and crossed to the other side.

'As far as I can see,' Thomas said, when we had gathered on the path he had found, 'this leads back to that village. It's a footpath, a shorter way than the main track. Watch for low branches.'

'Wait,' I said, before they could set off. 'I think we should avoid the village. The women are just as likely to tell the men following us where we have gone as they were to tell us what they had seen. Why should they care?'

'This side of the village,' Pyotr said, 'I saw there was a field with a belt of trees running along the boundary as a windbreak. We could cut through the field behind the trees and pick up the road north, beyond the village. I don't think we will be seen, unless someone is particularly on the watch.'

Thomas and I nodded our agreement, and we set off along the path in single file. Everything in me shrieked to kick my horse into a canter, but the path was criss-crossed with roots, boggy in places. We were forced to go carefully to spare the horses. We must have been halfway to the village when I heard faintly, away to our left beyond the trees on the far side of the stream, the sound of horsemen riding toward Godunov's house. Automatically Pyotr, who was leading, urged his horse to go faster, but was forced to rein him in again as he reached a patch of bright green bog grass.

At last we had come to the field. I was trying to calculate distances in my head. Would the horsemen had reached the house yet? Not quite, I thought. Pyotr turned his horse and headed up the field, breaking into a canter on the firmer ground. I followed, though the man behind me hung limp, sliding from one side to the other, nearly dragging me from the saddle. Thomas came alongside and reached over to push the man upright, but he slipped again at once.

I had a sudden hysterical desire to laugh. What if this was not Gregory Rocksley? He had not responded to the name. What if we were abducting someone else entirely?

No time to think now. Pyotr was pointing ahead to a way out of the field. As we broke out, down a bank and on to the road where we had been riding just a few hours before, I glanced back in the direction of the village. I could see the top of the roofs, for it lay in a dip beside the stream. There was no sign of pursuit yet.

Fortunately the road here must have lain over well-drained ground, for it was not churned up into mud. We gave the horses their heads and pounded up that road as fast as they could carry us. My poor beast laboured to keep up, but I was lighter than Pyotr and the man behind me was emaciated, his body pressed against my back felt bony and ill-fleshed. Together we cannot have weighed much more than the big Yorkshire man, but we were an ungainly burden, with my passenger constantly slipping sideways.

He continued to loll against my back, as an hour passed, and another. Helpless as a child's cloth doll, but more verminous. I imagined I could feel his lice migrating to my own hair and clothes, so that I had an almost irresistible urge to scratch, but I could not spare a hand from the reins.

It must have been at least fifteen miles to the post station, the one where we had acquired these horses early that morning. By the time we had extricated ourselves and our luggage from the exhausted animals, the groom had fetched his master, who began to berate us for ill using them. His ire was directed at Pyotr, but I drew out our permits and passports and handed them over. I doubted the man could read, but he recognise Godunov's seal and immediately began to bow and apologise. I could not follow all the words, but the tone was unmistakeable.

Thomas and I had managed to seat the rescued man on a bench outside the post station, then Thomas disappeared inside. He returned with a flagon of mead and cups, while Pyotr went off with the stable manager to select our fresh horses. I drank my mead quickly, but could not stop myself constantly glancing back down the road. Every minute's delay set my nerves jumping. We needed to be on our way.

I turned to the man seated on the bench. He had drunk the mead and was sitting up straighter now. Clearly he was ill, underfed, and exhausted, and . . . things . . . had been done to him, but he was beginning to revive. Curbing my impatience I sat down beside him.

'Are you Gregory Rocksley?' I asked bluntly.

'Aye.' His voice croaked, as though it had not been used recently.

'Thank God,' I said.

He regarded me warily. 'Who are you?'

'We work for the Muscovy Company. We've been searching for you.'

His lips parted in a weak smile. I saw that they were cracked and bleeding.

'Have some more mead,' I said, refilling his cup. 'Sickly stuff, but it will do you good.'

'Got any food?' He looked up at Thomas, who had returned from the post station again with a bag and a lidded basket.

'We'll eat later,' he said. 'Need to put a few more miles behind us.'

'You must be careful,' I said to Gregory. 'If you have been starved. Small amounts, often. Don't be a glutton.'

'Master Kit here is a doctor,' Thomas said. 'Though you might not think it to look at him. Wanted to stop and physic one of those murdering bastards – would you believe it? – just because I knifed him.'

'It's what I'm trained to do,' I said mildly. 'Give him a little bread, Thomas, but that is all for now.'

Pyotr emerged from the stable, leading two horses. Behind him, the stable master led two more.

'Will you be able to ride?' I asked Gregory.

'Have to, won't I? I don't think either of us could bear much more, two to a horse.'

I laughed. 'I don't suppose we could.'

As fast as we might, we secured our luggage and mounted, Thomas giving Gregory a leg up. I could tell by the way he adjusted his stirrups and gathered up his reins that he was an experienced horseman, but it was clear that he was terribly weak. What he needed was a bath, some simple food, and many days rest in bed. Instead, he must ride as fast as a government messenger at home in England, along these terrible Muscovite roads. He must endure, for there was no other option. I led the way, so that I would not have to watch how he suffered. Pyotr followed me, with Gregory behind him and Thomas bringing up the rear, to make sure we did not lose our man, now that we had found him.

I set as fast a pace as I dared. There was still no sign of pursuit, but we all knew it must be there. This was the only road we were likely to take. All they needed to do was to follow us.

At our second change of horses, we rested and ate a little of the food Thomas had bought. Gregory found a stream, where he managed to wash off some of the dirt. He borrowed a nit comb from Thomas, but the matting of his hair was too much for it. After he had broken two teeth of the comb he abandoned it.

'I do not suppose one of you has scissors,' he said.

'I carry scissors,' I said.

Of course I did. How did he suppose a physician could function without scissors?

He tried to hack off the lank clumps of hair that hung to his shoulders, but made a poor showing of it.

'Give them to me.' I held out my hand.

I trimmed all his hair close to the scalp, then treated the stubble with the potion against infestation I used on the dirtier Southwark children who were brought into St Thomas's. For good measure I rubbed some into my own hair.

'We'm had some queer looks at yon clothes,' Thomas said frankly, eying Gregory's rags.

'Worn the same for a year, I suppose,' he said dully. 'What month is this?'

I had lost track again, having other things on my mind. It seemed the others had too.

'Must be April,' Pyotr said. 'That gives us two, three months to reach St Nicholas and the fleet, easily.'

Thomas nodded agreement.

'We must stop at Moscow,' I said. 'Thomas can return to his duties there, and I can report to Master Holme before the three of us head for the White Sea. But before that we need to find something for Gregory to wear.'

I untied the roll of my winter clothes and took out the baggy trousers.

'You are only an inch or two taller than I am. These are over warm for this time of year, but they might serve.'

'I have a spare shirt,' Pyotr said.

Thomas provided a plain cloth doublet, but we could do nothing about footwear. Gregory used my scissors to cut off his hose below the knee. The lower parts and his boots were in better shape than the rest of his garments, for they had received little wear in the cellar. He carried everything off to the stream, to wash the rest of his body before he donned the relatively clean clothes, while we packed up the remaining food and readied the fresh horses.

'A'nt you going to ask him what they done to him?' Thomas said to me while he was gone.

214

'I can see for myself,' I said. 'That look in his eye? He's been tortured. Though thank God they had no torture instruments in that house. Still, there are other ways.'

He looked at me curiously. 'How do you know?'

'Experience,' I said, in a tone that brooked no further discussion.

When Gregory returned, he was somewhat oddly clad, but he no longer looked like a heap of rags dragged from the gutter. We mounted and went on our way.

The miles and days rolled behind us, still without sight of our pursuers, although we knew that they were there, biding their time. At night we slept under the trees, away from the road. It was then, in sleep, that Gregory's iron control gave way. He cried out, shrieked in pain, swore over and over that he would not speak. In the morning it was clear that he remembered nothing. We none of us mentioned what we had heard, although our own sleep had been broken and fearful.

The road was quite busy now, so the men following us would probably prefer a quieter spot to overtake us. We discussed turning off the main road north and trying to find our way along the minor tracks that led from village to village, but decided it would only lose us time and offer greater opportunity for attack. If we were to be attacked, better here on the open road.

We crossed the river junction by ferry again, and headed up the west side of the Moskva, eventually, to our great relief, reaching the post station in the large merchants' town where we had left the Company horses on the first day of our road south. We had decided to spend the night at the inn there, one of the few real inns to be found in Muscovy, and cover the final leg of the journey to Moscow the next day. As Pyotr sought the innkeeper to order a meal for us, Thomas, Gregory and I found a table in the crowded parlour. This was a busy trading station and we had passed a large market selling goods of every kind when we arrived.

'Dr Alvarez! Thomas!' A voice shouted from behind me.

I twisted round, then stood to see who could have recognised us. I was reluctant to move, for the long, hard riding had left me saddle-sore.

'Robert!'

It was Robert Farindon, sitting at a large table with a group of Muscovite merchants. He spoke to them, then rose, carrying his drinking cup, and came over to us.

'So, you have made it safely back from the south,' he said, pulling up a stool to our table. 'Is this . . .?'

I introduced Gregory and the two men bowed as Pyotr rejoined us.

Robert shook his head, seemingly in amazement. 'I thought you were on a fool's errand. After all this time, Master Rocksley, we had despaired of you.'

He reached out to pat Gregory's arm, as though he could not quite believe in his reality.

'Are you well? Have you been . . . are you recovered?'

'I am recovered,' Gregory said, 'I thank you.'

But that bleak look came into his eyes again. I shook my head slightly at Robert, who understood, and asked no more questions about what had happened to Gregory while he had been missing. Instead, Pyotr and Thomas regaled him with the story of our raid on the country house belonging to Godunov, and our flight north. Gregory and I said little, but ate the food the servant placed before us. I was hardly aware of what I was putting in my mouth.

I was conscious that there was something in Robert's manner that troubled me, something amiss, but was forced to wait until the meal was finished, when Robert asked if he might have a word with me. One fortunate aspect of being a physician is that when someone asks for a private word, everyone assumes that it is a personal medical matter, and shows no surprise. Robert and I strolled out of the inn and down toward the river, where a cluster of boats and barges was tied up at the wharf.

'You keep looking over your shoulder,' he said.

'Do I? We are certain that the men who pursued us to Godunov's house are still following us. I am surprised they have not acted before now. It would not have been difficult to overtake us. Hard as we rode, there was a point beyond which we could not try Gregory's strength. He is gradually recovering, but he was very frail when we found him.'

'Had he been tortured?

'Aye, I am sure of it, but I have not questioned him.'

'It is common practice in this place,' Robert said. 'I know we are far from blameless at home, but we generally have some grounds for such action. Here, they will seize a foreigner quite at random and apply torture, purely as a part of some political negotiation. Mark you, whole villages and towns of their own people can be wiped out at the whim of a Tsar.'

'Was there something you wanted to tell me, Robert?' I was very tired, and hoped he would get to the point.

'I want to ask you something first. Has Rocksley told you what he discovered that sent him haring away to the south?'

I shook my head. 'You don't know the state he was in when we found him. And since, we have been travelling so hard, there has been hardly time to think of anything else. I thought it best to leave all until we reached Moscow and could discuss it with Master Holme.'

'Then I need to tell you something as well as ask.'

He passed his hand over his face. It had been dark and smoky in the inn. Out here, in the spring twilight, I was suddenly aware of the strain in his eyes.

'Word has somehow reached the Kremlin,' he said, 'that Rocksley is released and is privy to some damaging information. Perhaps those men are not behind you but before, having overtaken you somewhere on the journey.'

I stared at him, startled.

'How do you know this? And so you knew we had found Rocksley?'

'We have our own people who are our eyes and ears in the Kremlin. So,' he said, 'it would be very dangerous for Rocksley to come to Moscow. He would be arrested the moment he entered the city. I was not at this inn entirely by chance.'

'What should we do, then? I think Master Holme should be informed.'

'We hoped you would make a stop here. I have been visiting regularly, using trade with the local merchants as my reason for coming. I will return to Moscow tomorrow to inform Master Holme that you have all four arrived. I am sure you will be safe here for the moment, though I would not stray far from the inn. The danger waits in Moscow. Get Rocksley to write a report of all he knows, for Master Holme. I'll return the day after tomorrow with instructions for what you should do.'

I agreed, and later that evening told the others of Robert's warning.

'Though I am uncertain which way we should travel,' I said.

'Clearly we will need to avoid Moscow,' Pyotr said, 'and make straight for Yaroslavl.'

I nodded. 'And we will see what instructions Robert brings from Master Holme.' I was glad to be able to shift the burden of decision on to someone else's shoulders.

'Robert has left us a supply of paper, ink, and quills,' I added, holding them out to Gregory. 'Do you feel able to write a report of your findings?'

I had already told him that the despatches he had intended for the Muscovy Company last year had been stolen.

'I will start on it now,' he said, taking the paper from me and pulling a stool over to the deep window sill to serve as a desk. We had a room to ourselves, the four of us, while Robert had gone for the night to stay with a Company man, whose house, unfortunately, was too small to accommodate all of us, for it would have been safer.

'No need to do it now,' I said. 'You will have the whole day tomorrow.'

'I would rather begin now. It is time it is all written down, lest something should happen.'

Lest he should be killed, he meant.

He lit a candle and set it on the window sill, for it was growing dark.

I prised off my boots and wriggled my toes. I suspected my feet had begun to stink almost as much as Gregory had done when we found him. I flung myself down on the bed, which was the usual narrow shelf attached to the wall, and turned my back on the light. And fell asleep at once.

Several times during the night I woke, for sooner or later a hip or a shoulder would protest at the hardness of those shelves. Every time I woke, I saw that the candle, or another, was still burning, and Gregory was still writing.

Robert returned in the morning of the second day, accompanied by two grooms, each leading an extra horse. He came to our room, so that we could talk in private, and Gregory handed him a thick packet of paper. Robert tucked it into the breast of his doublet.

'Now,' he said, 'Master Holme warns that you should not come to Moscow, any of you. As I told you before, Gregory is certain to be arrested, and as the rest of you are implicated in removing him from the custody of Godunov's household, you are likely to be arrested too, especially as you killed one of his retainers.'

'That was in self defence,' Thomas protested.

Robert shrugged. 'That will carry little weight. I am afraid you will need to go with the others to St Nicholas, Thomas, and return to London. I am sure the Company will be able to allocate you to other duties there.'

Thomas shrugged. 'I'll be glad to go. Seen enough of this b'yer lady country to last a lifetime.'

'Good. Now, Master Holme has made some funds available.' Robert unfastened a heavy purse from his belt and handed it to me. 'The Company does not want you to go short, after such unflinching service. It is good to know that it was not one of our former employees who was the traitor, but someone altogether more dangerous.'

He glanced around nervously, suddenly remembering that not all walls are a protection against spying eyes and ears.

'I have checked,' I said, to reassure him. 'We cannot be overheard here.'

He nodded. 'You are to skirt round to the west of Moscow. I will ride the first part of the way with you. I have brought Company horses for you, so you are to proceed at a reasonable pace, not changing horses, avoiding the post stations. It is possible that word of your movements up from the south was passed on from the post stations. Once I have set you on the alternative way, you can continue to Yaroslavl, then follow the route from there back to St Nicholas.'

'How bad are the roads?' Thomas asked.

'Not impassable at the moment,' Robert said. 'Or so we hear from those who have travelled down from Kolmogory. The worst part is likely to be from Kolmogory to St Nicholas. You may need to take a Company barge. Master Holme has written out an authorisation for you.'

He handed me a paper with Christopher's seal.

'Any of the Company houses will help you.'

I thought of the small packet I still carried, entrusted to me by Xenia.

'What if I were to pay a brief visit to my patient at Uglich?' I said.

He frowned.

'The Tsarevich? It would take you somewhat out of the way, but at least there will be no blizzards to contend with at this time of year. You must use your judgement when you reach Yaroslavl. I suppose it would be possible for you to go a roundabout way to Vologda. Provided you can reach St Nicholas in good time to meet this year's fleet . . . Probably there would be no harm in it. Make a decision when you are there.'

I had not told the others of Xenia's request and they seemed surprised that I should want to return to a place where Pyotr and I had virtually been held captive, but a promise is a promise. I would explain it to them when we reached Yaroslavl.

Christopher's instructions seemed to cover all contingencies. Before we set out, Gregory took me aside and gave me a copy of the report he had written.

'This is for the governor of the Company. Everything. Names. Places. Dates. Including individuals in London. So it should also be seen by Sir Francis.'

His words came as a shock. He did not know.

'Sir Francis is dead,' I said quietly. 'He died at the beginning of April last year. I am sorry. I did not realise I had not told you.'

A spasm passed over his face. Like all of us, he felt bereft with that great man gone.

'So what has become of the service? And this must be passed to the Queen and Privy Council. Urgently.'

'All Sir Francis's records were stolen. Everything was in confusion when I left London. There was a struggle for control between Essex and the Cecils. When we reach London, I think we should find Thomas Phelippes. He will know best what to do.'

He nodded, then sighed. 'I suppose there will always be work for an agent trained by Sir Francis.'

'What *you* must do,' I said, 'once we are back in England, is to take a long rest at home with your family. I speak as your physician.'

He gave me a wan smile. 'A man and his family must eat.'

'I am certain that the Company will take care of that. They owe you much. You have exonerated them and their employees, past and present, from acts of treachery.'

I smiled back at him. 'And if they do not reward you handsomely, then you and I will sit upon their doorstep until they do!'

The next day we set off early and Robert rode with us for two days, until we had passed by Moscow on the west, then he left us to return to the Company house.

'I wish you God speed,' he said. 'You should reach St Nicholas in good time. You can send us word of your safe arrival with the men bringing this year's merchandise down to Moscow.'

It goes smoothly and relentlessly on, I thought, this world of the merchants and traders. Poison, imprisonment, treachery, torture, conspiracy. Yet the fleet must still come every year, the English cloth be delivered, the Muscovy ropes and furs carried away. Through floods, storms, drought and snow, the goods must be moved across sea and land.

It was good to be back in the Company house at Yaroslavl, greeted warmly by the agent there, Walter Deynes, as if we had hardly been away. It was the first time we had been in what I called in my mind a *civilised* house since we had left Moscow weeks before, to head south. That night I crawled thankfully into an English bed, wearing a clean night shift instead of my filthy travelling clothes, and slept without stirring for nine blessed hours.

The next day I handed over my clothes to be washed by the Company laundress, and the others did the same. From amongst Company stores, Master Deynes found clothes for Gregory which were a better fit, so that he began to appear less like a pauper turned out from St Thomas's in a charity outfit. He was starting to lose the gaunt look in his face, but his eyes were still haunted by what they had done to him in Godunov's cellar.

While we waited for our clothes to be washed and dried, and rested from our seemingly endless journey, I explained to the others why I wanted to call at Uglich.

'The children are but pawns in the hands of unscrupulous adults,' I said. 'They are lonely, friendless, and afraid. It seems little enough to do.'

Pyotr was against it from the first. 'Master Holme's instructions were to make straight for St Nicholas. Robert was reluctant to agree to our travelling via Uglich.'

'It will not take us so very far out of our way,' Thomas said. 'No more than a day or two. I think there is no harm in it.'

'Kit has made a promise to the child,' Gregory said. 'We should keep our promises to children, if we can, else how are they to learn what is right? I think we should go to Uglich.'

I remembered. Gregory had children of his own.

Pyotr shook his head in annoyance. 'You forget. Although the Tsarina Maria Nagaya rules at Uglich, she is surrounded by spies. News of our whereabouts will wing its way back to Godunov. We will be seized before we can reach St Nicholas.'

I was annoyed in my turn, that he was trying to teach me my business.

'You need not come,' I said. 'My Russian is sufficient. I do not need an interpreter. I can join the rest of you at Vologda.'

I saw that I had hurt him by suggesting he was no more than an interpreter. After all we had endured together, he must feel I owed him more than that.

'Of course,' I added, 'I would much prefer it if we stayed together, the four of us.'

'If you go,' he said grimly, 'then we all go together. I will not let you enter that vipers' nest alone.'

So it was decided. Two days later, we all rode off to Uglich. It was the fifteenth of May. Plenty of time to make a brief visit to the Tsarevich, then travel north to Vologda, Kolmogory and St Nicholas, even if we had to hire a barge for the last part of the journey. We would, after all, travel down river with the current as the Dvina flowed toward the sea.

The road to Uglich was changed beyond all recognition from when Pyotr and I had come this way by sleigh last winter. Instead of bitter cold and dark, threatening forest, spring had reached even these northern parts. Sunlight flowed through the woods in shafts like liquid honey. The birches were in early leaf. Even the pines had shaken off the gloom of winter. Everywhere there was birdsong. Every tree was alive with them – calling, courting, nesting. Where we had glimpsed yellow eyes, sinister in the lamplight during our dark journey, now we saw a vixen sporting with two very young cubs. Deer poised, frozen, watching, then skittered away in real or pretended panic. Once, as we splashed across a stream – which must have been ice bound before – I caught a glimpse of a beavers' dam just a few yards away, and the surrounding trees showed the marks of their teeth.

Instead of a tiresome diversion, fraught with arguments, it had become a joyful ride through a countryside suddenly lovely. For the first time since coming to the country, I thought Muscovy beautiful. Even Pyotr had relaxed. I caught him whistling.

We stayed that night in one of the mean little rooms attached to a post station, though, as instructed by Robert, we made no use of the post horses. Perhaps it was a mistake to stay there. It was mild enough to have slept rough, but summer rain had come on at nightfall, not heavy but insidious, and I think none of us wanted to ride the rest of the way in sodden clothes. Aye, it was probably a mistake. Three English travellers and one half English, half Russian. It made us instantly recognisable.

The next morning the rain had ceased and all the woodland shone as if it had been polished. We set off merrily.

'At Uglich I shall simply tell them that I was passing on my journey back to England,' I said, 'and wished to make a brief call on my patient. I will slip him the present from Xenia, and then we can be on our way to Vologda.'

'You forget the single-mindedness of the Tsarina,' Pyotr said. 'She will try to keep you there.'

'I shall not let her,' I said firmly. 'She has my diagnosis. The boy is perfectly healthy. And she has my certificate, stating that he does *not* suffer from the falling sickness. She will be glad to be told that I am about to leave the country, which puts an end to her restriction on using the certificate.'

He shook his head, but did not protest any further.

We rode on. We were perhaps five miles from Uglich when we noticed groups of agitated people gathering in the corners of fields and outside the houses of two villages we passed.

'I do not like the look of this,' Thomas said when we reached the second of these. 'Something is afoot.'

'Aye,' Gregory agreed.

I wanted to argue, but I knew they were right. There was a vibration in the air, like the sense of an approaching thunder storm. I saw two women gather up their children and begin to run away into the forest.

'What can it be?' I tried to sound calm, but I do not think I succeeded.

'I will find out. Stay here.' Pyotr rode toward a group of men standing outside a village forge. As he leaned down from his horse to question them, they began gesticulating wildly, all talking at once. One man drew his finger across his throat in a gesture that needed no words.

'I like this even less,' Thomas said uneasily.

Pyotr galloped toward us and without a word, grabbed the slack of my reins to turn my horse.

'Back!' he said. 'We must go back!'

'What has happened?' I jerked my reins out of his grasp. I would not be manhandled like this with no explanation.

'The whole countryside is up,' he said. 'Ride back the way we came, for God's sake! There will be no getting through to Vologda. They are killing people indiscriminately.'

'But *why*?'

'The Tsarevich is dead. Cut his dog's throat and then his own. Had an epileptic fit and cut his own throat.'

223

Chapter Twelve

I wanted to howl, to rage against a heedless God who could let this happen to a child. Instead I dragged my horse to a stop and shouted.

'Never!' Tears were running down my face unchecked. 'Never! Dmitri would *never* harm Volk.'

So the wolfhound had tried to save the boy and been killed for it.

'He could not have cut his own throat,' I said. 'He was *not* epileptic*. And besides, someone in an epileptic fit could not cut his own throat. The hands are like this.'

I dropped my reins and held out both hands, splayed out like rigid starfish.

'He could not even have held a knife.'

'It seems the people here agree with you,' Pyotr said, grabbing my reins again and urging us all back the way we had come. 'They are running amok, killing anyone they think is connected to Godunov. Men and their families in the town. That supercilious steward at the palace. They are roaming the countryside, fired up with an insane blood lust. They loved that boy, and they believe Godunov had him killed.'

'Of course he did,' I said, suddenly exhausted.

'But they will not be a danger to us,' Thomas objected. 'They will not think we are supporters of Godunov.'

'We are strangers, that will be reason enough. I do not think they will stop to ask you for your allegiance. We are in danger from the crowds, but there's more.'

I held my breath, for I thought I knew what was coming.

'The Tsarina has produced the certificate Kit wrote, confirming that Dmitri did not have epilepsy. She has men copying it, to be sent out everywhere, as proof of the lies being perpetrated by Godunov's men, who have arrived with remarkable speed.'

'They weren't far away, then,' Thomas said. 'Convenient.'

'Exactly.'

'So Kit is in danger.'

'If Godunov's men catch us, I wouldn't give that for Kit's chances.' Pyotr snapped his fingers together. 'A sealed certificate from a respected English physician? Proving that the boy could not have had an epileptic fit? It would destroy their whole fabricated story.'

'But which way are we to go?' Thomas said. 'We cannot go back to Moscow.'

The two of them continued to debate as we headed back along the road toward Yaroslavl, as if Gregory and I were not there.

Suddenly Gregory reined in.

'Wait!' he said. 'If Godunov's men are in the area and have heard about the certificate, they will be bound to search for Kit at all the Company premises. Including the nearest one, at Yaroslavl.'

'They are protected by treaty,' Pyotr protested.

'And what is that worth? Look how Ambassador Bowes was kidnapped and held. These men would care nothing for any treaty. They would act first, on Godunov's orders, and the Company could argue all it wished, later, about infringement of the agreements, but it would be too late.'

If anyone should know, I thought, it would be Gregory.

'But we plan to travel back through all the Company houses,' I said. 'What other way is there to get to St Nicholas and our ship home?'

'By not going to St Nicholas,' Gregory said.

'I do not want to stay in this country a moment longer than I need to.' I was suddenly seized with a frantic wish to leave Muscovy immediately and never come back.

'I am not suggesting we should not leave,' Gregory said. 'I am suggesting we should go in a direction they will never suspect.'

'Where?' Pyotr said sceptically.

'Narva.'

'Narva! But Narva is in Swedish hands, and there is a war going on all along the border.' Pyotr stared at him as if he had gone mad. Perhaps he had. 'We could not get through to Narva.'

'We are not Russians,' Gregory said quietly. 'Three Englishmen and a man who can pass for an Englishman. Peter Aubery. Why should we not travel to Narva? It is a major trading centre. Everyone goes to Narva. Even Englishmen and English ships. There are ways past armies. I have made my way past armies and I daresay Kit has as well. And I speak Swedish. Not well, but enough to get by.'

They all looked at me.

'What do you say, doctor?' Thomas only called me that in his most serious moments.

'How far is it to Narva?' I asked. 'And do any of you know the way?'

They looked at one another. Thomas shrugged.

'Never been in those parts.'

Pyotr did not admit it, but I could read the same answer in his face.

'Gregory?' he said. 'You have been there.'

'It would be something like six hundred miles, I'd think. And I do not know the route from here, but I can guess. We cannot go north then west, because of the outbreak of violence and killing. We must go a short way south first, then take the first road leading west. I reckon Narva must be about due west of here.'

'And when we get there,' I said, 'if we survive that far – what then?'

'I know people in Narva,' he said vaguely. 'It was how I picked up information before. They will help us find a ship. Dutch or English.'

His confidence began to give me a glimmer of hope, despite the despair I felt at the murder of Dmitri.

'Then let us try for Narva,' I said. 'Only another six hundred miles.'

Gregory and Thomas led the way, and Pyotr and I were content to let them. Gregory had not traversed this particular part of Muscovy, but before he had been captured and imprisoned he had criss-crossed the country and gained a good deal of skill in finding his way. Thomas, the oldest of us and a soldier with campaigning experience, might not know this area of the country, but he had spent five years here and knew how to venture across uncharted and possibly enemy territory.

I am not sure how far we travelled that first day. I was still too numb with horror to pay much heed to my surroundings. Try as I might to blot it out, that terrible scene kept rising before my eyes. The armed men. The valiant dog attacking and dying, his throat cut. The child seized. The very last thing he must have seen before he was killed would have been his beloved Volk lying in a pool of blood at his feet.

It was unspeakable. It was obscene. Most obscene of all was the claim that the child, that gentle, brave child, had killed himself. In my

226

heart, I could not blame his mother for betraying her oath. She had proof that he could not have killed himself. Of course she would use it. I would have done the same.

Some time after we had ridden south, Gregory and Thomas found a track leading west. It was less than a road, but it led in the right direction, so we followed it, and this became the pattern of our days. Long days they were, as time drew nearer to the summer solstice, so we rode as long as we could see, then snatched a few hours' sleep on the ground under the trees, while the Company horses grazed. Robert had provided us with fine mounts, far better than the broken-winded post horses. Even so, we could not ride fast and hard, for we must spare the horses. Without them we would be lost in this country of forests, where men had left scarcely any mark.

There was one sizeable village I remember, Kalyazin or Kolyazin I think it was called, where we had to cross a river in boats which could barely hold a horse. The horses were frightened, but the river was too deep and too fast for them to swim, still carrying away the melted snow of winter. I had to pay the man heavily to make the trip four times, although Pyotr argued with him, and almost came to blows.

Pyotr was showing the strain almost more than any of us. It was foolish to draw attention to us by arguing, but he seemed unable to stop himself. I think he chafed at being unable to take the lead in this country which was partly his, but it was an unknown wilderness, far from the comfortable string of towns along the navigable rivers in the centre of the country which he knew so well.

After the river crossing, we seemed to ride for days through a land entirely devoid of people. If this was territory Sweden coveted, I could not help wondering why. There seemed to be nothing but forests, and surely they had enough of those themselves? Perhaps their purpose was merely to ensure that Muscovy was held back from its ambition to seize land along the Baltic coast.

After my months in this country, I had come to experience a sense of claustrophobia. To the south there were troublesome neighbours. Expansion to the east meant tackling the trackless wastes and bitter cold of Siberia. To the north, England had opened up a route through arctic seas, a lung, as it were, to catch a breath, but only during the short months of mid summer. No wonder the milder west, with the Baltic waterways providing a route to Europe, was a tempting prospect for the Muscovites.

At the end of a long, long ride we reached a place called Mednoye. By now we were growing weak with hunger, for there had been few places where we could buy anything to eat. Gregory and I waited on the outskirts of the large village with the horses, while Pyotr and Thomas went to try and buy food. I was so exhausted I fell asleep on the ground, only waking when they returned.

'You found food?' I said. It was all that concerned me at the moment.

Pyotr nodded. 'Food and news. There is fighting ahead of us, between the Swedish and Muscovite armies. If we want to reach Narva without being caught up in it, we must head north. It will add some time to the journey, but it cannot be helped.'

I groaned, but I seized one of the loaves and began tearing pieces off it. I knew I must not eat too quickly, but the bread was fresh and warm, better than any palace feast.

'Tell them the rest,' Thomas said grimly.

'The rest?' Gregory had cut himself a chunk of cheese and was poised with it on the tip of his knife, halfway to his mouth.

Pyotr grimaced. 'It seems we have been enquired for. A troop of men in government livery were asking for us two days ago.'

'What!' I said. 'How could that be?'

Gregory bit a morsel off his cheese.

'Simple tactics,' he said.

'Of course.' I came to my senses.

The men sent to look for us would have split up. We would not have gone north because of the riots. Some would have made a search quickly back to Yaroslavl and found no trace of us. That left only the way south and the way west. They would have known the roads and come more directly, while we had felt our way more slowly across country. So they were ahead of us now. Or were they?

'The people in the village,' I said, 'did they tell you which way the government men went? Did they also go north?'

Pyotr shook his head. 'They did not care to see. I had the impression they retired back into their homes and barred their doors.'

'So what should we do?'

'I think we must go north,' Gregory said. 'As it is, I think we have strayed a little too far south. All we can do is go on, but with caution.'

'I wish I had an astrolabe,' I said. 'I could calculate how far north we are. Though I do not suppose you know the latitude of Narva, Gregory?'

He shook his head, with a smile at my attempt at a diversion. 'I'm no mariner, Kit.'

So we went on. More of these endless forests. They no longer seemed beautiful to me, but a hateful barren country where no one would want to live or even linger. Once, we heard fighting in the distance to our left. Cannon fire. It meant continuing to travel north, until I began to wonder whether we would miss the way to Narva altogether and find ourselves in Lapland, the land of the Sami. By now there was almost no darkness, so that night differed from day only by a slightly greyish tinge to the light. The lingering daylight drove us to ride on and on each day. We were all, as well as the horses, growing exhausted.

At last, when our track met a road heading west, by mutual consent we turned on to it. Perhaps we had left the warring armies behind us, to the south, perhaps not, but we *must* head west if we were to hope to reach Narva.

Two days along this road, and I began to sense something different about our surroundings. The forest thinned out, certainly, and there were occasional farms, with fields cleared from the woodland. There were even a few poor villages. But it was something else. There was a mild west wind blowing toward us as we rode, and I lifted my face to it. I turned to Thomas, who was riding beside me.

'Do you smell anything?'

His raised his eyebrows in enquiry, but sniffed.

'Am I right?' I said.

His face broke into a smile. 'The sea! Hey, lads, we can smell the sea!'

I was suddenly back with my father, doing my lessons in Coimbra. It was the first Greek text I read right through. Xenophon's men, fleeing an enemy army across heartbreaking territory, then the cry of: 'Thalassa! Thalassa! The sea! The sea!'

At the next village Pyotr enquired how far it was to Narva. He came back smiling.

'We have done well to find this road. It will take us to Narva. About forty versts, they say.'

I did a quick calculation in my head. 'About twenty-five or twenty-six miles?'

'Aye. About that.'

It was almost unbelievable, for it had begun to feel as though we would go on riding for ever through this endless country. Sometime tomorrow, we should reach Narva, provided we did not encounter either army on the way.

We continued all the rest of that day until the horses needed to rest. In this more inhabited part of the country we had obtained food and even ale, which it seemed the local people brewed. We drank it gratefully after the endless mead, a drink I thought would surely rot my teeth with its clinging sweetness.

'We must have shaken off those government men,' Pyotr said, stretched out his legs on the carpet of pine needles and cradling his wooden cup. He closed his eyes. 'God's bones, I shall be glad to get out of the saddle. The blisters on my backside are developing blisters.'

I laughed sympathetically. 'We're all in the same state. I just want to find myself aboard ship again. These friends of yours in Narva, Gregory, you think they will be able to find us a ship?'

'Almost certainly, though perhaps not at once. Two are former Company men who have set up as merchants for themselves. Brought their families over from England and settled in the town. Although it belonged to Muscovy for a few years, you will find it more like a town in the Low Countries. Or Denmark. Have you been to Denmark, Kit?'

I shook my head. 'Never. You say "two" friends. There are others?'

'Aye. There's a Dutchman. Met him first in Amsterdam. He was in the same line of business as you and me, reported to the Earl Leicester, God rest his soul. Decided to give it up when the Earl went back to England and took up trade instead. If we can't find an English ship, we can probably sail to Amsterdam and take an English ship from there.'

It began to feel hopeful at last. Not many more miles to go, with the prospect of a ship home at the end of it. And here we were in peaceful countryside, well away from the fighting, with no sign of pursuit. This was still Muscovite territory, but we must be near the Swedish border, where Gregory said we might expect the road to be blocked and guarded. We were counting on his knowledge of Swedish to win our way through.

Thomas was to take the first watch. I curled up on the cushioning pine needles, with my knapsack under my head and soon fell asleep.

We made an early start the next morning. The forest thinned out to nothing more than scattered clumps of trees. The road now ran along a causeway, just wide enough for us to ride two abreast. The reason was soon clear, for here and there on both sides of us there were tussocks of bright green marsh grass, and between them patches of water flashed reflections of sunlight. The scent of salt water was unmistakable now.

'This looks as though it might flood at times,' I called out to Gregory, who was riding ahead with Thomas.

'Aye, it does,' he said over his shoulder. 'There's a network of small lakes and streams all around here. And Narva has a good harbour. Ships from every country call there.'

Including Spain, I thought. I hoped we might not encounter any Spanish sailors.

Suddenly Pyotr, who was riding beside me, reached out an grabbed my arm. 'Do you hear that?'

But before I could ask what he meant, Gregory stood up in his stirrups and pointed ahead. 'There is the border,' he said. 'They have put a barricade over the road, but I can only see a few men guarding it.'

I looked where he pointed. It was about a quarter of a mile ahead.

'Listen!' Pyotr yelled, shaking my arm. 'Behind us!'

We all twisted round. I could hear it now, the sound of many drumming hooves. We could see them too. A band of mounted troopers, about as far behind us as the border was in front, coming toward us at full gallop. Without a word we kicked our horses to the gallop and headed down the causeway at breakneck speed.

Like us, the troopers were forced to ride no more than two abreast, and could only move as fast as the two in front. They could not circle round us into the marsh. If we could outrun them, and if the Swedish soldiers would allow us through the barrier, we could escape them, but our horses were tired. It might be too much for them.

I risked a glance over my shoulder. They were nearer. But the leading riders seemed to have slowed. Then I saw why. They carried crossbows.

'Crossbows!' I shouted.

The troopers had no need to catch us. A crossbow shaft could cover the distance easily.

Desperately we urged our tired horses on. Something whistled past my ear and buried itself in the mud of the causeway. We thundered past it, but not before I saw it was a crossbow quarrel, still vibrating from its flight. That man would not be able to rewind his weapon quickly, not on horseback. The crossbow is a deadly weapon, but it is the longbow that can send a shower of arrows almost without pause.

'He's aiming for you!' Pyotr shouted. He was behind me now, his horse tiring. Then it stumbled.

I checked my horse, and nearly found myself flying over his head. If Pyotr's mount had floundered . . . I yanked my horse round.

'Go on! I'm all right!' He had his horse under control now.

But I saw what he was doing. He was putting himself between me and the pursuers.

'Pyotr!'

There was thump and a grunt, then Pyotr had slumped forward on his horse's neck, a crossbow quarrel protruding from his back.

Behind us the troopers had stopped and were changing position. They must be moving armed men to the front. I grabbed Pyotr's reins and urged both horses into a canter. Thomas and Gregory were too far ahead to realise what had happened.

Pyotr made a feeble grab at his horse's mane to stop himself sliding off. I spared a quick glance at his back. There was very little blood, but that meant nothing if the shaft had penetrated some vital internal organ. We were closing with the other two now, but the troopers were galloping on. There would be two fresh crossbows at the front.

Thomas and Gregory had reached the barrier and Gregory was speaking to the Swedish soldiers, gesturing back toward us. Thomas turned round and must have seen enough, for he tugged at Gregory's elbow.

'Not far now, Pyotr,' I gasped. My right arm was being nearly wrenched from my shoulder as I tried to control his frightened horse.

Another shaft flew between us, ripping the shoulder of my doublet. The troopers were having difficulty aiming while riding at speed.

The Lord be praised! The Swedish soldiers were removing the barrier. Thomas and Gregory were through. I spurred a last effort from my horse and we thundered after them, as the guards stumbled out of our way.

Then they were replacing the barrier and I slowed the two sweating horses to a halt. Pyotr had slipped sideways and would have fallen if Thomas had not grabbed him and eased him to the ground.

'Dear God,' Thomas said. 'He's hit.'

'Lay him on his front,' I said, sliding to the ground and scrabbling to unfasten my satchel from the saddle. I knelt in the dust of the road beside Pyotr.

'I'm done for,' he whispered. Thomas had laid him down carefully, his face turned to the side.

'Nay,' I said fiercely. 'Lie still.'

'Can't do much else.' He tried to smile.

I could hear the Swedish soldiers shouting. I thought they were shouting at us, but when I gave them a glance, I saw that they were shouting at the Muscovite soldiers who had ridden up to the barrier, just yards away. They were threatening to break it down. Suddenly there were more Swedish soldiers than we had realised, emerging from a hut beside the road. They were carrying muskets. The troopers began to back their horses. Crossbows were no match for muskets. I could spare them no more attention. I had my satchel open now.

I was thinking frantically. If the quarrel was not barbed, it would be possible to draw it out, but the damage would certainly be extensive. The shaft had gone deep. It might have punctured his left lung. It had missed his heart, or he would be dead by now. If the head of the bolt was barbed, I would do even more damage by trying to draw it out, for it would rip a wider gash.

My hands were shaking as I fumbled in my satchel. Extract of willow bark would ease the pain, though it would take time. And Pyotr had no time. Poppy juice would be better.

'Kit.' His voice was a whisper. His hand slid through the dust toward me and I dropped the poppy juice back into my satchel so that I could take it in both of mine.

'Pyotr, I'll do what I can.'

He tried to shake his head, but it was pressed to the ground and he could not lift it.

'Got to Sweden, didn't we?'

'We did. Just a few more miles to Narva.'

'Nearly made it.' He gave a weak cough and a thin trickle of blood ran from the corner of his mouth and sank into the ground.

'Let me give you something to ease the pain,' I said wretchedly.

'No point.' His voice was growing weaker, so that I had to lean closer to hear him. 'We did for them, didn't we? Found that fellow Rocksley. Pity about the boy.'

His breathing was so laboured I could feel the pain of it in my own chest.

'We were good comr–'

'Aye,' I said quietly. 'We were good comrades.'

I got to my feet. Thomas and Gregory were watching me. The horses had wandered along the road and two of the Swedish soldiers had gone to bring them back.

I shook my head.

We carried Pyotr to the church in the next village. He had never told me what his faith was. As a child he must have been brought up in the Orthodox church, but he had lived for almost as long with a Protestant

233

father. He had not spoken of religion, so I hoped he would have been content with burial in a Protestant Swedish graveyard. We spent the night in the village. The following morning the pastor held a simple funeral service, attended by the three of us who remained and two of the Swedish guards who had witnessed it all. Everyone was very kind to us.

By midday we were on our way, riding the last few miles to Narva, leading Pyotr's horse with us. His belongings were still strapped to the saddle. When we reached London, I would take them to the office of the Muscovy Company and enquire for his father's address. Someone must carry the news to his family. I supposed I had better do it.

All three of us were silent. It had happened so suddenly, so close to safety, that I think we could hardly believe that Pyotr was gone. Gregory and I were the intended targets, not Pyotr. If he had not interposed himself at the last moment, I would be the one lying in that cold Swedish graveyard. I thought of it as cold, deep under snow all through the winter months. Even in the summer sunshine, I shivered.

Over and over in my head I apologised to Pyotr. I am sorry I ever doubted you. I am sorry I condemned you as a mere interpreter. You were a friend, and a courageous one. I am sorry. *I am sorry.*

It was early evening when we reached Narva. Despite the lingering light of the sun, cheerful candlelight shone from the house Gregory led us to. A prosperous, sturdily built house of three storeys. The former Company man, William Waldren, it seemed, had done well for himself. I was suddenly so tired that I could hardly think and the next few hours are no more than a blur in my mind. Everyone was speaking English. Gregory was explaining, recounting briefly our last few weeks, but making no mention of his imprisonment. Thomas added a few words here and there. I left it to them.

I paid sufficient attention to gather that a small merchant ship, in which our host had a part share, would be leaving for London in two days' time. There would be room for us. Did we wish to take the horses? Probably, with a little contrivance, they could be accommodated.

'What do you think, Kit?' Gregory turned to me.

It was a problem I had not thought to confront before. The horses were Company property. They could not easily be returned to Muscovy.

234

'I suppose we had better take them with us,' I said, rousing myself. 'We can hand them over to the London office. Master Marler can decide what to do with them.'

I was glad, in a way, that we would not be abandoning them. They had given us faithful service on a long and gruelling journey. They deserved better than that.

'Good,' Master Waldren said. 'I will make the arrangements. You should all rest. My wife will be glad to feed you well.'

Mistress Waldren smiled. 'Indeed I shall. You look in need of a good meal.'

It was all so ordinary. So banal. My mind was filled with Dmitri and Pyotr. I had nothing to say.

Master Waldren's ship, which he owned jointly with another Englishman and a Welshman, all former Company men, was a round-bellied elderly merchant ship of practical design called the *Elizabeth Fortuna*. She was not beautiful, but I suppose to us she looked as beautiful as any fine modern vessel belonging to the Muscovy Company. She signified our escape, our means to reach home.

The port of Narva was prosperous and bustling. As Gregory had told us, ships from every nation of Europe traded here, though I was relieved to learn that the latest Spanish vessel had departed the previous week. Nevertheless, there were ships from England, Scotland, France, Denmark, Spanish Flanders, the United Provinces, Norway, even an Italian merchant ship all the way from Venice. And since this was now a Swedish possession, there were Swedish ships, though I did not think the Swedes carried out much long-distance trade.

An hour or two before the *Elizabeth Fortuna* was due to set sail on the ebb tide, we went aboard. Two of Master Waldren's grooms led our horses, one at a time, over a solid gangplank and stabled them in a makeshift canvas shelter which had been erected on the deck. Remembering difficulties I had experienced in the past, leading terrified horses across rippling gangplanks, I was happy to leave the task to someone else.

We had said our farewells and thanks to Mistress Waldren before leaving the house, but her husband accompanied us to the ship. By now he had heard our full story, including Gregory's experiences since he had last been in Narva – or as much of them as he was willing to tell anyone. He remained silent about his imprisonment. Master Waldren was clearly distressed, and could not do enough for us. The best of the cabins had been provided for our use, the ship's officers being required to double up as a result. I felt some guilt at this, but only a little. The voyage would take but a week or a little more, then the cabins could be reclaimed by their rightful owners.

Now that we were on the point of departure, I could hardly bear any further delay. Master Waldren's effusive remarks and his anxiety to see to our comfort became almost unendurable. At last he went ashore. The ship's pinnace threw across a tow rope, and the sailors aboard it bent to their oars. It was a difficult manoeuvre, towing a large ship out through the moored and anchored vessels, but at last we were clear. The pinnace was cast off and rowed round to the stern of the *Elizabeth Fortuna*, where she in turn was tied up to be towed, and the sailors scrambled up a rope ladder to join us on board.

The wind was light but favourable as we made our way out into the Baltic. We would head eventually for the east shore of Denmark, then follow it north to its northernmost cape. Once past the cape, we would be in the German ocean. I remembered the rough weather we had experienced at this season last year, but the weather now seemed set fair. Perhaps we would have a quiet crossing.

I turned to go to my cabin. We had sat up late the previous night, for after one of Mistress Waldren's enormous meals William Waldren had plied us with more questions about our time in Muscovy. I had had very little sleep. Then I noticed that one of the sailors who had rowed the pinnace was trying to catch my eye. He looked somehow familiar, but I could not place him.

He gave me a shy grin. 'Good day to you, Dr Alvarez,' he said.

'I know you,' I said, 'but I can't think where.'

'Aboard the *Bona Esperanza*,' he said. 'You picked a capful of metal shards out of me, what the b'yer lady pirates shot at us.'

'Of course!' I said, smiling at him. 'Jos, that's your name. Jos Needler.'

'That's me.'

'I thought you worked for the Muscovy Company.'

'Nay – one voyage a year? You couldn't live on that. They own some ships and hire some ships, but mostly they hire in crews. This year I'm doing the Baltic run.' He winked. 'Not so much risk of pirates here. And no ice.'

'And how do you fare, Jos? Are you quite recovered?'

'Oh, aye, I'm grand.' The sailor dragged up his rough tunic, exposing a criss-cross pattern of thin white lines on his side where the splinters of iron had lodged.

'Good,' I said. 'Quite healed.'

He winked again, pulling down his tunic. 'Works a treat with the wenches,' he said. 'You wouldn't credit what a hero I was, fighting them pirates. Speared three at once on my sword when they boarded us. It gets a bit better every time I tell it.'

I laughed. 'Well, good luck to you then, Jos.'

The meeting with Jos had cheered me, driving away a little of the cloud that hung over me. As the trumpet sounded for full canvas to be unfurled, Jos ran to the mainmast, gripped it with hands and bare feet, and began climbing it like a monkey. I headed to my cabin. I had myself been given the captain's cabin, a nod to my status as a London licensed physician, while Thomas and Gregory were to share the chief officer's rather smaller one.

I sat on the bunk and drew Gregory's bundle of paper containing his report from the breast of my tunic. I ought to read it, so that I could summarise the salient points for Thomas Phelippes, but I could not bring myself to make the effort. Not yet.

There was something else stowed here.

Xenia's small packet, unaddressed, lay in the palm of my hand. I remembered her words. *If you cannot give it to Dmitri, I would like you to keep it for yourself. As a remembrance.*

The packet was sealed with what looked like candle wax. She would not yet have a personal seal, and there would be no sealing wax in her apartments. She had made use, resourcefully, of what she had to hand.

I inserted my thumbnail under the edge of the wax and levered it off. Inside the outer sheet, blank and grubby from its long travels, was another, covered with round, childish writing in Cyrillic script, which I could not read. At the bottom Xenia had drawn a dog. Dmitri had drawn a picture of Volk for her, quite skilfully, which she had showed to me after she opened his packet. This drawing was not as good. The legs were too short and the head a little too large.

Did she know yet that both were dead? They would tell her that Dmitri had killed both the dog and himself. I prayed she would not believe them. Yet would it be any better if she knew that it was her father who had ordered their deaths?

Inside the letter was a small hard object, wrapped in a bit of cloth, which I recognised as the material used by those fiends to bind her limbs. I unwrapped it. It was a ring. Small but heavy. Solid gold. Set with a very large irregular turquoise. I had heard that these treasured gems were sometimes sent from Persia to Muscovy. The ring looked old. Perhaps it had belonged to an ancestor. A grandmother. The letter might say. Pyotr could have read it for me. It was a child's ring, but I slipped it on to the smallest finger of my right hand. Aye, I thought, I will wear it, as a remembrance of you both.

We crossed a wide stretch of the Baltic until we were in sight of the main southeast coast of Sweden, which we followed down to its southern cape, then headed up through the narrows between Sweden and Denmark. A ship flying the Danish king's flag intercepted us. We hove to while our captain lowered the toll money in a bag on the end of a long pole. The Danish captain counted the coins, signalled to us that we might continue, and we steered north.

'Easy money,' Thomas said.

Like me, he was watching this transaction from the railing.

'Aye. I wonder the Swedish king does not demand his share.'

'Too busy fighting the Muscovites, I expect.'

'Probably.'

'I miss that Russe, Pyotr,' he said.

'So do I.'

Having travelled west, then south, then west, we now sailed north along the coast of Denmark. It seemed a very zigzag course, this route through the Baltic. However, the weather held, the wind continued light but favourable. At last we reached the northern tip of Denmark and could head out into the wide expanse of the German Ocean.

In this part of the sea we were well north of London, probably, by my reckoning, about on the same latitude as northern Scotland, so we headed southwest, and now the winds blew less to our advantage, coming almost directly from the south. It brought warm weather, but made for difficult sailing. We were already more than a week out from Narva and it seemed that the final leg of the voyage would prove the slowest, tantalising us with the nearness of home.

Finally the coast of England came in sight. We were somewhere off the fen country.

'Now, if we had one of Thomas Harriot's perspective trunks,' I said, 'we should be able to see the fenlanders poling their boats among the reeds.'

Thomas and Gregory looked at me blankly.

'It is a clever new device,' I said. 'Using lenses.'

I explained how the perspective trunk worked, but I do not think they believed me.

'You would need to try it for yourselves,' I said. 'Perhaps you can come to one of the meetings at Durham House and see it there.'

Even as I spoke, I knew it would never happen. These were companions from another life. Back in London we would part.

At last the muddy, shoal-ridden estuary of the Thames came in sight. Recalling how long it had taken us on the outward voyage to travel from London to the estuary, I dreaded how many days it would take to make our way up river against the current. Briefly I contemplated going ashore with one of the horses and riding to London, but dismissed the idea. My responsibility at the moment was to Gregory and Thomas, to the report on Godunov's treachery, even to the horses. I would need to contain myself in patience.

However, our captain was skilful, there was a brisk wind from the east, and flood tides helped us on our way. It took us three days to reach Deptford. We anchored there overnight, knowing that with the morning's incoming tide we would reach the Customs House by midday.

That night I barely slept and before dawn I was on deck with my knapsack and satchel at my feet, watching the sailors hoist the anchor and unfurl the sails for the very last of this interminable voyage. It was not long before Thomas and Gregory joined me. As we watched the familiar poor outskirts on the north bank slip past, I was reminded sharply of standing with Simon and Pyotr on the *Bona Esperanza*. Simon would not know that I was coming. He would be expecting me to return with the Muscovy fleet early in September. In this fine summer weather, the players would be busy, performing a new piece every few days. He would be absorbed in his work, never thinking of me.

The captain came to stand beside us as we neared the Legal Quays.

'I sent word by messenger from Deptford,' he said. 'We have permission to moor at the Muscovy Company's St Botolph's Wharf. It will be easier to land the horses there than at some of the other moorings.'

'Thank you,' I said. 'You have been more than kind to us, and we are grateful.' I smiled. 'And now you may have your own cabin again.'

He bowed his acknowledgements, then hurried off to supervise the delicate mooring of the ship, which was towed once more by the pinnace until it was brought to rest beside the quay where I had embarked a year ago. It felt longer than a year. A lifetime.

The next two hours were filled with bustle and hard work. The horses were landed, but were unsteady on their legs after so long confined to their canvas shelter. Thomas led two of them, Gregory and I one each, through the streets to the London house of the Company. Gregory and I had agreed that we would go together to Master Marler the next day and arrange a meeting with him and with the governor, to report on everything that had happened in Muscovy. I would also make enquiries as to the whereabouts of Thomas Phelippes, so that we might ask his advice about presenting Gregory's report to the Privy Council. Gregory had occupied himself on the sea voyage making another copy, so that we now each held one.

After we had delivered the horses, with an explanation, to the grooms at Company House, Thomas, Gregory and I stood awkwardly in the street, knowing that it was time to part. Somehow the afternoon had disappeared.

'Let us go for a mug of decent English beer,' Thomas suggested, 'before we take our leave.'

'Tomorrow,' I said, 'I'll be glad to drink a beer with you. For you must come with us to see Master Marler, Thomas. Tonight I am really tired. I want to see whether I can reclaim my lodgings from the friend who has been occupying them. And I must fetch my dog.'

They agreed that we should all have not only a beer but a meal together the next day, so I bade them God speed and hurried away over the Bridge. All the time we were seeing to the horses I had been seized by a sudden fear that something might have happened to Rikki. As I struggled through the crowds, I thought I heard someone calling behind me, but I pretended not to hear. I would see them tomorrow. The Bridge was more crowded than ever. After our weeks in the vast emptiness of Muscovy, I felt penned in, so that I could hardly breathe. Near the southern end of the Bridge I broke into a run, my satchel flapping against my side.

There was the gatehouse of St Thomas's, and Tom Read sitting outside, as he liked to do at the end of a busy summer's day, taking the air and enjoying the sunshine. I could only see Swifty, lying across his master's feet.

Then a furry explosion burst from the other side of Tom's stool and was hurtling toward me. I dropped to my knees, else I would have been knocked over. I had my arms around his rough familiar coat and he was licking every bit of my face he could reach, licking away my tears.

I felt a hand on the back of my neck.

'Kit, are you weeping at seeing us again?'

'I was afraid something had happened to Rikki. Of course I am not weeping.' I rubbed the back of my hand across my face. 'How did you know I was back?'

'Oh,' he said vaguely, 'word gets around. You know that all players are gossips.'

He grabbed my hands and pulled me to my feet, though Rikki circled around me protectively.

'It is good to see you, Simon,' I said calmly, remembering how we had parted. *Did he know?*

He studied my face. 'It was bad, was it?'

'Aye,' I said. 'Some of it was very bad.'

He flung his arm round my shoulders in his familiar comradely way, and Rikki turned and trotted away along the river.

'Come along,' Simon said.

'I am coming.'

It was beginning to rain. A soft, warm, blessed, English rain. I didn't care. I was going home.

Historical Note

The Muscovy Company came about in a somewhat unexpected way. In 1553, an English expedition funded by a large group of merchants and noblemen set out to search for the so-called 'Northeast Passage', a sea route around the north of mainland Europe, via the Arctic Circle, and down into the China seas. If it existed, it would provide a much shorter journey for English merchant ships trading with India, China, and the Spice Islands than the vastly longer route around the bottom of Africa, which meant running the gauntlet of Spanish privateers. Geographical knowledge was growing apace at the time. The general shape and dimensions of the globe were understood, but the territory beyond the north of Norway was *terra incognita*.

Three ships set out; only one returned. The *Edward Bonaventure* commanded by Richard Chancellor had quite a tale to tell. They had discovered the White Sea and anchored at St Nicholas, where they realised they were in Muscovy. Chancellor travelled to Moscow, where he was received by the Tsar, Ivan the Terrible, and presented a letter from King Edward VI, explaining that England wanted to open up friendly trade routes with other lands. By the time Chancellor reached London again in the following year, the boy king was dead and his sister Mary, married to Philip of Spain, was on the throne.

Mary and Philip were prepared to support trade with Muscovy, so the original backers of the expedition created a new organisation, the first ever joint-stock company. Shareholders would invest their money to provide ships, merchandise, and paid employees. No individual would trade with Muscovy on a personal basis, all transactions would pass through the company. Losses would be sustained by the shareholders and profits would be shared between them. This new organisation, the Muscovy Company, was to provide the commercial model for all joint-stock companies of the future. Its best-known early successor was the East India Company.

Although the original plan had been to import luxury goods, like furs, it was soon discovered that more mundane products would provide the bulk of the merchandise, such as wax for candles and official seals, train oil (derived from blubber), canvas and cordage for the navy. The rope factory at Kolmogory (later Kholmogory) was another innovation which would subsequently prove a model for similar enterprises throughout the British Empire. The raw material and labour were cheap in Muscovy, but the country lacked skilled rope-makers, who were sent out from England to train the local men. Initially the Muscovy Company had exclusive trading rights throughout the Tsar's realms, although these were gradually whittled away over the years. Even so, the Company continued to trade, through the new city of Arkhangelsk built near St Nicholas, until the Revolution in 1917.

And what of the two lost ships? As is mentioned in the story, they were found intact, safely anchored in the estuary of the Varzina river the following year, plentifully supplied with food, all on board dead. At the time it was believed that they had died of the cold, although it was strange that they all seemed to have died at the same time, while occupied in various tasks. Today, another theory has been put forward. The shores of the estuary are scattered with sea coal, which the men seem to have gathered as fuel for their heating stoves. All the doors, windows, and hatches were tightly closed against the cold. It seems more than likely, therefore, that the men died of carbon monoxide poisoning.

By 1590-91, when Kit is in Muscovy, Ivan the Terrible was dead and his ineffectual son Fyodor sat on the throne, while Fyodor's brother-in-law Boris Godunov was the *de facto* ruler. Fyodor was childless, the only other possible heir to the throne being his eight-year-old half brother, Dmitri, whom Godunov had exiled to Uglich, fearing that a party of *boyars* would lead a coup to replace the useless Fyodor with Dmitri and snatch the reins of power from Godunov. The rest is history. Godunov became the next Tsar, and on his death civil war broke out, the Time of Troubles.

The search for the Northeast Passage continued to frustrate generations of mariners. It was finally discovered by the Finnish-Swedish explorer Adolf Erik Nordenskiöld in 1878, although it is claimed (possibly without evidence) that the Portuguese navigator David Melgueiro made the passage from east to west as early as 1660.

A number of the characters in this story were real historical figures. I have been as truthful to their appearance and nature as the historical sources make possible.

I owe a considerable debt of gratitude to Carolyn Pouncy, who has brought her formidable expertise to bear on Kit's travels in Muscovy. Any surviving *faux pas* are entirely my own responsibility.

The Author

Ann Swinfen spent her childhood partly in England and partly on the east coast of America. She was educated at Somerville College, Oxford, where she read Classics and Mathematics and married a fellow undergraduate, the historian David Swinfen. While bringing up their five children and studying for a postgraduate MSc in Mathematics and a BA and PhD in English Literature, she had a variety of jobs, including university lecturer, translator, freelance journalist and software designer. She served for nine years on the governing council of the Open University and for five years worked as a manager and editor in the technical author division of an international computer company, but gave up her full-time job to concentrate on her writing, while continuing part-time university teaching in English Literature. In 1995 she founded Dundee Book Events, a voluntary organisation promoting books and authors to the general public.

Her first three novels, *The Anniversary*, *The Travellers*, and *A Running Tide*, all with a contemporary setting but also an historical resonance, were published by Random House, with translations into Dutch and German. *The Testament of Mariam* marked something of a departure. Set in the first century, it recounts, from an unusual perspective, one of the most famous and yet ambiguous stories in human history. At the same time it explores life under a foreign occupying force, in lands still torn by conflict to this day. Her second historical novel, *Flood*, takes place in the fenlands of East Anglia during the seventeenth century, where the local people fought desperately to save their land from greedy and unscrupulous speculators. The second novel in the Fenland Series, *Betrayal*, continues the story of the search for legal redress and security for the embattled villagers. *This Rough Ocean* is a novel based on the real-life experiences of the Swinfen family during the 1640s, at the time of the English Civil War, when John Swynfen was imprisoned for opposing the killing of the king, and his wife Anne had to fight for the survival of her children and dependents.

Currently the author is working on a late sixteenth century series, featuring a young Marrano physician who is recruited as a code-breaker and spy in Walsingham's secret service. The first book in the series is *The Secret World of Christoval Alvarez*, the second is *The Enterprise of England*, the third is *The Portuguese Affair*, the fourth is *Bartholomew Fair*, the fifth is *Suffer the Little Children* and the sixth is *Voyage to Muscovy*.

She now lives in Broughty Ferry, on the northeast coast of Scotland, with her husband, formerly vice-principal of the University of Dundee, and a rescue kitten.

www.annswinfen.com

Printed in Great Britain
by Amazon